I0788166

THE ISOLATE

The Isolate

CHUCK WALSH

Rand-Smith Publishing
www.RandSmithBooks.com

Reviews

"Author Chuck Walsh offers a richly drawn portrait of the Tennessee community that raised and shaped Nick, only to be ultimately left behind. With empathy and insight, Walsh explores what led Nick to a life of isolation, tracing his transformation into a rugged mountain man and examining his profound bond with the land and its creatures that became his family. *The Isolate* is a compelling meditation on independence, belonging, and the wild spaces where the human spirit both struggles and thrives. - **Carla Damron, award-winning author of *The Orchid Tattoo* and *The Weird Girl***

"I'm going on record to say that readers (me!) will fall head over heels in love with Nick Grindstaff, the hero in Chuck Walsh's new historical novel, *The Isolate*. Nick is made of the right stuff, and the lengths he's willing to go to build a life for the woman he loves will capture your heart." - **Bren McClain, award-winning author of *One Good Mama Bone***

"There is a tenderness to Chuck Walsh's old-timey storytelling in his latest novel, *The Isolate: The Saga of Nick Grindstaff*. With a sense of reverence for his subject matter, the author attempts to bring to life the true story of Nick Grindstaff, who lived for forty years in isolation on Iron Mountain in east Tennessee. In his fictional rendering, Walsh imagines what might have caused a handsome young man with ambition and dreams to isolate himself from the rest of society and become a hermit. Steeped in legend and mystery, *The Isolate* will appeal to anyone who loves a good story, especially those readers looking for books set in the lush mountains of Appalachia." - **Kathleen M. Rodgers, author of The Llano County Mermaid Club - 2024 MWSA Writer of the Year**

"*The Isolate* by Chuck Walsh kept me glued to my seat. It took me deep into the heart of Appalachia with an intriguing story of love, redemption, and discovery. Chuck Walsh is a master storyteller who compels his readers to invest in his characters. He is, by far, one of the best writers of Appalachian mystery and suspense, so much so that readers are drawn into the story from the first sentence and can't let go until the very end." - **Joy Ross Davis, Grand Prize winner of Paranormal Fiction (Chanticleer Author Conference) for** *The Madwoman of Preacher's Cove*; **multi award-winning author of women's fiction**

"Unputdownable! *The Isolate* transports the reader to a remote 19th-century Appalachian region unaffected by the modern world, where its beauty and timeless traditions will steal your heart. A tale of ultimate resolve, this vastly appealing story is needed for today's beleaguered society." - **Parris Afton Bonds, New York Times Best Seller**

DEDICATION

Dedicated to the valiant spirit of the people of East Tennessee

CONTENTS

| 1 |

Nick stepped across the trodden path. The hinges moaned when he closed the gate. Standing on the bottom row of the wooden fence, he observed the cattle huddled around the bunk, a cursory inventory count. Pallid clouds had masked the progression of the day, but the entrails of smoke from the house confirmed the workday was done. With the cattle secured, Nick headed to the house, his boots heavy, overalls stained with remnants common to a farmhand. Beyond the house, Iron Mountain was cloaked in a mist of contrariness, the fog clinging to the dismal trees, shrouding the folds along the upper ridges.

He dipped his hands in the bucket behind the farmhouse. The creek water stung as he scrubbed his hands with lye soap. Before entering the back door, he removed his boots as Aunt Cora would never allow anyone to traipse mud across her floors. The table was set, the buttery aroma of cathead biscuits leading him through the kitchen. He sat in the chair that had been his designated spot for every meal since he was five. Tom gently slapped Nick on the back of his head as he passed. He took the seat across from Nick.

The room had an anticipatory air when Uncle Jerico entered, a gathering awaiting the proclamation of some edict. All was quiet when he took his seat, his face leathery in appearance in the dim light of the table lantern. The lines on his neck ran deep, interwoven, a hard-earned moniker from years working the farm. To Nick, it was the badge for a man who had earned his keep through the heavy toil of labor.

With Jerico seated at the head of the table, Cora took her seat across from him. "Bow your heads," Jerico said, matter-of-factly. "Lord, we thank you for the many blessings, and we give thanks for this meal. Bless Cora for all her work in preparing the food. Amen."

As the bowls were passed around the table, they settled into a familiar sense of comfort. Cora made sure their plates were full before filling her own. Jerico took pause after each bite as though acknowledging the work Cora put into preparing the meal. Tom and Nick gave no reflection or thought to the process, hurriedly eating as though it might be their last supper.

Tom took a sip of buttermilk. "Mama hog broke through the pen again," he said. "Found her outside the barn, chewing on old corn husks."

"That sow keeps it up, she's going to end up on the dinner table sooner than planned," Jerico said. "Can't escape the pen when your jowls are a featured item on a dinner plate."

"It weren't easy guiding her back to the pen. She plopped that old belly down on the roadside. Thought I was going to have to rope her and let Sally pull her to the pen."

"The last thing we need is Sally breaking a leg a movin' that ornery pig," Jerico said.

Nick sliced into breaded beef covered in flour gravy. He nestled it into his split biscuit. A day's wages could never measure up to the evening meal Cora prepared for them at the end of a workday. When dinner was finished and the table cleared, Tom and Nick took their seats at a small card table near the hearth. Friday was Old Maid night. A couple of times they had attempted to play penny poker, but Jerico quickly nixed it, reminding them that any form of gambling was not only forbidden, but a sin in the eyes of the Lord.

"Tonight, I get revenge for the whoopin' you gave me last week," Tom said as he dealt the cards.

"Surely you'll fare better," Nick said. "Can't do no worse, that's for certain."

"Well, unlucky in cards, lucky in love, is what they say."

"Son, you ain't too lucky in either."

"We don't all have the luck of the Irish. And you ain't got nary a drop of Irish blood, so I don't know how you qualify. Regardless, how a rube like you got a gal like Annabeth Parker to fancy you is one of life's great mysteries."

"It's the hard work of them Irish that gets the gold. I would argue that the same applies to me with Annabeth. Hard work and a heap of kindness thrown in. No luck involved."

Tom shrugged. "Horse manure. Luck or not, she's surely the prettiest gal in the state, I'd venture to say. And I been to Johnson City and Elizabethton, so I know what kind of ladyfolk Tennessee holds."

"I ain't hardly left the holler, much less the valley. So, I got a smaller herd size to compare. But it won't be much longer till that all changes."

"You need to get them thoughts out your head. Why would you want to leave Doe Valley? You got a roof above your head. Warm bed. And you get to court Annabeth."

"I got plans, cousin. Big plans. And that includes Miss Annabeth. But that's going to require leaving Johnson County for a while."

"You're a landowner. Build a house and try to convince that gal to marry you."

"The land my pa left me ain't the kind to build a farm. Make a life. It sets on the side of the hill. And that old, empty house still sits across the field from it. That place would be a constant reminder of the might-have-beens."

"Sell it and buy property someplace else in the valley. Far enough away from any reminders of that broken-down homestead."

"I gave John first chance at it, but he had no interest. Katherine and Sarah got no interest either."

"So, no offers?"

"E.S. Jordan offered to buy all four plots. I don't know what the girls will do, especially with them settled in with their families over in Abingdon. They got no reason to keep land around here. No matter what they do, I'm selling mine."

"Good. Find a nice piece of land and get to settlin'."

"Oh, I've got the land picked out. Daniel Stout is going to sell me that nice spot down Spear Branch way. The money I'll make from the sale of my land won't be enough to buy it. And I want the best there is for Annabeth. So, I got to go where the money is, at least for a while. The way I figure, with the sale of the land to E.S., combined with what I can make in St. Louis, I can pay cash for the Spear Branch property and build a house. And, Mr. Stout said he would wait till I get back to sell it to me. Said he wanted to make sure who owned it would take care of it. And I will take great care of it. Yessir, buddy. And, they's enough good timber on it for me to cut and build my own home. I have the skills to do it. A house suitable for Annabeth to live comfortably with her new husband. Me, being that person."

"I don't know, cousin. She's a high-cotton kind of gal. And you are just a simple farm hand."

Nick's expression turned dour.

"It's the truth. Boys like you and me. It's what we are. But that ain't nothin' to hang our heads over. We earn our keep the honest way. Annabeth's pa was able to take the sale of his land to the railroad company and parlay that into investments and such. He's earning money without getting his hands dirty. And that's the kind of man Annabeth is going to feel comfortable with."

"A woman don't care how her husband provides, just so long as he does. Annabeth don't get caught up in all the high-society dealings."

"If you're that sure about it, stake your claim and start your life together now. Before somebody else does it for you."

"Patience, Tom. I'm taking that job with Will Gentry in the big city, save every penny. I figure a year's wages will be enough to do it. And while I'm there, I'll see what the world outside Doe Valley is like. Check out the city life. I reckon the best way to appreciate what I got here is to have something to compare it to. No, sir, I best not pass up the opportunity."

"Will got you steady work, does he?"

"His foreman said they got plenty. St. Louis is bustling, and they can hardly find enough help. Tenant housing and food is provided. Six days a week. Shoot, I'll work on the seventh day if there's some to be found."

"That surely means Sundays, and you know what my pa says about working on the Lord's Day."

"He won't need to know about that."

"Sinner." They laughed in unison.

"And then I'll come back home, buy the land, and spend the rest of my life with Annabeth."

"The lovely Annabeth Parker."

Nick nodded, with a slight smile. "That's the one."

"Well, worry about all that later. For now, keep your focus on this here game because I'm getting ready to whip you like an egg in a teak wood bowl."

"You're going to need a mighty big bowl."

Tom finished dealing the cards, and the game began.

| 2 |

Annabeth Parker stood on the top step of the porch, waving at Nick as he approached. Grape vines ran along the underside of the tin roof above her head, making it appear as though she wore a purple veil. Nick tightened his grip on the reins as he brought Sally to a halt. The horse shook its head and whinnied as though to announce their arrival. Annabeth stepped off the porch and raised her dress slightly like she was in some form of curtsy, and Nick wondered if it was intended for him, or Sally.

"Morning, Mr. Grindstaff," she said with an air of comical aristocracy.

"Madam," he said with the same jovial air. He sprang from the buggy, removed his derby hat, and brushed his bushy hair from his forehead.

"Isn't it a *purdy* morning for a ride?" she asked, her humorous attempt at royalty already done with, though Nick felt her beauty should allow her to lord over any kingdom. Her caramel hair flowed delicately along her shoulders. Her green eyes sparkled in the morning light. Nick took her hand.

"It surely is," he said, guiding her by the elbow as she stepped onto the buggy. She slid across the seat, but just enough to where her dress brushed against Nick's pant leg. She took his hat and held it in her lap as though it were a cake on display. Nick guided Sally about, and the horse eased back down the narrow path to the earthen road. Annabeth took hold of his arm and touched her head to his shoulder. "I've missed you, Nick Grindstaff. A whole week is a long time to go without seeing you."

"Sorry I had to miss the church dinner. That sick colt had us tending to it day and night. He's on the mend now and will be running the fields again soon."

She slid her fingers along the contours of his face as though oblivious to his words. "I declare, you are the most handsome man I've ever laid eyes on."

"That's because you don't get out much."

She popped him on the wrist. "I have traveled farther away from Doe Valley than most people and seen more than my fair share of men, and they don't compare to you in the least. And you should be the one talking, Mr. Nick 'never left Doe Valley' Grindstaff. You've not even seen what the sun looks like rising beyond Doe or setting beyond Iron Mountain."

"I'll be fixing that real soon."

"How am I going to survive you being gone a whole year? Take me with you."

"What?"

"Hide me in your travel bag. I won't make a sound."

"I don't think they'd be too happy if I bring my gal to live at the work camp. Not lessin' you plan on doing construction work with the rest of us. Besides, Will Gentry says we'll be working six, maybe seven days a week at the site. And it's good money too. And when I get home, I'll have enough saved to buy the plot of land Mr. Stout had set aside for his boy Charles."

"That poor boy. Swept into Doe River, cart and all. I heard they found his body miles downstream. Just a tragic thing."

"That flash flood truly come out of nowhere. Never seen nothing like it."

"Can't we just start our life together now?"

"You know I got to marry you proper. And I want to build the prettiest girl in the state a home on the prettiest spot in the state."

"You already own a spot."

"Taking something passed down don't do nothing for a man. It weren't earned. And it's not a spot that's made for building a home.

Too hilly. Besides, the reminders of what happened in the house across the meadow would be too hard on this old boy's heart."

"Yes, you certainly don't need the daily reminders. I could ask Father for help to get us started on Mr. Stout's land. We can pay him back when we can. I'd venture to say he wouldn't want to be repaid at all."

"It's the responsibility of a man to provide for his wife. I can't let someone else pay for something I can do if I work hard enough. Look, Annabeth, I know it's a long time to be gone. But it will be a chance to make good money and carry my own weight. And I promise I'll make the wait worthwhile. I'll give you the best life I possibly can."

"Well, it's going to be monumentally sad around here while you're gone."

"You're going to have so much to occupy your time. Helping your ma and pa with the farm. The church choir. Before you know it, time will be ours for the rest of our lives. And as they say, 'absence makes the heart grow fonder.' By the time I get back, our hearts should be ready to explode."

"I don't want them to explode." She leaned her cheek against his shoulder. "You better write me weekly. Otherwise, my heart won't explode. It will collapse, and then all you will have will be faint memories of the sadness in my eyes this morning."

"I promise I'll write. And we still have a couple weeks before I head off on the train."

He brought the horse and buggy to a halt and reached behind him to the flat of the wooden cart. He took hold of a cloth-covered tray. "Looky here what Aunt Cora made." He handed the tray to Annabeth and she removed the cloth.

"Strawberry rhubarb pie," she said. She inhaled. "Ummm, don't that smell extra good? I think I'll just scoop some out with my fingers."

"Don't you do it. Wait till we get to where we're going."

She flashed an evil grin and eased her hand toward the dessert. "Uh, oh. My finger seems to have slipped right into the pastry." She curved her finger and scooped a chunk. "I certainly don't want to let any of Aunt Cora's dessert grow cold."

"You're as crafty as a bush fox," he said, shaking his head in mock disgust.

She carefully ate some and then held her finger in front of Nick's mouth. "Where's my manners?"

He opened his mouth, and she eased her finger into it, curving it so that it lay across his tongue. He surrounded her finger with his mouth, and a warmth rose within his midsection.

"Oh, my," she said as she watched his lips fold around her finger.

He winked.

"Where are you taking us?" she asked.

"To get a preview of our future."

They ambled through the valley, the narrow trail bordered to the west by grassy hills that canted to the base of Iron Mountain. To the east was a meadow laced with Virginia bluebells, trumpets tempered in arctic and cobalt blue that softened the green runners on which they grew. Beyond the meadow, Doe Mountain stood stoically, painted gray, the sun not yet high enough to cast it hunter green. A stream hugged the road, running along the meadow, providing a steady melody as the horse led them on. The road rose to a crest where cattle grazed. Nick pulled on the rein as Sally and the cart came to a stop.

"Is this not the most beautiful place you ever saw?" Nick asked, certain of her response.

"It truly is."

"The way I figure, we'll build the house right down there where the creek splits at the sand bar. I can build a lean-to on the sand bar for making molasses in the fall."

He eased off the cart and helped Annabeth down the footstep. Leading her by the hand, he guided her down the grassy slope to a two-by-four nailed to two stumps. When they had made it to the makeshift bench, Nick led her to sit. He stood beside her, and they regarded the land. "I think this spot is as pretty as any I've seen, and with you sitting on it, I know that it truly is."

"Nick Grindstaff, you just need to forget about this Missouri trip, marry me, and let's start our life together."

"Annabeth, I'd take you to the courthouse right now and make you my bride. Just the thought makes me want to cash in my train ticket. But I want us to be on stable ground, and I don't just mean this spot of land we're on right now. No, ma'am, that just won't do. I intend to make our lives, the lives of our future children, the best they can be. Free from debt. Owing no man. And it will give me a chance to see what the world is like outside this valley for a bit. To understand more of how the world operates."

"But look at what this world offers." She extended her arm and opened her hand as though presenting something not seen before. "And a whole year? I don't know how I'll be able to survive."

He knelt and touched her face. Staring into her eyes, he leaned forward and kissed her softly. "I promise it will be worth the wait. And when I get back, I'll spend the rest of my life making you feel like the queen of Johnson County. It will be Heaven on Earth."

She slid her arms around his neck. "Nick, as long as you're beside me, it truly will be."

He leaned forward and placed his hands on her slender waist. He sighed when he spotted a tear trickling down her cheek. In that moment, he saw her raw and exposed, and he knew he was a man of great fortune that had nothing to do with monetary value. He kissed her, his grip on her waist tightening. Her elegance made the inner fire within him ignite. When she pulled him closer, arms behind his neck, he wished to lay her on the soft grass, to explore her in ways he'd only imagined at night, lying in his bed. There was a force to her kisses, and when she sighed, pulling away from his lips as if to gauge his interest in pursuing something more, sweat formed inside his shirt. For a moment, he gave thought to the idea, but the innocence within her need not be compromised. He kissed her cheek.

"How about this—one year from today, you and I get married, and we return to this very spot, with a blanket spread out on what will be our rightful land, and give in to every desire. I'll build our home, and we can be together for the rest of our days. So, Miss Annabeth Parker, if you can be patient just a short while, I will deliver this promise."

She nodded, another tear sliding down her face. "I'll wait, Nick." She kissed him. "I'll surely wait."

The men gathered around the cart. The stack of hickory cast an aroma that oddly reminded Nick of the cured hams hanging from the ceiling in Crosswhite's Mercantile down Doe Valley way. The men took to unloading long planks from the wagon that had just arrived from the lumberyard. Jerico held the reins of the mules. From a nearby cart, the men took tools suited for the craft they were about to undertake.

Jerico orchestrated the construction project. They had planned a parlor at the back of the building where dinners and meetings of church matters could be held. They had battled the elements for years out back on the grass behind the church, and it certainly wore thin on the women who attempted to sit in ladylike fashion while on blankets serving chicken and biscuits and rhubarb pie. Nick and Tom carried planks to what was to be the eastern wall of the building. The crew took to aligning their duties, ready to lay the base of the walls. Jerico stood behind Tom and Nick, observing them intently. As the men began, Jerico stepped forward.

"Let me hold that hammer, Tom," he said. "Be accurate when driving the nail. Keep the wrist taut. Aim steady. Just like I showed you when we built the barn." He observed Nick measuring out the necessary distance between the boards and using precise detail in making sure the wood was perfectly perpendicular. With steady aim, he drove two nails into connecting beams. "That's the way, Nick. You always been a quick learner."

"Thank you, Uncle." Tom shook his head and grinned. Nick winked.

"Mr. Perfectionist," Tom said. "Look everybody at the way Nick sets the boards, the way he drives the nails, the way he makes the rest of us look like simpletons."

"You are a simpleton."

"What's your point?"

The day warmed and the men went at the construction like worker ants, the walls growing, the sound of steel driving into wood echoing across the valley. Hunger pangs began to grow in Nick's stomach, and when he saw the carts approach over the bald, he smiled.

"Looks like dinner has arrived, boys," Tom said.

"Praise the Lord," Jerico said. "I could see some of you men starting to buckle from lack of nourishment."

Four carts pulled into the grassy lot beside the church, each filled with food, lemonade, and spring water. Annabeth smiled and waved at Nick. He waved the hammer and returned the smile. The men gathered near the carts as the ladies took to fixing plates and filling cups. Annabeth brought Nick a plate. His heart fluttered, his chest poked forward, watching the most beautiful thing he'd ever seen walking toward him. He noticed the stares from the other men. Surely, she did too, though her eyes were set on him.

"I bet you are plumb starving," she said, handing the plate to Nick. In her other hand was a glass, a fork, and a cloth napkin. "A man needs his energy."

"You might say my belly and spine were nudging each other this morning." Her smile made him want to kiss her.

"Well, there should always be distance between spine and belly." She pointed at the plate. "Mama's stew beef. She said to give you an extra portion."

"My intention this morning was to help with the fellowship hall just for the kindness aspect, but I'd be telling a tale now that you brought this meal. Especially when served by a beauty like you."

"Come to the house afterward, and you can have plenty more."

"I won't refuse that offer."

Annabeth carefully removed a cloth from a satchel she carried over her shoulder. She unfolded it, revealing to Nick that beef stew was not his only menu item. He leaned forward and pulled back a corner flap of the cloth. "Apple stack cake?"

Annabeth raised her finger to her mouth. "Hush, now. I don't have but the one piece, and the boys will feel plumb left out if they see you're the only one to get a piece."

"Did you make this?"

"Lordy, no." She pointed to a woman who was removing plates from the back of a wagon. "Mrs. Veta Crosswhite made it. I begged her for a piece this morning at her place. She thought I wanted it for me."

"Is she kin to Ray Crosswhite, the man what owns the Mercantile place?"

"That would be her husband. Veta is a fine woman."

Nick looked about and saw no eyes looking his way. He took hold of the layered cake, took a large bite, and wiped apple butter from his mouth. "I swannie, this is mighty fine."

"You were supposed to wait until after you ate the stew." She lightly popped his arm.

"Couldn't help it." He stuffed the remainder in his mouth and tried to grin, reckoning he looked more like a chipmunk than a man at that point.

"Enjoy your meal, Mr. Grindstaff." She smiled, and he watched her walk away. She was going to make the perfect bride.

The ladies gathered in conversation around one of the carts as the workers ate. Veta seemed to orchestrate the collection of the plates and silverware by pointing the Reese sisters toward the workers. The men expressed thanks and resumed construction. The carts were loaded with dirty dishes, and the convoy began the trip home to tend to chores of their own. Over the hill appeared two horsemen. They stopped when they came upon the buggy driven by Annabeth.

"Well, if it ain't the baron of Johnson County," said Rory Peterson.

Tom and Nick stopped to look.

"Cody Swanson," Tom said. "That boy thinks he's God's gift to females everywhere."

The young man dismounted and held the reins as he stood next to Annabeth's buggy. He took her hand, kissing it before giving a slight bow.

"He's a snake, is what," Rory said.

"He sure seems to have an eye for Annabeth," Tom said. "Nick, old boy, you might need to stake your claim to that rich boy face-to-face. Make sure he knows without a doubt that she is your girl."

Nick shrugged.

The grassy field shimmered under the noonday sun. Cattle stood silent in their tracks, their black bodies as though silhouettes of beasts of legend told around the fire pit. Beyond them ran a barbed fence that separated the field from a thicket of hardwoods and Virginia spruce. Nick observed the cattle as they grazed. The corn-filled bucket he carried jingled as he walked toward the trough where two sows rooted in a nearby muddy bog. He spread the corn about the trough, and the pigs came running. When he returned to the barn, he spotted a slender figure beyond the fence, emerging from the trees. A diminutive shape, dressed in overalls and a floppy hat. Nick watched the figure slide carefully between two strands of the fence. As the stranger approached the cattle, Nick took hold of an ax handle that rested against the barn. Head lowered, face shielded, the visitor continued toward Nick. He tightened his grip on the handle. When the stranger removed the hat, the familiar mane of caramel hair spilled out. Annabeth's smile caused Nick's heart to flutter, and she continued on until she stood in front of him. She caressed his face and stared into his eyes. Placing her lips gently to his, she leaned forward so that their torsos touched. When she had deemed the kiss had accomplished its intention, she eased from him. He studied her manner of dress.

"Well, I never knew coveralls could look so good."

"I figured if I came waltzing up in a dress and bonnet, Mr. Jerico woulda spotted me and sent me on home so as not to interrupt you from your chores. So, I borrowed some of Daddy's clothes and decided to surprise you."

"Well, I can't think of a better surprise. Typically, the only things roaming beyond the boundary fence are coons and possums. And you certainly don't look like no possum I ever saw."

She reached inside a pocket of the overalls and removed a small, leather binder. With tears forming along the contours of her eyes, she lowered her head. Nick guided her chin upward with his finger until her eyes met his. "I hate to see sadness in those pretty green eyes," he said.

She handed him the binder. "I figured you'd need some writing materials out in St. Louis." She opened it. "Look, it's got a nice lead pencil in the center strap. You can write what your days are like out in St. Louis too if you have the desire. More important, though, you can use it to write letters to me." He wiped a tear from her cheek.

He took hold of the binder and studied it. "This is the nicest gift I ever did receive. I'll do all my letter writing with this, and I'll surely sleep with it under my pillow so I can feel like you're next to me." He guided her to a bench set up against the back of the barn. "Sit with me a spell."

They sat, shoulder to shoulder, surrounded in the silence of the day. Nick studied the valley that lay as if frozen in time, land that appeared untouched since creation.

"I dream about our life together," she said. "All the time. But before we start a family, can we see some of this world together, just you and me? We could walk alongside the ocean somewhere in the Carolinas. We could go to Gettysburg, where President Lincoln addressed the country. I want us to stand in the doorway at Monticello. The possibilities are endless. And to think we can see all these sites together, well, it just warms my soul."

"Let's write it all down in the binder. We'll make a list and check them off once we've done them."

"That's a great idea." She took the binder and removed the pencil. As she wrote, Nick regarded the aura of innocence and beauty that surrounded her. He studied her slender fingers as she created the list. "Okay, your turn. Tell me where you want us to go, and I'll write it down."

"Well, as long as it's you and me, I don't rightly care. But if I had the chance, I would like to visit Daniel Boone's birthplace. It's up in Pennsylvania somewhere. He trail-blazed all around this region. I've heard there's a tree up Jonesborough way where he carved *killed a bear* on it. He would go on them long hunts all alone. Something to be said about being just you and the land and nothing else. No one to rely on but yourself."

"Well, you won't ever need to worry about being in that situation." She put pencil to paper and wrote "Daniel Boone and his birthplace."

"Guess I'll put down 'tree with carving' too." She grinned. "I'm sure that will be easy to find."

"Sarcasm is just not necessary." He pinched her cheek.

"It might not be necessary, but it is an underappreciated art form." She leaned forward and kissed him.

After the kiss, he traced her face with his fingertips. "This has been an extra good surprise. It was nice of you to sneak on up here. And may I say you make the prettiest farmhand I ever did see."

She smiled and placed her cheek against the arm. "I love you, Nick. With all my heart."

"I feel the same."

"It sure is hard for you to say you love me. Why is that?"

He scratched his chin. "I don't know. It sounds strange coming from the mouth of a fella. The words just seem feminine in nature."

"Well, you would think if you truly loved me, you'd say it, and not make me have to guess one way or the other."

Nick took a deep breath. He stood and led Annabeth by the hand so that she was in front of him. He placed his hand on her face and caressed it, staring into her eyes. "You might have a good point there." He pressed his lips to hers, holding his gaze. Slowly, he pulled away and said, "Annabeth Parker, I love you."

She wrapped her arms around him and put her head to his chest. "Those words just penetrated my heart like no other words ever could. I know it wasn't easy coming from such a strapping man as yourself. I love you so, and I'll be counting down each day until you are back home and in my arms for good. You make the most of your time in St. Louis. See what you can. Make all the money you desire. But make no mistake—in one year, you better be home a marrying me."

"I promise you right here and now. I'll marry you, buy that land, and build our home, and we will experience all that life will allow and grow old together. You can take this promise to heart."

| 3 |

The sun had not yet cleared Doe Mountain, and yet the valley floor shimmered from a thin coating of frost, a sign that autumn would soon arrive. Nick tossed his canvas bag on the seat of the buggy. Sally turned and regarded Nick as though something was amiss. He patted her neck and rubbed his hand along her mane.

Sally's hooves provided a soothing tune on the earthen road as she led Nick down the valley. He needed to study the land again, worried it might somehow fade from memory once he crossed the county line. He guided Sally off the road onto a weed-laced path, ducking as the buggy dipped under drooping branches of a heavy elm. The path rose gently, and Sally's gait slowed as she maneuvered the long-dormant trail. A hundred yards between malachite, grassy knobs, the horse led them on. When they reached the peak, the trail flattened, and the base of the house became visible. The chimney stood tall, as though resigned to warm those of the unearthly kind, spirits gathered to escape the cold nights. Nick guided Sally to the front of the dilapidated house, the tin roof caved in, lying jagged across what used to be the kitchen. Flashes of memories played through his mind.

Being held near the fire by his father.

Sitting at a table eating something soft and warm. A biscuit. Heavily buttered.

Older children in conversation.

He was ten when he understood what took his mother and father's lives. The disease that had claimed them both, just months apart. Aunt Cora had explained it to him. He wasn't sure what Consumption was, but he decided it was a foolish name. After their deaths, the children were distributed about the homes of relatives. Catherine and Sarah were taken in by his mother's sister. John lived with Uncle Roby, Ma's brother, for what didn't seem long. Being ten years older, he was soon off to fight for the Confederates. When John returned, he was a changed man. Nick hadn't sent word to Catherine or Sarah that he was heading away from Johnson County. They had their own families, their own lives to worry about.

Nick studied the remains of the house as though some sort of revelation might present itself, something that would spark memories that had escaped him. He wondered if life was a constant state of contentment back then, or had it just appeared so through ragged memory? He wanted to believe that was the case, that the hardness of mountain life and the daily drudgery that it demanded was never a hindrance in that house. He gave thought to how life would have turned out had illness not destroyed the foundation, not of the house, but the family. Would Nick be heading west if that had been the case?

Annabeth stood stoically at the train station when Tom and Nick approached on the buggy. Nick's heart labored with a heavy beat. He had told Annabeth not to see him off if it would be too hard on her, but she insisted she couldn't miss the chance to see him one more time. Her reddened eyes did nothing to dim her beauty. Tom allowed Nick and Annabeth a quiet moment. "I'll take your gear to the baggage car," Tom said. "Morning, Annabeth." He tipped his cap.

Annabeth forced a smile and nodded. She approached quietly and then leaned forward, kissing Nick on the cheek as though his face was so delicate it might crack if her lips applied too much pressure. "I'm going to miss you terribly."

Nick fought back tears. "I'm going to miss you, too."

"You sure you have to go through with this? It would do my heart good if you just canceled the whole thing."

"I think the sacrifices we make are what make the reward that much sweeter." He wiped her tears. "Time will fly by, and I'll be coming back home on this train in the blink of an eye. We will have the rest of our lives together."

Tears rolled down her cheeks. "You take care of yourself, Nick. And please come back home to me."

"I promise I will. And I promise you a great life when I return. I'll write when I get there and will list my address so you can write me back."

"All aboard," the conductor yelled from the steps that boarded the engine.

Nick looked at the train and sighed. "Well, I guess I best head on before they leave me."

"Would that be so bad?" she asked.

He fought emotions and kissed her forehead. "I love you. Good-bye."

"Don't you dare say goodbye. That implies something permanent, and I will not say those words."

He touched her face. "See you soon."

Nick leaned out the window and waved. The whistle screamed across the valley, and the steel wheels began to churn as the train set to motion.

Tom waved his hat. "Don't get lost, cousin."

"I shall return," Nick yelled.

He smiled at Annabeth, who stood quietly beside Tom. Tears flowed as she forced a smile. In her green dress, her soft hair curled and brushed away from her face, she looked more beautiful than anything he'd ever seen. How easy it would have been to have canceled the trip, marry Annabeth, and build on the land willed to him. But the cost of a new home would require money he didn't have, and he was committed not to owe any man. Independence keeps a man free from others' control. He had learned that from Jerico. He had promised to give Annabeth a wonderful home, in the best spot in the county, and they would share independence together. And he remained confirmed that the experience away from Johnson County would provide him with some larger sense of understanding that would enhance his worth as a man, a husband, and hopefully, a father.

He continued his stare at Annabeth, and though the train led him further from where she stood, her loveliness remained bold and pronounced.

I will see you soon.

The train trudged northeast under a steady rhythm, soon entering the soft contours of Laurel Bloomery. To the west, Iron Mountain stood enigmatic, in plum hue, carving a jagged skyline below azure skies. The stories of Iron Mountain told to Nick when he was a boy gave the land some level of mystique, which had nothing to do with the physical aspect. Jerico had told Tom and Nick while sitting around the hearth that there were rumors and stories of folk who had tried to settle on the mountain, only to have the mountain spit them off the edge as their hearts were deemed impure. Iron found no one worthy of calling the mountain its home. Jerico spoke of bear hunters who came upon mountain spirits hovering above the land, ghosts who were shunned when they were alive, returned now in the afterlife to find refuge in a land that might offer them a second chance. Nick had also heard that Cherokee tribes once lived in caves in the far recesses of the mountain, bound to the land, unable to leave without suffering a violent death. No matter the teller of the stories, the common theme was that any wayfaring stranger stepping on the mountain should be wary of their footsteps.

After tipping his cap to Iron Mountain, Nick turned his attention eastward where grassy knobs rose and fell in giant waves of emerald, dotted with elm and sycamore where cattle sought refuge. The cattle, imposing in their stance, were spread about the balds, eating in silence as though oblivious to not only the train's passing, but the passing of time in general.

Beyond the hills, Nick came upon land his eyes had never seen or imagined, and he spotted mountains whose names he did not know. He marveled at the depth and expanse of those purple-tinted hills that carried on as though there was no end, melting silently into a blurry haze. He wondered if they rolled onto the sea. He had studied the names of the oceans in school. If the train tracks rose high enough, to the peaks of the mountains beyond, would he be able to see the Atlantic? A memory flashed of his mother telling Nick his eyes were the color of the sea. Had that happened, or was it something imagined? Had Mother lived, would she have told him about the sea? Had she stood at the ocean's edge before? A question he could never ask her. And what stories would Pa have told? Would he have talked of worlds with giants and dragons? Perhaps of bears bigger than any that roamed the valleys of Johnson County. Would Nick have trembled at the telling?

When he was deemed old enough, Cora told Nick how she tended to him and his siblings when Mother became bedridden. The bed was a place his ma would not leave until Jerico and Pa carried her away, wrapped in the sheets where she had taken her last breath. Later that day, Cora would place Mother in a dress that would be her eternal clothing. She told Nick how similar the scene played out less than six months later when Pa suffered the same illness and manner of death. The disease showed no partiality. People in the valley pooled their money and got Pa a suit for his burial. Being a farmer, a mountain man, his clothes were designed to accommodate a life of manual labor. But on his resting day, he was presented with much fancier clothing.

The train whistle alerted the narrow valley of its presence, and Nick placed his face to the window. Small gatherings of houses came into view, and he reckoned the town of Damascus lay ahead. Nick felt as though he now knew how the cattle felt when led through a gate into a new field. The land was a tight hollow, with houses in close proximity to a single, straight street of commerce.

Nick looked about the train car, having been so absorbed with the scenery and the approaching of a new world, realizing he had not spent time to observe the passengers. There appeared to be men of a business nature more interested in conversation than looking out the window at the undisturbed countryside. To them, surely the land held no importance unless it was land that they owned or could profit from. These men appeared as though a ledger and a quill pen awaited them, as though minutes sitting on the train prevented them from filling their coffers.

A man in dark clothing and a top hat announced that the train would be idle until eleven-thirty, and the depot had some basic goods available should the need arise. A privy was pointed out, and those on the car began to head to the door. Nick watched the passengers exit, and the man in the top hat looked at him peculiarly.

"Sir, could you tell me what time it is?"

The man pulled a watch from his pocket, where it was secured to his belt. "It's nine-eleven."

"We are in Virginia?"

"That is correct. Damascus, Virginia."

"I ain't never left Johnson County, much less the state of Tennessee."

The man regarded Nick peculiarly. "Never left the county? How old are you, young fella?"

"Twenty-six, sir. Going to let this train take me to St. Louis. That's in a state called Missouri."

"Well, the world awaits, young man." The man waved his arm as though he were parting a pool of water. "Best not keep it waiting."

| 4 |

He had slept little in the three days of the trip, primarily because he spent most of his time watching the world through the window. He had watched mountains fall away into what he would consider eternal valleys. He saw rivers wider than any creek that flowed in Johnson County. The train had passed small houses lined so closely to the tracks that it appeared someone could have handed the conductor a bread loaf right out their back window. The thought of bread made Nick's stomach growl. Cora had sent him on his way with cured ham and cathead biscuits filled with fig preserves, but he had finished the last biscuit soon after the sun shone through the open windows of the train car that morning. He pocketed what small change he had and decided he would purchase something to eat from the dining car.

He had listened to conversations taking place around him, dialects so vast and different from anything he'd ever heard in tiny Doe Valley. He pondered whether to strike up conversation with those sitting next or nearby, and he noticed the peculiar expressions when they heard him speak earlier when a steward asked if he cared for a warm cloth. He supposed he should be embarrassed speaking in a dialect different from the others, but he reckoned his homeland was as good as anybody's. It gave him a quiet pride that he hoped others might be, if not envious, then at least curious as to where his homeland might be.

He ventured through the four passenger cars, studying the riders. Some that looked like individual travelers, some of them collections of families. If they made eye contact, Nick gave a brief smile before looking away. He was curious to know their name, where they were from, and where they were headed. But he reasoned they had no desire to carry on a conversation with someone from a place so plain and simple. He worked his way back to his seat and spotted an elderly man facing him.

"Be okay if I set across from you a spell?" the man asked. He wore a beaver hat, with wiry strands of white hair flowing from underneath. His black wool pants and matching coat stood in strong contrast to the white shirt beneath his coat.

"Yes, sir. My name's Nick."

"I like to look at where I been before I regard the place I'm headed." The man's hand was wrinkled and dotted with age spots, but his handshake was strong. "Name's Oscar Morris."

"Why do you want to look at where you done been? Don't you want to see what's coming? This is all new territory to me. I can barely wait to see it."

"A man who only looks to what's coming can forget what's led him to this moment. It's the steps that got you here that matter. How can a man know how to deal with what lies ahead if he disregards his past? If he don't keep in his heart what led him to this point?"

"I don't aim to forget what got me to this point. But if a man don't look to the future, to the possibilities, how can he learn what the world has to offer?"

"The world is full of evil, if you want the God's honest truth. It lures men into the viper pit under false pretenses. It's designed to cut the strings of a man's foundation, like a sheep separated from the herd. And when man is isolated, he's easy prey." He removed his hat, ran his fingers through his flattened hair, and wiped his brow. He glanced out the window and returned his hat to his head. "Son, approach what waits ahead guarded and with tempered expectations. And don't forget to turn around from time to time to make sure you're still with the herd, and if you ain't, that you return in dire haste."

"I'll try and heed those words. But I don't aim to be gone long, so hopefully there won't be time enough for separation."

"You be fool to think that."

Nick shrugged.

"Where you headed?"

"St. Louis."

"Where you from?

"Doe Valley. East Tennessee."

"If I were you, I'd get off at Hopkinsville, buy a ticket back home. Get back to the herd."

"I aim to be back with the herd in a year. Going to make big city money, and in the meantime, see what life is like outside of Johnson County. The reason for it all is to buy a plot of land and marry the prettiest gal in all of Tennessee."

"The lure of wealth."

"It's not wealth I seek. Just enough to buy land and not be held in debt to any man. I can't make that kind of money working on the farm."

"Best watch yourself along the way. Wolves wait in the dark, son. They wait for sheep who wander." He slowly stood, removing his hat. He nodded at Nick. "Don't wander." He again placed the hat on his snowy locks. "Approach what lies ahead with the wariest of eyes." The man turned and walked away, soon disappearing through the door and out of the rail car.

They crossed the Kentucky state line at dusk. The steward announced the entry to the passengers. Nick studied the landscape to measure it against his homeland, but the land had changed considerably from East Tennessee, and it was hard to know what point from which to measure. The world outside his window had faded to black, and he would have to wait till morning's light to see what canvas of scenery awaited. Since the train had only traveled through Virginia briefly before venturing back into Tennessee, he was anxious to see a new state. He'd been awestruck when they passed through Nashville, the size of the town, the commerce, the people all gathered in one area. He could only imagine then what St. Louis would be like. By morning, he would find out.

| 5 |

Will Gentry shouted from the station as Nick hung from the window, waving back after he spotted his boyhood friend. The wooden platform of the station held hundreds of people, and there was much commotion as they awaited travelers to arrive. The train had barely come to a halt before Nick hurried down the steps, his canvas bag in hand. Will moved through the crowd and hugged Nick, causing Nick to briefly lose his balance.

"It's about time you got here," Will said. "I've done put the city on hold, alerting them to your impending arrival. They have been anxiously awaiting official confirmation before resuming normal activities."

"Lordy, this world is a big place. I had my head pressed against the window of the train like a chipmunk at a chestnut bin. Trying to see what I could of the landscape. I was worried they were going to run out of track."

"These tracks will take you to California if you have the time and money."

"Well, time I got. Money, well, that's why I'm here. Right now, it would be a struggle to find two nickels in my pocket to rub together."

"That's about to change, old pal. They got money to burn out here."

"I just want to make enough to buy that piece of land down by Spear Branch."

"The one Daniel Stout owns?"

"That's the one."

"Why in the world would he sell that spot? Son, that's prime real estate."

"Had it pegged for his boy, Charles. But the boy got swept away in a flood, two years ago this February. It took them days to find his body. After a time, Mr. Stout couldn't bear to hold onto the plot. Rather sell it and help put the past behind him I guess."

"Well, tomorrow you can start the Spear Branch fund. For now, let me take you around town to see what big city life is like."

They walked side by side, Nick clutching his bag as though it might tumble away. The gray skies held a starkness that appeared artificial in design, like God had swiped it with a brush dipped in a vat of apathy. Fog lingered along the skyline of brick buildings bunched together, and Nick became disoriented as to the time of day. He sought confirmation of where he stood relative to where he would be if he were back on the farm. The smoky buildings bordering the street made Nick feel as though he was walking through a holler made of brick and mortar.

"How are things back in Doe Valley? When's the last time you saw my folks? Does Pa still walk with a limp? I got a letter from them a while back, but they didn't go much into detail, other than to say they are getting along and that they hope I'll come back home someday soon to live."

"Church is the only place I see them. Your pa still is a bit gimpy, but it's hardly noticeable. I think the horse that threw him has been relegated to leading the cart to the market."

"I'm surprised Pa didn't shoot him right there in the middle of town when he got tossed. But when them dogs came out of the thick trees and nipped at that horse's leg, it reared up. Can't blame him for that."

"Surely, you can't."

The streets were a whir of activity, and Will had to tug on Nick's coat to keep him from walking in front of horse-drawn buggies and people busily scurrying about. A pungent aroma of smoke and tar filled the air, and the city appeared in a state of constant motion. Commerce was palpable, and Nick imagined that the townspeople were wound by some crankshaft. They came upon a street crossing perpendicular, with tracks in the middle of the road. When the one-car train clanged and slipped down the street, Nick was amazed at the number of passengers.

"A train with only one car," Nick said. "Never seen that before. Looks like a caboose that someone got to pushing down the track. Where in the world is the engine?"

Will laughed. "It's a streetcar. Don't need no engine. Works off electricity on that wire above it."

"Well, I'll be a suck egg mule. No engine, you say?"

"Nope. It rides up the street and then back down again. We'll ride on it later."

Nick circled behind the trolley, squatting to watch it glide along the tracks before studying the wire connected to the angled pole on top of the car.

They stopped at the window of Smithson's Mercantile. Nick pressed his nose to the glass and cupped his hands around his eyes to cut the glare. There were rows of shelving twenty-five feet high, and there were boots and shoes, shirts and jackets, hats and belts. The selection seemed endless. Patrons milled all about the store and men in white shirts and black ties tended to their needs. One climbed a tall ladder and fetched a fancy hat.

"We'll take you in there in a few weeks. You'll have enough saved to buy you a new pair of boots."

"I'm good with the ones I'm a wearin'. I got to save every dime I can. Take as much as I can to buy that land and make Annabeth Parker my bride."

"Annabeth Parker? Son, don't tell me Annabeth is sweet on a rube like you."

"Hard to believe, ain't it? We been courting for over a year. Going to marry her when I get back. She wanted to get married before I rode out here, but I thought it wouldn't be proper to marry and then leave her all alone."

"You make sure you hang on to that pretty one. Even though she weren't no more than sixteen when I last visited, she was like a spray of heaven. I'd venture to say she has only gotten prettier."

"I tell you, the shine from her eyes can dim a Doe Valley sunrise to where it looks like the dead of night."

"Well, with the wages you're going to earn, you can get a new pair of boots and still have plenty left in your pocket."

"I do like the look of that pair on the counter yonder. I reckon I'll see how the money supply looks when it's time to go home. I'd feel like some kind of high-falutin' sort if I stepped off the train in Taylorsville wearing a pair of those. I do want to look my best when I see Annabeth."

"Let's take you on over to the camp and let you see the place that's going to be your home for the next twelve months. And you best lay your head down early tonight because the boss man will aim to get all he can from you starting 'bout sunrise."

They walked somewhere around a mile, and the high rises began to thin, and they came upon an area more industrial in nature. Men hid in the shadows, and steam rose from smokestacks to where it became hard for Nick to know the difference between the fog and the smoke. An odor of sweat and smoldered embers hung heavy as though it had created its own presence. The smell was strange in nature, and Nick yearned for the earthy smell of hay in the barn back home. He imagined Tom tending to the cattle. More than that, he envisioned Annabeth handling the chores of the day. He hoped she was warm with contentment. Thoughts of her would surely be necessary company while in this new land. He remembered what he told her about absence making the heart grow fonder, and he certainly longed to see her right then and there. All along the trip, she was never far from his thoughts. He had also once heard someone say that out of sight meant out of mind, and he hoped that would never be the case for Annabeth.

They came upon a dozen wood structures, identical in design, split by a narrow dirt alley. Six buildings on each side, a mirror image of each other. Drab, faded wood shanties in rectangular design with gray pointed tin roofs. Men were scattered about in front of the buildings. Some played cards, and some leaned in straight-backed chairs against the front walls.

"Fellas, I want you to meet my buddy, Nick. He's from my homeland, and he's going to be working with us."

Nick smiled. "Hidy."

Before him were men with sullen, cynical eyes who appeared as though rumors of peril were forthcoming but not unexpected. Men void of anticipation of what news this stranger might bring. A cast caught in some great calamity, a play with no exit stage. Nick studied this wayward band of misfits and reckoned them vagabonds with no homeland. He gauged them for any reaction to the appearance of this Tennessee man, but there was none.

Nick looked at Will. "Ain't exactly a talkative bunch."

Will shrugged. "Never are."

A man removed a card from his hand and placed it begrudgingly on the table before regarding Nick as something of a nuisance. Will took that as a sign that the introduction need not go further, and he led Nick into one of the shacks. "Well, this is your home away from home for the next year," Will said. "That's your bunk in the corner. Put your carrying bag under the bed."

Nick looked about the drab, one-room shanty. No windows. Small cots, ten in all.

He tossed about on the rickety bed, the snores of others an angry chorus. Stale sweat hovered above the room like some affliction not quite rid of itself. Dogs yelped outside the row houses as though in pursuit of a moon not seen, or perhaps in pursuit of other beasts who knew where to find it. Nick retraced the day in his mind, overwhelmed at the sheer number of people he came across. A mass of humanity who appeared drawn by proximity only. In that clammy room, there wasn't space for peace within a man's soul, to give thanks for the day completed, to ponder what the morning might hold. His bed amounted to little more than a padded box spring, and he wished his goose-feathered pillow had followed him to St. Louis. How long till sunrise? Would he be able to handle the construction requirements? He wasn't afraid of hard work. He had been a farm hand since he was a young boy, and work was a necessary part of life. But this was a type of work he had no experience to draw from, though his comprehension skills in school made him confident he could learn the job quickly.

A faint whistle blew, rousing the men in the small quarters to life. Nick had finally found sleep, but concluded it wasn't nearly what would be required to work a full day. There was a wash sink with worn rags, and Nick waited blearily for the chance to wipe the sleep from his eyes. The outdoor privy was out back, and Nick found it to be a shorter walk than the outhouse behind Uncle Jerico's house. Nick followed the men across a small, elevated boardwalk that connected the shack to a kitchen area. There was a long plywood table in the kitchen that held three pots. The men took metal plates from a small side table, and with no form of communication amongst them, they served themselves. Some form of oats, thick sausage quarters, and eggs. Loafed bread sat on a plate beside the pots. The strong aroma of coffee filled the air. With plate filled, Nick followed Will to a small table with four chairs.

"These are the lumpiest grits I ever did see," Nick said.

"It's oatmeal," Will replied. "Might want to pour some buckwheat syrup on it." He reached the main table and retrieved a tin cup.

"Where's the butter?"

"There ain't none." Nick frowned. "Don't say anything. Just eat it."

He took a bite and gagged.

"What hole did you crawl out from to not know what oatmeal is?" a slender man sitting beside Nick asked. He wore a wool cap pushed up to the hairline, exposing a long forehead. "Grits? Ain't never heard of such."

"It's made from corn," Nick replied. "And they surely are serving it right now in East Tennessee."

"Don't sound like any place I want to visit," the man said. "If you boys are a good representation of the fellas that live there, I feel bad for the womenfolk."

"Russell here ain't exactly a morning person," Will said. "By dinner, he'll be as chummy as a well-fed pup."

"Well, I'd put a Tennessean up against any," Nick said. Will kicked him gently under the table and shook his head.

"Judging the likes of you, I'd say Tennesseans might be the dumbest to ever walk the Earth. Your mammies and pappies should have been sent to prison detail after bringing idiots like you into the world."

Nick bit his lip and glanced at Will.

"And just so you know, I'm from Oklahoma," Russell said. "I'd say an Oklahoman could whoop any man to ever step foot outside of Tennessee. If you need convincing, I'd be happy to test that theory right after we finish our work shift."

Nick studied Russell. "Why wait till after our work shift?"

"Your friend needs to show some respect," a man nearby chimed in to Will. "He ain't starting off on the right foot, so to speak."

"Can't blame a man for defending his homeland, Murle," Will responded. "He's just here to work like the rest of us. And I guarantee you he'll run circles around the whole lot of us."

After breakfast, Nick followed the other men out the door and across a muddied field. The sun rose shrouded above a row of buildings that seemed to be without people or purpose, and the sun's rays struggled to penetrate the gray haze that seemed frozen in some morose manner. Will led them to the foreman. A stocky man named Mickey, who had forearms the size of a man's thigh. His mouth clinched a cigar.

"Will says you can handle yourself," Mickey said.

"I'll do whatever you have a need for. If it's something I ain't done before, I'll catch on. I'm a quick learner."

"We got to get these border walls built on the factory, so I need all the brick layers I can get. You can work with Will."

"He'll be a good one, Mickey."

"You afraid of heights?"

"Not that I know of."

"What's that mean?"

"Well, the highest I ever been with some kind of foundation other than ground is in a barn. With ground under me, I've touched the clouds on Doe Mountain."

"More information than I needed," said Mickey. "Will, you boys get to work."

They walked around the west side of the partially built warehouse, where stacks of bricks were gathered in clumps like a slab maze. Will grabbed two pairs of gloves from a cart and handed a pair to Nick. After they slipped their gloves on, Will backed the cart to a stack. "Time to load up," he said.

They gathered bricks and began to make a stack of their own on the cart. The building blocks were cold and rugged along the edges. Dust kicked up as the men transferred them to the cart. They filled a second barrow and Nick followed Will's lead, grabbing the handles and pushing his to motion. The wheels creaked as they struggled toward the building. The carts were secured to a pulley that raised them twenty feet. After the second barrow was raised, the young men climbed a scaffold. With buckets of mortar and what looked to Nick like cake spatulas, the two positioned themselves on the platform. Nick looked in the distance, the streets coming to life. People setting up shop. Entrails of smoke drifted above the city, and Nick wondered if the sun would eventually show itself, and if so, what a Missouri sunrise might look like. Will demonstrated how to mix and lay the mortar and then took a brick and carefully handed it to Nick, who wiped the excess from the edges. Nick took a trowel and imitated Will's method.

"That'll work," Will says.

"It's like building a spring house."

"Except you only have to do about five hundred of them."

"Well, the factory ain't going to build itself, so we best get at it then," Will said.

The friends began their task, and Nick felt comfortable working alongside someone he'd known since childhood. He reckoned it might be more than he could handle being so far from home with no one he knew.

"What do you think they're doing in Doe Valley about now?"

"Well, I'd say Aunt Cora has done cleared the kitchen table and Jerico and Tom are feeding the chickens, getting ready to head the cows to pasture," Nick said. "With fall coming on, it won't be long before they get the molasses cabin ready."

"I ain't seen the sun rise above Doe Mountain in over two years now," Will said. "That's one of the things I miss back home. But city life has growed on me, and I don't think the country holds anything for me no more. There's nothing ever gonna happen in Johnson County for me."

"I can see where the city lights can put you in a trance, so to speak. And I want to see all the city has inside her. Get perspective on the world outside of Johnson County. But as soon as my time is done here, I'm heading back to Annabeth."

"I don't know. These city lights might get hold of you same as they done me."

"I'll be sure to keep my blinders on."

A horn sounded somewhere in the distance. Nick and Will laid their trowels on the platform and shimmied down the platform. A gathering of women began to hand out bread wrapped in wax paper. A line quickly formed, and after the men took their food, they moved to a dusty table that held a jug of water and tin cups. Nick pulled back the paper and touched some rubbery textured meat that he couldn't identify. The bread was hard and crusty, but Nick's hunger was strong, and he was not about to complain. With no pocket change, he was dependent on what the company fed him. Will identified the meat as salami as they grabbed cups and filled them with water. They found a seat nearby on two rickety wooden crates. Nick caught Will watching him eat.

"You act like you ain't eaten in months."

"Couldn't stomach that oatmeal this morning, so my belly is empty."

"You'll get used to the food. If not, you best suffer through it and eat what's placed in front of you. Otherwise, you'll wilt away like a dead petunia."

"Well, I don't mind saying I sure miss Cora's cooking."

"You can get plenty when you go back home. For now, eat the slop they give you."

| **6** |

The workers assembled in the camp house for dinner, similar to how they had done at breakfast. Little talk, and less enthusiasm. A gathering that looked like perhaps some story of ill telling might be shared. The briny aroma of meat simmering filled the air. Loaves of bread were beside a large pot of percolating stew, and the men broke off chunks that seemed to fit their appetite after they filled bowls with the main course. The only course.

Nick sat beside Will again, and he reasoned he'd be more able to fall asleep that evening.

"Looks like the Tennessee boy made it through the first day," Russell said.

"I could hardly keep up with him," Will said.

"That ain't hardly the truth," Nick said. "It was all I could do to keep up with my hometown friend."

"Same hometown?" asked a man sitting across from Will. "How big's the town?"

"Big enough, Curtis," Will said, "that there's a south end and a north."

"Way I hear it, your mamas and daddies are also brothers and sisters," Curtis said. The others laughed and Nick studied them. "What about you, Nick? Your mama and daddy brother and sister?"

Nick stood, reached across the table, snatching Curtis by the shirt. "You say another word about my ma and pa, I'll take you out back and wipe the dirt with your face."

Curtis tried to shake Nick's grip, but when he couldn't, he feigned a smile. "Can't take a joke, buddy?"

"His ma and pa passed away when he was a boy, Curtis," Will said. "Don't disparage the dead."

Will took hold of Nick's wrist. "As I said this morning, you don't need to start no trouble your first day on the job."

"I'll never sit quiet when defending my family. My homeland. It's what a true Tennessean does. Seems like you mighta forgot that."

Nick sat on his bed, the flickering light from the oil lamp making shadows dance upon the barren walls. He sought for memories of his mother and father, something to push the comments from Curtis out of his mind. Something warm to make it appear they were still in the world. With eyes closed, faint images appeared. He sat on a slender cow, big hands surrounding his waist to keep him from falling. A leather rein clenched tightly in his tiny hands. Mama gently guiding the cow, Pa walking alongside, the grip on Nick steady and secure. Everything else within the vision was blurred voices, the clucks of hens, the nicker of the horse as it eased down the grassy path.

The oil lanterns extinguished, Nick sought sleep in that strange world. Submerged in darkness for which he could not take measure. Had he not witnessed the hazy sun peek through the clouds earlier, he would venture it might not had followed him on his trip west. As his beleaguered body struggled to find a comfortable position, his thoughts turned to Annabeth. Was she in bed at that moment, thinking of him? He questioned the sensibility of his decision. From the sound of it, Will was in a deep slumber. Nick removed the leather binder kept in his canvas bag. He rubbed the soft binding and tried to will an aroma of Annabeth from his memory. A vision arose of her hand surrounding the binder when she had given it to him behind the barn. He touched the binder to his cheek and breathed. He would keep her presence with him each day. That was a promise he made to her and he would make sure to keep it.

When he thought of the days that would need to pass before he would again sit beside her, when he would again hold her, would again touch his lips to hers, a cold sweat surfaced. He resolved himself to focus on what his purpose was for being there. Being in St. Louis would give him a perspective of the world. It would allow him to view it with different eyes and provide a more perceptive understanding of how the world works, and how to translate that into being a great provider for Annabeth and their future children. These days were a necessary sacrifice to enable a life free from debt, from being in shackles that the businessman could place on him. On Annabeth. Every day of work would add another piece of land on Spear Branch that would be his. Would be theirs. And he reasoned he wasn't the only one sacrificing. Annabeth would have to perform her daily chores and go through the flatness of life, with no Saturday buggy rides with Nick to look forward to. No Wednesday church dinners with legs nuzzled under the fellowship table. No kisses under the moonlight along Doe Creek. He reckoned a man couldn't let his thoughts be absorbed by such memories, that they were just trivialities that shouldn't occupy his mind. He couldn't waste time and energy on the pleasures of the heart. He would keep his focus on the task before him. He had responsibilities to uphold so that when he arrived in Taylorsville, he could arrive knowing the sacrifice was worth it.

He eased from bed and brought a lantern to light, looking about to see if he had awakened any of the others. Seeing no movement and hearing no complaints, he removed the lead pencil from the binder. Glancing around at the bleak surroundings, the pain in his wrists and fingers from the day's work, he began to write:

Dear Annabeth,

Well, I made it to St. Louis. I thought the train would run out of track, but Will said it goes all the way to California. The maps of Tennessee don't do the state justice, and it ran further west than I thought possible. I went through four states to get here. This world is a lot bigger than I ever imagined. It was quite an experience riding the train. I can't believe how big the city of St. Louis is. I saw something called a trolley car today. It looked like a one car train, and it ran on electrics.

I have to tell you that I surely do miss you. I was excited to be heading out to see parts of the world outside Doe Valley, but it was truly hard leaving you. You've not left my thoughts since the train pulled out of the station. The distance between us can only apply to the physical if we stay strong. I will surely keep you in my thoughts but will not let it hinder the purpose and the plan for giving us the best life we can have together. I will sacrifice a year away for a lifetime with you on solid foundation. Just imagine that first morning watching the sun rise above Doe Mountain in our home on Spear Branch. And I know that I'm not the only one to sacrifice. It will be a hard row to hoe for both of us, being apart and all, but I promise to make it up to you when I get back. I already started my new job. It's tough work, but then again, work is supposed to be hard. Don't let Mr. Stout change his mind and sell the land on Spear Branch to someone else. I'm just funning with you. Mr. Stout promised he would hold the land for me till I get back.

I am putting my address on the envelope so you can know where to send letters to me. I hope you will write often so I can feel close to you and so we can still be a part of each other's lives.

With love and warm regards,
Nick

| **7** |

Doe Creek shimmered, the surface below it obscure and vague. The stream pushed along the footstep of Doe Mountain as though it sought some destination that perhaps the rising sun couldn't reach. Veta Crosswhite gripped the rusted bucket and knelt by the creek. As the bucket filled, she recalled a summer morning when Granny Ethel held her by the waist as she dipped the bucket into the icy waters. Veta regarded the stream in a manner that might elicit Granny's presence if she wished hard enough. Six years old, hanging onto Granny's apron wherever she walked, begging to help with the chores. It was in Granny's dimly lit kitchen that she learned how to mix flour and buttermilk, how to use the tin cup to section out the cathead biscuits from the dough. Granny told Veta to give each biscuit the shape of the moon. And so, moon biscuits were what Veta came to call them. With Granny passed on fourteen years now, that cold, worn bucket was the one thing that allowed her to imagine Granny beside her each morning when she visited the creek.

When she entered the house, Larry and Joan sat at the kitchen table. Larry had a pocketknife poking at a walnut, and Joan appeared ready to offer assistance in how best to crack it.

Veta studied the ongoing process. "You's gonna slice a finger off and then you'll never be able to play the banjo again."

"I ain't never played it yet."

"Well, make sure you can do it if the option arises. Let me set this pail down and I'll help you."

"I can do it," Larry said. "Daddy showed me." He dug the blade in between a slit and popped it. The kernel was exposed and Larry removed it. "See? Now that's how it's done."

"That's also how you slice a finger off. I need to have a talk with your daddy about what is, and what ain't, dangerous to the well-bein' of a young 'un."

"I'll be nine when summer comes."

"That don't mean a hill of beans," Joan said. "You still have to be hoisted onto the hinny."

"That's a lie. I can climb that horse in a flat second."

"More like end up flat on your back in a flat second."

The children scrambled to perform their morning duties. Veta took to making the biscuits and Ray walked in with a bundle of cut wood. He placed several logs in the wood stove and embers popped and rose as though newly released from some cryptic dungeon. "I'll get the horse hooked to the buggy. Need to be heading to the store. Asa Shoop will be settin' on the steps asking if I need a pocket watch so as to know what time the store opens."

"Why can't that old feller buy more than a day's supply of tobakker? He chews it like it's a goin' out of style, so you'd think he stock up."

"It's his excuse to get away from Liddie. That woman scolds him like a baby sow what keeps digging under the fence."

"He knew what he was a gettin' into when he married her. You get the buggy and Midnight hitched. Biscuits will be ready in just a few. Got a flank of ham to carve out. I'll send you on your way with a handful to keep your innards from rumbling 'fore dinner."

She stirred the wood with the poker and opened a separate door above the wood fire, sliding the biscuits on an iron tray. The warmth of the stove seeped across the kitchen, and it was a welcome relief from the cold that found residence in the house overnight. September had been warmer than most, and with the first frost of the season upon them, the woodstove was about to serve a dual purpose.

She sliced the ham and took a jar of fig preserves from the pantry shelf. Plates were filled for the children, and she placed three biscuits stuffed with cured ham in a canvas pouch. She poured a cup of black coffee into a tin cup and headed out the door. Ray was checking the straps to the horse's reins.

"Here'n you go," Veta said. Ray scaled the step, and the seat creaked when he sat. She reached his food and coffee to him. "I put you an extra biscuit in there in case you get hungry."

"Thanks, sweet one. I sure appreciate the way you look after my well-bein'."

"You have a good day. Love ya bunches."

Ray nodded and took the reins with one hand while holding the coffee in the other. "Veta, I'll be back before the whippoorwill calls."

After the children left for school, Veta gathered the bed sheets and headed to the creek to wash them. The sun warmed her face as she stepped off the porch. The sun had fully risen now about Doe Mountain, and even from the yard, she noticed the creek beyond the field was in some state of chaotic brilliance, and she pondered whether it ran the same pattern and rhythm since God wished it to life. A warbler called out from a chestnut near the barn, and somewhere in the distance another responded as though a conversation of great importance had commenced.

The day had passed in similar fashion as those before, and she gave brief wonder to whether days beyond would follow the same path, and she decided she was perfectly fine if that were the case. Time was quick in its passing, though she had no measure of what a day's progression might be like should she live in another world entirely. Her attention was drawn to a white horse pulling a wagon.

"How do, Miss Veta," the young woman said as she brought the horse to a stop.

Veta squinted and placed her hand above her eyes to shield the late afternoon sun. "Well, hello there, Annabeth. Don't you look purdy as a speckled trout?"

Annabeth blushed and rubbed her sleeve across her forehead. "Oh, I'm sure I look disheveled from the chores Mother had me doing this morning."

"Well, young 'un, if that's what disheveled looks like, give me plenty of it."

"Oh, stop that kind of talk. You are a pretty lady."

"Lordy, you have to love the imagination of youth."

"I'm not still a child, Miss Veta. I turned twenty this past August."

Veta shook her head. "Where is the time a goin'?"

Annabeth reached into a sack perched beside her on the buggy. "Mama made a batch of blackberry preserves. She thought you would like some. She would have come, but she had a mess of greens to clean."

"Your mama's blackberry preserves are the best in all the valley. What it does to a biscuit is beyond words." Veta turned. "Now, stay right there. I got something for you." She hurried into the cellar and returned with two jars. "These pole beans are as tender and tasty as it gets. You take these on home."

They exchanged goods while Annabeth remained on the buggy. "You surely have turned into the prettiest thing," Veta said. "Ain't no fella claimed you as their own yet?"

Annabeth lowered her head and blushed. "As a matter of fact, one has."

"Who's the lucky beau?"

"Nick Grindstaff."

"Ain't he one of them young 'uns whose ma and pa passed away years back from The Consumption? That was a plague of immense proportion. Hope we never have to deal with that again."

"His parents did indeed die from that disease. He and his siblings were raised by relatives. Nick was raised by his uncle, Mr. Jerico Grindstaff."

"Jerico's a good man. Cora is a fine gal herself." She brushed the hair from her face. "So, when you marryin' the young fella?"

"Well, he's gone to Missouri to work construction. The pay is real good, and he's going to save and buy some land down Spear Branch way that Daniel Stout owns. We are going to get married and live there."

"Well, that's just extra good. How long is he going to be gone?"

She sighed. "He figured he would be able to have enough saved in a year. Maybe eleven months if he works extra hard. He's been gone almost two weeks. The days are passing so slowly."

"You just keep yourself busy. Time will pass like a streak of lightnin', and your young fella will be back home in no time. I'll say a prayer for his safekeeping."

"Thank you, kindly. Well, I'll be heading back home now."

"Please come back and visit."

"Yes'm, I will."

Veta watched Annabeth turn the horse and buggy about. The vestal rider led the horse into the concentric splay of angled sunlight until the buggy was consumed entirely, vanishing as if carried into some portal, some new world altogether. Veta gave thought to following the path to see what that world might look like, but the sheets were still in need of cleaning.

| 8 |

Nick walked through the doors of the Midwestern Bank. Ornate poles and deep cherry railings. The counter was lined with customers. Four tellers stood behind glass windows; their eyes locked on the currency passing through the carved-out holes in the glass. Nick held the slender wallet firmly in his hand and studied his surroundings. The impressive building made the Taylorsville Bank appear as but a plow shed. He had accompanied Jerico to the bank a few times when they had errands to tend to in town.

He glanced to where a man sat behind a desk, looking quite official in the trade of money exchange.

"Can I help you?" the man asked.

Nick presented his wallet as though it was something encased in gold. "I would like to open an account. I need to start accumulating."

"Well, that's a smart plan. We will be happy to manage your money." He motioned to a chair in front of his desk. "Please, take a seat."

Nick placed the wallet on the desk beside the form he was told to fill out.

"So, how much would you like to deposit today?"

Nick removed the folded bills from his wallet. "I got thirty-two dollars. And I'll be coming in every Friday to see you and add to the pile."

The man poorly hid his grin. "Well, you won't need to bring it to me. Any of our tellers will be happy to take your deposit."

"It'll be like clockwork for the next year. I'm saving up to buy some land back home in Tennessee. Going to marry my sweetheart and build a home. Start a family. I'm working over at the Miller factory. Laying down brickwork."

"Say you're from Tennessee?"

"Born and raised. I come out here to make money that I just can't make back home on the farm. In the meantime, I'm seeing what the world is like outside Johnson County."

"What do you think of it so far?"

"Hard to get a handle on it."

"This town is driven by the almighty dollar. It's a giant stage where folks like you and me are controlled like puppets. Controlled by a select few who drain out the last drop of blood and sweat from the masses until they are broken and discarded for the next generation so that their lineage stays forever linear. It's a cycle that can't be broken, and it's the ones with power that make sure that it never changes."

"Every man deserves the right to prosper."

"Not in this town."

"Well, that's another reason to build my savings as fast as possible and go back home where life flows at a different pace."

"Leave before it changes you. Once you're woven into the fabric of this city, you can't be torn clear of it."

"I'll not let it pull me in. I'll do my time, build my savings, and head on back home. Every dollar will be coming to your bank."

"Just be aware that your dollar is not held in the same regard as a rich man's. Yours and mine are inconsequential. More of a nuisance than anything else."

"Well, I don't have the confidence that keeping it under my cot would be a wise decision. At least it will earn a little interest in your bank."

"*Little* is correct."

The man spoke, a dime store prophet in an uncomfortable suit. He appeared as one burdened with the responsibility of proclaiming the truth in hushed tones, as though the ears of others who held his fate in their briefcases might hear his warning and silence him so that no one else could be warned of the realities.

After the paperwork had been signed, the man took Nick's money and walked to a teller, where she made the deposit. Nick was instructed to head straight to the counter in future visits. He reckoned that a good plan, as further words of warning from the banker might cause Nick to alter his plans and leave town early. His focus had to be on staying in the city until that bank held enough money to allow him to become a Johnson County landowner.

Nick sat on the edge of the bed, his overalls unfastened. He rolled his aching neck before reaching for the muddied boots that lay under his cot. For three weeks, he had struggled to find sleep on that flimsy bed, and he gave thought to sleeping on the floor to see if that might be a better option. Sheer exhaustion helped him find pockets of sleep, but not the kind he had back home. Perhaps if Doe Creek could reach his doorstep, the steady patter of water over rock would put him to sleep like a newborn.

After breakfast, which had not changed in menu in the three weeks Nick had been there, the men gathered outside their small tenant houses. They stood in silence like a group who'd wandered off, waiting for someone to point them towards home. All were far from home except for Frank Morse, whose home was close enough to travel back on Sundays to see his family. But they had gathered for one common purpose, and that was to work for a day's wages to give their families a better life. St. Louis was booming, and the pay for able-bodied men was deemed worth the temporary separation from their homeland. A few had come without family to work for, to return to, and there were no roots to bind them. In those men appeared no purpose other than to pad the pockets until another gig came calling that would carry them to some other location. And still, there were some who seemed to be fleeing something, perhaps someone, wanting to go unnoticed, left alone.

Nick noticed the rise in the scaffold, the skyline expanding as the two Tennesseans' work of laying brick and mortar had expanded the eastern-facing wall. The hours trudged along like some galactic beast leaned its elbow against the world, slowing the rotation. Nick focused on the job, his purpose for being there, and the reward that awaited him when he returned home. He missed the mountains. There was something in those high-reaching hills of the Blue Ridge that provided comfort, as though they were a fortress constructed for his protection. In the flat land of Missouri, Nick felt exposed. He reminded himself that he had indeed wanted to see what the world was like beyond those Appalachian Mountains, but in the short time he'd been outside of it, he found himself more fond of his homeland than he imagined.

On Sunday morning, the tenant homes were quiet as the men took advantage of a day off to catch up on needed sleep. Sleep was elusive to Nick, and he reasoned he could find more eventful doings than staring at the weathered ceiling, listening to rough-edged snoring. He slipped his clothes on and headed out. Hopefully, the whole city was still asleep, and therefore unable to mar Nick's chance to observe the rising of a new Missouri day. Morning created the perfect canvas. At least it was so in Doe Valley. Nothing stirred in those early moments except the steady flow of the creeks, and Nick loved to sit on the porch as the night skies lightened to watch depth form in the valley. He reckoned that in the land of industry surrounding him, man's stirring would certainly pale the evolution of the new day. Perhaps he could find it before the city awakened.

Gas streetlights winked as the blanket of light they provided faded. The skies to the east bled plum, and for the first time, stars flickered, and he wondered if those same stars twinkled above Annabeth. That thought gave him comfort. He raised the collar of his coat as a breeze rolled down an alley where men lay sprawled, probably too drunk to make it home the night before, or perhaps the alley was the only place they had found to rest. He headed deeper into the city, and the mountains of brick and mortar cut a silhouette from the lilac sky. He saw no comfort in those high-rising buildings. A pair of mutts prowled around a metal can knocked off its axis, appearing to be searching for food.

He came upon a post office and wondered if a letter was there from Annabeth. He had given her the proper postal information in the letter he had mailed to her over three weeks prior. He envisioned her sitting next to him at the bank of Spear Branch, on their newly acquired land. In the quiet of dawn, Nick studied the landscape, intersections where brick joined commerce with convoluted dreams. He noted the names written on the buildings. Names that he had never seen, and some he wasn't sure how to pronounce. Had these people come from far away as he did, and was the common bond the pursuit of wealth? Nick reasoned it wasn't necessarily for a better way of life. He much preferred the quiet stillness of Doe Valley, and its splendor was etched in his heart. And yet there was a certain degree of magnificence to the landscape of the big city, more in the newness of witnessing it. City dwellers seemed more focused on the business at hand than on the presence of another's company. Nick knew his sample size wasn't big, but from what he had experienced so far, making money seemed their only goal. And for him, it was the same, for now. The end goal was in sight, and if it weren't, he would head back home on the next train.

Nick wandered the streets, observing the faces and interactions of the inhabitants more so than the buildings and tenant homes. In his searching, he hoped to find something in the eyes of at least one person that would give him belief the city was more than a collection of soulless beings. But in the eyes of those he came across that hazy morning were ones that appeared vacant, as though they were born into the world nameless, and nameless was the way they intended to go through life. He reckoned if they were to disappear from the face of the planet, no one would come forward to question their absence. Beings detached from the core of the earth, where no hope existed for the days that lay before them. No sense of wonder in them as to whether there might exist another place where life might hold true meaning. Through the streets he searched, but reckoned the city held no place for hope. No place for kindness.

He ambled back to the workhouse, and the pungent aroma of fried sausage filled the air. He walked to the room and spotted a letter on his bed. It was all he could do to keep from tearing the flap off, but he examined the writing style of his name, and just knowing Annabeth had written it made him trace his name on the envelope. He sat on the bed and quietly opened it, so as not to disturb Will.

Dear Nick,

I hope this letter finds you well. I was so excited to receive yours. I read it over and over as it, in some ways, put you right in the room with me. From what you said, St. Louis is a very big town with many people. Do they seem to be of the friendly sort? I know you are working hard, and it makes my heart swell with pride for the reason you are out there working. I'm trying to stay as busy as I can to quicken the time until you return. Sometimes when I get to thinking about how long you will be gone, I struggle to keep focus on the world around me. I miss you terribly and wish to see you. I envision meeting you at the train station, throwing my arms around you, and beginning our life together. Please write again soon, and I will do the same. In fact, let's make a pact to write to each other weekly.

There's not much news to tell around here. Ginny gave birth, and so we have a new calf on the farm. Uncle Bud saw a panther on Iron Mountain when he was hunting bear last week. Well, I guess that's all for now. You take care of yourself.

With all my love.

Annabeth

$$| \; 9 \; |$$

Veta entered the henhouse, took hold of a plump bird by the neck, and twisted it. The hen ran scattered for a moment before falling to the ground. The other chickens squawked and flapped about as though they might be next. The pot was readied over the fireplace and soon chunks of meat would be in the boiler, swimming amongst dumplings. The children would be home shortly from school, and Ray would be coming up the road before sundown. While the dumplings simmered, she took to the churn to make buttermilk.

They were better off than some around the valley, and some folks back in the hollers scraped by for enough food to keep them alive. If Ray's daddy hadn't left the store to Ray after he died, he would have become a logger with his brother in Kingsport and commuted back and forth. The store provided enough income and leftover meats and cheeses so that much of the garden vegetables could be canned and stored away for the winter months.

Veta noticed the sharp angle of the sunlight slicing through the window, and she studied the shadows under the big hickory beside the house. A clock more readable than any of the man-made kind. She turned her head slightly, hearing the voices of the younger variety. She reasoned their first request would be to hunt crawdads by the creek until dinner time.

Joan and Larry had cleaned up from their creek ventures, trying hard to get the lye soap to remove the smell of crawfish from their hands. While Veta set the table, she kept an eye on the window, wondering why she hadn't heard the clunk of hooves on the hard dirt road. Perhaps a customer had kept Ray past closing hours.

Veta had the children eat so as not to have a cold dinner. She would wait on Ray as it wouldn't be right for a man working hard all day to eat without companionship, even though most nights Ray ate without speaking.

Dusk was setting in, the valley fully shadowed. Veta led the mule up the road to Amelia's house.

"How do, Amelia. Would it be okay if the young 'uns stayed at your place while I run to the store to check on Ray?"

"Why, sure," the elderly woman said. Her hair was the color of newly fallen snow, standing in heavy contrast to her navy-blue sweater. "Come on in the house, young 'uns."

"Thank you, kindly," Veta said as she nudged the children through the doorway.

Veta guided the mule as she sat anxiously on the cold leather seat of the buggy. They inherited the animal after the father-in-law's passing. Veta thought it unnecessary to have a spare buggy and wondered if those in the valley might view them as being hifalutin. But at that moment, with the sun dipping beyond Iron Mountain, the chill of the evening nipping at her face, Veta was glad to have the means to travel faster than walking the mile to the store. When she pulled up in front, she spotted the hinny nibbling on wildflowers, creek side beyond the store, its reins dangling down its neck. A light was on inside, and with no other buggies or horses in sight, she figured whoever was inside with Ray had arrived on foot. Veta hurried into the store. All was quiet. An unexpected silence. Deciding the store was empty, she hurried outside and walked around back. Ray's buggy sat empty in the weeds. Veta called the horse, and it slowly meandered to her while she eyed the storage shed. The outbuilding was dark. She came around the back of the store and noticed the door slightly ajar. Her heart leapt when she spotted him slumped behind the meat and cheese counter. Rushing to his side, she cried out, "Ray!"

His body held warmth, but his eyes were fixed and cloudy as though he searched for something beyond the reaches of the world. She touched his neck for a pulse, and his skin was clammy and rubbery to the touch. She slapped his face and called his name. *Wake up. Please wake up.* She pulled him to her chest and sobbed.

| **10** |

The season had turned to winter in harsh manner. Throughout the night, the winds blew against the sleeping quarters as the flatlands had no way to stop it. Nick had struggled to find warmth under his slender, wool blanket. He longed to sit beside the wood stove back home, his sock-covered feet propped up near the black, iron belly. He rose, restless, the walls closing in on him like some one-dimensional creature. Relegated to another lost battle with sleep, he arose from the cot and slid his boots over his splayed wool socks. He removed the letters Annabeth had sent him. In the pale of dawn, he reread each one. Her words brought him comfort, and he imagined her voice speaking the words to him directly. He carefully placed the letters back in his writing satchel. He would write her again in the evening.

The door creaked when Nick opened it. He stepped out into the narrow alley between the shacks, the brisk winds reduced to a muted breeze. The damp chill in the air cut deep, and he slipped his hands into his coat pocket. Mist hung heavy, and the landscape lay in quiet gloom as though it wished not to be awakened, that it preferred the day be avoided. As Nick made his way down the lonely streets, it appeared as though no one else existed in the world except him, and there rose within him a feeling to shed that world altogether.

He headed toward the river. When the train had brought him to St. Louis four months prior, night had shrouded the wide shape of the Mississippi when the train crossed it. Will had taken him once to see what he called the Mighty Mississip, but a ruckus had started up on the way between what appeared a clash between a handful of men of different heritage. The fight had stumbled onto a market, and the destruction of vegetable stands commenced. When Nick and Will joined in to help break up the fighting, the errant fists that found their mark against the Tennessee boys' faces snuffed out all desire to walk to the river.

He walked past vast warehouses dulled by smokestacks. When he made it through the warehouse district, he came upon row houses that appeared dimensionless, abandoned, though surely their inhabitants had not been roused from their sleep. When he went through the shipyard, the land turned slightly downward, and the leaden water came into view. A fog hovered above the river, making it impossible to measure its mass from where he walked. He spotted an intricate bridge built on top of massive arches, and he headed toward it. There was a bronze sign at the base that said Eads Bridge, and Nick marveled at the size of the structure. He walked to where he was under the base of the bridge, and kneeling to water level, he spotted buildings on the far side, finally able to measure the width. Winds slipped from the water and brushed against Nick's face. His only sense of measure was the Watauga River west of Taylorsville, which paled in comparison. He searched the depths of the water's edge for stones, but the river bottom appeared smooth, and he closed his eyes and listened to the gentle movement of the water. There was something missing in its heartbeat. Missing were babbling sounds of water rushing over stones of endless shape and color. The lack of design made it appear as if it were an unfinished painting. The sight made him wish that he were standing on the bank of Doe Creek. He glanced down the river's edge, and the scenery blended into the mist. A steam ship broke the silence, and Nick watched the massive paddle wheel push through the ghostlike fog, as if something had risen from the depths on its way to worlds unimaginable. As it pushed off downstream and the fog swallowed it whole, Nick questioned whether his mind had conjured up the boat entirely.

Annabeth held the rein, guiding the horse down the lonesome road. The grazing fields along the hillsides had faded, their green luster chased away by the blustery, winter nights. Further beyond, the hardwoods on Iron Mountain stood barren, limbs intertwined, paled like bones under the midday sun. Stark walls of isolation. No sympathy for the forlorn.

"Sun of my soul, thou savior dear," Annabeth sang softly, so as not to disturb the solace in the valley. "It is not night if thou be near." Her audience consisted of the equine only, and she held no worries about how her voice might quiver. "Oh, may no earthborn cloud arise, to hide thee from thy servant's eyes." There was no purpose in this journey through the valley other than to pass the time, to let music soothe her, even if it was fleeting. Some days, she didn't care for the company of others, to be forced into conversation for which she had no interest.

She pulled up beside her house. An unfamiliar horse grazed in front of the porch. Its chocolate hide glistened in the afternoon sun, and its sinewy body was undoubtedly the result of good breeding. She guided her horse around back and dismantled him, leading him to the barn.

When she entered the kitchen through the back door, she heard voices. Her mother and father sat at the table, talking with someone with his back to her. The stranger stood and turned. He smiled and nodded at Annabeth.

"You remember Cody," Annabeth's mother said.

Cody slid from around his chair and held his hand out to Annabeth. When she extended it, he shook it gently. "Hello, Annabeth. It's good to see you."

She regarded her father oddly before speaking. "Hello, Cody. What brings you out here?"

"We have a big announcement, Annabeth," Mr. Parker said. "We are partnering with Cody's family. He has secured financial backing from his father, and combined with my investment, we're going to build an iron works plant. Cody will be plant manager."

"Isn't that exciting?" her mother asked.

There appeared to be some sort of fabricated excitement in her parents' faces. She felt Cody's stare upon her. "Yes, that's exciting."

"Cody will be spending a good bit of time around here as we lay out the plans for the plant," Mr. Parker said. "How many workers are needed and such. Payroll. Cody studied business at East Tennessee State and has the knowledge to take care of the company's every day running."

"How nice," her mother said to Annabeth. "Looks like you two can get to know each other better."

Annabeth glanced at Cody. Something crafty in his smile. "Yes, that's real nice," she said. "Well, if you'll excuse me, I need to write a letter to Nick." She left the room.

Will spread the wooden dominoes on the table. Nick assisted, and the dominoes were turned on their underside so as to hide their design. Will stirred them about, and they both chose seven of the dominoes before gathering them to where they could view the ones selected. Will laid down a double six, and the game commenced. Nick followed suit with a matching six, and Will quickly matched it. The dominoes shimmered under the lantern's light above them as the game progressed. The pungent aroma of grease hung in the air, and the kitchen workers were done for the day. The table where dishes and cups were kept for each meal made for a good place to play their game.

"Did you see how that young gal at the counter of Gleason's Market was batting her eyes at you yesterday?"

"Imagination is a powerful thing," Nick said. "She weren't anything but attentive to two customers who walked in the store."

"Sometimes I wonder how you've made it in the world this far. You are unmindful of what's going on around you. The people. That gal was smitten by you right from the get-go. I watched the way she spoke to you. Other people waiting in line, but she wanted to keep on conversing with you."

"You don't know nothin'. I'd wager she talks that way to all customers."

"She didn't talk to me. Son, she was a fine-looking gal."

"Why don't you go back on down there and start up a conversation? Since you are all wound up on her beauty."

"Oh, I wouldn't know what to say or where to start. Besides, I don't have the look that turns the ladies' heads like you do."

Nick drew from the bone pile and had to remove three pieces before he could find a match to Will's piece. "You know there's only one head that I want turning my way."

"You surely miss her."

"I surely do."

Will made another play as the collection of played dominoes grew, the pieces taking up more of the table. A grumbling arose from outside the kitchen, voices rising in anger. A dispute of some manner appeared in play, and the tone of the voices escalated, and both Will and Nick knew there was only one way the dispute would be settled. Bodies soon slammed against the wall, as though trapped beasts seeking release from some trap. The scuffling carried on as did the game of dominoes, and Nick reckoned the fighting might last longer than the game.

"I ain't never seen so much brawling that has to do about nothin'," Nick said. "Back home, a fight's only necessary if someone's reputation is on the line. Or when a man moves his fences to increase his land ownership from another."

"Or if someone steps over the line with another man's lady," Will said. "That's when all hell breaks loose. And I would agree that circumstance is the one where the use of fists is an allowable offense."

"In this town, it don't require more than giving one a suspect look. Fists seem to be the solution to anything. Ain't seen one fight that was for the defense of something worth defending."

"You sure jumped to your feet that first day."

"That was an attack on family and homeland. If that ain't worth defending, I don't know what is."

"These men are just restless. Bored. Got to have something to do."

"Seems like a waste of energy if you want my opinion."

"Speaking of opinion, why don't you head on back to Miss Annabeth? Leave all this foolishness behind?"

"You gettin' tired of me?"

"Like that would ever be the case. You have made all the hard work worthwhile. I'd prefer to have you here for always. But I know where your heart is, and this place ain't it. No, sir, it's back in that valley. Take what you have saved and head on back home. Marry that gal. If not, I might go back and marry her myself."

"I don't think you got the nerve, or the tools to accomplish the task."

"I know I don't. But a girl like that is bound to have to fend off the wolves. I'm sure her devotion to you is unwavering and all, but it would keep me awake at night knowing young bucks are trying to come to her aid, to console her sadness all under the guise of just being polite."

"Don't think those thoughts ain't entered my mind. But if I don't have faith in her, then what kind of relationship do we have? If it's not sturdy enough to deal with the separation, the miles between us, then I say it was nothin' but a house of twigs to begin with. I've set my course and got to see it through. The end is in sight, and it will be worth it all to buy the land we picked out, to build a home, and start a family. My bank account is expanding like a pig's belly that's been set free in the cornfield." He laid down his last domino. "No, sir, I can't let bad thoughts inside my head. I can't quit now. Too close to the end, and the beginning of a lifetime spent with Annabeth."

"Well, Bud, you are a stronger man than me."

"Tell me something I don't know."

They looked at the played dominoes, and when Will realized Nick had played his last one, he removed his hat and ran his fingers through his hair. "You are just a born winner. Don't matter the game. And it seems like the game that matters most is the one with Annabeth. And what a victory that is, Bud."

Nick entered the tenant shack. His hands ached. His back was tired and in need of a mattress, no matter how thin. He spotted the letter set up against his pillow. Excitedly, he sat and opened it. He put himself in a reclining position, the letter held above his face.

Dear Nick,

I am missing you so. The days move like molasses, and no matter what I do to occupy my time, to while the hours away, I am in a constant state of sadness and am at the point where making it through the day is futile. I wish I could fall into some deep sleep until the day you arrive, as the pain in my heart overwhelms me. I find myself daydreaming of being at the station, dressed in the finest clothes, watching you step off the train. I am so ready to start our life together. I took the horse and buggy to see the land on Spear Branch yesterday. I found a great spot to start a flower patch near the creek. We can put Goldenrod along the roadside leading to the house. It will be just the prettiest spot in the valley.

I've been tempted to take a train out to St. Louis to visit you, but Father would surely build a barricade on the tracks to prevent it from leaving the station. I've even thought of leaving out without telling them, with only a note placed on my bed for them to read after I'm gone. My mind just in a constant state of conjuring up ways to see you, whether it's there, here, or somewhere in between.

Please hurry home.

I love you more with each passing day.

Annabeth

Annabeth sat on a cane chair beside the house, stirring apples in the slow cooker over the fire pit. Her mind wandered. She mixed cinnamon and sugar in a wooden bowl. The fire dipped and fanned, the sweet aroma of the ingredients almost overwhelming.

"Hidy," she heard above the hum of the fire. She looked toward the house, and Cody approached. "Making preserves?"

Caught off guard, she wiped her hair away from her forehead. "Yes. Yes, I am."

"I love the smell of cinnamon, don't you?"

"I guess so." She looked beyond him, hoping her father was not far behind.

"Mind if I sit for a bit?" Before she could answer, he fetched a chair from the porch. He placed the chair beside hers, causing her to scoot hers to provide more space between the two. "You're looking very pretty today."

She stirred the contents of the pot. "I'm guessing it's Daddy you need to see."

"Well, it is. But I'm a little early, so I've got time to talk, if that's all right."

She shrugged. "I need to tend to the preserving, so I've not got much time for chit-chat."

"I don't bite." He grinned. "Just wanted to see how you are doing. How your day is going."

"It's going just fine."

"That's good." He looked about. "Say, would you like to go over to Abingdon sometime and catch a play? They have a nice theater. It's very entertaining."

"Thank you for the offer, but I have a steady beau."

"I heard something about that. Ned? Norman?"

"Nick."

"He went out west, right?"

"St. Louis."

"It's not serious, though, right?"

"Actually, it is. We plan on marrying when he gets back by summer's end."

"How long's he been gone?"

"Almost five months."

"That's an awfully long time to be gone from the one you love. Doesn't seem like you're much of a priority."

"Well, that's none of your concern. But just so you know, he's earning good wages so he can buy land down Spear Branch way where we can live."

"Sounds like an honorable fella."

"He is. Very much so."

Cody stood. "Well, I better find your pa." He held out his hand, and she extended hers. He kissed it. "If I was him, I'd a found a way to provide for you without leaving you all alone. I'd never leave someone as lovely as you. Not even for a day." He gave a slight nod. "Again, it was nice to see you."

She watched him walk away.

A gray mass had spread across the land as the cart led the men away from the city. Nick grasped a metal hitch of the side wall of the cart as it rumbled along the sallow road. The land appeared sparsely inhabited. A two-story wooden house sat stoically at the top of a gentle rise of a hill, its white columns dulled from the gray dawn. Two shacks sat off to the lower side of the white house, smoke coming from slender chimneys as though some early stirring had commenced, a preparation perhaps so that tending to those fortunate to live in the large house would soon begin.

Two men sat beside Nick, their feet dangling off the back of the cart as they watched the city fade behind them. Southward they headed, and through the haze in that morning sky, humidity began to build, and Nick's shirt began to cling to his skin.

"You done much wood cutting?" asked the slender man sitting next to Nick.

Nick nodded. "I cleared my share of woodlands back home. Cleared land for planting fields. Cut wood for building purposes. Barns, sheds, fencing. I never seen someone as good with the process as my uncle, Jerico. And it ain't just the wood cutting, but the structures he builds. You?"

"Cleared land down Oklahoma City way," he said. "When I heard they needed tree fellers for the lumber yard, and the pay better than anything I could find in Oklahoma, I headed this way. I ain't seen you before. First day?"

Nick gave a quick nod. "I can only work Sundays. Only day off from my job in the city. I'm trying to squirrel away as much money as I can."

"Ain't we all?"

"My name's Nick. I'm from the far corner of Tennessee, right near the Virginia line."

The man nodded. "Clyde. Born in Arkansas, but didn't live there long enough to call it home. We were a band of nomads. Moved from state to state, town to town. My pappy was as much a dreamer as he was a drinker. So, he couldn't hold onto jobs for long, and he figured there was always a better place waiting on him somewheres else."

The cart rattled and moaned as it led them past shanties strewn haphazardly like props discarded from some malefic play. A wasteland except to those who hid inside the shacks. When the cart had led them to their destination, the group dismounted. Twelve in all. There was a whir of activity beyond as what Nick guessed were a hundred men busy at work. Some guided cattle that pulled felled trees, encased in chains, to greased slopes where the trunks rolled until they crashed into the expansive Mississippi River. A man covered in sawdust awaited Nick and the others. When Nick informed the man he was good with an ax, the boss man directed him to a wagon where men climbed aboard. Nick hopped on, and the wagon headed toward a slender slope where massive fields lay, stripped of all timber. As far as Nick could see, the land appeared as something apocalyptic. The forest had been laid bare, discarded limbs and saplings strewn about the khaki-colored soil. The wagon cut through a gully and went beyond the destruction to where, in the distance, a deep, tree line was visible. A wagon approached them. Nick glanced into the cart as they passed. A half dozen men, casualties of some archaic battle. One lay on the cart, a blood-soaked sheet covering what appeared to be a nub of his elbow. Another had a kerchief pressed against his hand, at least two fingers missing. One man lay on his side, no movement at all. The other three must have had some degree of injury that Nick couldn't decipher. Their eyes were clouded and vague, as though what they had endured was nothing more than an imposition and not necessary of discussion. A hindrance to wages earned. One studied Nick as the carts passed, his dour expression a forewarning to this new batch of workers.

The cart ambled along to the base of a hill covered in hardwoods. The driver brought the cart to a halt. "Pair up and cut each tree to the base," he said. "They's bucksaws in a shed yonder if you prefer. Remember to judge the distance between you and the others so your tree don't come crashing down on somebody. Cut them so they fall down the slope. Cut limbs off before you move on to the next tree. Drivers will bring the wagons and drag the trees on out of here. You two new fellas follow the lead of the others. Remember--you cut yourself, you got nobody to blame but yourself. We will bandage you up, send you back home, and find a replacement. And stay aware of the land. It can turn slick, and you can end up tumbling to the bottom along with trees. You get hit by one and you're good as dead."

Nick entered the tree line with Clyde, his ax handle rough and brittle. He put on the worn gloves he had been given. When they had determined the separation between them and the others was sufficient, they chose a tall hardwood. Facing each other, Clyde nodded. "Let's cut the wedge."

The man from Oklahoma City drove his ax at a down angle, and when he cut into the tree, the crack of steel to wood reverberated across the hillside. When Nick drove his blade into the same crevice, it dug deep. "Damn," Clyde said. "That's the way to drive a blade."

Nick nodded and waited on Clyde to take his next swing. He followed with an uppercut blow that created a divot, and they took turns alternating angles until they had carved halfway into the tree. They moved to the back side of the hardwood and positioned themselves again. "We'll alternate again until we can make it fall just by breathing on it. Then we'll push the son of a bitch over."

They were efficient in their swings, and soon the tree fell. Nick nodded at Clyde, and they took to cutting the limbs. When they had deemed all limbs removed, Clyde said, "One down, ninety-nine to go." They spotted the next tree they intended to cut, so it began again. Soon, the cattle were brought to the base of the hill, and the timber was chained, and the cattle led them away. The land about them began to open up, the light from the hazy sun finding more ground to light. The hillside took on a pallid tone, as though something beneath the surface drained anything from the color spectrum.

Nick straightened his back and looked about, wondering if the intent was to wipe every tree from the state of Missouri. He'd seen the Doeville Timber Company clear fields of chestnut and elm, but it was done with some type of forethought so that it cleared fields for planting, or for grass for cattle to graze. The sparseness between them allowed the woods to reign supreme, still the prominent force of the hillsides.

Nick rubbed his hands together gently on the cart as they headed back to town. There were bloody callouses on the palms, and his fingers throbbed. His back ached, his stomach churned. When he made it back to the tenant house, he took a slice of bologna and a chunk of bread from the kitchen house and went to his bed. Lying on his side, he struggled to stay awake. Once he had finished the last bite of bread, he fell into a deep sleep.

Morning came too soon, and Nick sat on his bed rubbing the callouses. His back fell into a spasm, and he leaned forward to un-wrench it. He desired rest and was inclined to lie back on the cot and skip breakfast. Will sat on Nick's bed and began sliding his boots on. "You look like hell," he said.

"I hurt from head to toe."

"The logging industry not something you want to turn into a full-time career?"

"No, it's not. One day a week is more than enough."

"You sure you need to do this? Seven days a week is gonna be hard on a body. You might need to use that Sunday as a rest day so you don't end up keeling over like a shot groundhog."

"I can handle it. I need to fatten that bank account as fast as possible. Doing so should allow me to go home a little earlier than planned. I tell you, I'm missing Annabeth something fierce. I can hardly wait to lay creek side with her in the soft grass and do nothing but count bees and butterflies."

"Well, save the lying around till tonight. Get your ass out of bed and down to breakfast so I don't have to carry your workload today."

Nick nodded and ran his hand through his hair, the callouses tender to the thick hair on his head.

Annabeth rolled the dough with a wooden pin. Her mother tended to a skillet on the stove, the aroma of grease and beef filling the room. Annabeth took a metal cup and began carving the flour into round orbs that she put on a baking sheet. She glanced at the skillet.

"That's a big roast," she said. "An awful lot for just the three of us."

"We're having a guest for dinner."

"Who would that be?"

"Cody Swanson. Your father invited him."

"Don't they see enough of each other through the course of the workday? He's coming around the house almost daily now."

"He is such a fine young man. Smart, hardworking. Your father said if not for Cody, the iron plant would have never become reality."

"He seems to have more of an interest in just the plant."

"You should make an effort to spend time with him."

"I've got no interest in him."

"He's so handsome. And such a kind fellow. He has the kind of wealth that could provide for a wife, a family. Can't ask for more than that."

"Well, I have all I need in Nick. He might not be wealthy, but he's all those things you think Cody is, and then some. There's no need for me to spend time with Cody or any other man in this valley."

Nick approached the wagon. The headcount grew less and less each week. Clyde leaned against the wagon.

"You're as stubborn as me, it appears," Clyde said.

"Stubborn, or ignorant? I think both." He looked about. "At least we got more elbow room on the wagon."

"Well, some of them got hurt and are unable to work. Others, I guess, just figured it's not worth the risk of life and limb for fatter pockets."

Clyde and Nick hopped on the back of the cart, side by side. There was little conversation. They watched the buildings diminish in stature until the city became something etched into the skyline. Deathly quiet, like a town evacuated. Nick envisioned the cart riding into Doe Valley, Iron Mountain etched into the skyline. Annabeth waiting by Doe Creek.

When they made it to the lumber site, the cart ambled past log flumes where men were busy guiding the logs toward the river. The wood rolled with thundering motion, a mass of timber fighting to make it to the water below. Workers stood on both sides of the flume, anticipatory in their postures. As Nick observed the process, a massive log spun over the top of the stack, twisting out of control, as though trying to escape the river altogether. It wedged between two other trees, flipping so that one end rose skyward before slamming down into the flume like a javelin. In booming, crashing fashion, the logs coming from behind began to jam and stack like straw flowing into rocks of a bent stream. The timber below the jam pushed on into the river, but the conglomeration of the stuck logs creaked and slammed against each other until there was no movement at all. Two workers ran with a box where a cord-like wire fed from the back of the box as they scooted toward the logjam. One carried the box by a handle and carefully set it in the middle of the jumbled mess of timber. The driver of the cart in which Nick and the others sat brought the mule to a halt and turned to watch the scene unfold. When the man had placed the box under the log that had jackknifed and set the logjam to commence, he made his way back toward the other, who still held the cord. They were shouting to each other, the one holding the cord trying to hurry the other off the pile of logs. Once he had cleared the logjam, the two ran to where the cord connected to a detonator. "Lookout below," one yelled before pushing a handle downward. The explosion that soon followed reverberated across the ground, Nick feeling it from where he sat in the wagon. Logs shattered into pieces, some flying skyward fifty feet or more. As the jam began to loosen, the logs slowly started to slide down the flume, and two of the logs that were shot skyward tumbled off the flume. The man who had detonated the jam tried to run, but the powerful logs slammed down on him so that the only part visible was an arm and a leg. Nick leapt from the wagon and took to running to the downed worker. His partner reappeared from somewhere on the far side of the logs.

"Lordy, Lord, Monte. Hang on." He tried to lift one of the logs, but the weight was too much. Nick was the first to reach the scene, and he wrapped his arms around the end of a log.

"Help me with this end," he shouted. The man moved next to Nick, and they both surrounded the log as best they could with their arms and tried to lift. Clyde and another also joined in, and with panicked breath, they fought to lift the massive tree.

"We gettin' you out, Monte. Hang on."

There was no sound or movement from under the logs. A worker with a steel rod worked his way between the men and forced the rod in between the log and the one that ran angular under it, the one that lay across the injured man's torso. He found enough area between the logs to drive a wedge, and Nick joined in and pushed the rod upward. Two men took the end of the rod behind Nick and, with strained voices, pushed upward until the log rolled off to the side, lodging itself at the side of the flume. The men gathered around the log, and when the rod was jammed under it, they lifted the tree, and the man's partner pulled him out from beneath.

Nick knelt and took the man's hand. His skull was concave, his bloodied eyes staring skyward as though he was looking for an explanation of what had just occurred.

"Monte," his partner cried out. "Oh, Lordy, Monte. I'm sorry I couldn't save you."

Two men arrived in a wagon. They looked managerial and soon stood over the dead worker as if confirmation was in order. The assessment in their eyes was void of grief. Instead, a calculation of sorts appeared underway. A look as though they'd come upon a bridge washed away, and trying to determine if it was worth finding an alternate route. One of the men turned to those who had helped, who now looked down at the fallen worker. "Get on back to work now." The men appeared as though they had not heard the order. Nick imagined the grief that would soon overtake the dead man's family when the news was brought to them. "Go on, now. Get back to work. We're not paying you to stand around. There's nothing that can bring this fella back. So, move on and get to what we're paying you to do."

Nick watched from the wagon as Monte was lifted onto a small cart. A tarp was placed over the man so that the only part visible was his legs, which dangled off the back. As the men were led to the hill that would become the next one to be wiped clean, the next to be turned into an apocalyptic terrain, Nick couldn't shake the vision of what it might look like if Jerico and Cora were being told Nick had fallen into some tragic mishap. What would Annabeth's reaction be? Would she curse him for leaving her to work for wages he deemed would speed the process for going home early? Was the grand plan not so grand after all? When he and Clyde came to the tree they chose, Nick laid the first blow with the ax. The echoed sound made his stomach lurch.

His hands bloodied, his back wretched, Nick walked into the tenant house. The sight of the dead logger was fresh in his mind. He removed his binder from beneath his bed. He wiped his bloodied hand across his pants and sat.

Dear Annabeth,

It's been a hard day. To be truthful, it's been a hard nine months. I've been working Sundays for a timber company, and it's sped up the process of filling the bank account. My plan is to hop on the train back home in six weeks. You need to be prepared for the hug I'm going to give you. I fear the impact might knock you flat on your backside. I can't wait to marry you and build our home on Spear Branch. Just that thought is what carries me through. I wanted this trip to serve two purposes -- to make money, and to get a better perspective on how the world works. And I am accomplishing both. I believe the knowledge I've gained will benefit in being a good provider for us, and for our family.

Being a lumberjack is treacherous work, and today showed just how dangerous it is. One of the lumberjacks was killed this morning. I felt so helpless not being able to do anything to save him. All I could think of was how his family was going to feel when they were told the news. Seeing that dead man crumpled under a pile of logs made me realize that life is fragile and I don't want to be away from you any longer than I have to. I sure wish I was by your side right now. I promise I will head back in just a few weeks on the fastest train I can find and I will never leave you alone again.

I miss you and love you in monumental fashion.

See you soon.

Nick

| 11 |

Annabeth parted the coarse soil with a trowel. On her knees, she mirrored her mother, who moved along the row beside her. Together, they planted pole beans and cucumbers that would grow next to the collards and spring onions that were planted the day before. The clomp of hooves took her attention away from the task at hand. Cody approached, sitting tall and striking on the sleek horse. He dismounted and tied the rein to a post. He removed two bunches of flowers from a saddlebag. Mrs. Parker stood.

"Good morning," Cody said. He held a bunch in each hand, each a brilliant violet.

"Well, good morning, Cody," Mrs. Parker said.

"These are for you, ma'am." He handed them to the smiling woman. He looked at Annabeth. "And these are for you."

"Isn't that the sweetest thing?" Mrs. Parker put the flowers to her face and inhaled.

The young man shrugged. "I just thought ladies as pretty as you 'uns should have pretty flowers. Course, they don't hold a candle to how beautiful you both are."

"Now, stop that kind of talk," Mrs. Parker said, her cheeks rising to a delicate blush. "Let me get a vase. You two chat a bit while I'm gone."

Annabeth studied the flowers. "Moon orchids. Sure are beautiful."

"As are you." He removed his gray Stetson hat. "Annabeth, would you like to go for a buggy ride this evening? Spring sunsets are right impressive these days."

As Annabeth began to speak, her mother approached, holding a clear vase partially filled with water. "Why, I think a buggy ride would be splendid," she said. "You two go see that pretty sunset."

Annabeth shook her head. "I've got things to tend to this evening, but I appreciate the offer."

"Nonsense," her mother said. "Whatever it is, you can tend to later. Don't dismiss Cody's kind gesture."

"It's all right, Mrs. Parker. I apologize if I was being forward."

Mrs. Parker touched Cody's arm. "Nonsense. Annabeth would love to go, and it will do her good. She needs to get out and enjoy herself. Watching the sun set would do her wonders."

Annabeth glared at her mother.

"Well, then, if it's all right, Annabeth, I will pick you up around five. I just got a new buggy and it's built for comfort. I know a great spot down Campbell Creek. We can watch the sun dip behind Iron Mountain. It's quite the sight."

"Sounds lovely," Mrs. Parker said.

Annabeth seethed quietly and put her flowers in the vase.

Nick and Will sat on the back of a wooden cart, eating a piece of pork lathered in butter inside a cold biscuit. They examined the results of their work. Ten months of breathing mortar and brick dust, working on shaky scaffolds. Limiting the sun's ability to enter the eastern side of the factory a little more each day. Fighting through wind and rain. Days when the snow whipped above them, their fingers numb through the work gloves. But now the final brick had been laid. The factory wall completed. Three hundred feet of wall, enclosing the factory so that it was ready for production lines to be built.

The callouses from cutting timber had formed a thick wall of raised skin, ending the need to soak his bloody gloves. He'd counted fifteen trips with Clyde and the others to the timber site. The money he'd made cutting trees was deposited with the earnings from the previous week's work building the brick wall for Mickey. With money stuffed inside his pants pocket, he would flee to the bank each Monday while choking down whatever meager meal was provided, rushing to make sure he got back before the lunch break was over.

Annabeth sat at the vanity in her bedroom. She brushed her hair, staring at herself in the oval mirror. She had excused herself from the supper table, her appetite non-existent. A pensive vision stared back at her. The ache in her heart reflected in her eyes. She felt a presence at the doorway.

"Annabeth," her mother said, "your father and I would like to talk with you."

She watched them through the mirror. Her mother patted the bed. "Come sit."

Annabeth turned about on the stool. "I can listen from here."

Her father stood by the bed, arms folded. "Annabeth, you know we only want the best for you."

"We want to make sure you are taken care of," her mother said. "Not just for now. But for the rest of your life."

"Why the sudden concern?" Annabeth asked.

"The business partnership we have developed with the Swanson family has been a true blessing," her father said. "The joining of our family with theirs can lay down a foundation that will provide prosperity for years to come."

"Well, that's a good thing," Annabeth said. "But why do you make it sound like it's a concern?"

"Cody came to me the other day," her father said, taking a slight pause. "About you, to be exact. He has such high regard for you. Thinks you are the loveliest lady he has ever seen. He said he would love to ask you to marry him. He wanted my permission. Very admirable."

"Well, that's all well and good. But I'm to marry Nick when he returns. So, Cody can find himself another to marry. With his charm and money, I'm sure he won't have to search for long."

"Cody would make sure you never have any financial worries," her mother said. "He would take great care of you. You can enjoy the finer things in life."

"With Nick, you don't know what kind of financial shape you will be in," Mr. Parker said. "He doesn't have a lot in the way of income potential. And if you plan on raising a family, it will surely be hard on you."

"I don't care if we have a lot of money. As long as we have each other, that's all that matters."

"Annabeth," her mother said, "love is a wonderful thing. But you can't live off of it. Hard times make love take a back seat. Putting food on the table lessens the importance of being in love."

"I will be fine. And so will Cody."

The man looked at his wife in a way as though he sought emotional support. He took a deep breath and looked at his daughter. "It's not that simple." He rubbed his forehead. "I've gotten to know Mr. Swanson quite well since joining him in the iron ore venture. He sees a very strong future, with other business opportunities down the road. He wants our families to form a rock-solid partnership. We both agree that the ultimate way to secure that is to join in a legal sense. His son and our daughter."

"How dare you put that kind of pressure on me. You're free to do whatever business dealings you want with the man, but leave me out of it."

"Think about it, Annabeth. You and Cody, married, producing children with blood from both families. It will be a permanent bond that can't be broken."

"Cody is a good man and will be a great provider," her mother said. "You'll never want for anything."

"What I want is Nick."

Her father walked to where Annabeth sat, placing his hand on her shoulder. "Annabeth, sometimes we have to do what is best for the family. Selfishness must be cast aside for the good of all. This is a decision that will solidify our family's well-being for generations. You will never want for anything. Your children, your children's children, will never want for anything."

"There's more important things in a child's life than financial standing. Having Nick for a father will be worth more than all the wealth in the world."

"That's all speculation," Mrs. Parker said. "You have no idea what kind of husband or father Nick will turn out to be."

"And you have no idea what kind Cody will be. I'll take my chances with Nick."

"I'm sorry, Annabeth," her father said. "This is not up for debate."

Tears formed as she regarded her father in a way she had not done before.

"Remember, Annabeth," her mother said. "It's what's best for our family. Your future. Your children's future. And Cody is the key to make that happen."

They left the room. Annabeth lay across her bed and sobbed.

Nick's heart raced when he spotted the letter sitting on his bed. A perfect way to end the workday. He tore the envelope and lay on his bed to read it.

Dear Nick,

The news about the lumberjack is very sad. I prayed for his family. I'm sorry you had to witness that tragedy, and I know you would have done any-thing you could to have saved that man's life. That's just the kind of person you are. It amazes me how you have persevered in such hard country, so far from home. I admire your strength and resolve. I know I tried to dissuade you from going to St. Louis, and I realize that was selfish. I'd say the time apart has made us both surely more resilient. It's helped me become more in-dependent and given me an inner strength I didn't know I had. I realize the world is always changing, and I have to be prepared to face it no matter what comes my way.

I think back on the special times we've shared, and it makes me smile. I've never known anyone as kind as you. You have such a special heart, Nick.

Any girl in the state of Tennessee would love to have you as their beau. You will surely turn heads and stir hearts wherever you go.

I want you to know that my love for you will never die. I am blessed that you love me.

It's a busy time here in the valley. Lots of work to do on the farm and around the house. Mother and I have grown a bountiful garden. I've been practicing with the choir.

All my love forever,

Annabeth

There appeared an odd tone in the words. A resolution to some judgment that had no clarification. He read the letter again in hopes that he had simply misunderstood the intent. It only reinforced the confusion.

When they had finished their meal, the pair was surprised when Mickey told them to take the afternoon off. Through the complaining and basically hard-nosed tactics Mickey used to ensure deadlines were met, he didn't hide the fact that he was pleased with the work ethic of the boys from Johnson County. He'd even mentioned that he wished he had more like the Tennesseans.

"Well, Bud, I'm ready to wash this brick dust off of me," Will said as they entered the tenant house. "I'm heading to the shower house."

"You go ahead," Nick said. "I want to see if any mail has come."

"How long since you last heard from Annabeth?"

"Last letter I got was three weeks ago. It had me right confused. It seemed apologetic in nature. I sent her one right back, asking if she was okay. But I've not heard back."

"You're surely reading something into it that ain't there. The time away has just got you thinking crazy."

"This letter was different than any she had sent before. The words were distant. Said the time away had made her more independent. Thanked me for the special times as though there would be no special times going forward."

"Maybe she's trying to sound strong so you won't worry. You told her about the lumberjack getting killed. She probably don't want you distracted, so the same don't happen to you."

"That's not it. Something's wrong, and I just need to hear from her before I make the trip home next week."

"I wouldn't worry about it. You'll find out you worried for nothing when you get home." He left the room.

Nick looked on his bed. Searched under his pillow. What future was she preparing for? Why hadn't she responded to ease his concerns? If she cared about him, wouldn't she want him to be at ease?

He walked to the shack where Mickey and his wife lived. He dusted himself off best he could before entering. There was a woman brushing a cane chair with a whisk broom.

"Excuse me, Miss Mamie. Have you gotten any mail for me this week? I was expecting some, and nothing has been set on my bed."

"Whenever I get mail, I put it on the bed of the recipient," she said without stopping at her task. "So, if you don't see no mail on your bed, none has come to this office."

"Thank you, ma'am." He headed toward his shack, head down.

Thoughts that he didn't want crept in. Maybe she had become ill and was too sick to write. Maybe it was something else. He tried to push the warning from Tom that leaving a pretty gal like Annabeth unattended could lead to the wolves creeping in from the woods. Young men with hearts afire for Annabeth. But he knew her, knew her heart. She had cried so many times before he left, talking about how much she would miss him, making him promise to marry her as soon as he returned. All the letters she sent expressing her love, telling him how much she missed him.

But the time spent in St. Louis, in the big city, showed him that men by nature could be concerned with self-gratification. That the world was all about survival, about fulfilling the needs of the material and of the flesh. He'd passed by the bars at night and spotted men he worked with, the ones he shared a tenant house with, cuddled up next to women who appeared as though, for the right price, their love could be rented, at least for a short while. Men who had talked fondly of families back home, and the wives whose warm bodies they missed. Talked of their children and the pain of missing out on watching them grow. For men who shared their sadness, they surely didn't seem to have missed them on those nights in the bars. He witnessed some of them being led upstairs to rooms where affection could be offered in more intimate settings. The same ones who would proclaim the next day their only wish was to be home with their wife and children.

Perhaps the needs of the flesh had taken hold of Annabeth.

He questioned the path he had chosen. Decisions made. He envisioned her in another man's arms and broke out in a clammy sweat. How quickly could he pack his things and head to the train station? The distance between him and Doe Valley now seemed beyond calculation, as though it had become a land where no train track could reach. A place with no footpath to lead to it either.

Russell and two other workers sat at a small table, engaged in a game of cards. The smoke from stale cigarettes hung heavy in the air. Russell's chair leaned back against the tenant shack.

"Well, if it ain't Davy Crockett's bastard child," Russell said, placing two cards on the table. "Where's your musket? I saw a field mouse out back this morning. Maybe you can track him down and make us some rat stew for supper."

Nick bit his lip and kept his eyes on the dusty path that led to his tenant house. He passed the men without acknowledgment.

"That there is the look of a forlorn loser," Russell said. "You look like you just found out she's got another mountain man to keep her bed warm," Russell said. The others laughed.

Nick glared at Russell, who set his cards on the table. The gangly man stood, parted the others around the table, and walked toward Nick. "You got something you want to say?" He stood next to Nick, arms crossed. "What is it, you mountain piss ant? Something weighing on your mind?"

There were murmurs and muted laughter, an anticipation of events to unfold.

"Kick his country ass, Russell," one of them called out. Again, laughter.

"I ain't liked you from the get-go," Russell said. "You don't care much for the lot of us, do you? Tennessee this, Tennessee that. Maybe it's time you headed on back to them damn Tennessee hills. Though, by the look of things, I believe somebody back home don't care if you ever come back. Am I right? Annabeth? I heard you talking to Will about her. Sounds like a whore to me."

Those from around the card table had gathered up behind Russell. An uprising.

"Kick his teeth in," another said.

"Maybe I just oughta." Russell eased closer to where he stood nose to nose with Nick.

"Back away while you're still able," Nick said.

Will came running up the dusty road. "What's going on?"

"Stay out of this, Will," Russell said. "This is something I shoulda done months ago." He lowered his shoulders and wrapped his arms around Nick's waist, slamming him to the ground. The crowd erupted as Russell straddled Nick across the waist. He began throwing punches, several finding their mark about Nick's face. Blood seeped from his mouth. He struggled to gain leverage as Russell began delivering body blows, and the inability to free himself caused a fire to rise within him. The months of working so far from home, of wondering if his choice of laying a future for he and Annabeth had backfired, of being around people who didn't have any sense of pride in where they were from, of who they were, began to seethe in his heart and soul, and ultimately, his body. He let go a primal scream and pushed upward from the ground as though all forces of the world had bound together to join the fight, and he was able to grab hold of Russell's shirt. As he pushed his knees upward, he pulled Russell so that the man rolled over Nick's shoulder, landing him on the ground beyond Nick's head. Nick rose to his feet and tackled Russell as he tried to stand. Nick landed a fist to Russell's eye, and the man buckled. Nick took him by the shirt to keep him from falling, as there was work to be done, messages to be delivered. He drove an uppercut to the man's chin, causing Russell's head to snap back. He slumped to the ground. Nick knelt over him, and when Russell lifted his head, his eyes cloudy, one eye dripping in blood, Nick drove his fist into the man's nose.

"Get off me you son of a bitch," Russell said as he threw a punch that found air. He kicked his feet, but Nick lowered his body on Russell's chest, eyeing the man for any sense of fight left. He spat at Nick, and the Tennessean took the man by the shirt, delivering a blow to Russell's chin. Nick sensed that the lesson he intended to impress upon Russell and those who had egged on the fight had not been taken to heart. He again tightened his grip on Russell's shirt and sent his fist with full force into the man's cheek. Russell went limp. Nick observed his opponent, and when he realized he was out cold, turned to the others. "Anybody else got something to say to this Tennessee boy? If so, come on and take your ass-whipping."

They stood in silence. Nick wiped blood from his lip. "You'd be wise to learn the ways of a Tennessean. It, by God, might teach you what having a sense of pride is all about. From what I've seen, not one of you possesses that trait."

He turned and walked to the tenant house. Under his bed, he found his writing pad and sat. With bloodied hand, he wrote –

Dear Annabeth,

I have great news! I board the train next Tuesday. I'll close my bank account on Monday and withdraw my savings. As long as there's no risen rivers or streams covering the tracks back to Johnson County, I will be home on Saturday. I am so looking forward to seeing you, to starting our life together. I catch my mind drifting to the sight of you and me standing in front of our house by Spear Branch. What a great day that will be.

I've grown weary of the big city life, and the people that live here. They surely look down on people from Tennessee, and I don't rightly know why that is. Soon, I won't have to worry about the reason. I won't miss this place one bit as there is no sense of pride or loyalty. It's all about buildings and structures instead of land, animals, and the connection between man and the good Lord above.

This letter should precede my arrival by a couple of days. If I get there before the letter, I'll surprise you at your house, and when the letter arrives, you can read it while I'm sitting beside you. Shoot, I'll read it to you if you'd like.

See you soon.
With all my love,
Nick

| 12 |

Nick and Will embraced. The train whistle cut through the air, drowning out the clamor of voices around them.

"Tell them back home I said hidy," Will said.

"You can count on it," Nick said. "But you know it would be best if you told them yourself. They would plenty love to see you."

"I will make it back one of these days. You ain't the only one who's been saving for a new place. I've found a room at the Martin Hotel. Going to have a full-fledge bed, my own room. No more having to sleep in the same room with a bunch of snoring, smelly fellows. And having access to fresh bath water will be a nice change. Yes, sir, I'm getting out of the hog pen."

"That's great, Will. I can't thank you enough for getting me the job and looking out for me while I was here."

"I don't know how much looking out I did. You did fine all by yourself. I think Russell and the boys will attest to that."

"I won't be missing any of them fellows. St. Louis can have 'em."

"Make sure you spend your money on the land, and not on fancy jewelry and such for Annabeth."

He patted his satchel. "I did get her something. It's a necklace I saw a couple months back at Compton's. I'm anxious to see how it shines around her neck. The rest of her gift will be the land. And me, of course." He paused. "Hopefully, she is still set on us living on that land."

"Don't put no stock in that letter. That gal will melt in your arms when you get home. You'll see. And I hope it ain't nothing but wedded bliss for you the rest of your days."

Nick nodded and embraced his friend one last time.

He hopped aboard, held a side rail, and waved his hat at Will. The train chugged to life and slipped from the station, steam enveloping the platform, swallowing up those who remained into apparitions departing not the station, but perhaps the world itself. Uncaring clouds hung above the city, rendering the landscape vague and prosaic. Remnants from a bad dream, he wondered if he could ever shake loose.

The dining car was abuzz. Voices melding. Tinny clanging of dishes and silverware. The centerpiece of the train, the gathering of the jovial passengers. Perhaps it was just the ability to dine while watching the world go by that made it something worth reveling in. For Nick, it was a meal to celebrate.

A man in a black vest and top hat motioned for Nick to sit at a two-chair table. When Nick sat, the man asked, "Are you averse to sharing your dinner table?"

"No, I'm not," Nick replied.

"Here's the menu. If you don't mind me suggesting, the cut ham and corn is very tasty. The ham comes with a side of bread and mustard spread."

"That sounds good."

"You care for cider?"

"Yes, sir."

Nick looked about the car and wondered if any passengers were heading to East Tennessee. After spending so much time away, he wondered if he could spot one by dress or mannerisms. None seemed to fit that qualification. A young boy in a wool suit brought Nick's glass of cider, with a look as though he was doing a deed of great importance. Nick smiled, and the boy hurried away. The man who had seated Nick approached. Three people followed. The man lowered his head and said, "Sir, we have a party of three, and only one table left. May one of them sit with you?"

"That would be all right."

A young lady was the first of the three, and she smiled at Nick. She had deep brown eyes and wore a blue dress that clung tightly to the narrow shape of her body. Her hair was braided and hung over one shoulder like a sash. Her smile was in bold contrast to her ruby lips, and Nick became caught in a stare he struggled to break free from.

"If the gentleman doesn't mind," she said, "I'll sit with him."

Nick stood, and the *maître d* pulled her chair. The two men with her sat across the aisle at the other table. Nick wondered if they were siblings. The woman sat, and so did Nick.

"How do?" he said to the beauty.

"Pleasure to meet you." Her eyes fluttered. "My name is Rose."

Nick nodded. "Nick. Nick Grindstaff."

She glanced at the men who sat across from them. "This here is James and Paulie."

Nick nodded. "They kin to you?"

"We're her cousins," said the one she identified as Paulie. "James and me are brothers."

"Where are you headed?" Rose asked.

"Johnson County, Tennessee."

"Is it near Memphis?"

"No, it's at the opposite end of the state."

"Is it a pretty place?"

"Prettiest on Earth. The part where I live is called Doe Valley."

"Going to visit?"

"No. I'm heading home. I been in St. Louis working for the past year. And let me tell you I'm so ready to be back in those Tennessee hills. What about you? Where are you headed?"

"Philadelphia. Going to visit our grandmother. Sadly, she is deathly ill and we are trying to get to her before she passes. To say our good-byes and such."

"I'm sorry to hear that."

The *maître d* handed a leather-bound menu to Rose and, like Nick, she chose the man's recommendation for dinner. James and Paulie ordered whisky while Rose ordered lemonade.

"Why did you go all the way to St. Louis?" Rose asked. "Aren't there any jobs in the *prettiest* place on Earth?" She smiled, and her show of playfulness caught him off guard.

"What?" A sudden aloofness had him embarrassed. "Uh, well, most work around Johnson County is farm-related or working in commerce in town. Most businesses are small and employ family members. The only decent-sized towns, like Elizabethton and Johnson City, don't pay anything close to the kind of wages they pay in St. Louis. I wanted to earn as much as I could in the shortest time possible, and along the way, get an idea of what life was like outside Doe Valley. And I surely got a taste of it. Maybe more than I bargained for. Anyways, I'm buying a nice piece of land and I'm going to marry my sweetheart. Going to build a home and raise a family."

"Well, that's very admirable of you. What is the lucky lady's name?"

"Annabeth. I didn't realize how much I'd miss her. But I surely did. She's downright pretty, inside and out." He bent forward to open his satchel, and his money purse fell from his pocket. He quickly placed it back in his coat before removing the box with the necklace. "I picked this out from a fine store in St. Louis." He opened the box.

"Annabeth," she repeated. "What a pretty name." She peered into the box. "She is going to love that piece of jewelry."

"I surely hope so. She's worth every effort of work I did to earn the money to pay for it."

"I hope I can find someone such as you someday. Have a strong, handsome man of some means to settle down with. To raise a family with."

"Is that a fact?"

"You say you worked a whole year in St. Louis just to buy land, to marry and start a family?"

"Yes." Nick slipped a foot into the aisle. "I want to look nice when I first see her, so I did spend a little something on myself."

"Nice boots."

"I want to look presentable."

"Trust me—you'll look presentable."

 He blushed. "It's been such a long time since I've seen her. I don't mind saying that I'm quite anxious, and I surely wish this train could speed up."

She regarded him as though he were a piece of art worth studying. She made eye contact briefly with James. "Well, I'd be happy to keep you company, to help you from being so anxious. That is, if you don't mind. I don't want to overstep my bounds."

A young man placed plates of food on their table.

"No, that would be fine," Nick said as he nodded to the server. "Thank you, sir."

As they ate, they talked about the magnificence of the train, the articulate designs in the ceiling of the dining car. When Rose spoke, she looked deeply into his eyes, and he struggled to maintain eye contact, as though he might go blind if he stared at her too long, like looking at the sun. Her beauty overpowered him, and that puzzled him. His mind and focus had been set completely on Annabeth, and he could hardly wait to hold her in his arms. And yet, Rose held some mystique, a presence of refined beauty he had never witnessed, not even in that large city of St. Louis, and certainly not in the hills of East Tennessee. Perhaps Rose was right--spending time with her on the trip would surely pass the time and keep him from counting the minutes until Annabeth would be waiting at the depot. The wonder of why she had not written him near the end began to creep back in his mind, but Rose's smile pushed that worry from his thoughts. He reckoned he was fortunate to have Rose take his mind off the uncertainty.

When dinner was complete, James and Paulie excused themselves. Rose asked if she could sit a while longer with Nick, and he was obliged that she offered.

"What do you say we order a glass of brandy?" Rose asked. "I know some might not consider that very lady-like, but I don't really care what these strangers in this car think. We'll never see them again, am I right?"

"I'm not much of a drinking man," Nick said.

"Maybe just this once? So I don't have to drink alone? What do you say, Mr. Grindstaff?"

Nick shrugged. "Well, the homecoming that surely awaits is certainly worth celebrating."

"That's the tune." She got the attention of a man standing near the car door and ordered the drinks.

They toasted to Annabeth and Rose's grandmother. She talked about growing up in Jackson, Mississippi, being an only child, and wanting to escape the cotton fields and flat delta. Nick wasn't sure what a delta was and asked for an explanation. He told her Johnson County was the complete opposite of a delta. As they spoke, he became more at ease looking into her eyes. He had never seen skin so olive in tone. If pressed to speak the truth, he would admit that she was every bit as pretty as Annabeth. A feeling of shame overtook him for that thought, though a second glass of brandy made that shame fade. As the dining car thinned, Rose looked about.

"Looks like we own the place," she said, raising her glass.

"It surely does," Nick answered, and he touched his glass to hers.

"I know this might sound forward, but would you mind escorting me back to my berth? Crossing the connectors frightens me. And with the brandy in me, I'm not the steadiest person right now. If I have a steady arm to hold on to, I think I can make it."

"I feel confident I can get you safely to your room. And thank you for helping pass the time. I've enjoyed the company."

"It was a pleasure. I'll say it again—Annabeth is a lucky lady. I hope she realizes what a fine man she's got."

He followed behind as they made their way through the dining car, and when they came to the connector, he stepped across, reached back, and took her by the hand to guide her across. He repeated the process when they crossed the other connectors. Three cars back, they had walked.

"Well, this is my room." She stopped and placed her hand to his arm. "I hope you have a great life with Annabeth. If you weren't attached, I surely would like to be that special one in your life."

Flattered, Nick lowered his eyes to hide the embarrassment. "If I wasn't spoken for, I would be proud to have you as my girl."

She leaned forward and kissed him softly on the cheek. "Well, goodnight."

"Goodnight, Miss Rose."

His heart fluttered. It was best for him to find his bunk and put his thoughts all on the impending reunion with Annabeth.

"Oh, Nick," he heard her say, and he turned toward her. "I'm sorry to bother you, but could you help me with my trunk? It's jammed and I don't have the strength to open it."

Nick followed her into the slender quarters and spotted the trunk on the narrow bed. "Let's have a look," he said. He knelt and took hold of the metal fastener.

The impact of the blow to his head knocked him to the floor. Something heavy smashed the base of his neck. Angry voices. Kicks to his midsection. Fists finding their way between his folded arms, where he was unable to shield his head. "The wallet is in his coat pocket," he heard Rose say. "And grab that necklace in the satchel."

A blow from something blunt made him go limp, and all turned to darkness.

| 13 |

The sky appeared an apprehensive spectator of the world beneath it, a blend of incremental shades of iris caught in some hesitant metamorphosis. Stars glinted in the vast, western boundary, as the night sluggishly relented its hold on the land. The predawn light awakened wisps of fog. He studied the jagged skyline of Iron Mountain, the familiar shape that told him he was home. No longer on the shifting sand of the world. Nick's arm hung off the gurney, and he studied it to make sure the arm indeed belonged to his body. He was confused as to why he was in a lying state. He looked above, and a man, donned in black, smiled at him, an upside-down smile from the angle Nick held. In front of him, another man led the way carrying the gurney. When they placed him on the platform of the station, Cora and Jerico approached.

"Oh, my Lord," Cora said, squatting, placing her hand to Nick's cheek. He tried to raise his head, but intense pain coursed through it, and he lowered back on the gurney.

"Easy," Jerico said. "Just rest easy, Nick. Tom is bringing the wagon around. Going to take you on home. Doc Lunceford is meeting us there and will take a good look at you."

"What happened?" Nick asked.

"The conductor said he found you slumped over in the baggage car. Thought you were dead. You had been beaten badly."

Nick searched Jerico's eyes for confirmation that Cora's words were not some tall tale. He took Cora by the arm. "Annabeth. Where's Annabeth?"

Cora looked at Jerico as though guidance was needed. "Don't you worry about that. Let's get you home and in bed and let the doctor tend to you. I can't imagine how confusing this must be. They said when they roused you, you were speaking all kinds of crazy. Thank goodness you had your ticket in your pocket so they could know your final destination and get you home."

He touched his hand to the side of his head, bandages thick and wrapped tightly. He tried to retrace the memory. The trunk. Rose asking politely for assistance. He reached into his coat pocket for his wallet. The pocket was empty.

Veta pulled on the reins, bringing the horse to a halt. The children leapt from their seat and hurried to the back of the wagon. She winced when she stepped off the wagon. The pain in her knee had not diminished since she hurt it lifting Ray's lifeless body onto the wagon that fateful evening months prior. Images played in her head every night when she closed her eyes to sleep. The crack of the whip, the clomp of hooves when she tore off for Doc Lunceford's, the wagon wheels whining as they spun down the road. Haunting sounds she could not rid herself of. How futile her screams felt along the mile trip, how raw her plea for help when they reached the doctor's house. Mrs. Lunceford standing at the front steps. Veta held out some strange hope that the doctor could revive Ray, but the cold had crept into his face, along with that blank stare. Heart attack was what the doctor presumed had occurred, but to Veta, the cause wasn't important. The fact that her husband, her one and only love, had left her behind was all that mattered. Gone to streets of gold, she hoped.

Larry lifted the burlap sack from the wagon. Lumped inside were scrub pots and bleach for cleaning. Veta grabbed a separate sack with thin cuts of pork, bread, and butter. They hauled the sacks up the steps and into the store. Veta soon brought the oil lamp to life, and Larry filled the wood stove with cuttings he'd brought in from a stack out back. She hoped the patrons would continue to come, though she knew the reason many came was to solve the mysteries of life with

Ray. She had tried hard to learn Ray's inventory pricing sheet, a yellowed piece of paper kept in a tin box behind the counter. She struggled to remember what to charge and despised looking unprepared. Customers appeared to have patience, but she wondered how long that would continue.

The morning light angled one-dimensional through the front window, setting the building in an eerie sense of silence as though the world beyond that window had fled entirely. Or at least, fled the valley. Just past nine o'clock, the door creaked and John Payne entered. He removed his round-brimmed hat and approached the counter. "How you a doin', Miss Veta," he said, looking unsure as to whether to smile.

"I'm hangin' on like a hair in a biscuit," she replied. "What can I do for you, John?"

"I am in need of lard and flour. Priscilla is making batter bread tonight."

Veta searched the shelves and grabbed a can of lard. She found a ten-pound sack of flour and set it on her shoulder.

"I could have gotten those things, Miss Veta. Save your energy for more pressing requirements."

"Nonsense. Ray would have fetched it for you, and I gotta be able to do the same."

As he handed over the money, he said, "I surely do miss that ole boy. Weren't no finer man in all of Doe Valley, or for that much, all of Johnson County."

She nodded. "Big shoes to fill, that's for certain. I'm tryin' best I know how."

"Well, I think you're doin' a fine job. If I can ever be of help, let me know."

"I appreciate that."

Days and nights ran together, indistinguishable. Nick drifted in and out of what seemed like a continuous battle between dream and reality. He tried to identify the voices gathered around his bed. At times he saw vague visions, though he couldn't confirm their identities. Cora and Jerico. Tom. Surely they were there. Someone lifting his head to provide drinking water. Someone replacing bandages. Such thick bandages. Tender hands wiping blood from his forehead. Annabeth's?

He rose slowly on an elbow, pain pulsating through his head. He closed his eyes in an attempt to lessen the ache while sorting through his mind in patchwork effort of recent events. He had escorted Rose to her berth. She needed help with a chest. A stuck lock. Knelt to open it, and then came the sharp blow to his head. One and then another. He had tried to cover his head with his arms, but the object kept making contact. Multiple voices. Rose speaking, panicked instructions. A hand inside his coat pocket.

He looked about the room. His coat was folded across an oak chair. Fighting the intense ache in his head, he slipped off the bed to his knees and crawled to the chair. He pulled the coat to the floor and looked through the pockets. Empty. Cora walked in and rushed to Nick.

"Lord-a-mercy, what are you doing out of bed?"

"My savings. Where's my savings? Where's my money pouch?"

Cora watched as Nick looked about the floor. "I don't know. We took your coat and boots off and put them right there. Maybe it slipped out." She slid the chair and took to her knees. "I don't see any pouch. Are you sure you had it in your pocket?"

He sat up against the bed, placing his arms across his bent knees. He lowered his head to his forearms. "They stole it. Every bit of money I owned was in that wallet. All the money I earned in St. Louis, all that hard work. All for nothing."

"Oh, my." She took hold of his jacket and searched the pockets again as though maybe they had missed it in haste. She patted each pocket and put her hand in each one, trying to will the wallet to appear. "I'm sorry, Nick. There's nothing here." She knelt beside him, touching his cheek. "You don't need to worry about money. Jerico will pay you wages for working the farm, and this is your room for all your days if you choose. And you know you'll never want for a meal with me around."

"You don't understand. That money was going to buy the land on Spear Branch from Mr. Stout. Between that and the money from the sale of my land to E.S. Jordan, I would have had enough. I'm going to marry Annabeth, and that was where we were going to build a house. Now I have no way to buy it. That was my purpose for working in St. Louis. Working those long days, living in a tenant house, eating boiled cabbage and pork stew."

Cora placed her hand on his shoulder. "The Lord will provide. Right now, you just need to rest and heal up. The conductor fella said you were lucky to be alive. When they found you slumped in the baggage car, your head and face was all bloodied, and they just knew you were dead."

"Maybe it would have been best if they had just finished me off."

"Don't talk like that, Nick. You're going to be fine. Just fine. You're surrounded by family who are here to make sure of that."

Cora set the wooden tray on the dresser and removed the white cloth. She inspected the plate to confirm that she had prepared enough food. She bent slightly and gently rubbed Nick's hair. "Best eat it before it gets cold."

Nick opened his eyes and looked about the room. "How many days have I been back?"

"Pert near two weeks. Your body has been through a lot. I'd say the rest has done you good."

He raised up on his elbows. "I think I'd like to eat at the table this morning."

She studied his eyes and touched her hand to the bruised cheek. "I'll set your plate up there right now. With a big glass of sweet milk to go with it."

While he ate, Cora warmed water on the stove. She filled a porcelain basin in Nick's bedroom. The kitchen contained an odd silence. Tom and Jerico were surely working somewhere on the farm. After he was done, he bathed himself with a sponge at the basin. He studied his face in the dim reflection of the bedroom mirror. Someone he hardly recognized. It felt good to put on clean clothing. He slid on his boots and headed out the door.

Battling to sit upright in the seat, Nick steered Sally down the muddy road, the wagon wheels parting pools of rainwater. Sally, an equine metronome, interrupted the peace of the valley with her steady gait. The travelers were mired in gray under slate clouds that hung low and apathetic. The skyline of Doe Mountain was perceptible by imagination only, and other than cattle scattered about the hillsides, the land appeared as a place cast aside. The road snaked along the valley, rising and falling along hilly slopes. All was quiet in that land of ten thousand hills.

The road entered the tight hollow, and smoke from the chimney was a welcome sight. At least he perceived it as such. A combination of anticipation and caution rose within him. An unannounced arrival. When the road straightened, he spotted her on the porch. She appeared to be creating a blanket, a pattern of green and blue laid across her lap. Sally snorted and Annabeth turned her head toward the source. As Nick approached, he wondered if she looked the same. Was her hair still in soft ringlets, curling at the base of her neck? She moved the material from her lap and stood, walking to the edge of the porch. When he was close enough to see the sparkle in her green eyes, he raised his hand, a slow wave. She placed her arms around the corner post of the white porch. She wore a pale blue skirt and a white blouse, and Nick's heart hit a flutter he'd not felt in almost a year. He brought Sally to a halt, hoping his hat covered the cuts across his scalp. The bruises on his cheek and forehead couldn't be disguised, and he hoped it wouldn't startle her. She walked to the buggy, her warm smile giving confirmation that his surprise visit was okay. He eased off the seat and stood before her, tempted to pick her up in his arms and swing her around. But he held his composure, though being face-to-face made him realize how much he had truly missed her.

"Oh, Nick," she said, taking his hand in hers. "How are you feeling?"

"I expected you to be at the train station."

"I saw you from the road. When they carried you out on the gurney, you looked as close to dead as anything, and I figured they needed to get you home so the doctor could tend to you."

"You didn't think it was worth checking up on me?"

She lowered her eyes for a moment. "I'm sorry about that, Nick. I truly am." She glanced at his cheek and gently placed her fingers just below a bruise. "You poor man."

"I guess you must be preoccupied these days."

"Life has been one crazy cyclone. So many things going on." She sighed. "So many changes."

Nick's attention turned to the side of the house as Cody Swanson approached. "Annabeth," Cody said, "your mother is looking for the wash pail." He squinted. "Hidy."

"Hidy," Nick said, trying to hide the puzzlement stirring inside him.

Cody walked up and placed his arm around Annabeth. There was uneasiness in her eyes. He studied Nick's bruises. "You okay?"

"I'm doing all right."

"You must be Nick." Nick nodded. "I heard you had some trouble on the way home from Chicago."

"St. Louis."

"Right. St. Louis. You don't look like you're at full strength. Should you be out and about?"

Nick waited until Annabeth's stare moved to where their eyes met, confirming his fears. "Probably not. I just stopped by to say hello. Guess I should get on back home. Like you said--I'm not at full strength."

"You take care of yourself," Cody said.

Nick nodded and lowered his eyes. "You two do the same."

Annabeth's chin quivered. Moisture-filled eyes that appeared apologetic.

He climbed onto the seat and guided Sally around and they headed back down the road that before held peaceful reverence. As he guided the horse through the hollow, he stared at Iron Mountain to the west. He studied its curvature, trees hiding behind waves of mist. A sharp pain rose in his head, and he closed his eyes, bringing Sally to a halt. The fast clomp of hooves approached from behind, and Annabeth pulled up beside the buggy on a chocolate-colored horse.

"Nick," she said as her mare came to a stop.

"Well, that surely does explain why you didn't check on me while I was laid up in bed," he said. "And, you've answered the questions I had about the last letter you wrote me."

"I'm so sorry, Nick. I didn't want to hurt you."

Nick looked off into the distance. "Tom said Cody was a snake. I guess he was right. Just slithered on in while I was gone."

"A lot happened while you were gone. Things that I had no control over."

"No control over? You're a grown woman. You control your own life."

"It's not that simple."

"Seems simple to me. You were with me. Now you're with him."

"But that doesn't mean I love you any less," she continued. "You are my first love. That's something that can never be changed."

"Is that supposed to provide consolation? I worked till my hands bled, slept in a bunk that was barely more than a layer of cloth, to make money to buy that land that we both wanted, where we were going to build a life together."

"I begged you to stay. You should have never left the valley. Everything you loved was here."

"You're blaming this on me? You know why I left. To make sure we had security. Not in debt to anybody. And all the aches and pain would have been worth it because I was doing it for you. For us." He shrugged. "So much for that."

"Please let me explain."

"What's to explain? You found another. One in great financial standing. You'll never want for anything." He clicked the reins, and Sally began to walk. "You two have a nice life."

"Nick," she called out, but his eyes were set on the rain-slick road before him.

He led Sally on, riding through the mist as though interlopers newly entered from another world. Or, perhaps, seeking passage into a new world entirely.

| **14** |

Veta rolled in the bed, a dull pain racing across her back. She lay in darkness, but knew she needed to be frying eggs by the time the rooster welcomed the morning sun. She sat on the edge of the bed, wanting to flop back onto the mattress and rest her worn body just a few minutes more.

The children ate quietly as Veta placed some on a plate for herself. A nine-hour day awaited her at the store, and she prayed for strength to get through it. Though with the lack of patrons, she surely would have time to eat her cold pork sandwich at midday. She sent them on to school wrapped warmly in the cold.

The mare's breath rose toward the amber sky, the clomp of hooves cutting into the quiet of the morning. The gloves dimmed the cold of the reins, and she searched for warmth in the sun that had just appeared above Doe Mountain. She came upon the grassy bald where tombstones cut morbid silhouettes. It was coming up on two years since they laid Ray in his grave. In some ways, it seemed as though they had just covered his wooden casket with the cold soil. But the strain on her back, the pain in her bony fingers, made it feel like she'd been at it alone forever.

A man with a stubble beard entered the store. He was thick-shouldered and, what Veta assumed, a man of great strength.

"Hidy," she said as the man shifted his sight to the corners of the dimly lit store as though he needed confirmation of what he sought. "Help you find something?"

"I'm in need of an ax that strikes quick and true."

"Quick and true, you say?" She walked to a side wall and nodded. "Got three in stock."

"One is all I need." He chose one and slid his finger along the edge of the blade. He held it with both hands until the blade was above his head. He studied on it for a moment as if it were something that appearance alone could not solve. "Is this handle white ash?"

"I couldn't rightly say. But my husband had a good eye for tools. So, I think it's as good as quality as you would need."

He studied the shape near where it held the blade. "This one will do."

"Ain't you Cora Grindstaff's nephew?"

He nodded.

"I saw you at a Bethel Baptist homecoming dinner a dozen years or so ago. Nick, right?"

The man stood stoically as though pondering whether an answer should be given.

"Didn't you get all roughed up on the train coming back from someplace out west a year or so back?"

He gripped the blade. "Reckon I'll take this one."

Puzzled at the shortness in his reply, she led him to the counter. He removed a worn leather wallet from a pocket deep inside his coat. He fumbled his fingers across the bills as though contemptuous of their true significance, as though the impending transaction was something that should be avoided if not for necessity.

"You got that wallet buried deep. Can't nobody wrestle that away from you unless prior approval is given."

"That's the idea."

After a quick inventory assessment, he removed the necessary bills to complete the transaction.

"Thank you, kindly."

"Thank you for your business."

He turned toward the door as she tore the receipt from the book. "Here, don't you want your receipt?"

He stopped and turned, his eyes struggling to meet hers. "A transaction receipt implies lack of trust. In this world, trust is something there seems to be little of, and receipts can't change that fact."

"That may well be. In this case, it's just following basic rules of business. When I look in your eyes I don't see any ill notion." She regarded him closely. "But I do see a certain distrust."

"Wrongs can never be made right. Promises made don't amount to a hill of beans."

"Buddy, let me tell you, wrongs ain't always of an intentional nature or done with bad intent. My husband left me to fend for my young 'uns and myself almost two years back, but it weren't of his choosing. He made a promise to take care of his family, but, by golly, he didn't. His heart couldn't keep up its end of the deal. He passed in this very store. So, take to heart that no matter the reason a promise ain't kept don't matter. In the end, all that matters is the ones for who promises were broken; don't stew on the whys. All they can do is keep a movin' forward. Otherwise, the promise gets broken on both ends."

He gave a hesitant nod as though some revelation needed further thought. His scuffed boots echoed as he walked across the wooden floor. His dark wool pants were dirt-stained below the knees as though he had wandered through a bog. His black coat fit snug across his shoulders, but the edges dangled well below his backside, reminding Veta of pictures she'd seen of cowboys in the west. Regardless, he cut an imposing silhouette as he walked out the door.

Tom tossed the last bale of hay over the fence. Nick raked the remaining strands off the bed of the wagon. "What do you say we head to Lacy's tonight? They got a fiddle player and another what plays the banjo. Suppose to be some of the young ladies there. The Stout sisters. Maybe we could stir up a dance or two."

"You go ahead."

"You can't keep hiding from the world, Nick."

"From what I've learned of the world, I'd rather have a sack of cow shit. I can make good use of the cow pie. The world…can't make nothing from it."

"I know you been through the dickens, but you got to put that all behind you. You got your whole life ahead."

"Life," he repeated. "Everywhere I look in this valley are reminders of life. It's kicked me in the teeth, is what. The house where Ma and Pa died, right over that hill. The road down yonder leads to Annabeth's. Oh, I can ride down it. See Cody cozied up to her. That sounds like quite the life."

"You just happened to draw a couple of sorry hands at the card table. The odds from here on out are stacked in your favor."

"It's stacked, all right. Stacked so that there ain't a card worth playing. And that means it's time to find a new card game."

| 15 |

Sunlight angled hazy gray across the cherry floor. An oil lamp flickered on a desk cluttered with leather bindings and papers. Nick studied Daniel Stout as the man sat hunched over the desk, studying official-looking documents. "Mr. Stout?"

Daniel peered above his reading glasses, regarding the one before him as some apparition risen to human form. "Nick?"

"Yes, sir."

"I hardly recognized you. What with the beard and all. You look a might thinner than the last time I saw you." He pointed to a chair. "Have a seat."

Nick obliged. "I came to make an offer on your land."

"When you got home from St. Louis, in the condition you were in, I didn't want to put any pressure on you for that plot on Spear Branch. As time went by, I figured you had passed on the plan to buy it. I never put it back on the market, though, as I weren't sure what to do with it. But it looks like it all worked out in the end." He searched through a file cabinet behind the desk and removed a thin satchel. "I've still got the paperwork. It's such a fine spot." He paused. "I surely envisioned years ago that my boy would be the one living on it."

"I surely wish that were to be the case, Mr. Stout. Charles was a good fella. Sat next to him in the schoolhouse."

"Thank you, Nick. I wish the passage of time eased the ache, but it don't. But it will do my heart good knowing you will live on that land, make a home on it."

"About that," Nick said sheepishly. "I need to tell you something."

"How's that?"

"I'm not going to buy that plot. I was robbed of all my savings on the way home from St. Louis. And so, I can't afford it."

"I truly am sorry that happened to you, Nick. Such a tragic event."

"Even if I had the money, I got no use for that land no more. That plot is best suited for a family to settle on. Since that's not going to happen with regard to me, I got something else in mind." Nick postured himself at the front of the seat. "I'm told you own property on Iron Mountain."

"You want land for hunting? If it's for timber purposes, you'll need a whole lot more land than what I got up there to make it worth your while."

"No, sir. No timber business. I want to live on it."

"Why in the Sam Hill would you do that? It ain't fit for putting up living quarters. The winters alone would turn you to stone. The summers would be a constant battle with rattlers and copperheads. Bears and panthers. Not to mention the distance you'd be from anyone, anyplace. No, sir, the only thing it's good for is hunting."

"I'd like you to sell it to me all the same. I sold the share of my pa's property to E.S. Jordan, and I can pay that out to you for the land on the mountain. That is, if you will accept the amount I received from the sale." He removed the wallet from his inner coat pocket and placed the money on the table. "Would this equal out for the sale of your land? I've heard tell you got about twenty acres. I just sold my six acres, but being in the valley, surely it would be considered worth more per acre than your land on the mountain. So, I'm hoping they might equal out."

Daniel counted the money and scratched his chin. "Nick, you sure you want to do this? That's such remote land."

"Yes, sir, I'm sure."

"I'll draw up the papers."

The slope of the thick-timbered land angled skyward, and Nick used the ax handle to steady himself. He walked along Timothy Branch, mirroring the trail of the stream as it climbed the ridge. From afar, Nick had never realized that the ridge existed. Trunks of trees fallen long ago formed a strange web across the narrow creek, their limbs gnarled and void of foliage, colorless. The stream was laden with mossy rocks of various shapes, positioned as though God had placed them as obstacles for any who dared traverse it by foot. Nick held the ax handle tightly for support. Though the creek hummed, Nick was enveloped by a silence as though no creature existed but him on that land. He closed his eyes and reveled in the remoteness. King of nothing. Lord of the imagined. He looked below at the path he had ascended, at the graceful design in complexity. As he continued, he came upon laurel hells, intertwined walls of branches and leathery leaves, forcing Nick to push through them with eyes closed and head lowered. At some points, he cut limbs with his ax to carve enough space to push his way upward. The slowness of his ascension gave comfort that others would not be willing to follow his path.

He removed the property map and studied it. A familiar pain rushed through his head, the one that still frequented him since the incident on the train. He closed his eyes and rubbed his temple until the pain subsided. He recalled standing outside Daniel Stout's office, where the man had pointed to the highest ridge in the distance, the spot that looked like the head of a titmouse. Daniel told Nick that once he ascended it, he would be at the lower west corner of the property. He was told that chestnuts painted with blue stripes would indicate the boundaries. Daniel had told him the land held a peanut shape to it. Twenty acres in all.

The ridge leveled briefly, and the creek split. Nick followed the stream eastward. The laurels and underbrush gave way to hardwoods that stretched straight and true, and Nick struggled to find their pinnacle. Elms, maples, and poplars appeared to scrape the white, billowy clouds. Chestnuts were interspersed like titans lording over the land. There were bear droppings and bent saplings where the beasts used them as scratching posts. The angle of the land turned more vertical, and Nick used the ax handle to push himself forward. Pallid slivers of sunlight slipped through the trees, the only thing keeping the land from being blanketed in full shadow. The journey that had begun before daylight was still in progress even though the sun had risen to its apex.

The peak of Iron Mountain finally appeared, and the land about him had steepened as though a fortress constructed to protect something sacred at the top. His only way to ascend was to take hold of trunks and sapling limbs to pull himself upward. He slid the ax down his back and into his pants. The blade was cold to the touch. Near the pinnacle were a series of rock casings that appeared as though some beast borne in mountain lore had placed them there for decoration. There were slender gaps between the chalky rock accumulations, and Nick noticed dark shapes moving within. He removed his hand from a rock just as a copperhead lunged forward. He removed his ax like a warrior whose adversary had just made the first move in battle. With a swift blow, he severed the serpent's head, the body of the snake writing and tumbling down the slope. He broke into a sweat as he realized that there were other snakes in the rock casings. He scrambled the final yards until he reached the pinnacle, the thought of a snake attack providing a boost of adrenaline. He pulled himself above the edge and dropped to his knees, a wayfarer reaching the promised land. He lay on his back, catching his breath while staring at the ascent of the hardwoods above him. A world above the world. The shedding of something cumbersome.

He rose and regarded the landscape. Powerful, silent. He felt as though he'd entered a place where time had not yet begun, a location that had awaited his arrival since the beginning. As if the mountain had waited for him to start the clock in motion so the world could unfold to the design he chose. The land ran sleek and flat for a hundred yards, ferns and mayapple coating the floor a deep green. Scattered among the ferns were yellow and white flowers for which he had no name for. The trees ran arrow straight, and he wondered if he ascended one, what distant lands would become visible. Virginia was just ten miles to the north. North Carolina was just twenty to the east. Sunlight cut tiny swaths through the trees as though brushed by an errant hand, illuminating the greenery in some celestial manner. He reckoned no one in the world had ever reached such an ascension, observed such a sight. He took to one knee and bowed his head to acknowledge the purity of the mountain peak.

He glanced down the mountain. The tree line hid the valley from view, and it appeared as though all life below had been erased. He regarded the top of Doe Mountain in the eastern horizon. Beyond it, he saw mountains he had not seen before. Mountains he had heard of, but never confirmation given before that they were anything more than legend. A man at heaven's door, he considered himself blessed. From where he stood, the world below appeared as something he could no longer identify. He had found a world where he could remove all bindings to the place that had wronged him so.

He stood tall, surveying the mountaintop. Iron Mountain. The tales he'd heard growing up. A fortress. Impenetrable. Unbending. He recalled the tales of primitive inhabitants, but there was nothing visible from where he stood around that would indicate any one of human form had resided there. If others had come before him, he wondered how long ago their footsteps had been erased by cold winters, by the summer rains.

The summit enveloped him with a sense of belonging. He pondered the foolish desire he once had for living in the world below. He recalled the Good Book's warning not to love the world or the things in the world. He fashioned in his mind that the world he observed was not the one that God warned about.

He studied his surroundings as he moved about. A breeze rattled the treetops, speaking to him in some language he could not yet decipher. In time, he was certain he would. He came upon an elm and patted it. Looking behind him for clearance, he took the ax handle and eyed a spot a foot above the base. He drove the ax at a downward angle, and the echo of steel meeting wood called out to him, an announcement perhaps that some greater good had been set free. He gave it another lick, and then another, and he sufficed the wedge was deep enough. To the other side he moved, driving the ax in similar fashion. With three more cuts delivered, the tree crashed forward into a locust before twisting free, racing to the ground. He stepped back as the base of the tree hit with a thud and bounced several feet high before settling on the ground. Nick came to the locust that had tried to stop the fall of the elm, chose his spot, and drove the ax into the thick tree. The reverberation of the tree held some innocence, something pure, something untouched or tarnished by the hands of man.

The shadows that had stretched across the land earlier that day had returned, yet in the opposite direction, as the sun made its way toward the skyline of Holston Mountain to the north. Nick grew tired from the task, his hands blistered and bloodied. He surveyed the landscape. Twenty-two trees lay on the ground. A patch of sky was now visible, and Nick stood in wonder at the cobalt ceiling, where touches of red to the west gave warning that the sky would soon fade to black. The world around him warped, falling away concave in all directions as though he stood at the pinnacle. He balanced the ax so that it stood on its own volition. Nick knelt, paying homage as he designated it a flagpole for the independence the mountain offered.

Cora set the table. Sweet corn, pinto beans, batter bread, and beef shank, compliments of Burley Potter and his newly butchered cow. She walked outside and rang the dinner bell. Jerico and Tom tended to the hogs. Nick knelt beside the spring, searching the waters as though something cast haphazardly had been suddenly revealed as irreplaceable. Jerico and Tom made their way to the house, but Nick remained creek side. Cora stepped off the porch, shading her eyes from the angled late-afternoon sunlight, studying Nick as he snatched a stone from the stream before rising from his crouched position. He appeared as one misplaced, come to the bank seeking wise counsel. Seeking directions to a home far away, or perhaps to one that never existed. Cora searched for something within him, something familiar, but he appeared an apparition, something that could not take root on the ground below him. She placed her hand to her chest, seeking wise counsel of her own. He tossed the stone in the creek and headed for the house.

Talk was guarded. Nick sat silently, and Cora took the liberty of putting food on his plate. He picked at the corn with his fork.

"So, the Homecoming supper is Sunday," she said. "I need to fetch strawberry preserves from the cellar."

"You making strawberry cakes?" Tom asked.

"Sure am. Miss Louise is head of food planning and asked if I would make a few."

"You best make one that don't leave this kitchen," Jerico said. "The church folk will tear into every pie you bring, and I don't feel like fighting for crumbs of something prepared in my own home."

"I'll bake one for you boys. Guess it's only right my own family gets one they don't have to share." Cora studied Nick, his scruffy beard appearing as a veil to something more than his chin. He had barely touched his food. "You excited about Homecoming, Nick? They will have horseshoes and the log-totin' contest. You always do so good at those things. Especially the log-totin'. Don't know how you lift them heavy things and run them cross the field like you do. I hear Catherine and Sarah are coming. You haven't seen them since you went to St. Louis."

"Don't reckon I'll be going," Nick said.

"Not going?" Tom asked. "Don't you want to see your own sisters? That reason alone ought to get you there. Besides, there will be plenty of girls, all gussied up. Hap Elrod will be there with his banjo. Them gals will be surely looking for dance partners."

"There's some gals I don't care to see."

"Nick, you can't let Annabeth stop you from living. Much as I hate to admit it, all the girls 'round here think you're the catch of the county. Even with that bird's nest you got growing on your face there, the girls surely fancy you. You should be out there, making the most of your days."

"Tom is right," Cora added. "You got much to offer any young lady."

"I would like to be excused. Not much of an appetite tonight. Thank you, Aunt Cora, for the effort put into making this meal." He stood, eyes looking toward the table. "You 'uns have a good evening."

Nick walked to his bedroom.

Jerico walked into the kitchen. Cora was busy at work, scrubbing a cast-iron skillet. "I'm a headin' to town," he said. "Need anything?"

"We could use meal. Can you stop off at the gristmill?"

"I'll get the boys to grab a couple sacks of corn from the cellar." He looked about. "Where are they?"

"Tom is out back. Haven't seen Nick since breakfast."

"I'm worried about that boy. Ain't been the same since the whoopin' he got on the train."

"Well, I'd say losing Annabeth played as much a part. Even more so, I believe. It stands to reason he would be at such odd disposition."

"Long as he's able to do his duties around the farm, I guess he's all right."

"He don't just need to exist. He needs to have a purpose. Find a girl. Have a family of his own."

"I'd say them things are the furthest from his mind."

The sweet melody of a banjo and fiddle welcomed them as the mule led them over the rise. Doe Creek mirrored the road's path. A group of children ran alongside the creek as though trying to outrun it. Horses, recently unfastened from the buggies that had carried the participants, grazed in a grassy field next to the church. To the back of the field, saddled horses gathered under a sprawling oak, an elitist group of equines.

"Oh, look, Nick," Cora said. "There's Sarah. Lordy, she's all growed up. And such a pretty thing. Is that Katherine settin' on the wagon?"

Tom patted Nick on the back as they sat on the back of the buggy. "Aren't you glad you came now, cousin? You get to see your sisters. Hopefully John will come too."

"I'm here for the food," Jerico said. "Stick me under a shade tree with a plate and I'll be content until you 'uns is a ready to go home."

"Oh, stop that talk, Jerico," Cora said. "You being the head of the family, it's your duty to say hidy to the others. Make sure you tell Preacher Cole what a fine job he's doing."

"My duty is to run the farm. Make sure we got food and a house. And that takes all my energy. Visit with the other folk all you want. Just get me a plate of food and set me off to the side."

Jerico guided the buggy next to the others. Nick leapt from the back and helped Cora down from her seat before freeing Sally from the reins. She eased to the grassy field with the other horses. Cora instructed each to carry a pie that sat underneath a covered cloth on the back of the wagon.

Nick approached his sisters. It had been three years since he had seen them. They had grown roots in Abingdon. Even though they were married and had children, it was known that the sisters spent their days together, a joint effort in tending to the children, to the chores that were necessary for daily existence. Sarah lifted her dress hem above her ankles and raced toward Nick. When she hugged him, her bonnet fell, and Nick struggled to hold the pie he carried.

Nick stooped to fetch the hat. "Just leave it, Nick. It's nothing but an aggravation. One of the reasons I don't like coming to social gatherings." She tugged on his beard. "What's this mangled web?"

"Got tired of shaving, I guess." He ran his hand along his cheek. "I'm guessing you're not fond of it."

"I just wasn't expecting to see it. It does hide that handsome Grindstaff face. And there's no sense in that."

"I reckon I'll need it to keep me warm on the cold winter nights up on the mountain."

"Mountain? What mountain?"

He led her eyes to the outline of Iron Mountain with his chin. "That one."

"What in tarnation are you talking about?"

Katherine walked up. "Hello, there, sweet brother." She hugged him. Looking at them side by side, Nick realized how much alike his sisters appeared.

"Hidy, Sis. It appears you got the world by the tail."

"If not by the tail, at least by its hind leg."

"Nick was just saying something about winters on Iron Mountain," Sarah said.

"Iron Mountain?" Katherine asked. "You going on a hunting trip?"

"May as well tell you while you're both here. I bought land atop Iron Mountain. Building a dwelling. Going to be moving up there soon."

"Why would you want to do that?" Sarah asked. "It will be like living in another world."

"Another world is what I'm looking for."

"We heard about the trouble you encountered on the train back from St. Louis," Katherine said. "Is that what this is all about?"

"And speaking of the train, how come we had to find out about your trip to Missouri second-hand and after the fact?" Sarah asked. "Such a change of scenery deserves prior notice. We are your sisters, you know."

"You're the ones that moved two mountain ranges away from Doe Valley," he said.

"Well, you could at least sent word by mail," Katherine said.

"Well," he said quietly.

"So, you get roughed up on a train, and now that makes you want to live as far away from the world as possible," Sarah said, more statement than question.

"It's one reason." As he spoke, Annabeth and Cody approached on a shiny leather buggy with a brass pearl brake handle.

"Ain't that Annabeth?" Katherine asked. "She's your gal, right? Who's that fella she's with?"

Nick's eyes shifted toward the ground. "She *was* my girl."

"Was?"

"She found a better breed."

"So that's why you're running away," Sarah said. "Annabeth done broke your heart. I've got a mind to go over and sock her right on the nose." She stepped toward their buggy, and Nick took hold of her arm.

"No need to get physical," he said. "If that's who she wants, then let her have him. I'm not one to beg or plead my case. If time away from each other was all it took for her to run into the arms of another, then her love for me was a house of sticks."

"I still want to wail on her some," Sarah said. Nick took her by the waist as she tried to fight his grip.

"You're going to leave everything behind because of some dame?" Katherine asked. "That's malarkey. Your roots are planted here. If anyone should leave, it should be her and that rascal."

"Let's send her packing right now," Sarah said as she tried to break free.

"It's going to be all right. Don't worry none about me. You go make the most of your time today. Let me see them young 'uns of yours." He began guiding them back to their buggies, to their families.

"Does John know about your plans?" Sarah asked.

"I've not seen him," Nick said. "You know he don't venture far away from his farm. I don't think he cares one way or the other what I choose to do, just like he don't care where you live your lives."

"I'd say you're right about that," Katherine said. "But I would be interested to get his opinion."

"Enough of that," Nick said. "I need to help Aunt Cora with the food."

When they walked around back of the white, wooden church, Nick observed the fellowship hall, thinking back to the day they laid down the foundation, Annabeth bringing him a plate of food. How beautiful she looked that day, and how big his heart swelled when she passed all the others to bring his food to him.

Nick spotted Hap playing his fiddle, sidled by an elderly man he didn't recognize, playing a banjo. The duo serenaded the gathering while children chased each other. Ladies were busy finding spots on the tables for the food. Cora led her family to the dessert table, and when the men had placed their pies on the wooden structure, Cora disbursed them to do as they pleased. Tom spotted a couple of young men sitting on bales of hay. "Come on, Nick. There's Charlie and Benny Adams." Nick reluctantly followed.

"What do you say, boys?" Tom said as they stood in front of the bales.

"Is that Nick?" Charlie asked. "Son, I hardly recognize you with that beard. You look a might rugged."

Nick gave a slight nod.

"Yes, sir, Nick's going for that wild west look," Tom said. "St. Louis will do that to a man."

"Is that a fact?" Benny asked. "Nick's done settled into the ways of the trail blazers?" He tipped his cap. "Hidy, Nick. Good to see you again."

"You too," Nick responded.

"How was life in the big city?" Benny asked. "I expected to see you around town, at church, since you got back, but it appears you went into hiding."

"I've kept close to the farm for the most part."

"We thought maybe living in the big city had you all uppity, and you was too good to be hanging around the likes of us," Charlie said.

Nick shook his head. "No, nothing like that."

"I bet St. Louis makes Doe Valley seem paler than a sack of flour," Benny said. "Nothin' but tall buildings everywhere I reckon?"

"They sure had plenty," Nick said. "It made things tunnel-like. Hard to turn down a road and be able to see anything except street and storefronts. Tenant housing everywhere. A constant cover of smoke from chimneys and smokestacks."

"Bet you saw a lot of pretty gals out there," Charlie stated.

"Course he did," Tom said. "Word was the whole lot of 'em cried when Nick boarded the train for home. They all wore black cause they was in mourning."

"That certainly weren't the case," Nick said. He removed his hat and ran his fingers through his hair. As he spoke, Annabeth and Cody walked to the food tables. A large group gathered round them, abuzz with chatter. Nick tried to keep his eyes on Charlie and Benny, tuned in to their conversation, but he couldn't look away from the woman he had pledged to marry and carve out a life together. The murmur grew, and Preacher Cole stood by a nearby post where he rang a black bell.

"Welcome to Homecoming," he said. "Thanks to all who worked so hard in helping this event take place." He stepped forward. "Before I bless the food, I have some extra exciting news." As he spoke, Nick regarded Annabeth, who seemed a bit overwhelmed by the attention of those who stood around her and Cody. "I'm happy to say," the preacher continued, "that Cody Swanson and Annabeth Parker are to be betrothed next Saturday in the church, and all of you are welcome to attend. The Swanson family will provide food and such after the wedding. It promises to be an outstanding event."

The gathering clapped and made public their approval. As someone patted Annabeth on her shoulder, she caught Nick's stare. She flashed a sad smile, something apologetic for the just-mentioned news. Cody leaned and kissed Annabeth on the cheek before shaking hands and acknowledging the congratulations coming his way.

"Well, I'll be damn," Charlie said. "She's going to marry that snake?"

"He's a bit too prideful for me," Tom said. "Anytime a body's around him, he makes sure to let them know he comes from better stock."

"He's got a wanderin' eye," Charlie said. "I guarantee you if Annabeth excused herself to the privy, Cody would be eyeballing any pretty thing he could find."

"I had the feeling that she would end up marrying you, Nick," Charlie said. "You had her corralled and ready to go. But, I guess while you was gone, Cody opened the gate and slipped into the pen."

"Yes, sir," Benny added, "the wrong bull jumped in the pasture."

Their conversation faded to jumbled words as Nick watched Annabeth and Cody accept well-wishes. Within the festive atmosphere, Nick realized his lot had been cast into a stream he forged against but couldn't stop. The torrent held all the power, held the strength to determine the path his fate would flow, as though a hook from the pole of some dark-souled fisherman had landed deep in Nick's soul. The world had snatched hold of Nick Grindstaff, holding him up for all to see, reveling at the captured fish that could no longer put up the good fight.

Nick headed for home, disregarding the pleas from Cora. He followed Doe Creek, the steady hoarseness of its water rushing over the vast array of stones and rocks. Standing creek side, he reckoned the water had more control of its destiny than he. And so, it was time to release the grip the world had of him, to spit free the prong lodged deep in his soul, and dive free into deeper waters where he could no longer be found.

| **16** |

The blade ripped into the fallen trunk. He'd measured it four steps long. He carved a notch on one end and set the ax against another of the cut tree trunks. He dragged the notched trunk and laid it onto the base log below so that the notch gripped tightly. Three rows high now, with a gap for the fireplace. Iron Mountain was scattered with stones, and he reasoned they would form a sufficient fireplace. He looked at the widening landscape, the sun's rays gleaming, unimpeded, warmth spreading wide on his face and shoulders. His body ached, and he sought rest, but the vision of Preacher Cole announcing Annabeth and Cody's engagement six months prior at Homecoming pushed him on to complete the task. So much more to do. He envisioned a planting field. He would have to be particular in his choices. Taters. Rhubarb. Maybe corn. A supplanted apple tree beyond Jerico's pasture. Maybe two. Tomorrow he would return with a cart and a froe. A splitter.

He continued through the day, the sweat building under his clothes. The walls were growing in height. He carved out space for the doorway, and when he measured the walls three feet high, he laid a long log across to start the row above the doorway. No windows would be necessary. Would only bring in cold on winter nights. When he wanted to look at the world, he reckoned he would go outside. The chimney would be against the back wall. A new world taking shape.

Shadowed treetops under the amethyst sky guided Nick along the dirt road as he made his way down Timothy Branch. The lanterns were aglow through the windows of Bert Greer's house when Nick passed, the yard opaque and dreamlike. A buttery aroma came from within, and Nick guessed Nadine had supper ready. He guessed Cora had as well, and he wondered if she was worried about him.

Nick sat at the kitchen table, his appetite strong. For the first time since he'd returned home from St. Louis, he desired food. It was hard to believe it had been two years since the beating he suffered. More devastating was the pummeling administered to his heart. But that was all behind him now, and there was purpose within him again. He had cleaned his plate before the others settled into their first bites, and when Cora passed him the bowl of pintos, he nodded his appreciation. Talk was small as the others appeared worn from the day.

"Where you been?" Tom asked. "You missed a good day at the creek. Me and John loaded up on trout. He asked me to pass along his regards."

"How's he doing?" Nick asked.

"Taller than a locust. He hadn't heard about your misfortune on the train. Was hoping to see you. Waited on the porch after we finished dressing the fish. Said he'd come back another day."

"Said he spends most of his days in Laurel Bloomery working the pottery mill and tending to his farm," Cora said. "I invited him to church. Maybe you could come along. You two can get caught up. Surely you would enjoy time together."

"I am truly glad you had kin to raise you and your siblings after Mary and Isaac passed," Jerico said.

"Isaac would be proud knowing his brother did such a fine job raising one of his young 'uns," Cora said.

"Nick has been a blessing to us all." He nodded toward his nephew.

"I appreciate you raising me like your own," Nick said. "You could have felt pity and not held me to a high standard."

"That wouldn't have been fair to you."

"If you were held to such a high standard," Tom said, "how come I got more whoopins?"

"Cause you were more mischievous in your ways," Cora said with a grin.

"I would argue my case," Tom said, "but I'll just eat another slice of cornbread instead."

Nick entered the store. Veta was sweeping next to the box stove. She smiled when she spotted him. "Why, hidy, Nick. How you a doin'?"

"Miss Veta." He nodded.

"Say, how's that ax working out for you?"

"Just fine. Now I'm in need of a cart. A pull wagon of some sort."

"You must be workin' on some kind of project."

"It's a might big one."

"Well, if you been cuttin' trees ever since you got the ax last winter, you surely have carved out a whole valley somewheres."

"I'm carving it, but it's a little higher up than the valley."

"What do you mean?"

"I bought land on Iron Mountain. Building a home."

"More power to you. Foller me out back and see if the cart will serve your purpose."

Beyond the back door was an overhang where various wooden crates twirled in the breeze, hanging from the tin ceiling with narrow twine. All but two were empty. Two saddles were stacked next to a pair of reins hanging from nails on the back wall.

"As you can see, inventory is dwindling," Veta said. "I can't get suppliers to lend me credit to sell their wares. I don't know how much longer I can keep the store a goin'."

"I hear tell Mr. Ozzie has got the shiny gadgets, but he surely can't compare to your kindness with customers. Good people see the difference."

"It don't seem like their vision's too good. It appears them gadgets is what draws them in. I don't mind admitting I wish I had me some of them shiny things in my store. Yonder is the cart."

Nick placed the ax and froe in the cart. A pair of work gloves. A jug of water. Tom approached from around the side of the house.

"What are you doing?" Tom asked. "We got enough firewood to get us through three winters."

"Ain't cuttin' firewood. I'll be a cuttin' trees for the barn up on the property."

Tom regarded Nick peculiarly. "Barn? I thought you were just building a lean-to or some such to hunt or maybe escape to when summer bears down on us."

"It's more of the permanent kind."

"You been going up on that mountain for a good while now. Taking tools and such. Working till sundown. I knew it was of some intent, but didn't realize it was to relocate. Seems like it would be a might less dicey here in the valley. You got a plan on how to survive up there?"

A shrug. "The Bible says God knows the plans He has for me. Plans to prosper and not harm me. Well, that plan rode straight into the ditch. I figure if I can get closer to the heavens, maybe God can explain directly why things got so out of sorts. I sure ain't been able to figure it out down here. Besides, I trust the mountain has better plans for me to prosper than what the world down here has in mind."

"There ain't nothing on that mountain to provide trust."

"And there's no one there who needs to be trusted."

Mist crept along the folds of the hillsides, the valley hushed and dreamlike. The faultless clouds hung bleak and unyielding, the higher peaks of the land hidden from view. Nick wished for the sun to appear and warm the day, but he figured the energy he would generate on the mountain would create heat enough to keep any cold winds from chilling his bones. Pushing the cart up the ridge became a struggle, and the slope of the land turned to where he began to pull the wagon behind him. He searched the crevices and ridges for gentler slopes, taking time to examine and study the shape of the land for more favorable ascension. The barren trees allowed for a clearer view of the slants, and except for laurels and firs spread about the land, the mountainside was an endless bound of tall trunks and far-reaching limbs. He looked to a ridge east of where he stood, one he had not noticed before. There were folds in the mountain less angular and he headed for them. He came upon natural switchbacks, the ascension less taxing on his body. When he came upon saplings, he kicked at that them with his boots. The initial stages of creating a trail had begun. It appeared he was ascending the mountain sideways, the elevation more tempered. When he reached the top, he traced with his eyes the way he had come, committing it to memory. The sun had burned through the clouds, the mist dissipated. Nick headed westerly.

Winter had flattened the underbrush, and Nick eased his way through the hardwoods, a trailblazer pulling a wagon along a boundless array of timber. He listened carefully for whispering among the treetops, as though instruction was forthcoming of how to best maneuver the land. He studied the area, noting trees that had odd growth patterns. Markers that would help guide him back to the newly made path that would help him descend the mountain. He came upon massive rock formations near the eastern edge that looked out toward Doe Valley. He came upon a rise in the terrain where he had to lean forward for leverage to pull the wagon. He spotted a small branch and studied the flow. Kneeling, he scooped water into his hand. The icy drink held a mild flavor of minerals. Of earth. He scooped again and drank, assuring himself he had never tasted something so pure.

When he spotted the cabin, he estimated he had walked three miles from where he had ascended the mountain. He set the cart beside his newly designed workplace, two tree trunks lodged a few feet above the ground, held in place by smaller logs wedged into the soil beside the trunks. The trunks formed a small V, a foot apart at their widest diameter, inches apart at the closest. He took a small log from a pile and with a wooden mallet, tapped it between the two trunks. With his froe, he split the piece of wood oblong with the tapping of the mallet. Soon, he had carved a narrow plank board. The creation of the roof was now underway.

The day carried on, Nick unaware of its passing. He stopped to rest and inspect the work. The creation of the roof gave the house a look of impending completion, a fortress from the world. Shelter from storms, God and man-made. The stars would soon light his darkness. The winds would surely serenade him. Creatures of the night would stand guard as he slept. No shortcomings of the world would be able to pass through his door.

He headed east for the stream, an empty pail in each hand. Through heavy timber he walked, a man lost in discovery. Subtle differences in each rise, each dip of the terrain laid opposite from the way he observed it on the way to the cabin. Hardwoods caught the afternoon sun, sparked fiery orange. The back side of those trees hid in gray shadow as though some sort of concealment was underway. He came across laurel hell bound so tightly they appeared to be an entrance to some portal where no entry was permitted. When he had made it to the slender creek, he observed the shape the water took. Shallow, sliding past rocks that seemed part of the mountain, not separate like the rocks at the bottom of Doe Creek. He filled the buckets and headed homeward.

Back at the cabin, he dug soil and scooped it in a metal tub. Adding the water, the soil soon turned to mud, and he began pasting it between the log walls.

The waning crescent moon hung wearily in the western sky, its dull shine rendering the dark skyline of Iron Mountain cavernous. To the east, the marigold contour of the sky whispered the new day would soon unfold. Nick's breath wisped white in the chilled air. The world appeared vacated, as though a mass exodus had taken place through the night, where the news had somehow not reached the valley. The roadway lay dim before him, yet more pronounced than the valley, as though some massive paring knife had separated the land. He wore the solitude like a coat, anticipating how much greater that seclusion would be atop the mountain. Fifteen straight days he had returned to his new homeland to finish the race to independence of the most primal kind.

By the time he had ascended the trail, the morning air had warmed, and the sun appeared a ball of white. At the top of the world, he felt as one peering down at lesser beings. With hammer and chisel, he peeled away soft limbs of ferns, searching for stones that would fill his need. The smooth rocks were dusted gray and tan, a look that mirrored the soil around it. He spotted one the length of his hand and examined its pale-yellow texture. Out of curiosity, he wiped it, studying the smooth design. He ran the rock along his tongue. The dampness turned the rock to where veins the color of blood appeared. Legend had it that iron in the mountain's rocks would show itself if moisture was added. He touched the stone to his face as though a pulse might vibrate from it. He took his knife and began carving into the smooth underside. When he was done, he observed what he had written. Satisfied, he removed a kerchief from the pocket of his over-alls and slipped the rock inside before returning the kerchief to his pocket.

With the collection of stones added to the circular stack of rocks, he packed them with mud, and day by day it grew until it was higher than the ceiling. The fireplace was complete.

The days had grown longer, and the warmth of the early summer sun was suitable for the labor needed for a man with such an un-dertaking. For a man burdened. The house was completed, and Nick turned to other tasks, clearing more land and felling trees of smaller girth. A barn was built. Metamorphosis almost complete. The shed-ding of old skin. The cutting of burdensome ties. A settler in a new land. He'd read of pioneers in schoolbooks and was ready to test his mettle against theirs. He believed he had found the most desirable world possible, but only for himself. There would be no sharing of this world. No trailblazing. He aimed to stake his claim as that of a singular kind. And though many explorers sought distant lands, Nick had found a wilderness of beauty hidden simply beyond the hardwoods seen by those in the valley where he was born and raised. And there was something special in that comfort.

| 17 |

Cora fought back tears as she handed the small burlap sack to Nick. "This is for you to eat when you get up to the new homestead," she said, not ashamed of the motherly tone of her voice.

Nick took the bag. "Thank you, Aunt Cora. And not just for the food. For everything you've done for me."

She hugged him, staring out at Iron Mountain in the distance. She never gave thought that one day it would be the call of a dreary mountaintop that would take him from her house for good. Flashbacks of Jerico bringing Nick to the house in the wagon arose, the boy a newly coined orphan, her wondering how that three-year-old would do without his ma and pa.

Jerico placed his hand on Nick's shoulder after Cora eased her grip. "You know you always got a place to stay. This house is just as much your'n as it is ours, and if you decide that mountain ain't to your liking, you surely come on back."

Nick nodded. "Appreciate all you done. Rearing me when I wasn't even your child. I'll always be indebted."

"Families take care of their own," Cora said. "Now, you make sure you take good care of yourself up on that old mountain. And you come back any time a need arises."

"Yes'm." He nodded and took a breath. "Well, I best get a movin'."

"You got that sack of cornmeal?" Cora said. "When that runs out, you come right down here and we'll have another for you."

"I'll head to the mill when I need more."

"They don't hand it out for free," Jerico said.

"I know they don't. I'll be growing corn. And rhubarbs and taters and wild leeks that I can barter with."

"Not everybody is inclined to work in trade. It's currency that they deal with."

"Then I'll seek out ones that work with something other than money."

"I just don't know about all this," Cora said, putting her hands to her mouth as though she were about to pray. He adjusted the denim shoulder sack, smiled, and turned. As he approached the dusty road, Tom waited, kicking halfheartedly at something on the ground as though doing so might help him gather his thoughts.

"I guess this is it, then," Tom said.

"It is," Nick replied as he placed the burlap sack on the cart next to the sack of corn. A small iron pot, a box of friction matches, and a spindle of clothing. Long-handled underwear. A wool coat. Three wool blankets. Gloves. His Winchester rifle and a sack of ammunition.

"I hope you make your way back down from time to time. Maybe I'll come check on you soon. I'm sure I can find your cabin."

"Someday. For now, I think it's best to adjust to the new land on my own, without a body to lean on or turn to."

"You sure this is what you want?"

"It ain't so much a want to, but a have to. I've played the hand the Lord dealt me, and I wagered and lost it all. Now, I need to find a new table with a new hand. See if I can win when there's nobody settin' across from me in human form. I like my odds better playing a'gin nature."

"I wouldn't be so sure that nature don't have a few cards up her sleeve." They embraced. "Go on if you're going," Tom said. "It ain't going to be daylight forever, you know."

Nick made sure to meet Tom's eyes one last time and smiled.

He took hold of the cart and headed toward the mountain.

Nick sat in the rickety cane chair he'd constructed, his first creative work outside the home building. By the fire pit, he carved a limb of an elm branch as he waited on the sun to rise. The fire's glow, muted by the iron pot above it where grits churned and popped, struggled to provide light for Nick to see the shape of the limb he whittled, but the process was just a distraction to pass the time for what would soon unfold. Dawn would soon give shape to the mountain, and Nick would become witness to a metamorphosis that couldn't be duplicated or explained. There were subtle differences and variations in each sunrise. He found something mystical in that passing of darkness to light, in the perpetual rebirth of the mountain. In it, he found something tangible that wiped away the fear and insecurity that the dark incubated, something that dimmed misfortune, that washed away heartache and heartbreak.

The skies lightened, and a thin layer of clouds woven orange and purple appeared above Doe Mountain, a celestial veil for the sun's appearance. For those in the valley, it was an alert that it was time to tend to the tasks of the day, to the beasts of the field, to the crops that would make it to the dinner table in the fall. For Nick, it was a chance to observe at Heaven's door what surely only the eyes of God and Nick viewed. A breeze stirred the morning chill, confirmation that he was emancipated, free to watch the world shape and evolve to his choosing. Embers rose from the dimmed fire, and he knew the ground corn in the pot would soon provide his meal. The hardwoods had begun to bud, spring making its appearance known. The firs and mountain laurels were prominent in their appearance, their perpetual state of green shortening the depth of the mountain.

He had survived the first winter. He would admit to no one but himself that on some nights, under wool blankets, donned in wool coat and beaver hat, trying to keep the fire alive in the cabin, he had perhaps underestimated the ferocity of the brutal winter winds that would shake his cabin, his soul, to the core. But with spring newly arrived, his focus turned to the prospects of what knowledge the mountain could teach him.

With the bowl filled, Nick carved a chunk of butter with his knife and watched the grits swallow it up. He'd harvested apples from the two transplanted trees. He'd grown corn, rhubarb, potatoes, and onions in that first summer on the mountain, and was able to barter at William Dowell's store in Stoney Creek for lard, flour, and hardtack. He had the corn turned into meal. Cubes of butter. Salt. He'd found the route down the backside of Iron Mountain toward Stoney Creek a might easier to traverse. It held not the sheer steepness of the mountain slope approaching from the Doe Valley side. He also found William Dowell to be fair in his bartering, especially after he found out that Nick was living alone on top of the remote mountain.

With an easy breath to cool the food, he spooned a small amount, looking westward toward the barn. To the north, Holston Mountain carved a slight silhouette against a plum sky, the sun's light not yet reaching that narrow mountain. There was movement beneath the barn's overhang, a dark figure slouching about the corn crib. Nick set the bowl on a stump he'd carved out for a table setting. Moving slowly toward the doorway, he removed his rifle from beside his split-log bed. He eased back to the fire pit, resuming his spot in his chair, rifle laid across his lap. A shadow emerged from the barn, sleek and long. Too slender to be a bear, yet black as any bear he had ever seen. Its movement was deliberate, and when the big cat was within thirty yards of Nick, its green eyes sparkled from the sun. It's raven shape carved emptiness from the shadows, a darker shade yet itself, as though it had stolen light from the dawn. The cat emitted a low scream, as though a child crying. It froze in its tracks, curiously eyeing the one who watched him. A counterpart to his existence on the mountain, perhaps. It gave a slight wag of its tail and looked about as though to measure any adversaries lurking. When it appeared satisfied, it gave a parting glance to Nick, who watched the cat slink toward the edge where the mountain fell sharply toward the valley. It stopped and looked toward the shadowed land below, as though proclaiming dominion over it all. It roused another scream to the risen sun as though to curse its arrival before disappearing over the edge.

Nick heard one final cry, and hoped the panther understood it held more dominion over Iron Mountain than Nick ever could.

He knelt, placing the potato seed in the cool soil. After covering it with the dirt he'd plowed the day before, he moved down the row, sweat building under his long-handle shirt. The callouses on his hands ached from working the plow. He had repaired a leak in the roof of Veta's store in exchange for an old sawmill blade. He fastened the blade onto a discarded wagon wheel and tied two pieces of seasoned beech tree limbs together to make the apparatus. It was primitive in nature, but so was his existence.

He moved along the field, placing the small seeds in the open vein, his knees throbbing. Above him, a hawk screeched as though the world had wronged it and due penance was in order. When Nick had returned from St. Louis, he had screeched internally in like manner until he realized that no penance would be paid no matter how loud the shriek. The world moved at its own choosing, the experience had taught him, and there was nothing man nor beast could do to alter that course, and cursing served no useful purpose.

He finished planting two rows of potatoes. Rhubarbs had been already planted, and he would lay the seeds for corn in the morning. Nick just needed the spring rains to come, to provide the growth for the planting season. He made his way back to the house, a well-worn path that gave him pause as to how long he'd made the mountain top his home. A bucket of spring water hung from the outside wall under the overhang. When he dipped the ladle into the shimmering water, he was certain he was drinking God's most perfect drink. A familiar dull ache rose in his head, and he knelt and closed his eyes until the pain was gone. He reckoned the remnants from the beating on the train would be with him for the rest of his days.

He walked into the cabin, the light from the midday sun carving shape from the murky corners. The ashes from the fireplace held a muted, amber glow. He sat on his split-log bed. A short break from the chores. The cabin served the purpose for sleeping or cooking when the cold or rain wouldn't permit it at the outdoor pit. Other than that, Nick was outdoors. Free, alive, not beholden to anything, nor anybody. He leaned forward to check the lacing in his boot, and a rattle caused him to halt all movement. His head still, his eyes glanced beside the fireplace. Curled, wrapped over itself in layers, its tail rose like a warning flag, shaking gently. Its tongue slithered.

"Looks like I got company," Nick said, careful not to make any movement as the rattler lay three feet from Nick's boot. "If you come looking for food, you're out of luck. Ain't seen nary a mouse in this cabin and I been here going on two years now. If you've come for the warmth of the fire, stay as long as you need."

Nick slowly stroked his beard, pondering the next move, if any should be taken. He eased out of the cabin and took hold of his spade. Walking to the barn, and the wire screen corn crib, he rummaged around small amounts of corn shelling and shuckings. He tapped the screen where it met the side of the barn, and a field mouse scampered. Nick turned the shovel and came down hard on the rodent, freezing it in its tracks. He scooped the barely breathing mouse and walked to the house. When Nick entered the cabin, the snake raised its head, and the rattle sang the warning song again. Nick dropped the mouse in front of the rattler, and it hissed.

"I'll leave you to eat in peace."

He walked outside the cabin and headed for the apple tree to gauge its bloom. A good apple crop would help the barter process of things Nick could not produce on his own.

A clanking of metal and tin roused Nick from the cane chair where he sharpened his knife. He grabbed the rifle that leaned against a nearby stump and moved up the ridge. When he spotted the stocky woman leading a steer, confusion overtook him. Surely, she wasn't passing through. There was nowhere to pass through to. He met her as she approached.

"Hidy, Nick," the woman said with a wave.

"Miss Billie? What in heaven's name brings you way up this mountain, and with an ox no less?"

"Your sister, Sarah, said you moved up here all alone. She is with child and didn't need to be scalin' any mountains right now. She's worried about you and wanted you to have some items to make sure you ain't a starvin' to death. You surely can't survive turnin' fox squirrels over a spit. So, she sent utensils and pots and such so you can cook and not live like some cave dweller. I'm always up for adventure, so I gladly volunteered. I needed to go down Shady anyway, and the climb up here ain't too steep from that side of the mountain. And I ain't seen you in a coon's age, so, here I am. Besides, I was curious to see for myself what a mountain man's life is all about."

"This is way beyond the degree of kindness."

"That gal has looked out for me for years since Rollin passed. It does me extry good to be able to return the kindness. As you can see, I'm a bit thick in the loins, but I can still scale a mountain with the best of them."

"How is Sarah?"

"Busier than a one-legged gal in a mule kickin' contest."

"She's going to have another child, you say?"

A vision of chasing butterflies along Doe Creek with Sarah arose. He couldn't have been more than seven or eight. The older sister, giving instruction on how best to get butterflies to light on his arm is what he recalled. He could never coax those butterflies to land on him. "Please give her my best."

"You should do that y'sef. And to Katherine too."

"They got enough to worry about than entertaining me."

"Hell, it ain't entertainin' when it comes to kin. Would do them both a world of good to see you." Billie wore a stained scarf around her neck. A floppy hat with the front brim flipped skyward. A toothless mouth made her chin and nose almost touch.

"I'm not much of a conversationalist these days. I ain't spoke to another in months."

"Well, you can practice on me to get your pipes a workin'. You need to see them little 'uns too. You got four nieces and one nephew that don't know you from a cow pie. Need to do somethin' about that."

"Someday."

"Sounds like talk of the dismissive kind."

Nick studied the cart. "You shouldn't have gone to all this trouble, Miss Billie. Making the trek up here weren't necessary, but I can certainly use the cooking items." He led her to two trees where he had hammered a plank between them. "Wrap the reins to the ox around the plank and follow me to the fire pit. I got chilled cider in the shade."

"There's work yet to be done. We'll tote these pots and such to the shack, and then we can worry about the cider."

It took two trips to carry the cooking provisions, the skillet, and the small pot. Secured on the steer's back was a small ceramic baker, which impressed Nick that the steer could maneuver the mountain with the weight of it on its back. Billie helped Nick carry it to the cabin, laying them under the overhang near the door.

They sat in cane chairs around the dormant fire pit, sipping on the cool drink.

Billie looked about. "Lordy, how do you handle the isolation?"

"There ain't none. Deer along the planting field. Coons and possums in the underbrush. Squirrels watching me eye from the treetops, surely to see when I come in close proximity of my gun. The occasional wolf. Seen a panther twice."

"They, lawd. And what about the bears?"

"They pass by from time to time, but leave me be. We have an understanding, so to speak."

"Hope you don't find out firsthand what their idy of understandin' is."

Nick shrugged. "When they are in their own element, their own world, they don't carry animosity."

"I wouldn't be able to relax for a second."

"How's Katherine? Does she and Sarah see much of each other?"

"The proverbial peas in a pod. Live less than a stone's throw from each other down Chestnut holler. Katherine with the two young 'uns and Sarah with three boys. Course, the new one on the way. Maybe this 'un will be a girl."

"Again, please give them my regards."

"Again, you should do that y'sef. I'm sure they would be happy as hogs in slop to see you."

"I don't venture off the mountain much. When there's trading to be done mostly."

"A peculiar way to live."

"I reckon if I didn't need supplies, I'd not leave this land at all."

"I passed a branch a ways back. Is that your closest water source?"

"It is."

"Have to a make a day's trip just for a sip of drinkin' water."

"I take a couple buckets each trip."

"More power to ya." She patted her knees. "Well, guess I better get on back down the mountain. Need to get home 'fore dark."

"I surely appreciate your effort. Let me send you home with some apples. I'll pull a couple rhubarbs from the field. Winter preserved them well. The apples taste sweet as honey. Everything comin' from the ground up here has a taste that I've not found anywhere else."

Billie walked to where she stood under the overhang above the entrance to the door. There were shelves which held pots and bottles. A ladle. Glass jars that held what looked like jerky. Near the door a wooden barrel, tightly closed. Nick reached up and grabbed a burlap sack.

"This is unlike any homestead I ever saw," she said. "All your wares are outside."

"The inside is for the bed and fireplace."

She peeked in through the open doorway, the room in heavy shade except for the sluice of light coming through the doorway. "You barely got room to turn around. Heaven help ya if you got to scratch an itch."

He let go a brief laugh. "Let me get them food items." Nick went to the planting field. She watched him carve several rhubarbs from the ground. After placing them in the poke, he went to the apple stump and picked out a dozen.

"You plantin' shuck beans?" she asked.

"Hadn't given it any thought. Not sure how I'd keep them preserved."

"You get needle and thread. Hook through 'em and hang 'em from the shanty lattice. They will shrivel and go into a natural state of preservin'. Can make several britches. Toss 'em in the pot with fatback and sliced onion. Now that's a tasty dinner."

"I'll have to do that." He handed the poke to Billie as she stood next to the cabin, looking about. One last examination of the mountain.

"Yessir, you're as removed from the world as is humanly possible. Don't look for me to be a frequent visitor."

"Safe travels, Miss Billie. And thank you again."

"You take good care of yourself, Nick. And if you get the urge, come see your sisters. See your nieces and nephews. Let 'em know Uncle Nick is alive and well."

"Maybe some day."

He watched her ease down the trail. He regarded the sturdiness in her gait. Something in the way she carried herself, the way she guided the beast, the raw simplicity. Life without burden, a slight nuisance perhaps.

She fell from view and the clomp of the animal's hooves faded into the quiet of the mountain.

Larry held the rope as Veta tied it to the worn handle. When it was secure, Larry eased the pail down the narrow well.

"How we going to keep the piglets from getting out?" he asked. "That fencing is so weak, it wouldn't take much of a breeze to knock it over and them little 'uns will have full access to the valley. May as well just sell them than to let them wander off."

"I'm working to save enough for new fencing. My supplier will give me a fair price, but I got to sell some more goods at the store to have the money."

"I can cut posts from some of the locusts out back. Should be plenty sturdy to keep the wire sturdy."

"Lordy, how in the world would I make it without you and your sister. Sometimes a body takes what someone else does for granted. Since your pa passed, I realize now what all he did. Running the store, working the farm. Making sure we had food on the table, shoes on our feet. Yes, sir, buddy, he was a hardworking man." She took hold of the filled pail of water. "If my foggy mind is thinking clearly, somebody's about to have a birthday."

Larry nodded. "Twelve years old."

"Almost fully growed. I'd say you're entitled to some pie. What would you like? How about blackberry fig?"

"Sounds good, Mama."

"Now, you get on inside and get your sister. Don't forget your learnin' books. I best get to the store. I pray we have customers."

Larry headed into the house. "Bye, Mama."

"Bye little'un. I love you bunches."

Veta pulled the wagon to the side of the house. She heard Larry and Joan in the distance, busy in some sort of play. She took to unloading the fencing wire from the wagon bed, staggering from the weight. She heard footsteps approaching and leaned against the wagon, flinching when she noticed the tall figure.

"Didn't mean to startle you."

When she detected the familiar voice, she patted her chest. "Well, hidy, Nick. You had me shook for a second."

"I certainly didn't mean to."

"Don't give it another thought." She regarded him. "Well, what about that wad of beard runnin' down your face? Ain't you heard of shavin' razors?"

Her ran his fingers along his beard and grinned. "How do, Miss Veta."

"Well, buddy, I'd say it's been at least a year since I seen you last. How's life on the mountain?"

He nodded. "Good."

"Anyone keeping you company beside the bears?"

"No, ma'am."

"Well."

He took hold of the wire bundle. "How about you let me build that fence for you?"

"I ain't got money to pay you."

"I don't want money. But I would surely accept a meal."

"I can toss some flour in the sweet milk and make some dumplin's. I'll fetch Larry to help you with the fence."

"I prefer to work alone if you don't mind. Helps me think more clearly of the task at hand. Let the boy run and play like boys are want to do. I'll be fine on my own."

"Well, at least let him take the old locust poles around back. Can use the firewood."

"Well, I best get to work."

Veta and Nick carried the wire to the hog pen. Veta pointed to the stack of locust posts that Larry had cut and accumulated over the course of the past three weeks. She explained her plan to replace all posts and rewire. Nick nodded. "I'll just need the necessary tools," he said.

"I'll fetch them while you lay flat the wire."

Nick put his coat on the wagon. He rolled the sleeves of the stained cotton shirt he wore when he worked on Jerico's farm. Overalls faded pale blue. Veta soon returned with a basket of tools and a tin of nails. "Ray always had a collection of tools. It gives me comfort seeing them put to good use."

"Yes'm. I'll take great care in handling them."

Dusk settled into the valley, the mountains vague, maya-blue, fading into the folds of the expansive dark. The air contained a chill, the warmth of the day dissipating, cooling the sweat under Nick's shirt. He bundled the old posts that would make good firewood for the cooking stove. He remembered Cora saying locust held a strong flame. He had a load surrounded by his thick arms, when Veta appeared from behind the house. "You let Larry take those around back. Supper's a ready and you need to get washed up."

His stomach growled when the buttery aroma of dumplings tickled his nostrils. His meals on Iron Mountain were out of necessity, to survive. To enjoy a meal for the sake of satisfying taste buds, in the company of others, gave him pause.

When gathered at the table, Veta blessed the meal. Joan stared oddly at Nick. "Uncle Nick, is it true you live with bears and panthers and such?"

"Now, Joan, don't be a botherin' our guest with questions. Let the man enjoy his meal in peace."

Nick gave a quick smile. "It's all right."

"You ever tangled with one?" Larry asked. "Which is scariest, bear or panther?"

"I've not tangled with either," Nick said, the innocence of the boy's question causing him to smile. He regarded Larry. "But as far as which one is scariest—the bear's growl is mighty powerful, but there ain't nothing that causes me to take notice as when I hear the panther's cry."

"Do you hunt?" Joan asked.

He nodded. "Squirrel and rabbit. Coons on occasion. I trap beaver. I'll snatch a trout or two from the creek with a net from time to time."

"So, you ain't never had to shoot a bear?" Larry asked.

"They come around the camp from time to time. More out of curiosity than anything. I don't look like something they are a used to seeing. Maybe they come to get a closer look to what's cooking over the fire. So far, they've not come close enough to share a meal."

After dinner was finished, Nick thanked Veta and headed for the door. He looked out at the darkness. "Miss Veta, could I trouble you for use of a lantern? I didn't reckon this morning that I'd be out past nighttime. I promise to return it end of the week. I'll bring you some rhubarb and corn freshly grown."

"Now, buddy, that's a deal. I been wanting to make a rhubarb pie for the longest time."

Standing at the road, he turned and nodded his gratitude to Veta. He headed down the road, the lantern casting it in circular glow, pale yellow. The sound of his boots on the dry dirt was his only company as he made his way towards Timothy Branch. A wayfarer passing through a world he no longer understood. No longer needed. He passed houses with darkened windows, the inhabitants seeking rest for their tired bones. Some, perhaps, stirring around woodstoves for warmth and company, giving thanks for the day's blessings, or mulling over the chores awaiting when tomorrow would arrive. Perhaps both.

When Nick passed Preacher Cole's house, he noticed the front window aglow and the preacher in a rocker by a hearth, a soft fire beyond it. He appeared to be studying a Bible as though truths might be revealed that had escaped him in prior readings. Nick reflected on Sunday mornings in Bethel Baptist, sitting on the first pew with Uncle Jerico and Aunt Cora, trying to keep from jumping when young Cole's voice rose to a high-tenored pitch when he warned against the evils of the world. The age of the preacher's face showed in the firelight. In that progression of time, how much wisdom had been acquired? He came upon a farmhouse where cattle lay near the roadside fence. He extended his lantern to get a better look. Beasts dead silent, their legs tucked under themselves to where, in the darkness, they appeared as mounds of ash. The moonless night gave the stars immense boldness, scattered across that vast sky. Orion stood guard, his sword ready to defend the constellations. To perhaps write lyrics on the walls of Heaven.

Nick took to whistling a tune he had heard somewhere in his past. In St. Louis, probably, based on the somber tone. He came upon an abandoned house where Timothy Branch bent northward along the base of Iron Mountain. He noticed a dim light inside the decrepit shanty. He stopped at the road, setting the lantern at his feet to get a better look through the darkness. The quiet rumble of the branch out in that black of night comforted him. The sweet aroma of wild grass at the dirt road's edge arose. He studied the house for movement, confused as to why he had never noticed an inhabitant. Picking up the lantern, he resumed whistling and commenced to walking. The shape of something in front of the shack caught his attention. He raised the lantern, and a silhouette detached itself from the darkness.

"'Tis a fool that whistles of a night," a scraggly voice said. Warily, Nick stepped off the road toward the figure. The light from the lantern revealed an elderly woman. She wore a long, pale dress that hung loosely about her shoulders. The sleeves were bunched, yet only her hands were visible. Her silver hair was matted against her temples.

"What do you mean?" Nick asked.

"Your whistle rouses demons and haints and setch from the dark."

"Is that so?"

"They's all among us in the night, callin' out. A whistle tells them you hear their call, and it conjures them up in human form. You surely got them stirrin' about this evenin'." She came closer into the lantern's light. Her face was sullen, her cheekbones pronounced, eyes receded and hidden as though there might be none at all. "Why do you wander of a night? A strange interloper lookin' to speak with the undead."

"Just passing through on my way up the mountain."

She turned her head to the vast black behind her. "Iron?"

"Yes'm."

"You'll not be walkin' it alone tonight. You got no idy what night spirits you done stirred up."

"A walking companion might not be a bad thing tonight."

"These ain't of the walkin' kind. If you're easily spooked, best not look up in the trees. Them haints will be hoverin' above you, curious to your every step."

He studied her. Her dress touched the ground. She appeared to be hovering. He searched her eyes for movement, but they appeared as barren sockets. His spine tingled. "Well, I got a lot of ground to cover. You have a good evening."

Under the glow of Nick's lantern, she regarded him as something undecipherable. He regarded her in like manner.

When Nick reached the first ridge, the lantern's light led him to the path he had carved out from his travels up and down the mountain. The land began to rise, the depth of the woods forming a tight barrier. Trees gathered, conspiring in the distance. He kept his gaze to the ground, the warning from the woman in the shadow fresh in his mind. Returning to the world where peace came in the isolation, he was unable to find peace in his walk. He felt stares from the trees, heard voices in the distance. He began to imagine eyes of the damned watching from above, following him, waiting for millennium to communicate with the living. Those were not eyes he sought. His pace quickened, and a rush of air rose from the valley. When he finally ascended the top and hurried down the path to the cabin, a breeze whistled through the trees. The laurels swallowed the darkness into something beyond darkness. When the light from the lantern shined upon them, their leaves appeared as faces of some backwoods entities staring at him as he passed. Had the haints dropped from the trees to the land about him? He began to run, the wind singing something hollow, and he flipped the lapel of his coat to cut into the bite. Shadow leading shadow, he longed for the safety of the cabin.

Lying on his bed, the flicker of the lantern casting shadows on the ceiling, he listened to the wind, trying to decipher if they carried voices from the afterlife. He killed the flame of the lantern and lay under his wool blanket in the darkness. Waiting. Listening.

Nick added apples to the carved-out stump, and the aroma reminded him of pies at church dinners on summer evenings. The production levels would provide an ample supply of apple butter. He could barter for lard and flour at William Dowell's, and have plenty for the black bear and her two cubs that had taken residence nearby. The summer rains led to a bountiful crop of corn, potatoes, and rhubarb.

He carried two pails to the brook, stopping to glance through a break in the trees at the vast valley. In the far reach of the dale, he spotted the new house that sat across from Annabeth's. Veta had told him that Annabeth and Cody were the talk of the town. A baby was due come winter. Cody had the home built across the road so her parents could be near the baby. Veta learned Cody had purchased a broad expanse of acreage, which he stocked with horses and cattle. Just one big happy clan, Nick presumed.

Nick continued along the path. The land angled before him, the mountain floor deep, floral green where sunlight splashed the landscape like a painter's brush slung forward to rid itself of remnants. Squirrels traversed a group of elms, and Nick made a mental note of their location. Squirrel stew had become one of his most desired meals. He also made note that his ammunition supply was low and needed to see what chores Veta had for him that could be paid in bullets. He worried about her ability to keep the store open. There was worry in her eyes the last time he visited. She was hanging on the best she could, and he performed what repair work he could when she needed it. She stirred a desire in him to help her battle the hardness that was her life. He reckoned he was partly to blame for the grueling path he'd been led down. Veta, on the other hand, had nothing to do with the hard-fisted fate that came her way. She was an innocent bystander to an unfolding tragedy.

He knelt at the stream, filling his bucket when bursting through a group of laurels was a large bear, the color of coal. It trampled through underbrush and disappeared beyond the ridge like something briefly transposed from another world. Nick pondered what had set the animal to run at such a frenzied pace.

With pails filled, Nick trekked back up the sharp rise. From the thicket a man emerged with a long-barreled rifle. The interloper turned his rifle toward Nick and aimed. Nick stood frozen. The man studied Nick and lowered his gun as though confirming Nick was not the prey he sought. The man looked about and slowly approached Nick. Glancing at Nick's buckets, the man said, "Lessen you found a way to hunt with a metal pail, I'm guessin' you's here for another reason. Surely you don't reside on this mountain top."

"What business is it of yours?"

"It would make sense if you was a carryin' a gun. But to be fetchin' water when there's ample supply in the valleys below is a bit curious."

"This water is the best I've found."

"Was surely a long trek to get some." He regarded Nick peculiarly. "You reside on this mountain?"

Nick nodded and began walking, a bucket in each hand. The man took to walking beside him. "Never imagined anybody ever livin' up here." He rested the rifle over his shoulder. "You sure don't have to travel far to commence the hunt."

"Don't do much hunting. Squirrel. Trap beaver. Fish the stream for trout and horny head."

"All the bear in these parts and you choose squirrel? Seems like wasted opportunities." He tipped his cap. "Name's Sam Lowe. They call me Bear Huntin' Sam cause, well, that's self-explanatory. Speaking of bear, I ran one through here not long ago. You seen it?"

"Only seen you."

"You ain't carryin' no gun. You leave yourself vulnerable."

"I got weaponry." He opened his wool coat, exposing the large knife resting in its sheath.

"Hell of a knife. But that's no match for a black bear. All right if I travel alongside you?"

"You feel the need to kill bear at such high elevation?"

"I feel the need to kill bear no matter the elevation. It pays well. Just the bearskins alone fetch a nice price."

"I'd rather you hunt them somewheres else. The ones here have developed what you might say is a kinship with me, and some have cubs. I'd like for them to live without hindrance or worry of a hunter's bullet."

"How big a spot of land you talkin' about? Do you own legal residence here?"

"My cabin sets over the next ridge. I purchased it outright and legally four years back. Got twenty acres and aim to keep it where I can walk upon it without worry of getting shot." He pointed with his chin. "Surely there's plenty of bear on other mountains. I'd be obliged if your bullets flew through other woods."

"Always thought this mountain was free from ownership."

"It surely might be in other places, but not this spot."

Sam scratched his beard. "My guess is other hunters might not oblige to your hunting ban."

"You're the only hunter I've seen. If I come across others, I'll pass on the news to them same as I did you. Bear hunting is not up for debate."

They walked to the cabin as though adversaries just notified of a recent truce. They studied each other in silence as they made it to the cabin door. Sam peeked inside and regarded the living quarters. "You build this?"

"It ain't fancy, but it serves its purpose."

"Mind if I take a load off? My feet are a bit heavy."

"Have a seat and I'll give you some spring water."

Sam sat on the edge of the bed as Nick took hold of a water pail sitting on a small oak table near the fireplace. Nick removed a ladle which hung from a hook on the wall. When Nick reached the ladle toward the visitor, he spotted Sam pointing a pistol.

"What are you doing?" Nick asked.

"It's a damn rattler. Gonna kill him before he strikes me dead."

Nick guided the barrel upward so that it pointed at the ceiling. "You'll not harm him. He keeps me company."

"Company? His skin should be pinned on the wall and his rattlers hangin' from your knife sheath."

"I got no fear of him. And he's got no fear of me."

"I wouldn't trust a snake a lick." Sam rose and walked to the door. "I think I'd prefer to be where I'm less likely to get bit."

"They are all around us, and less friendly than this'n."

Nick led Sam to the fire pit, carrying the water pails with him.

"How long you had that critter in your cabin?"

"I'd say two years. I feed him mice from the barn and he serenades me with the rattle."

"I prefer the fiddler's melody."

"Well."

Nick took hold of the ax that leaned against the exterior wall and removed a circular stone from a shelf above the ax. He sat on the cane chair and proceeded to rub the smooth stone against the blade. He felt no need to sit idle just for the purpose of conversation.

"You seem quite the skilled woodsman," Sam said before dipping a ladle in one of the buckets. "You a carpenter by trade?"

"No. A farm hand. Spent some time in St. Louis in construction. Was a tree feller as well. My uncle taught me the skills of the ax, and how to construct something from nothing. The roofing part of the cabin, I figured out on my own."

"Where you from?"

"Down Doe Valley." He pointed with his chin to the valley below.

"I'm from Stoney Creek. Down the backside of the mountain."

"I'm familiar with Stoney Creek. Do a lot of trading with William Dowell."

"He's a fair and honest man."

"How long you been known as Bear Huntin' Sam?"

"I been huntin' bear and small game since I was sixteen. Hell, that's nearly thirty years ago if my calculatin' is correct. Kind of built up a reputation from that point on. Like I said, there's decent money in bear hides, though not like it was in the old days. Nowadays it's the meat what brings in the money. A bear can feed a dozen families."

Nick kept to his work. "Don't understand the reasoning. Bears represent the freedom of this mountain like no other, except maybe the black cat. Wild. Free. There's a lot to be said for that. I say stick to the smaller game. Rabbit, beaver, squirrel. Even deer, I suppose, though they are a pretty sight to behold. But the bear--leave it be. Let it have free rein. Panther too. You kill them, you kill part of the mountain's spirit."

"Perhaps. A man can't survive off just squirrel and beaver."

"Like I said, if you feel the need, do your killin' on other land. Do that and we'll get along fine."

"Well."

"How much of this mountain you cover?"

"Roan Creek to Shady Crossroad. Won't go no further north than that."

"Why is that?"

"Cherokee burial grounds. Don't desire to disturb the eternal sleep of the spirits. You wake 'em and they latch hold of you forever." He rubbed his beard and studied the trees. "Visions of war and malevolence and unspeakable deeds will forever haunt the one who wakes 'em, even in death."

"Where are these grounds? How would you know if you come upon them?"

"They's dead pines all about. Evil lookin'. Jagged limbs. Trunks the color of bone, creakin' in the wind though the winds ain't a blowin'."

"I'll be sure to stay clear."

Sam stood. "Since you've declared no bears are to be hunted up here, I think I'll wander back down Stoney Creek way." As he regarded Nick, the wind drew up the mountainside, adding a bite to the morning air. "This sure is hardened land to be a livin' on."

"Life is best when it tests a man's spirit."

"Is that a fact?" Sam placed his rifle over his shoulder and commenced to walking. "That's a might more testin' than my spirit desires. May God watch over you with favor."

| **18** |

Veta set the table. She scooped boiled greens onto Larry's plate next to the pinto beans. He tore a chunk of buttermilk cornbread from the iron pan and cut a large shank of butter from the dish. "If I gotta eat greens, might as well hide the taste with bread and butter," he said.

"We ever going to eat anything made of meat again?" Joan asked. "I'd like to eat something ever once in a while that had parents."

"Vegetables are good for a body," Veta said.

"Not every meal," Larry said, looking at the glob of greens on his fork.

"Well, you are 'bout old enough to start hunting," Veta said. "How about you bring in a squirrel or rabbit. Even a groundhog would do."

"Will you teach me?"

"I guess I better."

Larry took aim at the empty can Veta had set on the fence post. She stood behind him next to Joan. His fingers were sweaty where they gripped the barrel. He had watched his father shoot many times, and it looked easy enough. He took a deep breath, fired, the recoil knocking his shoulder backward. After staring for any sign that he'd hit the can, and not seeing any, he lowered the gun and rubbed his shoulder. "That gun throws a mighty kick," he said.

"You got to keep the stock pressed up a'gin your shoulder," Veta said. "Then take a deep breath, and exhale right 'fore you pull that trigger. And keep your eye looking right down the sight."

Larry nodded and tried again. The jolt of the rifle hurt even worse. The can still untouched. "Must be something wrong with the sight," Larry said. "I'm sure I was aiming right at the can."

"Maybe it ain't the gun," Joan said. "Maybe you ain't cut out to be a hunter."

"That ain't so," he responded. "I just got to practice some." He took aim again, and the can went flying off the post. "See, I told you."

"Now all we got to do is find a squirrel or rabbit to sit still on the post, and you just might have a chance," Joan said.

"Hush'n up," Veta said. "Larry just needs to practice. Now, don't go shooting all the bullets in the box. We don't have an unlimited supply. And don't shoot nothing but the can. Folks won't take it too kindly if you start popping off rounds at thin air. Or at them or their livestock." She patted him on the shoulder. "I got to get to the store and clear out the woodstove. Smoke's been building up in the store and making the place a cloudy haze. I'll be back in time to fix dinner."

"Hopefully something besides collards and soup beans," Larry said.

"You just be thankful for what you got."

"Yes'm."

Veta opened the side door of the stove and on bent knee, shoveled ashes and dead embers from the belly. Dust stirred as she scooped the remnants of fires that had quelled morning chills, that had kept winter winds from making the store an icebox. She was not fond of working on the Lord's Day, but the Lord took Ray from her, and on her own, she could only do so much during store hours. Besides, she wouldn't want to kick up soot and dust with what few customers were in the store, sending them running out for fresh air and possibly incentive to shop at Ozzie's.

She took a stool and stood on it next to the stove. Removing and cleaning the stove pipe was typically a two-man job, though she reckoned she was up to the task herself. After she had laid old cloths around the base of the stove, she laid another over the stove itself. She strained upwards so she could reach the binder and loosen the screws. She removed the first screw and placed it between her teeth. When she reached behind to fit the screwdriver in the split of a second screw, the stool turned sideways. She had nothing to take hold of, and she fell hard on top of the stove. The impact to her midsection slammed the breath from her, and as she tumbled off the stove and hit the floor, she had no air to cry out. For a moment, she lay there, unable to move. She rolled over slowly and touched her ribs. The pain was sharp, and she began to perspire at the thought of the damage to both body and stove.

She heard the creak of the door opening.

"Miss Veta," Nick said as he rushed to her side. "Are you all right?"

She nodded. "I don't guess I've got much of a future in the stove cleaning business."

Nick helped her to a sitting position. Her midsection hurt when she breathed, but the pain had already begun to subside.

"Miss Veta, let me first tend to your injuries and then I'll finish cleaning the stove."

"Notice how you keep coming to my rescue?"

"I was scouting trout holes down Doe Creek. Saw your buggy when I passed by. Thought I'd stop in and say howdy."

"Well, the Lord must-a whispered in your ear. I'd be in a world of trouble if you hadn't stopped."

"Life must surely be hard for one who has to run a farm, a business, and rear a family all on their own. You are a wonder to behold."

"I'm a wonder, all right. Wonderin' what in the world I'm a doin in it. I'll tell you this—you clean that pipe, and I'll take you home and fix you dinner. That is, if you don't mind cabbage, pinto beans, and cornbread. I do have a caramel cake I baked just yesterday that is itching for somebody to eat."

"It's been the longest while since I had cake."

When they drove up in the buggy, Larry and Joan stood waiting at the road. "Ma, I got to where I can knock the can off the post every time."

"That's good, Son," Veta replied.

"Hidy, Uncle Nick," Joan said.

Nick nodded before easing Veta off the buggy.

"Lord-a-mercy, Mama," Joan said. "What happened?"

Veta held her arm to her midsection. "Oh, just had a little spill at the store. Nick was Johnny-on-the-spot and came to my rescue. He's going to eat with us tonight."

As Nick guided Veta up to the house, he regarded Larry's rifle. "Looks like a nice squirrel gun."

"I been practicing. Getting pretty good at it."

"That's good. How are you at hitting a moving target?"

"Not good at all," Joan said.

"Pay my sister no mind," Larry said, admiring the gun as he held it. "Think you could show me, Uncle Nick?"

"Let's tend to your ma first."

"I'm okay. Be much obliged if you can help Larry with his shooting skills. We need somebody who can put a little meat on the table."

Nick took hold of the rifle and traced the blue calcite stone set in the stock. "That's a pretty stone."

"My pa put in there years back," Larry said. "Said he never saw such a bright stone."

"It certainly gives it a fancy look." He handed the gun to Larry. "Okay, let's see how good you are."

Nick headed up Campbell Creek Road. With no lantern, he hurried to make it home before the sun had completely set. His belly full of garden vegetables and caramel cake, he reckoned it would be a great night to sleep under the stars. He'd been told since he was a boy that Iron Mountain was the tallest spot in all of East Tennessee. Some nights he would lie near the planting field where he seemed close enough to grab a star if he would only extend his arm. On that spot, he saw storm clouds move across the valley, lightning furiously seeking exit points from the mass of clouds, giving sinister shape to the skyline as though some evil conspiracy was underway. Thunder reverberating as though to quell a diabolical scheme that had been uncovered.

With evening approaching, Nick kept a steady gait. A horse and buggy approached, the sun beyond drawn at such an angle that the riders were but silhouettes. As the buggy came closer, he recognized the horse. He knew that buggy. And in a moment, he knew the shape of the face of both riders. In between them appeared a smaller shadow.

"How do, Nick," Annabeth said.

Cody brought the horse to a stop. "Hello, Nick."

Nick glanced at them, shading one eye to keep the sun from blocking his ability to see. He gave a polite nod.

"How in the world are you?" she asked. "I heard you moved somewhere up on Iron Mountain."

Nick looked at the child sitting beside Annabeth. "That is correct."

"Nick, this here is Sarah Jane." She placed her arms around the young girl's shoulder. An air of awkwardness arose.

Nick nodded. "Hidy," he said softly. The girl leaned into her mother and looked at her feet.

"She's a bit shy."

"But she's as smart as a whip," Cody added.

Annabeth lowered her head. "I worry about you, Nick."

"No need."

"Seems to suit him, Annabeth," Cody said. "Let the man be."

"Why don't you come to the Fellowship picnic Sunday week?" Annabeth asked.

"I got much to do at the homestead."

"What brought you to the valley?" Annabeth asked. "Visiting kin?"

He raised his can. "Oil for the lantern."

"You been to McQueen's place?" Cody asked. "He's got all the gadgets."

He shook his head. "I get my supplies from Veta Crosswhite's store."

"Is that still open for business?" Cody asked. "I thought she had to close down."

"Still open. Not sure for how much longer. Kind lady, that one, trying to raise young 'uns, run a farm, and a business all by her lonesome."

"I think Mr. Ray's been dead, what, seven, eight years now," Annabeth said. "It's got to be a hard life for that sweet woman."

An odd silence fell over them, as though they awaited instruction from someone who had not yet arrived. Annabeth regarded Nick in a passing glance, a faint semblance of regret in her eyes. It appeared as though she searched for something stirring in his eyes, only to realize that all ties to the physical, as well as to the heart, had been severed.

"Well, I best be moving on," Nick said. "Got to get to the cabin before sundown or it's going to be a task scaling the mountain on a moonless night. You take care."

"Nick, please come to the picnic," she said as he started forward on the road home. "Jerico and Cora are coming. I'm sure Tom will be there."

"Give them my regards."

The wheels groaned a sad tune. The steady clop of the horse's hooves announced their arrival. When Veta brought the horse to a halt outside Muse's Mercantile, Larry hopped off the wagon and took off for the privy beside the store. Joan stood and stretched her back. "Thought we'd never get here. Why do we live so far from town?"

"Because we's on family land," Veta said. "It belonged to our kin before Taylorsville ever got started."

"Maybe they can move the town closer to us."

"Maybe a tornado will come down the mountain and lift every building and set it right across from our farmhouse."

"Mama, now you're talking nonsense."

"Nonsense," she repeated. "I wish this world had a little more nonsense. Would make it easier to handle the hardness."

Veta eased off the buggy and tied the reins to a post. "Well, I best get the material for you 'un's blankets. Those on your bed are as thin as a gnat's tongue, and winter will be sneaking up on us before we know it."

The store was long and narrow. The mahogany ceiling, hidden in shadow from the light of the window beside the doorway, gave the appearance that something sinister hid in its corners. Rolls of fabric were centered in the store, and Veta began to search for wool material.

"What about this 'un?" Joan asked as she pointed to a flowery pattern of blue and white.

"That ain't thick enough to keep the cold off you."

"But ain't it purdy?"

"It is that. But we need fabric of the more practical kind."

"Howdy, Miss Veta," a woman said as she walked from behind a counter. "Ain't seen you in town for the longest time."

"Hidy, Isa Mae. It has been a while. Too much to tend to at home and the store."

"How's business?"

"Slower than a snail in molasses. McQueen seems to be getting most of the business."

"I need to get Russell to ride out to your store when he needs supplies."

"That's quite a ride for him."

"It's the least we can do to help keep someone as kind as you. If you ever have a need for anything, let us know. Speaking of that, I've got some fig preserves in the back. I'll fetch you some."

"That's kind of you."

"What can I help you with today?"

"I need material to make the young 'un's blankets. The thicker the better for them cold nights."

Isa Mae led her to a spindle wrapped with gray wool. "This is the thickest we got. Not the most comfortable material in the world."

"Don't need to worry about comfort. Only warmth." She ran her hand along the pattern. "This should do just fine. Can you cut two pieces? Both six by eight?"

"Let me get Russell. He's the expert with that cutting tool. Be right back with those preserves."

"Thank you, Isa Mae."

Isa Mae headed down the end of the long store and disappeared through a doorway.

"Go check on your brother," Veta said. "Make sure he ain't gettin' into no mischief."

"Yes'm." Joan walked out the front door.

Two ladies entered. One Veta knew but not well. Pansy Graybeale. Her daddy was the county judge, and she always carried an air about her that she was a bit better than everybody else. Royalty without the legal title. The woman with Pansy didn't look familiar. Veta nodded a smile, but there was no acknowledgment. A grinding reverberation rose up from the road beyond the doorway. Through the window, a man could be seen dragging a wooden sled. He had a rope around his chest that was tied to the sled, and he leaned forward for leverage. Pansy turned and looked through the window. "Would you just look at that," she stated, more a command than a suggestion.

"Who in the world is that?" the other young lady asked. "Or, should I say, what in the world is that?"

"Nick Grindstaff. He's turned plum peculiar. Moved up on Iron Mountain several years back. He's nothing more than a retched hermit."

"Well, he's an embarrassing sight. Appears there's no bathwater on Iron Mountain. Looks like his clothes could stand on their own from all the dirt."

"Oh, he's too far out of his mind to care about that. He's oblivious to the world now. I heard it's because Annabeth Parker married that Cody Swanson boy."

"Word goes all the way up to Elizabethton that they are the most handsome couple in the county."

"He certainly is a fine-looking one. She is pretty, I suppose, in an unrefined sort of way."

"Doesn't sound like she comes from good bloodlines."

"Regardless, she once belonged to Nick. Some say it wasn't so much losing Annabeth to Cody, but rather, he got beat up real bad coming home from out west, and it messed up his way of thinking. Made him crazy. From the looks of it, he's as crazy as they say. I'd just as soon be happy if he didn't set foot in town. He's an embarrassment, and I hear he's become a mean one."

"He might keep to himself, but he ain't a mean one," Veta said.

Pansy turned about. "Oh, hello, Veta."

"Pansy."

"And how would you know he's not a mean one?"

"He helps me around the farm from time to time. I feed him for his efforts. Can't afford to do no more than that, and I don't think he'd let me pay him if I could."

"Like a stray dog. Feed him and he keeps coming back."

"Hello, Miss Veta," Russell said as he approached from behind. "Isa Mae said you need some material."

Veta turned and nodded. "Yes, please. Two six by eights." She turned back toward Pansy. "You should find out more about someone afore you go off spreadin' fabrications. Nick is a good man. Life knocked him down, but he's doing the best he can."

"Perhaps you should head on back to your sad, dreary place in the hills, Veta. Kill a possum or something."

"I'd just as soon knock that snotty smirk off your face."

"Whoa, now," Russell said. "Let's not get carried away here, ladies."

"Come on, Margaret," Pansy said. "Let's come back when the vermin is gone."

"Go find some cat so you can grab it by the tail. You're full of meanness, is what you are."

"Well, I've never been so insulted."

"Then you should get out more."

Veta paid for the materials and took the sack which held them. Isa Mae handed her the poke of fig preserves. Veta thanked Russell and Isa Mae and returned to the buggy. Larry and Joan were watching a man shoe a horse at the blacksmith, and Veta called out to them that it was time to go. She gave thought to catching up to Nick, but decided it best to start the trek home.

Nick brought the sled to a halt. Dropping the rope to the ground, he straightened his back. He removed a sack tied to the sled and tossed it across his shoulder. The smell of seasoned apples filled the air, and he knew it was an aroma that would bring him fair trade for necessaries. Judd Tate would sell some and turn the rest into apple butter, which would surely be bought up quickly once word spread. He entered the store and spotted Judd stacking string in a thread box. Nick's shadow darkened the doorway, and it brought the man's task to a halt. "Well, how do, Nick."

"Judd."

Judd walked to the counter, and Nick set the sack on top of it. "If my nose ain't failin' me, you got a sweet batch of apples in that sack."

"Got a good crop for you."

"How's life on the mountain?"

"Can't complain."

"What do you think of the name change?"

"What name?"

"The town. You're no longer standing in Taylorsville."

Nick looked about the building. "Where am I standing?"

"Mountain City."

"What happened to Taylorsville?"

"Folks with some say-so figure Mountain City is a more suitable name. I say if anyplace needs the name, mountain, in it, it's where your cabin sits. Maybe you should start your own town. Iron Mountain City. Has a nice ring to it, don't you think?"

"As long as it can remain a city of one, I got no problem with it."

Nick came upon the Taylorsville Hotel and wondered if they'd not yet received the word that the city had been renamed. Maybe they were just waiting on the new sign to arrive. The two-story structure with its spindled balcony was abuzz with patrons on the front lawn. There were men in suits with derby hats, pocket watch chains hanging from their vests. There were women in long dresses and children at play, and they all appeared as though they were waiting for arrival of great news, or perhaps, someone of great standing. Nick observed them, a curious lot in his eyes. They appeared as ones who chased something they could never quite take hold of, to something to which they thought they were entitled. Nick reckoned if they did take hold, it would be hollow in the grasping once realization set in that lies had been told to them. Lies that the world owed them something.

As he passed the hotel, he caught the movement of someone approaching.

"Hello," the soft voice said.

Nick regarded the young woman who now stood before him. She wore a crème-colored dress that buttoned to her chin. Her auburn hair was pinned behind her head, and her face held a glow as if some form of royalty flowed through her veins.

"Are you Nick?"

He studied her. "Have we met?"

"No. My family is staying at the inn. I am from Charlottesville, originally. My father is here on business. His work takes him to many places, and so our home changes frequently." She paused. "We've been here almost two weeks and there's been talk in the hotel of a man named Nick, that some call the Hermit, who comes down from some remote mountain from time to time. I thought it was just a fairy tale they tell the guests to keep them entertained. When you walked up, someone said, 'here comes Nick.' So, I decided to come ask you directly."

"I do live on a mountain," he said as though an apology should follow. "That one." He nodded toward the massive skyline to the north.

She nodded. "My name is Adeline."

"Hidy, Miss Adeline." He looked beyond her shoulder. "If you will excuse me, I need to head toward home." He tugged on the rope, putting the sled to motion.

"Surely you don't have to be in such a hurry." She glanced briefly toward the inn. "I'm so bored. Talking with a true mountain man would surely add some excitement to my day."

He regarded her peculiarly. "I'm not some sideshow at a carnival. I just come to trade apples for flour and such. If I tarry, nighttime will sneak up on me, and that will make for treacherous travel up the mountain. Especially since I don't have my lantern."

"I don't mean to slow down the necessary progression of your day. Is it okay to walk with you a spell?"

Nick made a sweeping movement with his boot over the dirt road on which he stood. So many reasons to decline her offer. He turned his glance from his boot to her eyes, trying not to regard her in any serious manner. Her muddy-blue eyes held an undeniable manner of warmth, something that told him the beauty of her face might not be a mask to some sort of evil within. Though he'd been fooled by those kinds of eyes before.

"I don't know. People around here see you walking with a recluse, might be inclined to think you are a bit tetched yourself."

"I couldn't give two hoots what others think."

"Based on the outfit you're wearin', I don't know if I believe that."

"Oh, if I had my druthers, I'd trade this dress and hat for some denim pants and some canvas shoes. But Mother would tan my hide if I did."

"Following a path someone else has laid out for you might not be the one that's best for you."

"I agree. Lord knows I'm getting tired of just doing as I'm told."

"As I was saying, I need to head on home."

"You worried I might just follow you up the mountain? Think the town would stir up some good gossip on us?"

"I don't care what others think."

"I'm a fast walker, and I promise not to slow you down. And I promise to turn and head back to the hotel when you've had enough of me."

Nick looked down the quiet dirt road. "I guess it wouldn't hurt to have a walking companion." He took to pulling the sled, and she lifted her long dress above her shoes so as not to hinder her gait. She walked alongside him.

"Are you from the area, originally?" she asked.

"Yes'm. Grew up about six miles west." He stopped and turned. "But it's on top of Iron Mountain that is home now. See where it peaks?" He pointed. "Where it rises like the head of a titmouse."

"My goodness. You have to climb to the top of that just to get home?"

He nodded. "Course, like I said, I prefer to climb it during daylight."

"Aren't you afraid?"

"Of what?"

"All sorts of things. Indians, bears, mountain lions. Snakes. Lord, just the thought of a snake would have me hightailing it down the mountain."

"Indians? What year do you think this is?"

She laughed. "I don't know. You hear all kinds of stories. I hear of Cherokee who hid in the backwoods when they tried to move all the Indians out west."

"Well, if there are any hiding out on Iron Mountain, they surely do a good job of staying hid. Though I might not mind visitors of that nature. I surely would have some questions on how to better run a plow. How to get crops watered when the rains stay away."

"Why do you live up there all alone?"

"It's a long story."

"I've got nothing but time."

"It ain't worth discussing."

"Do you have family around here?"

"I have a brother and two sisters. The brother lives over Laurel Bloomery way. The sisters not too far apart from each other across the state line in Virginia. Abingdon."

"Mother and father?"

"They died a few months apart when I was three."

"I'm sorry to hear that."

"It's okay. I was raised by kin."

Nick's attention turned to the intersection where a buggy approached from a side street. Annabeth sat stoically, holding the reins, guiding the horse along the road. Nick's eyes met hers, and in hers a look of shock drew as she took in the scene unfolding before her. Something in the way of jealousy. As she rode on by, Nick turned his shoulder and regarded her intently, their eyes locked on each other.

"That's why you live up there all far from the rest of humanity, isn't it?" Adeline asked. "Because of her. I could see it in the way you looked at each other."

Nick shrugged and resumed walking.

"She broke your heart is my guess. It makes perfect sense." She pressed her hand to her chest. "Well, if that isn't the most romantic, heartbreaking thing."

Nick walked in silence, Adeline at his heels like a dog in hopes of food scraps.

"She surely is a pretty thing. But I would venture to say she couldn't have found someone more handsome as you. If you don't mind me saying, you make quite the dashing form, and frankly, not something I expected to see in a hidden part of the world like Taylorsville."

"I think your mind has gotten the best of your imagination."

"I do admit, it would be nice to see more of what that beard is hiding." She tugged on the edge of the facial hair and regarded him intently. "Beard or not, that's one special kind of face."

He removed her grip.

She surrounded his arm with hers as though she just realized she needed an escort. "And my imagination is fine, thank you very much. It has nothing to do with what I see is going on. So, you're a victim of heartache. Let's talk about that."

Nick eased his arm from her grip and slid the sack off his shoulder. "It was nice meeting you, Adeline. If you'll excuse me, I've got to get on up the trail. You enjoy the rest of your stay in Taylorsville. I mean Mountain City."

He shielded his eyes with his hand. The sun beat down on him as he headed for home.

| 19 |

The stump resonated when the ax made contact, the split log dropping off the stump onto the rugged soil. Nick tossed the two pieces onto the cart. He sized up the inventory of wood and reckoned there was now plenty to carry him through the upcoming winter. He took hold of the shirt he had laid across a sapling. The sun had warmed his shoulders while he had split the wood, as though a conduit to the energy his body expended. He draped the shirt across his shoulder and took the cart handle, starting it to motion toward the barn. His shoulders and arms tightened as he pulled the wagon, and he laughed in reminder of how hard he'd struggled to pull the cart up the mountain six years prior when he first moved on the mountain. His breath was steady and smooth as he began the trek back home. He had learned to search for recently fallen trees about the mountain. He didn't want to cut live trees as it felt as though he were taking from the mountain something for which he had not received permission. Besides, he didn't care to wait for the wood to dry and age.

Above him, wood thrush and catbirds volleyed back and forth as though a debate of great importance was underway. An argument of sorts, perhaps. Hazy shards of light slipped through the trees, onto the deep green of the foliage, as though patches of snow from winters past had yet to melt. The mountain was vibrant on that August morning, a revelry in the warmth of summer. A disregard of the fact that bitter winds would soon return. But not on that day. Nick convinced himself with little effort the mountain was putting on the performance in his honor.

He poured cold water from the bucket over his head, and it chilled the sweat that had gathered along his torso. After he had emptied the bucket, he slipped into a spot of sunlight to dry his upper body. He shook his head and ran his fingers through his wet hair. Tugging on his beard, he reckoned he might trim it when after he checked on the herbs.

A bear cub scurried nearby in the ferns, and another soon followed. They scampered up a tree, as though to show their climbing skills. Nick eased behind a thick maple, watching as they looked about, perhaps rethinking what they had done, or perhaps miscalculating the height they needed to scale to impress Mama. They looked about, baying as though in need of assistance. A large bear ambled up to the tree, huffing at her cubs as though she had little patience for them on that warm afternoon. Rising on her back legs, she took one by the back of the neck and peeled it off the tree, setting it gently on the ground. She did the same with its sibling, and the cubs soon scampered away as though eager to find what other trouble they could get into. Nick remained still, not just so he could observe the antics of the cubs, but to keep mama bear from thinking he was a potential threat to their well-being. He watched them disappear over the ridge.

Nick stood over the wire rack, inspecting the row of ginseng. Next to the planting field, where the sun bore down on the rack in that midday hour, the earthy aroma, the coarseness of the roots confirmed they were ready for slicing. In a poke, he placed the lumpy roots. He took a seat in a cane chair near the fire pit. The faint aroma of dormant embers from the previous night's fire hung in the air, and it elicited the wonders of that night. A peaceful evening it had been, corn and tater stew bubbling over the outdoor pit. Johnnycakes baking on the iron pan. A gentle breeze had settled into that night air, and he had wondered what creatures roamed in the shadows. He had listened carefully in hopes their words might be translated through the breeze. Enveloped in assurance that the plagues of the world could not reach him, existing in a state of timelessness, where mortal clocks had no way to measure.

Over a stump, he took one of the roots and began slicing it. Ginseng would command much in the way of barter for its medicinal benefits. He chopped a few roots into small pieces and set them aside for the pot that would later boil over his firepit, seeping with a touch of honey to warm him before he went to bed. When he had finished slicing, he placed them back in the poke. Tightening the leather string, he spotted two squirrels flitting along the branches of a maple. He fetched his rifle from the cabin. He had learned from the panther, the fox, and the coyote. The stealthiness in the way they moved toward their prey. Deliberate silence. Disregarding the shirt that lay across the chair by the firepit, he eased under the canopy of green toward what he hoped would provide the evening meal. The squirrels ran along the trees toward the edge where the mountain turned sharply downward toward Doe Valley. He followed along, drawn into the game. The chase. When he stopped and took aim, he spotted movement behind a rhododendron on the trail below. Perhaps the mama bear and her cubs were in search of berries, or maybe a deer trying to maneuver the steep incline. When he spotted the flowery bonnet, he took hold of a sapling to lean further, puzzled as to what, or more aptly, whom, was climbing the mountain. Through an opening of the trees, he watched as the person below stopped, removed her shoes, and shimmied off a brightly colored dress. She tossed the bonnet on top of the dress. Nick slipped behind a thick elm, curiosity building in many ways as to what was unfolding.

When the woman removed her slip, she was bare except for the undergarment covering her backside. The sleekness of her midsection, the gentle curve of her shoulders where her hair draped, was something he couldn't turn his eyes from. She opened a sack that sat on the ground, removing what looked like denim pants and a shirt. A feeling of guilt overtook him, but a fascination of what he observed grew, a curiosity to the delicate entity that had presented itself to the mountain. She slipped on the dark blue pants and was soon buttoning a sleeveless shirt. She slipped a pair of canvas shoes on her feet. When she turned to where she faced the mountaintop, her face exposed, he shook his head. Adeline placed the dress and bonnet in the sack and left it behind a tree. She took to climbing the trail, and he was impressed with her agility. There appeared a burst of energy in her demeanor, and she scurried quickly upward. When she was within a hundred yards, Nick listened to the squirrels playing above as though they had realized they were the last thing the hunter sought, at least for that day. Nick rested the gun against the elm and began walking toward Adeline. She spotted him and waved. Even though she was still sixty yards away, her smile cut through the shade of the land as though it contained its own light source.

"I was beginning to wonder if you were funning with me about living up here," she said.

"How did you know where to look?"

"I followed the shape of the titmouse. You know, you aren't the only one who can climb a mountain. I watched the path you led out of town yesterday. And I got bored with the prospects of another dreadful day today at the inn, and decided it was a perfect day for adventure. I came upon a man in the valley tending to his crops and asked if he knew of you and where best to scale this unbelievably high mountain. He pointed to where that trail below began, and I decided to give it a try. I hid these clothes in a sack and figured once I got away enough from the valley, I'd change and climb to the top."

He noticed her eyes studying his chest, and he remembered he was shirtless. "I apologize for the way I'm dressed."

"I don't have a problem with it." She looked down to where she had come and appeared to spot where she had hidden her dress. "You weren't looking at me change out of my dress, where you?"

He placed his hand to his forehead and glanced downward. "Well, I wasn't sure what was unfolding, and I wasn't sure if you were in distress. To be honest, at first I thought you might be a bear."

She walked to where she stood in front of him. "Are you saying I look like a bear?"

He struggled to make eye contact. Her eyes held a sense of fascination as though they sought things far from the ordinary. Sought things separate from what her life had become. "A bear is the furthest thing I'd compare you to."

"Then you were watching me. You sly mountain devil."

She took him by the hand. "Show me this cabin you built all by your lonesome. I want to see where the famous Hermit lives."

He looked at his gun and gave thought to walking to the tree which it leaned against, but the firm grip of her hand, the tug she gave toward the cabin, made him decide he would come back for it later.

"Is it this way?"

"Down that ridge."

Leading him on as though it was her land, they came upon a copperhead at the base of a shrub along the path, and it recoiled as though preparing to strike. He took her by the waist and pulled her behind him. She gasped. Nick broke a poplar limb, quickly stripping side limbs so that the only ones remaining formed a prong-shaped piece of wood. She took hold of his shoulders, her soft hands warm to his skin. Nick scooped the snake, the prongs gathering the slithering serpent along its underbelly. He tossed it several yards into the ferns.

"You're not going to kill it?" she asked.

"He has as much right to the mountain as we do. I just want to make sure he didn't hinder our walk."

"Well, this wasn't the kind of entrance I was expecting," she said, removing her hands as though she just realized they rested on his shoulders.

Nick turned to make sure the fright had left her. "You sure have come a long way just to visit."

"Curiosity got the best of me, I guess you could say. I wanted to see where you live." Her tone was apologetic. "I had no idea it was such a steep climb. Only mountain goats should be living at such altitude." She looked toward the cabin, now in view. "Well, I've come this far. Take me the rest of the way."

"There's not much to see."

She smiled. "I'll be the judge of that."

He carefully guided her along the path, checking for any other creatures that might convince her to retreat to where she'd come. "I can see why you limit your trips off the mountain," she said. "The climb is ridiculous."

"It certainly cuts down on unwanted visitors. Though, the incline on the backside of the mountain to Stoney Creek and Shady Valley is much easier for visitors to maneuver.

"I hope I'm not considered unwanted."

"For you, I'll make an exception."

She looked past Nick to the cabin. "So, there it is. The home of Nick Grindstaff. The Recluse. The Hermit. You got any other names you go by?"

"I'm sure there are others that people have given me. Some of the little 'uns do call me Uncle Nick." He led her to a cane chair and caught her eyes on him as he slipped on the shirt. He scooped water from a drinking bucket and poured some in a tin cup.

After she took a sip, she regarded him as though he were some myth verified, a tall tale proven to be a reality. "I wasn't sure what to expect when I got up here. Part of me thought this was some joke you and the town were playing on me, but sure enough, here you are. A true mountain man. And that's your living quarters."

"Folks aspire for possessions. I only care that this spot of land is called my own. I see no need for any other possessions."

"That woman on the buggy. What did she do that sent you running up this mountain? Must of been something of great magnitude."

"It always is to the parties involved."

"Well, I've lived such a sheltered life, I have no basis to understand what great magnitude means."

"Ignorance can be an adequate protector."

"I'm overrun with ignorance. I desire knowledge not found in a book, but in the heart. Something with substance. Good or bad. Anything to pull me out of the emotionless quagmire that is my life."

"Gird yourself when you open the book of the heart. You might find the writer had ill intent in mind. As I was once told, when God made the world, the Devil was by his side. There's hints of the Devil's work in everything. In the world. In mankind. Surely this wasn't in God's grand design."

"I don't pretend to know God's thought process, what the grand design was from the get-go. Maybe the Devil did alter the original blueprint a bit. Regardless, I choose to believe there's more good than bad in all things of this world. And I aim to find out if that belief is warranted."

"I don't doubt you will find out either way."

Adeline took a deep breath. "That's one reason I made the hike. I figured if I could see the world from up here, from a perspective of one who lives so far away from the world I live in, I could gain some sort of knowledge so that when I head back to town, I could formulate a plan to find out exactly what great magnitude means to me. And, buddy, from this perspective, great magnitude has endless possibilities." She looked about. "I can see why this mountain gives you contentment. Gives you freedom. I stay in that little hotel where I'm expected to act like some movable statue with my mouth sewn shut. But that is about to end. Freedom will soon come. Well, as soon as I figure out how to tell Father without him trying to lock me in my room."

"It sounds like you still have some convincing to do of your own before you try and convince him."

"You don't know my father. For every chain I unlock, he'll have another set ready to shackle me with. He's even got me a marrying partner. Some fella from a family held in high regard."

"What do you think of the man?"

"He's as dull as a pail of rainwater. He'll want me to be nothing more than keeper of the flock of children he's planning on me producing. I got news for him. I ain't the mothering type. I want to let fate decide each day where to lead me. There will be no moss gathering on this rolling stone."

"Well, I hope it all works out for you." He stood. "Set right there. I want to get you something." He walked to the apple stump and opened the ragged-wood door, removing a handful of apples, the crisp, sweet aroma wafting from the stump. He closed the lid and hurried to a shelf outside his cabin, where he placed one apple on the shelf before placing the others in a small burlap sack. On the shelf was a jar of apple butter. In a poke on the shelf, he removed a chunk of bread. With a small knife he took from an empty jar, he spread apple butter on the bread and took it to Adeline. "Take these apples back with you. You don't have to mention where you got them. My guess is your pa would not be pleased that you came to my cabin. In the meantime, here's some bread and apple butter. Surely you're hungry from the walk."

She smiled and took the sack. "Thank you, kindly. He certainly wouldn't approve, though I have a mind to tell him I came just to get him riled. At least it would provoke some kind of reaction." She took a bite. "Oh, my, this is very good. You made this apple butter?"

Nick nodded. "Contrary to popular belief, I'm not up here just chewing on tree bark." He pointed to the planting field. "Vegetables. Apples. Preserves. Sometimes I'll make squirrel jerky." He grinned. "Would you like some?"

"Squirrel jerky? I believe I would rather eat the tree bark."

"Suit yourself."

"Squirrel jerky aside, I am impressed with your setup. You are quite the pioneer."

Her eyes sparkled. He studied her smile. Nervousness brushed up against him like a fragrance vaguely familiar. Feeling as though she may have gained some emotional upper hand, he glanced at the skyline through the treetops. "If you don't want to be caught walking home in the dark, you should head on back within the hour."

"The dark does not frighten me."

"A panther or bear just might. They are nocturnal by nature. If they smell those apples, they might figure you've saved them the trouble of hunting down dinner. And I'm not talking just the apples."

"Since you put it that way…" She took another bite. "So very good," she said with a nod. She wiped butter from the corner of her mouth with her sleeve. "Pardon my manners."

Nick waved her off.

"This might be the best thing I've ever eaten."

"Well."

She ate, studying him all the while, and he wondered if she regarded him as something amusing, or perhaps, just entertaining. They sat in quiet company of each other for a while, both seemingly content just to be in the presence of each other. She appeared as a bird newly freed from its cage. She closed her eyes, slowly chewing. Nick studied her face, the pronounced cheekbones, the gentle curve of her cheeks. Her skin was smooth, as white as the sweet milk Cora made. There appeared no sense of concern about her, as though she had been kept free from all things concerning the toils of mankind. But something in that expression made it appear as though she sought to break free from walls that bound her.

For a moment, Nick thought she had fallen into some gentle sleep until she opened her eyes and smiled. "I've got a mind to never rise from this chair."

"I'm sure your pa would organize the largest posse imaginable to find you. And what would he do if it was here where he found you?"

"Perhaps it's the awakening he needs to realize I'm not something he can keep hid from the world."

"I have a feeling the world will find out about you soon enough. Like a wildcat in a cyclone."

She laughed precociously. "When it does, I'll let you know its response."

He walked alongside her to the main trail. He didn't care for visitors to occupy his time for long. But, on that day, there was sadness to see her go. He fancied the gentle bouquet of her hair. He wondered how her skin carried such a light scent of lavender in all the heat and sweat she had surely mustered in her ascension up the mountain. When he had led her to the tree that hid the sack of her proper clothing, he stopped. Looking about, a nervousness arose. "Don't tarry in getting down the trail." He checked the height of the sun in the afternoon sky. "I hope the trip was more than just a walk up a mountain."

"It was worth every step." She took him by the hands and leaned toward him. She kissed him gently, her eyes regarding his. Studying his reaction, perhaps. She eased away from him. "You take care of yourself, Nick Grindstaff."

"May you find all good things in life."

"I just found one of the best right here, I am quite certain." She smiled. "Goodbye, Nick." She picked up the sack of clothing.

He watched her descend until she disappeared from sight. But though she faded from view, her presence lingered. And that gave him comfort.

He stopped at the doorway of the cabin, catching a glimpse of himself in the round mirror hanging from a nail post. He stood before it as if to confirm that the one staring back was the same as he. The reflection appeared as one who peered at him from another dimension altogether, a look of curiosity to who met his gaze. There were lines in the face of this stranger he didn't recognize. There was a sprinkling of gray in the beard. He studied the man's eyes, looking to see if youth hid in there somewhere. In those eyes, he sought remnants of something from a different life, a different circumstance. A different outcome. He touched his lips, and he could still taste hers. Could smell the aroma of her hair. For a brief moment, the eyes of the one whom he studied in the glass sparked something from the depths that he'd considered forever dormant. He turned toward the valley as though something rare had been presented, a spirit come to life that he wondered if he might ever feel again.

Winds slammed against the cabin walls like a plague newly freed. Nick stirred the fire, trying to command it to a stronger force. Two wool blankets were draped across him as he sat on his bed. He searched for warmth but could not find it. Above the cabin, the hardwoods creaked and wailed, as though being beaten into submission.

Ice and snow popped against the wall, and Nick envisioned some malevolent enemy seeking control of the mountain. It reminded Nick of stories told by Dudley Lever at Cora's dinner table after he had returned from the war, describing Union soldiers' attacks on Confederate strongholds. Nick was just a teenager when Dudley, a distant relative of some degree, described the fierce events. Nick was enthralled, asking questions, wanting specifics on the battles, what it was like to be under attack, the will it must have taken to charge forward amid bullets flying. In the talk about gun battles, what appeared to weigh heaviest on Dudley's mind was the pitting of friend against friend, brother against brother. Nick questioned why that was so, and Cora interrupted to provide insight. Johnson County had many who decided that what the Northern armies were fighting for what was of the most compassionate kind, the freedom of others. Those who fought for the Confederates thought the North only wanted control of their land, their money, their way of life, all things certainly worth fighting for. Cora added that the Home Guard was more dangerous than either the Union or the Confederates, installing their own set of laws to ensure that able-bodied men were not deserting the cause. She told of how they shot Clyburn Stevens up around Neva in front of his family for leaving the war to tend to his crops. He only had two young daughters and a wife. With no men to tend to the crops, to bring in the harvest, his family would not have food to get through the winter. Clyburn's wife, Olivia, cold-cocked the one who shot her husband with a skillet. Word was that the leader of the Guard was so impressed with the swiftness of the blow, he acknowledged Olivia's prowess before leaving her farm. Nick was intrigued by the stories, his concept of war being that enemies were supposed to be from separate corners. When Dudley showed Nick the wound from a bullet that penetrated his upper arm, Cora put an end to conversations of war.

Nick's beard crackled when he ran his fingers across it, pondering the wars that had plagued man since the beginning of time, and to what thoughts God must have had of each. Had there been some miscalculation in the initial blueprint? A grand design gone awry? At some point, had He attempted to correct the flaw, resigned when He realized it was beyond repair? Nick reckoned God turned his focus on the land itself, something man could co-exist with without taking up weapons to survive. Nick's breath hung white in the cabin until the faint heat of the fire erased any proof it existed. He took hold of a burlap sack set near the fire and removed the remaining strips of squirrel jerky. Food supply getting scarce. He studied on how many days the snow and the winds had hammered the mountain, confining him to his cabin. and he reckoned the number was four. With snow mounting, the wind battering nonstop, he found himself in some form of hibernation to where he couldn't remember if it was night or day. When he had peered out the barely opened door, the snow had nearly reached the top of the door facing. The dim skies and the opaque landscape made it appear as though the world was stuck in some constant state of dusk from which there was no escape. Eyes closed, breathing in the cold that seeped through, he searched for the peace that only Iron Mountain could provide, and he finally found the warmth he sought. The winds became melodic in sound, and a tune rose inside Nick's soul. A storm perfect in its deliverance. A message to remind him that there were purposes of an otherworldly kind that he was not meant to understand. Absolutes in the form of bitter wind and snow.

After he ate, he added the last of the logs to the fire. He would soon have to plow through the doorway to retrieve more from the barn. He tried to move his toes inside his boots to verify that frostbite had not taken hold, and though movement was slow, all toes indeed moved. He set his feet in front of the fire in hopes the warmth from the flames would penetrate the leather. The winds rattled the walls, and he tightened the grip on the blankets. He summoned the words of Preacher Cole's reading from the Bible in church when Nick was a little boy. *Be strong and courageous; do not be frightened or dismayed, for the Lord your God is with you wherever you go.* He opened up the well-worn book, *The Last of the Mohicans*. He reckoned he should find new books to read, but he loved the story. The battles and struggles of the Hurons, the disappearance of the Native tribes, made Nick ponder whether the spirit of the Cherokee people died when they were forced to leave for Oklahoma.

Nick woke to the sound of embers popping. The fire was extinguished, the coals fighting to produce the last waves of heat. His blankets were rigid, and he struggled to rise from his bed. His bones creaked. He turned his head to better listen, to gauge the situation outside the cabin. No howling winds. No pinging of ice or snow against the walls. When he opened the door, the wall of snow was above the top of the doorway. He forced his way through the white barricade. Once outside and out from under the overhang, he found his boots submerged, the snow above his knees. He shielded his eyes from the brilliance of the morning sun, which hung white in the eastern sky as though the words, *let there be light,* had just been spoken for the very first time. The world was a linen land of perfection. The firs and mountain laurels were powdered white, a purity about them that seemed to cast the trunks and limbs of the naked hardwoods into some glow of tranquility, verification the trees didn't need the spring foliage of green to show that they contained a vibrancy.

Nick took hold of a gray sack tied to a thick board made of elm. The sack contained a shoulder harness he placed across his neck. Slowly, he waded through the snow to the barn. The work he had put in cutting and gathering firewood during the fall was a wise decision. He kept no calendar, but signs the mountain offered, told him winter had a month or more to go before spring would warm the mountain. His stomach churned, and he reckoned his wasn't the only one. He scouted the edge of the dormant field, and he spotted the pair of deer that had taken up residency. He guessed the steady supply of corn was what kept them near. He knew the thick snow had made it hard for them to find food, and they waited as though they were solely dependent on Nick. In the rafters of the barn, he took hold of the metal bucket and headed across the field. The deer circled into the trees when Nick approached, their huge eyes watching with anticipation.

"Hungry, are you?" he said, before sprinkling the cold corn onto the snow. After he had placed what he thought would fill their bellies, he backpedaled, holding the bucket. Slowly, the deer eased from the trees. As Nick slowly retreated, they approached the corn. They eyed him while they ate, and he wondered how they would have found food otherwise under that snowy landscape. How many more beasts on the mountain searched for food, their bellies empty? "Don't be greedy," he said to the buck. "Give the lady her fair share." He observed them, their gray hides holding soft contrast against the snowy backdrop. They appeared to regard him as something not to be fearful of, but rather, something given acceptance to their land. When they had finished, the deer shook their tails as though to show appreciation. They took a few bounds until they were beyond the field and stood in front of a spruce where snow had settled in the curvature formed by its needles, and the serenity of the scene caused Nick to smile. He nodded when the deer looked back at him before disappearing into the thick woods.

Nick placed the bucket back on the rafter, took his shoulder harness, filled it with wood for the fire, and headed back to the cabin.

| **20** |

Jerico led the steer outside the gate, patting its haunches as Nick laid a rope around its neck. Nick noticed the slowness in his uncle's step. Tom closed the gate and followed alongside the ox.

"You sure you can get this gal up the mountain?" Jerico asked.

"I carved out a good path up Campbell Creek way," Nick said. "Plenty of switchbacks to lessen the incline. I worry that path might one day become a maneuverable trail for others."

"You could pave that trail with gold, and you still wouldn't get any homesteaders," Tom said.

"You doing okay up on the mountaintop, Nick?" Cora asked.

"Yes'm."

"You need any other supplies?" Jerico asked. "Whatever is ours is yours."

"I appreciate the offer, Uncle Jerico. Getting this steer is more than I could ever expect. I'll be eternally grateful."

"We love you bunches, Nick," Cora said. "Always have. Always will."

"Come back when you got time to fish," Tom said. "We'll empty the creek of horny heads and put on a fish fry to feed the valley. We'll charge a quarter a head and buy ourselves new rods and a couple of them fancy fishing hats with the proceeds."

Nick nodded. "How have you all been doin'?" He looked about the farm. "Looks like you got the place running smooth as an eel's belly."

"Pa works me like a belligerent mule. Pulls the whip out on me daily."

"Oh, you stop that kind of talk," Cora said, popping Tom on the forearm. "If you ask me, he treats you more like an Arabian steed, not wanting you to get dirtied in the mud."

Tom let go a laugh. "If that don't beat anything I ever heard."

Jerico regarded Nick. "See what kind of foolishness I have to put up with? You got room in that cabin for one more? I just might move up there with you."

"See what kind of meals you get on that mountain," Cora said. "You won't make it two days before running back here for cathead biscuits and sausage gravy."

"Well, I guess I best guide this gal on up the mountain," Nick said.

"Hitch her to that wagon yonder. It goes with the ox."

"This is way beyond kindness," Nick said. "She will be a huge help in plowing my garden."

"This gal is made for it," Jerico said.

"I can't thank you enough."

"Wait one minute before you head out," Cora said. She hurried to the house and soon returned with a sack of food from the house. "Pork biscuits. Freshly made."

"Thank you all," Nick said. "For everything."

"You take care, Nick," Cora said. "And please, come back soon."

Nick's trips off the mountain became relegated to the Stoney Creek side. Those in Doe Valley carried what seemed a perpetual curiousness to Nick's well-being, and had turned him into a spectacle, something to be dissected, to be ridiculed by those who reckoned their judgment of the world was saner than his. Or perhaps, his residence on Iron Mountain provided a conversation point, a source of entertainment to the townspeople. The more time passed, the less he wanted to deal with it. William Dowell seemed to understand, so much so that conversation between them stayed business in nature. And maneuvering the back side of Iron Mountain to Stoney Creek took less of a toll on his body. With William, Nick found him fair in the trading for Nick's produce, allowing Nick to stock up on items he could not produce himself.

The garden plowed, the seeds planted, Nick prayed for Mother Nature to take over with steady rains and warm sunshine. With the alfalfa that had grown, the steer had plenty to eat. Nick rubbed his lower back as he walked to the cabin. The joints were stiff, and the flexibility within him was not as they were in the earlier days. Fourteen planting seasons had taken its toll. Nick reckoned the winters had played an equal part in the wear and tear of his body. He had a growing appreciation for the way Jerico was still able to work the farm. As he neared the cabin from the planting field, he spotted a pair of men approaching. They headed for the cabin as did Nick, and when they appeared out of the backdrop of hardwoods, Nick was greeted by a smile and a wave.

"Howdy, Nick," Tom said.

The man with Tom stood stoically as though waiting for proper introduction.

"Tom," Nick said with a nod.

"How you been, cousin?"

"Still alive. And that's as much as a man can ask."

"I want you to meet the new preacher," Tom said.

The stranger stepped forward, Bible in hand. "Hello, brother Grindstaff. Preacher Hill is my name. It's a pleasure to meet you." He extended his hand toward Nick, who reluctantly shook it. "Brother Tom tells me you live all alone on this mountain. I have to say, that's quite a feat."

"It suits me."

"Preacher Hill has been the pastor of Bethel Baptist what, three months now?" Tom asked.

"Four, actually."

"Four? Time is a movin' on."

"Nick, we are making an effort to grow the flock, so to speak. Tom tells me you grew up in the church."

Nick nodded. "Long time ago."

"Well, we sure would like to have you join us on Sundays. We feel the sheep are safest when they are among the flock."

"Is that a fact?"

"Yes, indeed." The preacher was slender, his high-waisted pants held loosely in place by a slender, black belt. His sandy-blonde hair held a defined part on the side. His eyes held the look of something hopeful, yet something verified. "And with you so far away, on your own, we thought it would be prudent to have you under the church's wings. Look out for your well-being."

"I appreciate the concern, but my *well-being* is fine."

"Well, you might have heard the saying, 'where two or more are gathered in His name.'"

"You sound as though I'm a discarded man." He glanced briefly at the mountain floor. "I suppose I'm just a flock of one."

"He don't mean that you ain't part of God's flock, Nick. He, we, think it would do you good to be part of the church again."

"I appreciate the concern."

"We just wish you lived a little closer to the family," Tom said. "I want you to meet my wife, my little boy."

"Wife?"

"Yes, Nick. You are so far removed you don't know all the goings on in Doe. I got married two years ago. Thelma Gay. Her family moved in from Bristol. Got a little baby boy. Named him after you."

"Why would you do such a thing? He should be named after someone highly regarded. One who has accomplished much in this world."

"You might not realize it, Nick, but your family holds you in high regard. You are a man of grit and fortitude."

"I don't know about all that."

"What your cousin is trying to say is that the people of the valley could benefit from your presence," the preacher said. "Your influence could be inspirational, a way for others to see what courage is all about."

Nick studied the tree line beyond the planting field. Courage? What kind of courage did it take for a man to run from the meanness of the world? What kind of spirit was required to run defeated from the murky shadows of fate, convinced that happiness could not be found among the company of others? He shook his head. "The world is doing just fine without me, and me without it."

"So many bad things can happen up here with you all alone," Tom said. "Bears, snakes. Harsh winters. Wanderers. Heck, you could cut yourself with a saw blade and bleed out without a doctor's care."

"Your kin are worried about you, Nick," the preacher said. "And to be honest, worried about your salvation."

"So that's what it all adds up to—a tally of the blessed. Round up the lost souls before it's too late. Let me tell you, I'm nearer to God here than I ever was living in the world below. And I don't mean proximity-wise. Salvation resides in these hills. The ground is so hallowed we should all remove our boots when standing on it."

"That's mighty fine and all, Nick," Tom said. "But you got family who love you and miss you."

"Just think about it, Nick," the preacher said. "Maybe a Sunday morning soon there might be a tugging on your heart to come to Bethel and worship with us. Would certainly bring joy to the congregation. Joy to your family."

"I'll keep the thought in the back of my mind."

"That would be good, cousin." Tom regarded the preacher. "Well, I guess we best head down the mountain. You take care, Nick."

"You too, Tom." The men turned and headed back from where they had come.

Dogwoods painted the valley in wisps of white and pink as though it might usher winter away by inference alone. But there were still cold nights ahead before winter would release its grip on the land. The sun warmed Nick's shoulders as he guided the ox. The wheels squealed a lonesome tune as the cart ambled down Campbell Creek Road. Wheat strands swayed on the hillsides, a dance of thankfulness perhaps for bringing winter to an end. Larkspur and zinnia cast the roadside in blue and yellow, a gentle buzzing from the bees who darted about the tall flowers.

Curiosity had led him down the mountain on the Doe Valley side. He wanted to see if spring had brought the valley to life, and it appeared to be showing off a little extra, perhaps for his benefit. Perhaps to entice him to move back to the valley. He spotted the familiar chimney, the sharply rising tin roof beyond the grass-laden hill. The place where generations of Grindstaffs had declared their homeland. He wondered how many were buried on the nearby hill. How peaceful was their sleep? The faded tablet headstones on the hillside, strewn about as though little forethought was given as to their placement, seemed a contradiction on land where time held no purpose. Yet the bleached etchings, a permanent census of those buried beneath, appeared as though to dispel rumor to anyone who might consider themselves as the first inhabitants. Nick brought the wagon to a halt and regarded the tombstones, darkened and dim from the passage of time. From the elements. What stories could the bones below them tell? He turned his ear toward the hill in case any accounts were being offered.

The faint aroma of smoke rose as Nick guided the ox around the sharp turn. Dormant grass covered a steep slope to the side of the road. He was anxious to see that house, the one where his father and Jerico grew up. Jerico had taken Nick and Tom to the house one day when they were boys, but the new owners weren't in the mood to give them a guided tour. Chores that needed tending to, was the reason they gave that day. And so, sitting on the cart in front of the house, Jerico resorted to telling stories of the past as though it might kindle up visions for the boys that they could at least see in their minds. He told of how he and Nick's father once chased a skunk up onto the porch, and the punishment that ensued after their grandma was sprayed by the frightened animal when she stepped outside to sweep the porch. The switch marks that the woman laid on them that day was a reminder for quite some time to never repeat the tomfoolery.

When Nick had rounded the curve, the house now in view, there was commotion in front. A woman held an infant in her arms while calling for a young girl to stay next to her. On the downslope of the road, a cart lay overturned, a horse on its side, fighting to right itself. A man was frantically trying to lift the cart. Nick led his ox to the side of the road and took to running. As he approached the overturned cart, he noticed legs and arms squirming under the edge of the wagon. The horse whinnied in distress, and the cries of the one pinned underneath caused Nick's heart to leap. When the woman called the man by name, Nick ran toward the cart. He rushed to the side of the man who was squatting, trying to lift the bulky wagon. A familiar face.

"Let me help you, Rodrick," Nick said.

"Nick?"

"On the count of three," Nick said as he slipped one hand under the wood, the other hand on a metal latch connector. The two men lifted upward, Nick feeling the strain in his wrists, in his lower back. The fear in the voice of the boy beneath the cart heightened the urgency of the situation. The men lifted the cart momentarily before the weight caused them to lose their grip. The horse kicked and wailed and the cart shook.

"Lord-a-mercy," the woman yelled. "You 'uns have to lift that cart now. It's crushing Dennis."

"Again, on three," Nick said. Again, they strained and grunted, and Rodrick tugged at the boy's leg with one hand as he held the cart with the other. As he tried to pull the boy from underneath, the cart slipped, and Rodrick lost his grip. The cart dropped and pushed down on the boy's leg. His scream echoed along the countryside. The woman yelled her displeasure, one hand on the little toddler who tried to run toward Rodrick. Nick rushed to his cart and soon returned with a pickax. "When I lift the cart, Rodrick, you drive the wedge of the ax underneath the wood."

"Daddy!" the voice under the cart cried out.

"Hold on, Dennis," he said. "We are gonna get you out."

Nick centered himself along the overturned cart, the horse kicking, the mother and her young ones now in full cry. Rodrick took the pickax. "You got to help me get that cart lifted, Nick. Else my boy's going to suffocate."

Nick took a breath and squatted. He forced his fingers underneath the splintered wood. He closed his eyes and drew in anger from the wrongs the world had laid upon him. The disillusionment and the distrust birthed a strength within him. With a cry, he pulled upward. The cart moaned as it rose inches off the ground. "Slide the blade underneath the mid-brace," he shouted. Rodrick slid the black steel underneath and turned the handle upright. With one hand, Nick took the ax handle. He let go of the cart with his other hand, and when he had both hands on the ax handle, he pulled it toward his body. As the blade on the exposed side of the pickax found traction with the road, the side of the blade under the cart locked in. Nick moaned and strained as he pulled. The cart slowly began to rise. Rodrick took hold of a leg and dragged the boy from underneath. After the child was safely removed, Nick eased on the handle, and the cart lay flat again. Upon seeing the boy being tended to by his father, Nick hurried to the front of the cart. He removed his knife from the belt sheath and sliced the reins on the upper side of the downed cart. He knelt and did the same to the reins on the underside, part of it wrapped under the leg of the horse. With the reins now cut, the horse freed, Nick shifted to the horse's shoulder and lifted. The horse kicked and flailed, and Nick was able to slide his arms further under the animal. With rocking motion, the horse's momentum lifted upward, enabling it to get to its knees. Nick grabbed hold of the bit that crossed the mouth and pulled upward to where the horse was able to stand. It stomped about, appearing as much angry as confused. Nick held the cut reins, clinging to the horse's neck. "Easy, now. You're okay." He patted the horse along its neck, and it stood calmly beside him.

With the horse at ease, Nick walked to the boy. By all appearances, he looked fine, obviously shaken. The mother gathered an arm around him while still holding onto the infant. Rodrick extended his hand. "Nick, it's been forever since I saw you, but if there ever was a time to see you again, this was it. You saved my boy."

Nick shrugged. "He appears to be a tough little 'un. As I recall, you were as tough as they came when we were running round the schoolyard all those years ago."

"Acting tough was the only way to keep from getting a whoopin' on that schoolyard." He looked at his son. "But that was nothing compared to what Dennis just went through."

"Don't look like he suffered much in the way of physical harm."

"If you hadn't come along, I hate to think what the outcome would have been."

"Yes, thank you, sir," the mother said. "Thank you so much."

"Tess, this is Nick Grindstaff. We grew up together. Nick, this is my wife, Tess." Her family roots is over in Trade."

"There's no call for thanks. Anyone woulda done the same had they come upon you 'uns."

"But you are the one who came," the mother said. "God sent you. I know He did."

"That I couldn't rightly begin to know," Nick responded. "But, as it says in Deuteronomy, don't sit idle if you see a man's donkey fall to the roadside."

"I don't recall the parable mentioning anything about a child pinned under the donkey," Rodrick said. "What you did goes way beyond that Bible story." He shook Nick's hand forcefully. "I never been so glad to see a familiar face in all my born days. I'll be grateful for as long as I live."

Dennis wiped dirt from his clothes and tears from his face. The fear that had been in the boy's heart was still evident. Tess guided the boy toward Nick. "You need to thank this kind man." The boy lowered his head and walked up to Nick. When he extended his hand, Nick took it and knelt.

"You sure are a tough buck. I don't think many boys could have kept their wits about them like you did." The boy smiled. "If it had been me, I would have kicked and screamed so loud the whole valley would have heard me."

"The boy hung his head. "Thank you, sir."

"Did I hear your name right? Dennis?"

"Yessir." The boy clung to his father's leg.

Tess studied Nick. Studied the ox and the old cart. "You wouldn't happen to be the one that lives up on the mountain all alone?"

"Unless there's someone who lives up there I don't know about, then, yes'm, that would be me."

"I see Tom from time to time," Rodrick said. "He updates me with how you're doing. Of late he hasn't had much to update. You must not venture off the mountain much these days."

"I tend to go to the Stoney Creek side when necessary. Got enough to keep me busy atop the mountain. Today, some sort of curiousness set in to come down Doe."

"I think it was God sending you off the mountain to save our boy."

Nick shrugged.

"You got quite the reputation around town," Rodrick said.

"A questionable reputation is my guess."

"Not by folks with any sense. Any others are just ignorant and need to be ignored. What you did today will just add to the legend."

Nick smiled. "I got enough to concern myself with than what others think."

"We talked about you at school a while back," Dennis said. "Murle said you was a haint. Said you snatched children from their beds at night."

Tess took Dennis by the arm. "That's nonsense talk. You apologize to Mr. Grindstaff."

"I'm sorry. I never paid no mind to Murle. I just figgered you was a made-up story."

Nick knelt. "What do you think now?"

"I think you's a real lifesaver."

"Then I don't think you need to worry no more about getting snatched from your bed."

"Stay for dinner," Rodrick asked.

"I need to be a movin' on."

"I've got a fresh mincemeat pie just waiting to be et," Tess said. "Please, Mr. Grindstaff. Come in and visit."

Nick looked toward the wide porch and what looked to be cane-back rocking chairs. "My pa grew up in this house. I wouldn't mind seeing if I can feel his presence once again." He smiled at Dennis. "I guess I can do it while sharing a slice of pie with this young 'un."

"That sounds like a square deal to me," Rodrick said. "Dennis? You want to eat some pie with Uncle Nick?"

Dennis nodded.

The mother placed her hand on Dennis' shoulder and smiled. "Pie is the least we can give you."

"Just glad the boy is okay." He looked toward his ox, who munched on grass on the roadside. "Before we commence with the partaking of dinner, we best hook my steer to your cart and let her righten it. She's got the strength to do it."

"That would be a big help."

Nick patted Dennis on the shoulder. "You head on inside and let your ma tend to your bumps and bruises, young fella. Then we'll meet you at the dinner table."

The men hooked a harness to the steer and with their help, righted the cart. Rodrick led the horse to the barn.

Veta struggled to stand. The night had found her restless. She had retraced memories of Larry when he was little, how much he reminded her of Ray. Both with an untamed spirit. Stubborn, proud, loyal to a fault. Larry stood a half-foot taller than Ray did, much more solid in his stature. Where had the time gone?

Veta worked busily at the stove, fighting tears. Eggs fried in a slab of lard, pork patties next to it. The aroma of food and embers inside the woodstove awakened tender memories of mornings when the family gathered to start a new day. Sitting at the table, words unnecessary, the presence of each other, was all they needed. Larry entered through the kitchen door, his son in his arms.

"Morning, Mama." He walked to where Veta stood and leaned forward with his child, who gave Veta a kiss on her cheek.

"There's my little pole cat," she said. "You 'uns have a seat and I'll have your food ready in a snap."

Larry walked to the table. "Set right here, Carter," he said, placing the boy in a chair. Larry came up from behind Veta and kissed her on the cheek. "Love you bunches." Those words tugged on her heartstrings. She had said that to Larry and Joan every day before they would head off to school.

"Love you more," she managed quietly.

Larry talked with Carter at the table, sitting beside the boy that Veta said was a spitting image of Ray. In between, he watched his mother do what she did every morning for what must have been her entire life. Veta sensed he was watching her cook. Perhaps he wanted the memory to stay with him after he rode off on the wagon to Richmond. Jobs were scarce around Johnson County, and with a wife and child, he had to take the opportunity. She would miss the daily visits. She would miss the busyness of the house with Larry and his family there. Most of all, she would miss him.

"You 'uns all packed?" Veta asked while sliding the eggs onto a plate.

"Yes'm. Got the wagon loaded up."

"Carter, you ready to move into your new house?"

Carter scrunched his shoulders.

"I bet you will make all kinds of friends. Your daddy will find some fishin' hole nearby and you 'uns can catch all kinds of trout and such. Yeah, buddy, you will have a grand time."

"I wanna stay here with you."

She placed food on the table and knelt, her bones cracking from the strain. She brushed her hand through his hair. "I'll keep maple syrup candy in the cupboard just for you, so you come back anytime to visit. Now, eat while it's hot."

"I'm gonna miss your cooking, Mama."

Tears flowed. She had always kept a stoic exterior. The one time she cried was when she watched the undertaker lower Ray in the ground. "I'm sure the food in Richmond is better than what these old rattlin' pots and pans can put together."

"No, ma'am. Yours is best in all the land."

Joan entered through the kitchen door, sleep still in her eyes. "There's that rascal, Carter Crosswhite." She came to the table and tugged on the boy's ear. "You ready to ride the wagon?" He bit into a biscuit that Veta had stuffed with strawberry preserves.

"Too busy eatin' to talk, I suppose," Joan said. After kissing her mother and whispering a "good morning," she sat next to Larry, lowering her head against his shoulder. "Not gonna be the same around here without my breakfast eatin' buddy. Course, I won't have to worry about your daddy eatin' off my plate."

"You won't have to guard your plate no more," Larry said.

Veta brought a plate of food for Joan and took to cleaning the skillet.

"Sit and eat with us, Mama," Larry said. "This is our last chance to eat together for a while."

Veta lowered her head, and the tears poured down her cheeks. She shook her head and left the room. It took a few minutes to regain her composure, and she sat at the table, though she didn't eat.

When Larry had placed Carter on the seat of the wagon, he turned and regarded his mother and sister on the porch. He gave them a slight wave. The sun's light reflected the tears in Larry's eyes.

| **21** |

Signs of winter. A hardened land. The hardwoods barren, their mangled limbs paled under leaden clouds as though sentinels assembled from a world born of calamity. A mist clung to the bleak terrain, a gray entity that fell away on both sides of the path he walked. The vapors appeared as something of Cimmerian lore, a mist to assure souls from long ago laid in perpetual ambiguity. The sky hung one-dimensional, a flattened ceiling constructed while Nick slept. The air held a stillness, and only the call of a wood thrush broke the silence. There was a sense of wandering within him, to walk on land perhaps never walked upon. Could he regard himself a mountain man if he didn't search for something not searched before? He had fled the world, but what of it existed beyond where he called home? Remote land no longer remote. The backwoods rolled endlessly beyond, but to where? The trail he had carved up above Campbell Creek had been named the Cross Mountain trail. It enabled travelers to climb Iron Mountain to Stoney Creek or Shady Valley and beyond to Damascus. That's what Veta had told him. She said he had become a legend of sorts. Again, that word. What claim to legend could he truly make? Best to be left alone and not regarded at all.

He couldn't shed the worry that the trail he had created would lead to more people to cross the mountain. And ultimately, that might lead some to settle on it. It would no longer be his alone, and that thought had led to restless nights.

He stopped when he came upon a canopy of laurels. Patches of snow held to otherwise muddy ground. He looked skyward at stark hardwoods, their trunks and limbs dimmed lifeless as though nothing could grow on them, no matter how warm the spring sun and air might touch them. The fog held some distance to it now, as though it had become continually in retreat, making the land around him fall away to where a world beyond could not be confirmed with any certainty. When he made it to the Cross Mountain trail, he looked east where it faded into the mist, and felt odd comfort how Doe Valley evaporated into some lore, the perils of it nothing more than hearsay. To the west, the land leveled to where it would eventually ease downward to Stoney Creek and Shady Valley. The trail was silent, no sign of travelers, and Nick was glad it was so. He crossed the trail and took a slope northward. A deer path perhaps. The woods were in heavy shadow with chestnut trees towering above the other hardwoods. He stood at the base of one of the chestnuts, the width of it larger than his cabin. His ax would not be able to take down such a tree. As he walked, he searched for signs of life in any form, but none were found. The land contained an unfamiliarity that led Nick on with a feeling more of curiosity than discovery. Soon, he found himself on a slope rising westward and realized the land where his cabin was sitting was not the highest on the mountain. He came upon a steep, bowl-shaped gap and spotted a spring flowing from a crevice below. A water source. Mist clung to the depths, and the stream disappeared into the downslope. He came upon a laurel hell gathered tightly before him, reaching skyward, limbs extended and curved so that they formed a tunnel of emerald. He walked through them as though some new world awaited on the other side. Once past, he came upon woods deep in firs and Virginia spruce, and he imagined he'd passed through the entrance to another mountain altogether. He looked over the hollowed gap, still mired in the mist. In the skyline, above the fog to the west, he regarded Shady Valley and the base of Holston Mountain to where it disappeared into opaque clouds. Beyond Holston lay Damascus, though he knew that only by memory, as the clouds closed off the world beyond that gentle landscape. He recalled the day when he entered the town on the train, the nervousness of leaving Doe Valley for St. Louis, the ache in his heart of leaving Annabeth.

The land was a continual ebb and flow of hardened terrain with jagged inclines and slight descensions as though the mountain hadn't decided where its true peak lay. He came upon a rise where sunlight appeared to have slipped through the clouds, though only on that crest. Curiosity drew him closer. The climb became more difficult, and he took hold of trees and saplings to keep from sliding. When he made it to the top, he found himself in a land where dead pines stood tall. Barren, jagged limbs. Something sinister in the design. Trees creaked some odd tune as they swayed in a place where no breeze blew. Sam Lowe's warning to Nick at the cabin that day arose. The warning of spirits risen. Spirits disturbed. He knew he was a stranger in that land, uninvited. Turning about, he hurried away from the burial grounds.

When he had gained a sizeable distance from the land of dead pines, he found himself above a hollow. Below, smoky entrails slipped through the trees, an ominous presence that gave him pause. There was a singed odor of sugar, of wood burning. Nick looked below and spotted a worn path that headed toward a ravine. There was something deliberate in the design of the trail, some backwoods malefaction. The odor of fire made him think it was something else. A hunter's camp, perhaps. Hopefully not one who had come to hunt bear. Again, curiosity drew him in, and he eased down the slope, using the hardwoods as cover. He peered from behind an elm, spotting a man crouched beside a large, copper pot. The man was adding logs to a fire below the pot. When he was done, he stood and took hold of a long-barreled rifle, staring at the flame. His stained shirt struggled to keep his pale belly from exposure. His short-brimmed hat appeared darkened from soot. There was something devious in his posture, as though he were orchestrating some procedure that was best kept secret. Nick turned to ascend the slope, to ease back to where he had come. Above him, a man stood, pointing a rifle. Nick froze, eyeing the barrel of the rifle with guarded respect. The man wore suspenders that kept his pants from sliding down his slender waist. He wore a beaver hat that was frayed along the bill. The man descended, and Nick gave brief thought to running.

"What the hell you a doin', nosin' round the shadders?" the man asked, exposing pink gums and jagged teeth. "We got a gravesite yonder filled with federal men who come to put down our still."

With hands raised, Nick said, "I'm not a federal man. I just came upon your camp and realized it was not a place I wanted to be. I'll just leave you be and head home."

The man looked about. "Home? Ain't no man what lives on this mountain."

"Well, there's one that I know of. So, if it's all right with you, I'll head that way."

The man regarded Nick with distrust and pointed the rifle down the hill. "Git on down the hill."

"I'm not here to cause trouble."

"You should have thought about that 'fore you snook up on our camp. Now, git on down the hill before I split your skull with a bullet."

The mist parted as they descended. There was a decrepit shanty propped by cut wood on the downslope as if to keep the shack from tipping over. A clapboard structure surrounded by thick laurels. The man beside the fire watched as the men approached. He wore a necklace made of bear claws.

"Who you got there, Clete?" the man asked.

"This feller was hidin' up yonder. I think he's a federal man."

The man approached to where he stood before Nick. He regarded this interloper with peculiarity, took a deep breath, and patted the barrel of the rifle in his hand. "A fed, ya say?"

"He said he lives on the mountain somers, but ain't no man that crazy. Not unless he's a hidin' from the law."

The man studied Nick. Studied his manner of dress. "You runnin' from the law?"

Nick shook his head. "I'm not runnin' from anyone."

"Well, you sure as hell shoulda been runnin' from us."

"What you figger we should do with him, Porter? Shoot his ass and be done with him?"

"We can worry about that later," Porter said. "Might as well get some use out of him before we go to the trouble to shoot him." Porter studied the downslope as it fell away into the mist. They led him to a fire pit below the shack. On a wire tied between two hardwoods were two bear hides hanging like blankets needing a breeze to dry them. Around the fire pit were sapling posts with bear skulls resting on them. Claws dangled from rawhide loops draped over the jawbones. Clete nudged Nick to sit on a stump by the fire.

"Did you look to see was anybody with him?" Porter asked.

"There weren't nobody. I come down from above, and when I saw him hidin' behind a tree, I studied the mountainside just to see if it was some ambush about to commence. He's here all on his own accord."

"Then why was you nosin' around?" Porter asked.

"Was doing some exploring, I guess you could say."

"You's trespassin'."

"Squatters can't be landowners. Makin' corn liquor, sell it tax-free. And by the look of it, you are thinning out the bear population."

"Bear hides bring in good money. The meat provides months of food. So, you might say we're shiners who subsidize our livin' expenses dealin' in the bear market."

"You should leave them bears be."

"There's nothin' like takin' down a giant beast. Kind of reinforces the fact that man holds dominion over the animals of the world."

Porter poked Nick's pocket. "What kind of change you carryin'?"

"I carry no money."

"Well, then it's time to earn your pay," Porter said, pointing the gun. "Don't look for any earnings of the monetary kind, though."

The hunters stepped toward the shanty, Porter glancing back at Nick to ensure he was not about to seek escape. Nick observed the men, voices muted, as two men haggling over some inventory of goods and the value attributed to it. Nick eased his hand to his calf as though an itch had commenced and verified the positioning of the knife strapped above his boot. He eased the snap, loosening the knife from the leather crevice. The men wore stains of slain animals, wore the remnants of tasks of survival, and they appeared as macabre actors in some wicked play void of a protagonist. There appeared to be some reconciliation, and they approached their newly acquired prisoner.

"Git your ass up," Clete said, pushing the rifle barrel into Nick's shoulder.

They led Nick down the ravine, below the shack. They came upon a pen of barbed wire cornered by elm and maple. Within the makeshift fence, a cub lay weakened on its side. It cried out and tried to burrow under the fencing when it saw them approaching. Nick's gut roiled at the sight. They led him down to where the land flattened and a mule stood tied to a tree. On its back were four burlap sacks that the mule fought to keep from pushing its prostate to the ground.

"We'd like to get involved in the slave labor trade," Porter said. "We'll start with you a carryin' them sacks up the hill to the homestead. After that, you can cut wood. We need to stock up for the fires that will cook our highly regarded elixir."

Clete pushed Nick's backside with his boot, causing Nick to stumble in front of the donkey. With two guns pointed at him, he lifted one of the sacks and placed it over his shoulder. He began walking toward the men, and they guided him back up the mountainside. He fought to keep his balance, holding the sack with one arm and using the other to hold on to hardwoods and saplings. When he came upon the pen, he studied the cub, dried blood from lashings. The cub again clawed at the fence, the barbs cutting the animal's paws as it fiercely tried to part the wires.

When they reached the shack, Clete guided him to the door and instructed him to place the sack inside. He repeated the process for the other three sacks as the men hurled insults and found amusement with the slave they had just acquired. After he had taken the last sack and placed it in the shack, he took to the stump and sat.

"This ain't no time for restin'," Porter said. "We got to get as much outta you before we toss you in a shaller grave."

"Give me just a minute to catch my breath," Nick said.

Porter turned to a bucket and removed water with a ladle. "Don't tarry," he said. "I've worked up a thirst watchin' you work."

Nick slipped his knife from the sheath, wheeled about, and came up behind Clete, placing the knife to his throat. When Porter spotted the turn of events, he pointed the gun toward the pair. Nick placed his arm to where he turned Clete's head to the side.

"Drop the gun or I'll slice his throat."

Clete took hold of Nick's arm with both hands trying to tug it away. Nick tightened the grip to where he was pressing against Clete's neck.

"Do what he says, Porter," Clete said.

Porter hesitantly set the rifle on the ground.

"Back on away from it," Nick said as Porter backpedaled. Nick eyed Clete's gun and twirled Clete loose. He reached and grabbed the gun, pointing it at the two as Porter charged forward. Nick shot above Porter's head, the crack of the rifle echoing throughout the mountainside. "The next one goes between your eyes."

Nick backed them away and took Porter's gun from the ground. With one draped across his arm, the other pointing at them, he motioned them down the ravine. When they got to the pen, Nick said to Porter, "Step on across that pen and ease that cub back over the fencing."

"It'll claw the piss out of me."

"I hope so. Now get in there before I shoot your partner's ass off."

Porter crawled over the fence, the barbs cutting his wrist. "Damn, that stings," he said.

"How you think it feels for that little cub, you heartless bastard?"

The cub ran to the furthest corner, and its crying was as if one caught in the grips of terror. Its claws tore into Porter's shirt and overalls as its legs flailed away.

"Now set it on the other side," Nick said. "Set it down easy."

Porter tried to set the cub down over the fence, but it flopped from his arms and landed hard in the underbrush. It bayed as it took off running.

Nick walked to the still and kicked it on its side. Liquid poured through the coils and pipes. With the butt of the rifle he smashed the pot, damaging it beyond repair.

"Now, both of you walk down to that mule and carry it on out of here. I got the rifles pointed right at you. I suggest you choose another line of work. And if I ever come upon a scene again with you keepin' a cub trapped for your amusement, you'll be the ones ending up in shallow graves."

"We ain't gonna forget this, mister," Clete said.

"I hope that's the case, cause I don't think you want to go through this jackpot again." He pointed one of the rifles down the slope. "Go on, now."

The men headed down the mountainside, a defeated army of two. They led the mule down a narrow path of switchbacks. Rendered mute by the growing distance between them and the one who pointed the rifle, perhaps they plotted a new strategy. Nick placed one of the rifles on the ground and, with the other, fired two shots above their heads to dissuade any planning that might be taking place. He picked up the other rifle and hurried up the ravine until he had found the path from where he had walked. He turned from time just to verify he was the only one on the trail, on that mountaintop. When he came to the spot where the bowl-shaped curvature of the land dropped to the mountain spring, he emptied the bullets from the rifles. He smashed one against a poplar, pounding it again and again until the barrel separated from the stock. He tossed it down the gulley and watched it tumble through the limbs of the trees until they reached the ground, tumbling and flipping until they disappeared into the mist. He studied the other rifle and decided it would look nice next to his split-log bed.

| 22 |

The road was muddied, remnants of rain that had fallen through the night. The valley green and vibrant, spring unfolding. The land contained a silence that grew with each step Veta took. A place timeless as though the spinning of the world was something hypothetical. On a rise beyond the field, she imagined a pretty house where Ray waited for her on the porch. She missed him so.

An easy breeze carried across the valley, and she found a soft spot of clover just off the road. She set her walking stick on the ground and sat, her legs angled sideways. She leaned against her elbow. New life was all about her, pushing the dreariness of winter away. The morning sun warmed her shoulders, and she lifted her hair so that her neck was exposed. Veta studied the land about her as if she were an artist ready to bring the scene to life on canvas. Her legs now rested, she resumed the walk toward the base of Iron Mountain. She noted the first ridge of the mountain bathed in charcoal gray, a wave of hardwoods where spring had not yet arrived. She followed the path Baxter McEwen had told her to take. She had not been on top of the mountain since Ray took her when they had begun courting. With strong legs and stronger desire, a mountaintop picnic provided a chance to express the newness of their love with no one else within miles. And so, they had carried a blanket, a basket of pork biscuits and fig preserves, a small jug of cider, and kindred hearts to the furthest reaches they could find.

Veta came upon a ridge descending low to the east until it flattened out into the hollow. Andy Branch murmured its presence somewhere to the west as though a vast collection of voices spoke some language she could not decipher. Isolation enveloped her as though she had entered a doorway that closed behind her. After a brief thought to turn for home, she pushed on through the trees and came upon a second ridge. Andy Branch came into view, winding its way along moss-covered rocks. She'd forgotten how the stream appeared more rock than water. She assumed a fisherman would have nothing for the frying pan unless it was a salamander they sought. Limbs long fallen draped the creek, discouraging any thought to travelling up the stream. Using the walking stick, Veta followed the creek as the land rose opposite to the way the water flowed. Hardwoods thickened, raising the level of her insignificance in the grand scheme of things. She found saplings and dogwoods to grab hold of to help ease her climb. Where was that Cross Mountain trail she heard about? She angled further eastward through heavy underbrush, a realization she had miscalculated the entrance to the trail. Holding on to saplings and laurels, she made her way on the sloped land until she spotted a slice in the tree line.

When she made it to the trail, she looked from where she came. *A route fit only for a mountain goat.* As she disparaged her initial route choice under her breath, she began the climb. The talk she'd heard about the Cross Mountain trail proved to be true, and she guaranteed herself that the next time she climbed it, it would be sitting on a buggy leading a horse. Veta gave brief thought to the lack of protection she had if she came across a bear. When she was a young girl, helping Grandpappy feed the hog one morning, she had spotted a bear on a nearby hillside. The dark beast seemed the size of an elephant, and she quizzed her grandfather on how something so beautiful could be so dangerous. He told her that it was the way of nature, and there was no use questioning. He told her if she ever was confronted by one, she should rise up, arms raised, yelling and screaming, and move towards the bear. She guessed the yelling and screaming wouldn't be a problem. Approaching the bear was something she questioned her ability to do.

Her denim shirt clung tightly to her skin from perspiration. Her wool pants itched, and she found rest on a stump. Looking down the mountain, regarding the valley, she tried to measure the distance. Sitting so far above the world, she felt as though in a place where a clock or a calendar had no purpose. Far beyond the valley, Doe Mountain stood in grayed silence. She looked behind her to judge the distance to the mountaintop, to the end of the climb. The mountaintop wasn't coming to meet her, she reasoned, and she took a deep breath and continued on.

When she had reached the top, she gave another glance to the valley, to Doe Mountain. She spotted a narrow footpath that headed southwesterly and took to walking it. The land about her held a peacefulness that gave odd comfort, as though some tale of woe had been revealed as a falsehood. She had walked for some while down the path, giving pause as to whether she might be heading only further into the wilderness. Soon, the aroma of embers from a fire arose, confirmation that she was heading in the right direction. A small cabin came into view, and she wondered if she should announce her presence. Nick came around from the back of the cabin, carrying a spade over his shoulder like a weapon held for marching. He stopped when he spotted her. At first, he appeared in some form of defense, but as she approached, he raised his hand in a slight wave.

"Could you live any further from civilization?" Veta asked. She took a seat on a cane chair near a fire pit to catch her breath. "If I had gone any further up, I'd be on the moon."

"Miss Veta, what in the world brings you up here?" His stoic impression gave her pause, as she had hoped for a warmer welcome.

"I ain't seen hide nor hair of you in close to a year, and I was worried you might been et by a panther, or a bear had decided to make a winter coat out of your hide."

He shrugged. "Winter was a hard one. I been busy trying to recover. Summer's not far off, and this planting season will determine if I can make it through the next winter."

"I feel a blackberry winter comin'. Can feel it in my bones. So don't let these warm days fool you into thinking winter has closed up shop just yet. You don't want them crops to get froze from the get-go."

Veta looked about. The deep timber. Barren. Colorless, except for the laurels and firs that dotted the land. Treetops clanked in the soundless breeze like antlers of primeval beasts. "I was in town week prior and couldn't find a soul who could confirm a Nick Grindstaff sighting. And you sure ain't darkened my doorstep in forever. So, I figured you either tired of the company or you been kilt up here rasslin' a creature of the wild."

"I'm sorry about that, Miss Veta. I ain't climbed down Doe in a good while. When I do leave the mountain, it's to the Stoney Creek side. Much easier maneuvering."

She looked about. "Don't have to worry about rubbin' elbows with nobody, do you?"

"Only the bears."

"I wouldn't want to rub elbows with a chipmunk, much less a bear."

"How have you been, Miss Veta?"

"Middlin'. Livin' by myself now. Larry and Joan all growed up and gone. To tell you the truth, it's mighty lonesome in that old house. You know, it sure would be nice if you'd visit ever once in a blue moon."

"When you're a one-man crew, your days are mapped out." He seemed to wish he could retrieve those words. "I know you know that as much as anybody, Miss Veta. I didn't mean to lessen what you've endured through the years keeping a family, farm, and business going on your own. I'm right impressed with how you've handled the load put upon your shoulders."

"I don't know how impressed you should be. The load puts me on my knees somedays." She looked about. "At least I have civilization nearby when I need something. You, on the other hand, got nothing but trees and frosty air."

He took a ladle and scooped water from a pail. He poured it into a tin cup, handing it to Veta.

"Much obliged," she said. "I did work up a thirst." She studied the cabin. A shelf hung above the doorway. Jars and bottles. Tin cans.

Wooden crates. Two narrow tree trunks that anchored an overhang above the doorway. "Quite the set up you got here."

"It provides."

"How much property you got?"

"To the back of the crops," he said while pointing, "and to the edge of where the land drops east on the opposite end. It's about a twenty-acre spread."

"You've a deed of some sort for it?"

"Bought it from Daniel Stout. He wore a puzzled look the day I told him I wanted this land instead of the spot down Spear Branch." He studied the horizon beyond the planting fields. "I'm sure it didn't take long to sell it. That land was the prettiest spot in the valley."

"Don't spend time on somethin' that ain't part of your life." She took a sip of the water. "You findin' enough meat to put on the table? You's gettin' to be a skinny 'un."

"I hunt and trap small game."

"Surely you got deer on the mountain. That'd leave you enough venison to last a cycle of seasons."

"I can't bring myself to do it. They got gentle souls."

She shrugged. "They got tender meat too. What crops you got growin' yonder in the plantin' field?"

"Corn, taters, rhubarb. Rutabagas. Volunteer onions along the back edge."

Veta took another sip. "Say, since I walked halfway to Mars to visit, how about I get a tour of the castle?"

She followed him to the door. "Not much to see," he told her. She eased her head through the narrow door. The cabin was square, no more than eight or nine feet deep, and the same width across. There was a bed made of a split chestnut log. On it was a slender bedding and two wool blankets. At the head of it was a circular wood table with three books. A bible. There was a fireplace against the back wall, and there was an iron hook with a pot hanging above where food was cooked and surely coffee brewed. There were no windows. The sunlight slipped through the doorway, casting the small room pale gray. The ceiling was angled with hand-hewn boards. Veta wondered how it handled the bitter, winter winds. In between the logs that formed the walls appeared to be dried mud. "Well, I reckon it's homey enough," she said.

When she turned from the doorway she heard a hum. A rattle. She looked back into the cabin. "Good Lord. Nick, you got a rattler in there."

"He's a resident."

"A resident? Why, he'll fill you full of poison and make you surely suffer a painful death."

"He's a young one. Had another one but he must have crawled out and died. This one keeps my cabin free of varmints and he warms himself by the fire in return."

"I think I'd stick with a yard cat. If you don't mind, I prefer to sit outside."

He pulled up a cane chair and placed it next to a wooden barrel. After instructing her to sit, he removed a pottery jug from a shelf above the doorway. He filled her cup and one he had grabbed beside the jug. "Try this cider."

"All right."

As they sipped the apple drink, Veta looked at the planting field, puzzled that crops grew at such high elevation. "It's a purdy spot, but surely you miss the company of others."

"I talk to the wind when I'm lonely."

"Well, what about that?" She let go a chuckle. "Don't tell me it talks back. What does it say? How much your body's a goin' to ache when it blows right through you?"

"It whispers the sweetest song if you listen closely."

"You're a talkin' nonsense." She looked through the trees and regarded the smooth skyline of Doe Mountain. "I bet them sunrises are a sight. Seein' that big orange ball rise above Doe at eye level."

"It makes the morning meal more enjoyable." He sighed. "So, tell me about the young 'uns."

"Larry lives in Richmond. Works at a textile mill. He writes weekly. Joan got married in April. Moved on off to Elizabethton. And now the house ain't nothin' but a collection of memories." Her eyes watered, but she decided not to fight it. "Business got so bad, I had to sell the store. Ozzie bought it for next to nothing. But it beats gettin' nothing. I just couldn't compete with him anymore. He had more knowledge in the ways of commerce. He knew more about building materials, had vendors jumpin' at the chance to do business with him. Now he has two stores to carry on all that business."

"I'm sorry to hear that, Miss Veta. What are you doing to get by?"

"Bout like you, I reckon. I work the garden best I can. I can the surplus to get me through the winter. Larry sends a few dollars each month. Helps me buy flour and meal. Baxter McEwen brings meat when he slays a beef cow." She nodded, a revelation just arrived. "Makes you and me pretty much the same, other than geography."

Nick ran his fingers through his oily hair. "You might be right. But for different reasons. I ran from the world, and it appears the world ran from you."

"Well, the Good Book says, 'do not be conformed to the world.' I guess you and me have got that command pretty much mastered."

"I'd say so."

Nick escorted Veta to the Cross Mountain trail. Tears formed in the corners of her eyes when she hugged him. "Come to visit."

"I'll do my best."

He watched her amble down the road that had transformed from the path he carved by ax and foot years ago, into a trail that now led people from the valley over the mountain to Shady Valley and Stoney Creek. The soft light of the afternoon sun painted Veta's shadow flat and angled below her, as though it laid forth the path it wanted her to walk. In fragile gait, she moved in a manner that appeared she had escorts at each elbow, guided perhaps by ones who had long awaited her arrival. The path's bend led her from sight, a specter absorbed into the bowels of the mountain. A creature of mountain mythology that had temporarily assumed human form.

There was a familiar chill in the valley. Reminders of mornings tending to the cattle with Tom, the quiet of those days disturbed only by the bellows of the cows for the hay that would be laid down for them. Nick studied the road, the slow rises, the gentle curves, the way it worked its way up the holler toward Jerico's house. A mist. A grayness to the sky that cast a shadow of loneliness. Nick gave thought to venture up and say hello to the family, but the day was approaching midday, and he had six miles to go to make it to town. He had heard a rumor that the county wanted to take ownership of the Cross Mountain trail with plans to make it a designated road. Would the troubles of the valley soon work its way to his doorstep?

There were new homes on the road to Mountain City. Growth. Families expanding. He entered the outskirts of town and spotted the steeple of the First Baptist Church. There was a buzz of activity on the street. People rode on buggies or walked toward the center of town. When Nick neared the courthouse, he noticed a wooden structure on the lawn in front of the two-story building. There were people gathered in front. More people than he had ever seen gathered in Johnson County. In the distance, people standing on the structure parted. Between them, up steps that rose up from behind the scaffolding, several men appeared.

"There he is," a man in front of Nick said, pointing to the group of men who had just arrived.

"It surely is," the woman beside him said. "Lord, have mercy on his soul."

"It's too late for that, Nadine. He's done carved out a path straight to Hell."

A loud murmur rose above the crowd. Anticipation of some performance. Nick studied those around him, a mesmerized group. A dark-skinned man was led to the front of the scaffold. Nick noticed a rope hanging from a beam next to where the man stood. Behind him were two men who looked as though assigned a task of grave importance.

"Nick, you come down the mountain to watch this?"

Nick turned and spotted Judd. "What is it that appears to be taking place?"

"Why, the hanging of Finley Preston is what."

"Hanging," Nick repeated. "What did he do?"

"He murdered Lillie Shaw," a woman near him said. "Killed her and cut her all to pieces. She's buried all over the county." Nick regarded the woman, pride welling in her eyes in being able to pass the news on to him.

"Finley's wife should never have allowed Lillie to move in with them," a man nearby said. "A young, pretty gal like that. Was asking for trouble."

"I think Finley's wife caught them wallerin' in bed and made him kill her as penance," another woman said.

"I think they both killed her," an elderly woman said. "They's two sets of footprints near the place where her midsection was found."

Nick felt like he had come upon some diabolical circus. He looked to the galley and the two men led the condemned man to where he stood under the noose. It appeared as though they were in some manner of conversation with the prisoner.

"By proclamation of the Circuit Court of Mountain City, on this day, November seven, in the year of our Lord, nineteen-o-five, Finley Preston is to be hanged by the neck until dead. Be witness all who have come."

The man, with hands tied in front, stepped forward. Though he stood a hundred feet away, Nick saw the fear in the man's dark eyes. His expression was something of wonder, as though he wasn't sure of why there was such a gathering. As though an event had been planned without his knowledge. A morbid party where he was the surprise guest. The bloody toast of the town. Shakily, he looked about the crowd, studying the eyes of those who had come. He knelt his head for a moment, took a deep breath, and said, "I guess I'll see you on the other side."

The lawmen guided him back to where he stood under the noose. A few words spoken to him, perhaps instructions. A black hood was placed over his head, and a murmur again floated among the audience. Nick backed away from the crowd, turning toward the road. He came upon more people rushing to the scene, those who didn't want to miss out on such an occasion. He pushed through them and hurried to the main road that would lead him home. On the horizon, Iron Mountain stood, its skyline hidden by gray clouds that hung flat and motionless.

Behind him, the distressing creak of a gate swinging open, the thud of something forcing the tautness of a rope, the gasp of the crowd, made him rue the decision to come off the mountain.

Nick studied the planting fields. A plague set upon the land. Pestilence. Something biblical in the air. The sun bore on his shoulders, on his balding head. His beard dripped with sweat. The plants lay wilted, the drought now two years running. His hands ached from countless trips to the spring, trying to keep the plants watered enough to produce a harvest. A harvest that wouldn't come.

In the bin were two apples. Nick examined them, the mushiness and ill-shape of them both confirmation they were good for nothing except a meal for the raccoons. He took his hat, took a sip of water from the pail, and headed down the mountain.

When he arrived in front of the familiar home, memories of childhood rose dreamlike, emotion stirring the visual. He recalled Aunt Cora taking him to the barn to see the newborn calf not long after he came to live with them. The earthy smell of hay. Cora's long dress and apron. Dark boots. Watching from between wooden rails, the spindly animal ran in small circles as if putting on a show for the young boy. Nick was fascinated with the speed the calf had generated. When her hooves sprayed a cow pie onto Nick's shirt, it caused him to fall on his backside. Cora was quick to pick him up before cleaning his shirt with her apron. He recalled the two horses that Uncle Jerico led into the pasture one evening. Both animals black as coal, their hooves clomping in unison as Jerico coaxed them along with gentle words. Jerico was dwarfed by the horses, and Nick was in awe of how the man was able to assert dominance over such large beasts. Those events occurred not long after Pa had Ma had passed. Tuberculosis had hit the county hard. There was talk about it everywhere, though Nick was too young to understand it. All he knew was that they both got sick around the same time. When they passed, staying with Jerico and Cora seemed natural as they had taken over the duties his stricken parents could not perform. He wasn't sure how it was determined where he and his siblings would be distributed. He had been sent to Jerico's, Sarah and Katherine to Uncle George's, and John placed in the care of Uncle Roby. Had they had been set upon some bidding table, items of some family co-op?

Doe Valley held a quiet reverence as Nick walked through it, the midday sun appearing as though its motion had been stopped, as if it would remain at its apex forever. The searing heat had caused the world to retreat, and he was glad it was so. Or had he perhaps become so calloused to the world that he was unable to feel anything below the mountain top? There was a sense of embarrassment in the reason for his visit, but he reasoned survival superseded pride.

There was hesitation in the knocking. He had spent over twenty years just walking through the door, as it was his home. But now he darkened the doorstep a stranger, and the house seemed a faded picture from a time long ago. In some regards, it was. When Cora opened the door, Nick noticed the aging in her face. Her once smooth skin was deeply wrinkled. Her neck sagged, and her hair was dull silver, pulled tightly into a bun. Her blue eyes still sparkled, a perpetual youth, and it caused Nick to smile. He removed his hat.

"Nick," she said, placing her hand to her chest. "Oh, it does my heart good to see you at our doorstep." When he crossed the threshold, she hugged him, though he was hesitant to do the same, as shame had risen inside him for staying away for so long.

"Hello, Aunt Cora. How you a doin'?"

"Fair to middling. Please come in and stay awhile."

He smelled buttered biscuits and ham simmering in pole beans, and his stomach growled. "Thank you."

"We are just sitting down to eat. Would be a pleasure if you join us."

"I would like that." He followed her to the kitchen table where Tom sat next to a woman and a teenage boy.

"Hello, cousin," Tom said.

Nick raised a hand. "Tom."

Tom stood, and when Nick walked around the table, they embraced.

"It's good to see you, Nick," Tom said. "I want you to meet my wife, Thelma. And this is our son, Nicholas."

The hearing of the name gave him pause. "Pleased to meet you," Nick said. The boy regarded Nick with trepidation. Nick looked about the room. "I hope I'm not interrupting."

"Fiddlesticks," Cora said. She took a chair from against the wall and placed it next to hers at the table. "Sit." She fetched a plate and utensils from the cabinet. Nick stared at the empty plate, hunger roiling through his midsection, guilt preventing him from taking food from the table. Cora surely sensed it, and she scooped pole beans and pinto beans from bowls, carved a piece of beef from the gravied saucer, and removed two cathead biscuits from a bowl.

He nodded his thanks and looked about. "Shouldn't we wait for Uncle Jerico?"

There was an uncomfortable pause. "Pa passed two years back," Tom said.

A pain knifed through Nick's heart. "I'm sorry. I didn't know."

"Maybe if you came off that mountain more than once a decade, you'd know when kin passes," Tom said. Cora touched Tom's hand.

Nick stared at his plate of food, tempted to leave the table. Cora placed her hand on his shoulder. "Well, let's all eat before it gets cold."

Talk was limited. Tom's wife spoke of the sighting of an automobile passing through Mountain City, and how people crowded the street to watch it drive by. Nicholas regarded Nick peculiarly as though not sure what to make of this odd man who shared the same name as him. Nick offered up little to the conversation, responding to questions about life on Iron Mountain with short answers. He felt his daily life had no merit with regard to those in the valley. The news of

Jerico's passing caused Nick's stomach to roil, and yet he forced himself to eat as the primal desire for nourishment took precedent.

Like a man who had lost his bearings in unfamiliar surroundings, Nick thanked Cora for the meal, gave cursory comments on the pleasure it was to meet Tom's family, before patting Tom on the shoulder and heading out the door.

"It was so good to have you, Nick," Cora said at the door. "Please come back soon."

Nick lowered his head, fighting tears. "I'm so sorry about the passing of Uncle Jerico. He reared me just like I was his own boy."

Cora wrapped her arms around his chest. "He surely loved you."

"Yes'm," he whispered before turning toward the road.

On the walk home, Nick pondered not the path he walked, but the path that had led him to this point. He passed by D.W. Lewis' farmhouse, recalling summer mornings picking strawberries. He remembered the battle with bees when he tried to fill his bucket before Will and Tom filled theirs. It was there when Will told them of his plans to leave Doe Valley for St. Louis for fame and riches. If only Nick knew back then what the outcome of St. Louis would lead to, the heartache he could have avoided. Could have stayed and married Annabeth. How different life might have been.

Nick searched the porch for signs of life. Still, it held only desolation, a house relegated to nothing more than a remnant, a testament to a place where voices once echoed, where footsteps once reverberated across the wooden floor. Evidence of lives long passed, now strangled by weeds and sumac and briar strands that would choke out all but the spirits of those who once inhabited it.

Shadows crept long and quiet across the valley, confirmation that night was coming on. He was approaching the first ridge when he spotted something coming from a field of wildflowers. He assumed a deer had emerged, but when he saw the face, the eyes, the perkiness of the dog's ears, he knelt. The dog circled Nick as if unsure as to what treatment might be doled out, and it lowered itself to its belly, paws forward.

"Now, where did you come from?"

With his hand out, the dog crawled toward him. When Nick rubbed the dog's head, the animal wagged its tail. Nick looked about to see if the dog might have an owner nearby. The dog certainly didn't appear as a hunting dog. It didn't have the sleekness of a coon dog or one good for hunting rabbits. The hound was black with three white markings on its head as though someone had dipped their fingers in paint and pressed them above the animal's eyes. When it rose to a sitting position, Nick noticed his undercarriage was colored white in the shape of a cross. "You lost?" Nick looked about again as he petted the dog. "I ain't got no food, so you best run on home." The dog stood when Nick did. "I got to get up the mountain, little one. Nighttime is coming on. You go on home, now."

Nick gave the dog another pat and headed up the ridge. He stood at the base of Cross Mountain Road, as it had become officially named. Concrete evidence that he was a true pioneer to some degree. He reckoned he would not be remembered after his time on Earth was over, but the road he'd carved out might perhaps cause those crossing it to wonder its origin. Without the road, darkness would surely come while he was on his way home. With no moon to guide him, the journey would be treacherous. When he had made it halfway to the top, he turned to catch the jagged, amber skyline of Doe Mountain, the mountaintop as though afire from the final moments of the setting sun. Below him, the dog dropped to its knees, tail wagging.

"Listen, little 'un. You best get on home before you get caught in the darkness. Too many animals of the night would love to make a meal of you." Nick clapped his hands together. "Go on, now. Hurry home." The dog lay still, studying Nick. "Suit yourself." Nick resumed his climb.

The cabin had recessed into dusk's shadows, absorbed into the night air as though faded from the world altogether. He sparked an oil lantern to life under the overhang. He held it away from his body, and the eyes of the dog sparkled from the glow. He walked into the house and returned with two Johnny Cakes. "This should get you through the night."

Inside the cabin, the flame danced, the walls swimming, his own reflection a ghostly blur of movement as though trapped, searching for escape. He soon found comfort on the bed, the lamp snuffed out, swallowed by the darkness that Iron Mountain brought each night. Restless, his thoughts turned to Jerico. Had his uncle died a quiet death?

The predawn light slipped under the doorway, carving shape from the corners of the cabin. Nick lay quietly in his bed. Grackles sang out in the distance, as if to alert all living creatures that the mountain had awakened. He listened to them and wondered their conversation. He had come to look forward to their morning calls. A sweeter call to be awakened by than a cackling rooster, for certain. He ground coffee after he had built a fire. Soon, the earthy smell would compete with the burning embers of the fireplace.

With the tin cup of coffee and a jerky stick, Nick stepped outside to watch the sun rise above Doe Mountain. He sat in his chair, positioned toward the east. In the underbrush, he spotted movement and eyed his rifle beside the doorway. Too early for squirrels to be stirring. Perhaps a raccoon searching its resting place. There was heavy panting, and the movement through the ferns came closer. An animal in distress, perhaps. When he saw the dog's snout, the longing in its eyes, Nick shook his head. "Well, it's clear you decided not to head on home."

The dog inched closer, on all fours, crawling on his belly like he'd done the evening before. Nick reached his hand forward, and the dog made its way so that he was soon being petted. "You must be part mountain goat." The dog continued to pant, and Nick poured water from the pail into a wooden bowl. "You're a thirsty one." The dog lapped up the water, and when it was empty, he lay next to Nick's boot. "Well, you got a belly full of water, so why you still pantin'?" The dog rolled on its back, and Nick scratched his belly. "Well, this place ain't exactly a palace, and food might get a might scarce, but if you are in need of a home, I will accommodate you." The dog rolled upright and rubbed his paw against Nick's leg. The dog continued to pant. Nick poured more water and then went inside and fetched two pieces of jerky. As he watched the dog tear into the spindly meat, Nick studied him. "Well, we got to name you, I guess." The dog choked down the food and returned to Nick on the chair, panting as it eyed Nick for the possibility of more food. "How about we call you Panter? You sure do enough of it."

Summer showed no signs of relenting. Nick constantly sought the coolness of shade. The air was oppressively humid, a vice-like grip on the mountain that made Nick wonder if autumn would be able to ease the grip summer had on the land. Whatever shelter Nick sought, Panter was by his side. The dog had assumed the role of lead investigator, watching Nick's every move when he performed chores or prepared dinner. When Nick went to the planting field, Panter would run ahead, tail wagging, looking about as if trying to run off any creature that might have taken root. Field mice, squirrels. Birds searching for seeds. Earning his keep. When the field was deemed animal-free, Panter would circle the edges, peering into the woods for larger prey. Nick wondered what Panter's reaction would be should a bear or panther amble by. Based on the way it stomped and stamped toward a buck that had entered the field two days prior, Nick worried that his will to protect would lead the dog to run right into direct danger.

| **24** |

The moon hung incandescent, the sky cobalt blue. Treetops painted silver. The mountain floor was aglow in some neon sheen, except where shadows slipped into the abyss where the moonlight could not reach. Nick walked toward the planting field. Curiosity had crept under the doorway with the thin splay of moonlight, leading him to rise from his bed. When he stood in his doorway, the brilliance of the moon lured him from his cabin.

As he walked toward the field, Panter following at his heel, bush crickets sang in angry chorus. They chanted as though grievances were being aired with no recourse for satisfaction. He made it to the crest just beyond his planting field, and all around him the land fell away. A summit of its own. Were there a way to get closer to the moon, he would surely make the ascension, though he reckoned the moon's light could not gain in magnitude. Iron Mountain had transformed itself into colors that Nick couldn't name. A landscape only possible in a dream state until that moment. Nick found an opening where the moonlight penetrated the woods unobstructed, nature's spotlight. He stood in the middle, himself awash in silver. Shadows lay circular beyond where he stood. He rolled his sleeves back so that his forearms were exposed. A warmth from an unknown source lit upon them, reminding him of the arms of a mannequin he had once seen in St. Louis.

He removed his shirt, the cool air tingling his skin, and kicked off his boots. When he had removed his overalls, his body now fully exposed to the moon, Panter sat, puzzled as to the intent of this bizarre event. Nick studied the bluish-gray glow of his skin, the light so strong he could make out the individual hairs across his legs and arms. He marveled at the clarity, to see so brilliantly in the deepest part of night. He closed his eyes and felt the hum of the katydids' song reverberate through his body. He tilted his head and stared at the moon. Within the shape of it, his mother's face appeared. Tears welled, and he reached his hands toward the orb as though he might cradle its shape in his palms. The face held a pensive smile, as though the vision of her son looking up at her brought both sadness and joy. He longed for her to drop down and stand beside him, to hold him, and perhaps whisper words that she had waited years to tell him.

Like an affliction newly born, separation enveloped him. For the first time, he felt alone. Discarded. Sweat formed, and he struggled to breathe. He searched the moon for his father's face but could not find it. A soul that could not be reached. Where was he? He thought about his sisters. Were they okay? John? How long had it been since he'd seen his brother? Questions of a deeper kind, a deeper level, arose. Why had he run from the world? Where was the will to fight? How hard had Ma and Pa fought The Consumption? Tears flowed. Annabeth. What if he had stayed and married her? What would life be like? What kind of father would he have been? Panter peered up at him as though unsure how to provide comfort. It moved in front of Nick and lay on all fours, whimpering. As tears continued, a vision of his mother evolved, standing before him, healthy, no longer frail and bedridden. He recalled the coldness in her hand that final day before Cora led him to her house. Memories of childhood were scarce, but the one of that day was engraved in his mind. The faint smile she gave him. Final words.

"Go on, Nicholas. Go with Aunt Cora. You be strong and don't worry one lick about your ma. I'll be on ahead waitin' for you. Always remember that." The creak of the door played in his head when Cora led him outside, never to return to the house where he was born.

He removed a blanket from his bed and found a spot near the fire pit. There was a need to sleep under that moon, with mother watching over him. He lay on his back and searched through the treetops.

Her vision had faded, but her presence was all about him. He fought thoughts about giving the world another chance, that perhaps he had rushed into a stream without giving thought to its depth, or its ability to place him on the far side of the bank without means to return to where he had first entered the water. He rubbed his head. The scar still under his hairline from the blow he took on the train. He recalled the intense pain when he tried to rise from his bed at Aunt Cora's when he had returned home. The emptiness of the chair beside his bed, where he anticipated Annabeth would be sitting, nursing him back to health, talking of the plans for buying the land by Spear Branch. There was excitement in her eyes as she talked about the wedding. The vision he had of her on their wedding night, a consummation of the boundless love they shared. Instead, the vision of her sharing her bed with Cody attacked his soul, a tight fist that squeezed any will his heart had mustered.

The sled carved a crevice in the dirt road. His footprints had not left an imprint on that road in seasons. A collection of rain showers and snowstorms through long winters had long since washed away all traces of his steps. Nothing remained except perhaps faint apparitions in the minds of those who had crossed paths with him. With the Hermit. Uncle Nick. And there he was, walking the road to what was once called Taylorsville. "Mountain City," he spoke under guarded breath. What did he care if the name had changed? It wasn't his town any longer.

The one well-versed in the hardship of trail blazing knew the route he walked had been blazed long before he came into the world, and he walked the road with indifference. As the metal bindings of the sled rumbled, a steady hum competed with the steady beat of clops from the steer's hooves. It was the animal's first trip off the mountain in years. Panter followed along at Nick's heel. Main Street was active as merchants peddled their wares. Window fronts contained cooking supplies, dresses and hats, glassware, tins of candy, and dried fruits.

There were wooden racks draped with fabric and rugs. Commerce was thriving, it appeared.

Three children chased a dog across the road into an alley, and Panter watched intently. Nick pulled the steer to a stop and tied a rope to a hitching post. He removed a burlap sack tied to the sled. The mild, musty smell of rhubarb made Nick certain he'd fetch a fair amount in trade. He ambled through the door of Lunceford's Market. Panter followed behind.

"Hidy, Nick," said the slender man behind a dark cherry counter. His face contained a warm smile.

"Judd," Nick said with a nod.

"Nice to see you on the Doe Valley side of the mountain. I heard tell you only dealt with the folks from Stoney Creek now."

"I am in need of ammunition, and McDowell is out of what fits my gun. And to tell the truth, I grew a bit curious to see how the town has grown. The name changed. Figured the town must have too."

"It's growing, this little town." He looked at the sack. "What have you got for me today?" He inhaled. "Rhubarb?"

"Three dozen. Fresh from the ground." He handed the bag to Judd. "And I got two dozen ear o' corn."

"Extry good! Folks around here had given up hope that they would ever eat your produce again. What kind of horse trading you got in mind today?"

"A sack of meal." Panter sat at the doorway as he'd been taught to do. "And the ammunition. Two boxes should do it."

Judd turned around to where boxes of ammo were stacked. "I believe I recall the gun you use." He grabbed two boxes. "See if my memory is correct."

Nick read the box and nodded. "Those are the ones." He studied a bundle of jerky on the counter. "Reckon you could toss a little of that into the trade?"

"I'd call that a square deal." He slid the bundle to Nick. "Folks swear your crops taste better than any around. If I didn't care about you putting me out of business, I'd tell you to set up shop here in town.

You wouldn't be able to keep anything in stock, and it would sell so fast."

Nick fetched a sack of cornmeal lying against the wall. Judd took the burlap sack and emptied the vegetables onto the counter.

"That sack of meal sure looks tiny in that big old hand of yours, Nick. It wouldn't surprise me if you could put your hands clear round the neck of that steer of yore'n."

Nick regarded his hands and saw nothing extraordinary about them.

"How's life on the mountain?" Judd asked.

"It sustains me."

Judd scratched his chin. "Say, why don't you come for dinner sometime? Eula will load you up on rump roast and gravy over mashed taters."

"Maybe one day." He tossed the sack of meal over his shoulder and carried the boxes of bullets. The jerky was placed in his shirt pocket. Nodding his thanks, he turned for the door.

"Stay awhile. I got a good rocker by the woodstove. Take a load off and we'll solve the world's problems and aggravate anybody who walks in."

"I need to be a movin' on."

"Well."

Beside the sled, Nick placed the meal in his sack. The bullets he wrapped in a coat and secured it on the sled. He set the jerky on the seat as it would settle hunger pains on the way back. Panter circled behind Nick as though trying to get a good view of what was being placed on the sled, and quickly winced as a barrage of stones flew at him. Several hit Nick in the leg. He raised up, and two teenage-looking boys stood in the street laughing. "Which one is the stupid animal, Artie?" one asked.

"Surely it's that old hermit," Artie replied. "Anyone dumb enough to live up on that mountain has to be a fool. And he looks like something what crawled out the shitter."

They approached as Nick checked Panter to make sure he wasn't hurt. Nick untied the rope and turned the steer around. He pointed it back down the road from where they came.

"Word is you're a crazy sumbitch," Artie said.

"Notice how the whole town starts to stink when you show up," the other said. "You smell like a possum crawled up your ass and died."

Nick led the steer down the road, eyes straight ahead. The boys followed alongside. "Hey, mister, how come you ain't et your dog yet?" Artie's companion asked. "I bet he'd be tasty if you roast him over the fire." The boy kicked his leg out toward the dog, and Nick took hold of the boy by his jacket.

"You so much as look at my dog again, and you'll be the one roasting over the fire."

The boy's eyes grew wide. "You're crazy, old man. I'm going to tell my pa what you said."

"Tell him whatever you want. But make sure you tell him what a disrespectful boy you are. Come on, Panter. Time to head home."

They traveled through the valley, transients easing through deep-green fields and shimmering brooks. The land appeared dreamlike, as though it resided in Nick's mind only. Shadows moved across the valley below isolated clouds that passed beneath the sun. They came upon a brook close to the road, and Nick stopped to let Panter drink. Nick spotted Ruben Johnson working on a fence post. Beyond the fence, Angus cows grazed. Ruben looked up and waved. Nick nodded.

"Come on up for a spell, Nick," Ruben yelled.

"Ain't got time," Nick replied.

"Hang on a minute." Ruben eased down the hill, hammer in his hand.

"How in the world are you, Nick?"

"I'm making it."

"We were talking about you last week at church. Would love to see you visit. I'm sure the good Lord above would, too."

"I don't need to be a settin' in church for God to see me."

Panter circled them both before sitting in the road, appearing intent on listening to the conversation.

"He sees you wherever you are. Jonah found that out when that whale swallered him."

"I think the chances of me being swallowed by a whale 'round these parts are pretty slim."

"They's other ways besides a giant fish to grab your attention."

"Don't need nothin', or nobody, to get my attention. I'll just keep a goin' at it on my own."

"You're never goin' at it on your own. He knows your path and is always ahead waiting on you, clearing the way."

"You make it seem like God knows what's going to unfold beforehand. I say He observes it as happens, just as we do."

He waved his hand in the air. "I disagree."

"He decided a long time ago to create man. To make Adam and Eve, right?"

"He breathed them to life."

"But did he know about the serpent? About the apple?"

"Surely he did."

"If so, then it stands to reason that He knew everything that would unfold, right?"

"That's right."

"So, He purposely planned for evil and destruction for all of mankind?"

"No, of course not. That's free will that has brought on evil."

"That's not what you said. You said the Lord knows everything that is going to happen before it does."

"Yes, but..."

"Then, that means God designed the world with the intent that the general nature of man would be evil."

"Well, no."

"It only stands to reason."

"How do you figure?"

"If God knows the future, then that means He decided at the beginning to have his first two creations fall into sin from the get-go. That they would disobey Him and be condemned. And all those who came after would be condemned as well with sickness and death and evil and betrayal."

Ruben scratched his chin and appeared in search of words, words that wouldn't come. "I'm sure the Lord would have a response to that, but He's not telling me what that is. You might need to talk to Him direct for the answer."

"He's not going to provide the answer. When Job had suffered so and asked God why he deserved it, God replied, 'Who has put wisdom in the inward parts, or given understanding to the mind?'" He looked skyward. "He rebuffed the need to answer His own question when He asked Job, 'Is it by your wisdom that the hawk soars, and spreads its wings toward the south?' It was his way of sayin', 'I don't have to explain myself to you or anybody.'" He gave a tug on the reins, and the steer took to walking. "God don't yet know what's going to happen down the road. He's letting it unfold and observing it like you and me. To think otherwise means you believe He's purposefully created us to fail Him, and to suffer because of it." He motioned for Panter, who had lain at Nick's feet. "Come on, boy."

| **25** |

Nick rested the ax on his shoulder as he descended the mountain. His stomach churned. His inventory of canned vegetables had dwindled. The apple trees were weeks away from producing fruit. He had grown tired of eating squirrel stew. The trout he caught weren't big enough to make a meal. The groundhogs had become more elusive. He had reckoned he could kill a deer, but they had been spooked by a panther that had taken residence above the ridge near Nick's cabin. His trading worth was nonexistent. He studied the blade, sliding his finger along the edge to make sure he had sharpened it well. Panter pranced alongside his master, nose to the ground as though something worth eating or chasing waited ahead.

The winding, earthen road was in a constant state of descent, angled switchbacks hugged by hardwoods as though some form of reluctance had risen against letting Nick off the mountain. Though it was a road he walked, there was hardly light from above as the tree line stretched to the clouds. A constant state of shadow as though the world was asleep. The angles of the road soon began to soften, the twists less harsh, the trees easing their tightness on the path Nick walked. He entered the hollow that was Stoney Creek. The land flattened, and he came upon a small farmhouse that he had passed many times on his way to barter his produce. He had spotted an elderly woman on the porch a time or two. He had Panter sit in the yard and set the ax against the porch. He stepped upon the wobbly stone slats that led him to the door. After he knocked, there appeared at the door the elderly woman.

"Excuse me, ma'am," Nick began, "but I didn't notice any wood pile alongside your house. Are you in need of firewood? I'm quite the lumberjack and have a sharp ax, and if you would like me to cut you some wood, I would be certainly glad to oblige."

She studied him through the barely open door before looking past him as if to see if there were others with him. She spotted Panter with a suspicious eye. "I ain't got money to pay fer any wood cuttin'. I got an old broke-down shed out back that I just use when I'm in need of a fire."

"I'm not asking for money. I would be willing to do the work in exchange for food." He stepped back and pointed to the distance. "I live up on Iron Mountain, and my food supply has dwindled. I don't want handouts or charity. Just want to work for a meal."

"I heard tell of you. They say you's plum crazy."

Nick chuckled. "I may be a little peculiar, but I wouldn't say I'm crazy." He regarded her intently. She was dwarfish in stature, hidden in shadow in the dimly lit house. Beady eyes. Ashen face, she wore a look of one who dreaded news of the world, good or bad. One who could hide from it all with the simple closing of the door.

"I don't care what you are. I want you off my porch. Go on, now. Git."

"I didn't mean to startle you. Just looking to earn a meal."

"Find your meal somers else."

Nick took the ax and led Panter on down the austere road. He came upon another house with a stack of wood stored next to a shed. Another had wood next to their barn. He fought the pains in his stomach as the aroma of food cooking came from a home set close to the road. He spotted a group through a small window. They were busy passing bowls of food, and Nick craved a tasting.

The sun had risen high above, casting the small valley in gold shimmer. The planting fields were just beginning to sprout, making it appear as though some giant being had painted lines of green into the otherwise gray bottomland. Sweat began to build beneath his flannel shirt. He spotted a narrow stream and was soon kneeling beside it.

Panter stepped into the creek and drank. Nick scooped water from the creek with his hands. The water tasted heavy in minerals, as though it flowed from the rocks directly. After he had his fill, he sat by the bank. Panter sat next to him. Nick rubbed his chin.

"I don't know about you, but I'm in monumental need of food." Panter studied him as though deciphering what was spoken.

A slender trout flittered about in the shallow water, and Nick wished for his pole net. Bees hummed, hovering above jonquils and dwarf iris that grew creek side. Nick studied the movement of the rotund insects, impressed with their persistence in finding an open bloom. The babble of water distracted Panter, and he appeared mesmerized by the constant push of water downstream. Nick looked about the concave valley. Cloaked in its own reverence, tangled in its own serenity, as though the inhabitants had either fled to other valleys, or word had perhaps spread that a crazy mountain man was roaming their hollow.

Nick stood, looking about. If he was to make it home by dusk, he needed to find work soon. He chose to walk the opposite direction. He came upon a narrow flatland where the valley tightened into a separate hollow, and in the distance, someone was on their knees working a small planting field. Ax again placed over his shoulder, he approached, the road narrowing. The person working the field wore a khaki bonnet. She was busy at her task, and Nick stayed at the roadside.

"Hidy," he said, the ax blade resting on the dirt road.

The woman straightened her back and peered from underneath the bonnet. "Hidy."

"Don't mean to be a bother, but would you be in need of firewood? I got my ax all sharpened and I'm quite good at fellin' trees." She rubbed her hand along her forehead, moving long strands of hair from her face. "I don't want any money. Just a meal is all I ask."

The woman stood, looking about as though to see from where the stranger had come.

"If it's food you need, I will gladly give you some. No need to work for it."

"That's mighty kind of you, ma'am, but I don't allow charity. Do you have a need for firewood?"

"Well, I'm sure I could use some. My woodstove devours it like it's made of air."

Nick looked beyond the field to the woods. "I spot a couple of trees that appear to be dead. I can cut them, and the wood won't need to age."

She looked to where Nick gazed. "Well, that sounds like a deal. Tell you what—you get started on the tree felling. I need a good reason to stop weeding, and I'll go in and start up a meal."

"Thank you, kindly."

"I got a fat pullet that I was going to use to make dumplin's. How's that sound? I'm sure I got something the pup can eat, too."

"That sounds extra good. I'll get to cutting. Where you want the wood stacked?"

"In that shed yonder."

He approached carefully. "My name is Nick. I surely do appreciate your kindness."

"Hidy, Nick. My name is Martha. And the way I see it, I'm getting the best end of this deal."

"How do you figure?"

"I was going to fix dinner regardless. Now, I'll do that and watch my stack of firewood grow in the process. My bones have gotten too brittle to start taking an ax to a tree trunk."

He felled three trees and split the logs, Panter biting at the limbs each time a tree would fall. The aroma of the center wood roused memories of the hillsides outside St. Louis. The vision arose of the worker lying dead under the massive tree trunks sprayed about like straw. The emotionless faces of the men as they cleared that land. Like nomads with no place to call home, to wander endlessly, they carried on with their tasks as though there was nothing waiting at the end of the day other than to add some coin to their worn pockets.

Once he had stacked the wood in the shed, he spotted a well off to the side of the tiny farmhouse. A pail sat next to a hook that held the pulley. Nick was about to attach the rope to the pail when he heard, "Fill that and bring it in, would you? Dinner is ready, and you can drink all the well water you want. I have fresh buttermilk too if you care to have some."

He sat at a small table. Panter lay on the porch, a bowl of water beside him. Nick had drunk two glasses of water and a glass of buttermilk by the time Martha set the table. The warm fragrance of flour filled the air when she set the dumplings on the table. She placed a basket of biscuits with butter and preserves on the table. Crumbling two biscuits on a small plate, she poured the broth of the dumplings over them and took it outside. She smiled as Panter devoured it. She returned to the kitchen.

"Miss Martha, you have gone above and beyond. I didn't mean for you to make such a fuss."

"Nick, I haven't shared a meal with someone other than the yard cat since my husband passed six years ago. It feels good to make food for more than just me for a change. I think the pup enjoyed his too."

Martha blessed the food, and Nick gave a silent thanks as well. He waited on Martha to eat first, even though his stomach churned.

"Where are you from?" Martha asked. Her long, dark hair was streaked silver, pulled in a tight bun. Her cobalt-blue eyes sparkled, and her cheekbones were pronounced as though some aristocracy flowed through her blood. Her skin smooth and taut. Nick guessed her age to be around sixty but didn't care to ask. Sixty. Wasn't that the age he himself had reached a few years back?

"Iron Mountain," he said after the realization of his own age sunk in. "Well, Doe Valley originally."

"Iron Mountain?" she repeated. "I didn't think a body could live up on that hardened land."

"I believe I'm its only inhabitant."

"How long have you lived up there?"

"The passage of time clouds my memory. I would say around thirty years. Maybe a few more."

"Outstanding."

"In what way?"

"You built a life where no one else has. Least that we know of. That makes you a pioneer in the truest sense. I wish I had done something so daring. When I was young, I had dreams of the big city, on my own, experiencing the things that this part of the world could never bring. I dreamt of New York, of Paris. I wanted to be among those who had come for the same purpose as me, living off spur-of-the-moment whims that the city might bring to life. Living it the way I saw fit instead of how this primeval society expected me to live. But I was too afraid. Scared of the unknown. And so, I chose the safe and comfortable route."

"I wouldn't say what I done should be considered daring. I just did what was best for me."

"I say it's both daring and admirable. I only wish I could say the same about mine. It was anything but daring."

Nick placed his fork on the plate and sat back in his chair. He regarded the woman. "Do you have children?"

"Two. Joseph lives in Atlanta. Works for a large accounting firm. Silas lives in Chattanooga. Works for the Nashville and Chattanooga Railway."

"Sounds like they are quite successful."

"Oh, they are."

"Then what you accomplished in life is quite admirable. You raised a family. Raised those sons into good men. So, if we are comparing lives, I'd say you have lived the more admirable of the two."

"I guess it's normal to see our own lives as nothing of great importance."

"Perhaps. All we can do is carry on the best we can with the life we choose."

"Can I ask you something, Nick?"

After taking a sip of milk, he nodded.

"Before you retreated to the top of Iron Mountain, were you ever in kind favor of a woman?" She studied him. "Forgive me if I'm being forward."

"It's alright." He noticed Panter looking at him from the porch. "Yes, once."

"Was it a true love?"

"I thought it was." He lightly shook his head.

"Love can be fleeting."

"That is true. So, I just direct mine toward the mountain." He nodded toward the door. "And Panter."

She waved his words away. "Love the pup all you can. He will love you back. But the mountain--it's simply a collection of earth and trees." She took a breath.

Nick studied on those words and quietly finished his meal.

He scaled the road from Stoney Creek homeward, using the ax as a walking stick to steady his gait, the landscape a steady incline. The sun angled low behind him, casting his shadow long and flat as he pondered the words Martha had spoken. He studied the hardwoods at the top of the mountain, a blaze of orange from where the sun's rays flared unimpeded. Panter, stomach full, skittered about the trail, content in the journey. When they had ascended the last of the vast array of bends of the mountain trail, Nick stopped and studied the mountain floor below his boots. He was certain a pulse beat within the ground below him, for him, disproving Martha's claim that the mountain was just a collection of earth and trees.

They made their way down the narrow trail to the cabin. Through the trees, Nick noticed the skies had taken an odd shape, the plum hue replaced by something sinister in design. Leaves of the hardwoods soon bent and shook in odd silence, a forewarning of the winds that would soon race across the mountain top. A dull rumble of thunder. Nick quickened his pace. Panter whimpered and clung beside his master. The strong breeze made Nick's sweaty shirt cling to his body, chilling him as though he had descended directly into December. Lightning arced the sky, and the mountain floor rumbled beneath his feet. Rain moved slanted through the trees, and when the spray of water hit his face, he raised the ax blade to shield his eyes. He leaned forward with his head and shoulders, and the wind pushed against him as though warning him to stay away from some impending doom, from witnessing something that he need not see. The land about him flashed silver, and the crack of thunder that followed was immediate.

A tree sizzled on the ridge above him, a conglomeration of sparks as the tree split in half. Nick squatted as though he could hide, as though the storm was seeking souls that he was not willing to part with. He gathered Panter underneath him, trying to soothe the animal. Again, a bold flash ripped through the trees, and again the mountain shook. The rain came in sheets, and Nick struggled to keep his eyes open. The storm was above him now, lightning boring out from the black clouds at treetop level. Nick sat with his back against the tree, his head down, wiping the water from his eyes. The dog cowered under Nick's bent knees. It appeared as though the storm was only gaining in strength, and Nick stood, took the ax, and led Panter down the trail. He struggled to keep his balance as winds swirled from all directions. Rainwater rushed down the trail, a makeshift creek where no water source existed except from the skies above. He scooped the dog in his arms, the fur matted and soaked. The land held an ominous tone, as though night had wrested control from the daylight. An eclipse of a sordid kind. Evil appearing in each crack of lightning, in the rain beating the land into submission.

When he made it to the cabin, the storm eased. Soaked to the bone, he set the ax against the side of the cabin. Lightning had fled to the valley, thunder rumbling conspiratorial as though the method of attack below required something different altogether. As the storm pushed on to the east, dusk settled in, a different look of dark. The normal kind. Panter shook and sprayed water all about him. "It's okay, boy. The storm's over." Panter followed his master inside the cabin.

Veta noticed the shadow pass by the kitchen window. Footsteps on the porch. Early for visitors. The sun newly risen above Doe Mountain, the task of chasing shade from the flat of the valley was underway. She dried her hands on her apron and headed for the front door. She froze when she saw it open. A man stood in the doorway, in ragged clothes. A bowler hat with a hole near the crown. The room was cast gray as she had not yet built a fire, and the sun had not yet peered through the window by the door. The man stood more in silhouette than in human form.

"A stranger ain't supposed to enter a home unannounced," she said. She eyed the rifle standing in the corner near the fireplace.

His eyes followed her to the gun. "Don't get no foolish notions," he said. He turned his head as if to detect motion in the house. Veta caught the movement of something to the doorway of the kitchen, and there stood another man.

"I don't particularly care for uninvited guests, so I need you boys to leave. Get on to the porch and then ask me while I stand at my door what you are in need of."

"We can take care of ourselves just fine without your instruction," the one at the door said.

The other man walked to the corner and took the rifle. "A man could use something like this," he said. "Never know when he might come upon a dire situation." He examined the stock. "And ain't that the bluest stone you ever did see?" He looked about the room. Veta gave thought to running into the kitchen. Maybe she could make it out the back door and yell so that Bud Johnson might hear her if he were milking his cows. The man who had stood at the door glanced at a desk as if doing inventory. He picked up the trinket Ray had brought Veta from Boone when they were newly married. He put the item in his pocket.

"If you's in need of food, I'll fix you some and send you on your way," Veta said. "But you ain't got no right to my belongings."

The one with the rifle pointed it in Veta's direction. "We got right to whatever we want."

The other pointed Veta to the kitchen. "And we will take you up on your offer for food. You get in there and get to cookin', and we'll let you know when we are ready to be on our way. You appear quite lonely, so you'd think you'd be happy for company."

"You ain't company in the least. I'll fix you boys something, and then I will ask you kindly to be on your way."

She spooned lard into a skillet and placed it on the stove. Soon, the greasy chunk slid about the surface and dissolved. Keeping watch from the corner of her eye, she placed sausage patties in the skillet. Pouring water from a pail into another pan, she fidgeted as she waited on it to boil. The one who wore the hat stood in the doorway, and Veta heard rummaging coming from her bedroom. Eggs rested in a chilled basket near the door, and when she bent down to pick it up, she took a deep breath and bolted for the kitchen door. She burst through the screen, and the chickens clucked and scattered as she ran across the yard. She made it to the road as footsteps grew from behind, and when he placed his arms around her waist, she screamed. He covered her mouth, and she bit his finger. He tossed her about as though she were a ragdoll, and with legs dangling, he dragged her around the side of the house. The one with the gun waited, the rifle pointing at her. "I'll shoot you graveyard dead if you so much as make a whisper. Now get your ass inside and finish cookin'." She turned and looked over her shoulder at the Johnson farmhouse. It was eerily silent.

Her hands shook as she flipped the eggs. The pair had taken seats at the table, the one with the gun keeping it pointed at her. She thought about how much she loved Larry and Joan and hoped neither would be the one to find their mother dead on the dusty floor. She brought the food to the table and made sure to provide them with enough so they would not be disappointed with her generosity. He set the rifle across the table, his hand resting on the stock as she filled their plates. His fingers traced the blue calcite stone as though there might be some inscription of great importance.

"You got any sweet milk?" the one with the hat asked.

She nodded and walked to the icebox and removed the metal pitcher.

She stood in the kitchen while they ate, avoiding eye contact. She prayed that they simply wanted food and the rifle. Ray had gotten the rifle for his eighteenth birthday, and the gun was more for sentimental value than for hunting, as it was a reminder to Veta of days when familiar voices filled the house. When they had finished eating, they headed to the kitchen. A burlap sack lay in the corner. The one with the gun pointed at Veta. "Fill that with any meats and bread you got. Preserves." He took silver from a narrow basket. "Put this in there, too. No need to eat like animals."

Veta emptied all she had. "Okay, you got what you need. I'd like for you to leave."

The one with the gun walked up and took hold of Veta by the roots of her hair. "That ain't very neighborly of you."

"I'd never claim the likes of you as neighbors. I hope you take a train to the furthest reaches of the world. No place in Doe Valley for the likes of you 'uns."

The blow to the back of her neck knocked her to her knees. A boot came upside her jaw, knocking her against the stove. The butt of the rifle hit her midsection, and she rolled over and placed her arms around her head. The blows from the stock of the gun against her back and hind legs caused her to become nauseous. When a boot made contact with the side of her head, everything turned to black.

Nick sat on the stump, carving limbs from a newly cut elm. He wanted climbing sticks for tomatoes and pole beans for the new crops next spring. He had prayed God would bless the mountain with rain when the planting season arrived. The recent lack of production had him figuring he should be better prepared, ready for the elements, and allow for growing food so that there would be no dependence on those in the valley. As he whittled away side limbs and greenery, Panter rose from beside Nick's feet, growling. He took for the trees, barking, and Nick stood to see what had caught his attention. Sam Lowe waved, a rifle leaning over his shoulder. Nick called Panter back to his side, taking hold of the kerchief collar he'd draped around the dog's neck days earlier. "Easy, pup," Nick said. "This 'un means us no harm."

Nick filled a cup with water and handed it to Sam when he entered the camp. "Much obliged," Sam said. "The day has warmed."

"Surely you've not come for bear," Nick said.

"You made it clear bear weren't to be hunted on Iron Mountain. It's deer I'm after. Can't you tell by the size of my gun? It wouldn't do nothing to a bear except agitate him."

"I appreciate you biding by my request. If you're hungry, I got persimmon preserves and hardtack. Hand me that water jug of your'n and I'll refill it."

"Much obliged. You got you a new house guest, I see." The dog sat next to Nick, eyeing the visitor.

"He's a good mate. Panter's his name."

Sam observed the dog breathing heavily. "Fittin' name." Sam took a seat in the cane chair and drank water. "It sure was a dry summer."

"That it was."

"Bet it was hard plowing that soil."

"It was a battle. A losing one, I'm afraid."

"You need an ox or a mule. I know of a man in Shady who has one for sale. He buys bearskins from me. I could see if he was interested in selling it at a fair price."

Nick pointed to the barn. "I got me one. My uncle, Jerico, give it to me. Makes plowing tolerable. But when the land is this dry, it's all the steer can do to move that plow."

"You got all the necessities to make it work."

"As long as the rains come. It's looking fairly bleak as of now."

"We stand at the mercy of our Creator. That's why I hunt instead of working the plow. As long as there are furry beasts and fowls of the air, I've got a surefire way to keep hunger from visiting my table."

"If the rains don't come soon, you might be a findin' that the animals have headed off for better circumstances. Bear and deer won't stay where there's no foliage, no berries, no honeysuckle. Then what will you do?"

"I guess I'll grab a fishing pole. Long as the creeks don't dry up, I got a way to keep fed."

"Well, won't do us good to talk about things we can't control."

"I agree."

"I'll put the hardtack and preserves in a poke for you."

"Appreciate the kindness, Nick."

The sun dropped beyond Holston Mountain. The hardwoods were losing shape, their features dissolving into the grainy canvas, the painter's brush relegating the scene to memory. The lilac sky appeared unwilling to relinquish its hold on the world, fighting to keep the crystal display of stars from appearing. Nick set two logs on the fire pit. He had shot a groundhog earlier that day, and under the warmth of the fall afternoon, he added the dark, coarse meat to the briny water where taters and rhubarb rolled and turned in the iron pot. He placed the pot on the hook above the fire. Panter lay beside the chair, his eyes following Nick's every move. Nick removed a jug from the shelf above the doorway. With nothing else to barter, Ed Shealy had offered the jug of moonshine for squirrel jerky. Nick had offered the meat for free, but Ed wouldn't accept charity. Nick never had much desire for the drink, but looking out at the peace of the early evening, the purity of what God had presented to him on the mountain, he reckoned a toast was in order.

He raised the cup, nodded his appreciation, and took a sip. "Lord-a-mercy, Panter. This is potent. You best stick to the spring water."

Panter rose to his feet, growling. Nick spotted two figures approaching. Unfamiliar silhouettes. He stood and moved around the cook fire so that the light of the flame wouldn't shield his view. One carried a rifle over his shoulder. Hunters, perhaps. Nick touched the knife strapped to his belt and verified the location of his rifle in the doorway. When they came into close proximity, the light from the fire gave shape to their faces. Hunters or not, they were new to Iron Mountain.

"Hidy," the one with the rifle said.

Nick nodded, studying the pair. Panter growled, and when he began to charge the men, Nick took hold of his collar. "Easy, pup. Easy." The dog sat and eyed the visitors. "You boys been hunting?"

The other one held up a sack he carried. "Yep."

Nick studied the outline of the sack best he could in the faded light. "Squirrel?"

"You'd be right."

"Late to be hunting. You don't appear to be carrying a light source."

"We got a campsite a ways back over the ridge. Saw your fire and thought we'd stop." He looked at the jug. "Say, we have worked up quite a thirst. Mind if we share your jug with you?" Panter growled as the man came closer. Nick placed his hand to the dog's head. "The pup can get a bit protective." He studied the man. "Let me get you spring water. This here drink ain't of the thirst-quenching kind."

The man placed the sack on the ground and sat on the stump. Nick again regarded the peculiar shapes within the sack. The other man took the straight-backed chair and sat. He wore a bowler hat. There appeared to be a tear in it, though perhaps it was just the fire's light distorting the hat's pattern. Nick walked around the fire, and Panter retreated to his side, standing. The one with the gun set it across the barrel drum. "To be honest, it's the liquid in the jug that I have a hankerin' for this evenin'. Mind if I have a taste?"

The one on the stump stood and came around the fire to where Nick stood. "I'll be happy to go first." The stranger took the handle by the jug and walked back to the stump. He turned the jug back and gasped. "Damn, that's good squeezin's." He handed it to his partner, and he took a sip.

"Never seen you fellas before," Nick said. "Where you from?"

The one who'd carried the rifle turned the jug back and took another long sip. Sitting down, he said, "Aberdeen."

"You crossed the state line and scaled Iron Mountain just for squirrels? Surely there are plenty around the hills of Aberdeen."

"Let's just say we were looking for a change of scenery and to compare the meat of Iron Mountain squirrel to them mealy ones we got back home."

"I went through Aberdeen by train back in seventy-seven," Nick said. "I wonder if it's changed much since then." Nick walked around the fire to retrieve the jug. He glanced at the rifle and returned to his seat. He turned the jug back in a fake sipping motion. The men regarded each other. Nick studied the darkening skies. "Going to be hard to find your way back to camp soon."

"We're used to scurrying around at night," said the one next to the rifle. "Nocturnal, I think, is the word. We got coon eyes you might say."

Nick nodded.

"This is mighty fine liquor. Would you happen to have a spare jug we might take with us to camp?" The one on the stump studied the cabin, peering through the open door where the gentle fire lit up the one-room shanty. Nick tried to follow the man's gaze to the cabin.

"I got a spare jug." He stood. "Panter and me will fetch it from the cabin. If he don't accompany me, he might be tempted to take a bite out of your legs." He headed to the doorway.

"We don't mind gettin' it for you," the one with the gun said. "You take a seat."

"Just being neighborly. You're guests." Nick walked inside and returned with his rifle pointed at the one who sat next to the barrel.

"Easy, old man," the stranger said. "No need to pull out weapons."

"Where did you get that rifle?" Nick asked. Panter scurried around the side of the fire and growled at the man who sat in the chair. Nick walked around the other side of the fire and pointed the gun at the other one.

"I got it from my pappy years ago." He slid his hand to the barrel.

"Don't get no ideas," Nick said, the barrel of his rifle pointed at the man's face. He slowly lifted the rifle from the wooden barrel. He held it closer and studied the stone. "That rifle belongs to Miss Veta in Doe Valley. What the hell are you doing with it?"

"I don't know what you're talking about. I told you, that's my rifle."

"You better hope you ain't hurt the woman. I'll shoot you both. Carry you back up yonder. Let the creatures of the night have their fill of you. No one will ever know where the hell you went. And Hell is where you'll be going, I'll guarantee you that."

While pointing the rifle, Nick took two pieces of rope from a nearby box which held a small ax and gloves. He tossed one to the man seated by the fire. "Take this and tie your friend to that tree." Panter stood next to Nick, who stood next to the fire, pointing the rifle at the men. The one with the hat sat against the maple, staring at Nick as he placed his hands behind the tree to where they met. His partner tied the wrists together, and Nick eased forward. "Make it tight and secure." After he was done, Nick guided him to sit against another tree. Panter stood in front of the man, a slight growl. Nick removed his belt and placed it around the front of the man's neck, pulling it tight and around the tree to where his head was flush against the trunk. Once it was secured, Nick tied the man's hands around the back of the trunk. When it was knotted, Nick removed the belt. He fetched two wool blankets from the cabin and placed them over the torso of the men. "It might get a bit cold during the night."

"It would be wise for you to let us go," said the one who had carried Veta's gun into camp. "We'll head off the mountain and forget this ever happened. Otherwise, we might return some night when you's fast asleep and slice your throat and hang that dog from a tree."

"I reckon it would be a better plan to take this rifle on back to its rightful owner in the morning. You better pray she's in good enough shape to accept it."

"I would sleep with my eyes open if I were you." Panter growled and approached the man, who kicked at the dog. "You're gonna make a tasty meal for the buzzards."

Nick drove his gun barrel into the man's knee, and the man winced.

"The hell?"

"Don't badger my dog."

Veta lay in her bed, eyes caked with dried tears. She placed her hand cautiously to her cheek. Dull pain throbbed along her face. She attempted to roll on her side, but her ribs ached as though they were cutting a hole inside her. She wanted to tend to the gash in her face, but her body was in too much pain for her to rise. When she heard the creak of wagon wheels, she broke into a sweat. Had they returned? She forced herself from the bed and made her way to the kitchen, grabbing a carving knife. Her heart pounded. She thought to run, but she would not give in. She would protect her home or die in the process. She ran to the door and peered out the edge of the window. Nick was placing the rein of his ox to the fence post. He carried a rifle. As he walked to the door, she slowly opened it. When his eyes met hers, his face filled with anger. She fell into his arms.

"Miss Veta, are you alright?"

She nodded as she cried against his coat.

"I brought your gun back."

She pulled away from him and looked at the stock. "I thought that was gone forever. Where did you find it?"

He nodded toward the cart. "They wandered on up to my cabin last evenin'. Knew there was something untrusting about them and then I saw they had your gun." He studied her face. "My Lord, are you okay?"

Again, she nodded, her eyes fixated on the men in the back of the cart.

"I'm taking them to the jail. My guess is Sheriff Adams is going to need you to identify the two and explain what happened. Do you think you can do that?"

"Ain't gonna let what they did scare me from doing what needs to be done. I've got a mind to take that rifle and blow their guts out all over the valley."

"I can't blame you for doing so, but we best let the sheriff administer justice."

"I can't thank you enough for bringing the gun back. This was one of the few things I have that was Ray's. Getting the tar whooped out of me weren't nothin' in comparison. Thinking of Ray's gun gone forever, in the hands of them cowards, is what would have hurt me most."

"You don't have to worry about that, Miss Veta. Now, you go tend to yourself and let me haul these two to the jailer. I'll be back shortly and carry you to the sheriff if he's ready for you."

"Don't need no tending to." She caressed the gun. "Thank you again."

The man with the bowler hat glanced at her. A smirk.

"Well, I best get a move on," Nick said. He returned to the post and loosened the leather strap. He turned the ox toward the road and began to walk alongside the animal. When the shot of the rifle cracked across the valley, he pulled on the rein to steady the ox. A hat landed in the dusty road. The man on the cart's eyes grew wide when he spotted Veta pointing her rifle at him.

"Consider yourself lucky I only shot the hat off your head," she said. "I've a mind to make the next shot right between your eyes."

Nick hurried to Veta and lowered the gun. "Miss Veta, we can't take matters into our own hands. Let the law run its course."

"They ever come back on my land, the law will run its course, all right. My law. And the penalty will be death, I'll guarantee you that."

She stared at them, measuring the fear in their eyes as Nick led them down the road.

| 26 |

Nick folded the blanket and spread it across the shadowed ground. Panter's silhouette moved beside him when he dropped to his knees. The ground was cool beneath him as he rolled onto his back. The night sky was strange, foreign. The planting field next to where they laid held vague depth. Panter laid his head across Nick's chest. Nick nestled the dog's head into the fold of his arms, an added pillow on the wool blanket. Above them, stars were scattered across the vast sky and Nick wondered if even God knew their number. And yet on that night, their sparkle was muted as violet and mint-green streaks and waves rose above the horizon as though some beast, born in folklore, had cast bands of preternatural colors into the heavens from some mountaintop beyond Nick's view. He reckoned this occurrence to be one never seen, as surely this phenomenon would have been told to him by prior generations. Beyond the waves and bands, the stars appeared to expand concentric to the corners of the heavens as though they sought to flee something they didn't understand. Nick marveled at the sight and chuckled, thinking God had created it just for Nick's eyes, for his entertainment. *Do not be conformed to this world.* He recalled Preacher Cole reading that verse from the pulpit when he was a boy. Had God conjured the view to reward Nick for not falling into the ways of the world? Nick wondered if some day, long after he had departed this world, would he be able to look down upon Iron Mountain. Would he recall it? Would he remember how it saved him?

He rubbed Panter's back, and the dog licked Nick's cheek. "Sure glad you paid me no mind when I told you not to follow me up the mountain that first evenin'." He scratched the dog's chin. A shooting star emerged behind the violet and green shroud, racing as though it might outrun its own demise. Its silent death appeared merciful in nature, its existence relegated to rumor, something that may have just been the mind playing tricks on The Hermit.

The newly fallen snow held Shady Valley in deep slumber. Shrouded in silence, the sun made its appearance above the skyline of Iron Mountain. Nick stood beside the bank of Low Gap Branch, watching the crested sun crystallize the shadowy, snow-laced valley until it appeared embers seared beneath it. The mountaintop above the valley was tinged white from the ice that had formed in that high country, a sharp contrast to the pale, leafless hardwoods at the base of the mountain.

The hum of Low Gap kept Nick company as he walked along the narrow creek. The canvas glove covering his hand surrounded the maple stick of the gill net he carried. He held the twine toward the rising sun, checking for kinks or inconsistencies. He checked the four sticks that held the cylindrical net, and the weighted stones tied to the mouth of the device. He gave the twine a gentle tug to test its durability. Easing to the bank, he studied the shallow stream for movement outside of the normal flow of water. The creek ran fast, a continual churning where water lapped white and frothy against the endless assemblage of rocks. Kneeling, a burlap sack lying across his shoulder, he searched for the orange and gray brook trout that inhabited Low Gap. The creek was transparent on that morning, the sun not yet high enough to elicit a reflection of the sky above the waters.

He moved alongside the stream, studying, watching. He noticed where rocks had narrowed the flow of the water, pushing it to the right flank of the bank. He stepped into the creek, the force against his boots making him steady himself as he walked. He placed the net where the water narrowed, positioning it so that the stones sat on the creek bottom to prevent the force of the water from carrying the net downstream. With a rope tied to one of the sticks, he loosened the slack and exited the creek.

Sitting on the burlap sack to keep his overalls from getting wet from the snowy bank, Nick held the rope and waited. He missed having Panter beside him, but the snow and wet conditions were something that would have slowed the journey off the mountain. He had left the pup fed and happy, sleeping dreamily in the cabin.

Nick looked at his coat sleeves. They were frayed and brittle, offering little protection against the morning cold. Idle time could lead a man to ponder decisions made, roads chosen, and it was this idleness that Nick sought to avoid. He followed the shadows from the tree line, running long and one-dimensional across the valley, curious as to how the sun could flatten the shape of something as mighty as the chestnuts, elms, and maples. Symbolic, perhaps, of the flattening the world could make of a man's spirit. He looked along the bank to where a tiny pool had gathered, the smooth rocks gray and purple. Something dull and odd-shaped caught his attention. When he had knelt by the pool, he removed his glove and ran his fingers along the bottom. The water stung. He felt a sharp edge and loosened it from the creek floor. He held the arrowhead to where the sun hit it directly and examined it. Half the length of his forefinger. A faded shade of purple. He ran his finger along the body, wondering if the ridged texture had been there since it was constructed, or whether the constant flow of creek water had created the texture through the passage of time.

He felt a tug and turned his gaze toward the creek. He placed the arrowhead in his coat pocket and spotted movement in the net. Alternating hands, he pulled the rope to keep it taut. Cautiously, he waded the creek, lifting the rope, the net now clear of the water. He carried it to the bank, where he emptied the trout into the sack. The burlap bag flopped as he set it in the small pool where he had found the arrowhead. He returned the net to the spot in the creek. The ground was cold against his backside as the sack that had kept him dry now kept the captured fish from swimming away.

When Nick had caught his seventh fish, the sun was at its apex. The snow under him had melted from the body heat, and the day had warmed to where he had removed his hat and canvas gloves. He lifted the sack, shook what water he could from it, and placed it over his shoulder. He carried the trap with his free hand and began the trip home. The valley still appeared as though it was in some form of hibernation. He spotted a farmhouse on the hill just below the tree line, where a man tossed bales of hay over a log fence. A handful of cows had gathered along the railing, waiting impatiently for their food. A caramel-colored horse came running from underneath the overhang of a barn, sprinting across the snowy field to join in the feast.

As he walked the powdered road toward Iron Mountain, he came upon a small, faded-wood home set close to the road. Beside the house, three children of various ages and sizes had assembled snow into the shape of a small person. The oldest, a boy who appeared to be perhaps ten, pushed sticks into the snowman, giving it the appearance of arms. The two younger ones, both girls, stood by, holding items to complete the look. One, who appeared not quite as old as the boy, placed a gray wool scarf around the neck. The boy placed two pieces of coal into the head of the snowman, giving it the appearance of eyes. The smallest of the group, who looked to be about five, was lifted by the boy, and she gently pushed a corncob pipe into the snow orb. When the boy set her down, he removed his wool cap and placed it on the head of their creation. While admiring their work, the littlest one spotted Nick, who stood roadside watching the transformation unfold. She removed something from her coat pocket and ran to where Nick stood. Standing before the stranger, she opened her hand, and on the glove was a piece of maple candy. She offered it up to Nick.

"Git away from that man," came a gruff shout from the flimsy porch. In the doorway, a woman donned in a green sweater and scarf tied tightly around her head, a broom in her hand, approached the porch steps. "Come back into the yard, Mary."

The girl turned back toward the house and regarded the woman. "I's just giving him some candy, Mama. He looks to be hungry."

"I don't care what he looks to be. He's that hermit what lives way back in the mountain. You git from that man right now and back in this house before I tan yore hide."

Mary frowned and took to running until she stood in front of the porch. When the front door closed, she smiled and waved at Nick. He returned the wave before continuing his walk. The road soon bent, and the land before him rose like some wave newly formed. The backside of the mountain was painted crystal white, and he reckoned the welcoming of it the one constant of his world. Standing in the road, regarding the peacefulness of it all, the soft sound of snow crunching beneath boots came upon him. He turned and spotted Mary running. Nick was fearful of the impending trouble awaiting the child if her mother caught her.

When she had reached him, he knelt, and she handed him the candy. "Here, mister. You don't look like you et in a while. Take this candy."

Nick smiled. "Thank you, Miss Mary." He set his poke on the snow and removed the Indian arrowhead from his coat pocket. "Now, you take this. I just found it down in Low Gap. No need to tell anybody where it come from." She took the arrowhead. "It's supposed to bring the owner prosperity."

"Prosperity? Never heard of such."

Nick laughed. "That means you'll always have taters on the table when you's hungry. Maybe some candy too when you been extra good."

She smiled and rubbed the arrowhead.

"Now, you best get on back home before you get into trouble. And thank you kindly for the candy. I'm going to save it till I get home so I'll have something to look forward to."

She regarded the arrowhead as something mystical and smiled. He watched her tiny legs churn through the snow back home. When she had reached the front yard, she turned and waved. Nick returned the wave.

| 27 |

His bones ached. There was a slowness to his gait as he walked from the privy to the cabin. Glancing in the mirror that hung from the sideboard near the cabin door, he noticed a slight arch in his once broad shoulders. The mirror had become useless other than to confirm that the days of the world were fleeting, that any news he sought from that mirror would be only that he still existed. Other than formulating the daily plan to ensure survival, his thoughts had become obscure, as though trying to recall past dreams. There were fleeting visions in the depths of the night of Annabeth. The what-ifs. Even an ardent mountain man couldn't help but wonder. Though the mountain had provided him with more than he could have imagined, he did miss the touch of Annabeth's skin. The tenderness of her kiss. The saltiness of her tears. He recalled the kiss from Adeline. How soft, how gentle. The innocence in her eyes. Had that innocence become stained yet by the world's iniquities?

Sunday morning. The fields of the valley were cast in a golden hue, except where shadows ran long and one-dimensional alongside the hardwoods interspersed along the dale. Doe Mountain was in a metamorphosis, shedding its bluish coat to hunter green as the sun climbed in the eastern sky. Nick was surrounded in silence, the sun warming his shoulders as he walked along the chert road of Campbell Creek. When he came upon Bethel Baptist Church, he slipped into the thick woods behind the church. He found a soft gathering of ferns and sat, hidden from view. A small window near the back of the church was open, and Nick studied the familiar design of the building as he listened to the choir singing. *Rock of ages, cleft for me, let me hide myself in*

Thee. Nick closed his eyes and took a deep breath. The congregation seemed filled with the Spirit as their voices rang out along with the choir. Nick softly hummed along, visions rising of days sitting in the front row next to Tom, struggling to keep daydreams from blurring the words of Preacher Cole. When the song was complete, a gentle stirring commenced as the churchgoers took their seats in the pews. Nick listened as the preacher began his sermon. The voice was unfamiliar. A new preacher. A new shepherd, keeping the flock safe from the perils wrought by the Evil One.

"Lookin' out at the valley as I walked to church this mornin', I marveled at the splendor of the Lord," the preacher said. "His presence is everywhere. His work is in every detail. I watched a hawk soar high above, and I gave thanks to the Lord for its power and beauty. I walked along the creek and saw trout flitterin' upstream. What a beautiful sight." There was a slight pause. "But in all the beauty of the valley, hidin' in the weeds and shadows, the Devil sets, waitin' for his chance to steal, kill, and destroy. Amen?"

"Amen," came from the congregation.

"Was that amen, or oh my?"

"Amen!"

As the preacher spoke, Nick looked beyond the church to the defiant skyline of Iron Mountain. The physical distance paled in comparison to the emotional chasm. He reasoned the spiritual distance was minimal, though Nick's church was a congregation of one, on land where the splendor of God rebuked any ill intent the Devil might have.

He lay back on the ferns and closed his eyes. He listened to the preacher's sermon, his fiery words, the urgency in saving lost souls. When the reverend had decided his message had been sufficient, his voice morphed into a soothing tone, as though to remind the congregation that all was right in God's world. The choir led them in song again, and Nick quietly slipped through the trees and back to the road. As he walked back up Campbell Creek, he began to sing. "Though like the wanderer, the sun gone down, darkness be over me, my rest a stone. Yet in my dreams, I'd be nearer, my God, to thee." The sun warmed his face. A bluebird sang out from atop a fence post.

Nick left the cabin, the burlap sack hoisted over his shoulder. He headed for the stream, Panter strutting ahead along the well-worn footpath. They walked among the bright green mayapple and ferns. The sun hung white and bold above Doe Mountain, dimming the sky to powder blue. Nick found an opening in the trees and observed Doe Valley below, a land that appeared asleep. A memory arose of him sitting next to Cora on the porch, holding a metal bucket that seemed as big as he was. Pole beans snapped between Cora's fingers, a mound of green cylinders on her lap. Nick had held the metal bucket with both hands, leaning toward her so she could add the beans to it. The memory played like a fading dream, so that the memory was relegated to short bursts of scene and dialogue.

The terrain leveled, and the rumble of the brook hummed in the distance. Nick anticipated the crisp taste of beaver tail for dinner. He planned to line his coat with the pelt to ward off the winter winds that would return in a few months. He made it to the stream, Panter stooping to drink. Through the trees, a voice echoed. A tone of strict command. A whinny, a pop of a whip, and the voice yelling out instruction. Nick walked beyond the creek and down the slight dip in the mountain to Cross Mountain Trail. He spotted a horse and buggy ascending it. When the horse had led the buggy to the peak, a second voice was heard, and a conversation began that drew Nick closer. He observed a man beside a Palomino, holding it by the reins. He appeared to be giving the horse a close inspection. He lifted the horse's front right leg and ran his fingers across the hoof. On the back of the buggy sat a young man, a fiddle across his lap. He appeared to be staring across the valley at Doe Mountain, though his gaze seemed to be focused on something within, an inner soul-searching perhaps. He sat quietly, his eyes simply gazing at what lay in the distance. As the driver checked the other legs of the horse, the young man on the buggy took his bow and held the fiddle oddly to his chest. He began to play. The melody was haunting and sad, as though a revelation of some poor fate was being acknowledged. Nick snapped his fingers and pointed to his foot, instructing Panter to remain at his heel. Nick and the dog approached carefully so as not to disturb the man's playing, and when they emerged from the woods, the man tending to the horse regarded them in some curious manner.

"Hidy," the man said, stepping in front of the horse and taking it by the reins as though it might get spooked. "Didn't expect to see anybody wanderin' round up here. If you're a huntin', I'd like to see how you coax your prey into that sack."

Nick eyed the man and patted the sack sitting across his shoulder to verify it was there. "Checking beaver traps." When he snapped his finger, Panter sat. Nick regarded the one sitting on the cart, watching him return the fiddle to his lap. He turned toward Nick.

"How do, stranger?" the fiddle player asked, as though he awaited confirmation from voice, not from sight.

Nick nodded. "You 'uns headed on over to Stoney Creek?"

"Shady Valley," the man next to the horse said, seemingly satisfied that the horse was at ease with the approaching stranger. "You travelled a might high to catch a beaver."

"I didn't travel high at all. It was downhill if anything." He couldn't help being drawn to the distant stare in the young man's eyes.

"That's a right smart-lookin' dog you got there."

"He's a good 'un."

"You set up camp around here?"

"Something like that."

"You mean of a permanent sort?'

"Got a cabin down the trail yonder."

"I heard tell of some mountain man lived somers up here in the backwoods. Would you be him?"

"That would be me."

"How about that?" the fiddler interjected. "You ain't just a made-up, tall tale."

"Shady Valley, you say?" Nick asked, trying to deflect attention. "Visiting kin?"

"No," said the older man as he patted the horse. "G.B., here, has got a concert of sorts to play at some shindig Squar Lloyd is a puttin' on. I think it's more a reminder to the folks of Shady that he is still the wealthiest man in East Tennessee."

"Step closer," G.B. said to Nick. "Come to the buggy if you will."

Nick warily approached, the dog following closely. When Nick stood in front of the musician, the stature of him gave Nick thought that he was just a boy. But upon closer inspection, he could see he was a man, though, perhaps, not yet exposed to the hard ways of life. Studying the man's face, he noticed his eyes lacked depth, a shallowness as though the eyes served no purpose other than to occupy the space of their own sockets. G.B. turned his head slightly as though he searched for some sound that had no source.

"Hidy," the young man said with a nod. He extended his hand. "Name is G.B. Grayson. From down Laurel Bloomery way."

"Grayson, from Laurel Bloomery," Nick repeated. "Any relation to the Grayson that tracked down Tom Dula?"

"That'd be my uncle, James. He caught Tom somers down Doe Valley."

"It was down Doe Creek, a stone's throw from where I was raised by kin."

"Is that a fact?"

"Word was that the James wanted to catch Tom before the posse got to him, as they would have tossed a rope across a tree limb and hung him right there and then."

"Uncle James wanted Tom to get a fair trial and weren't about to let some gang of men decide Tom's fate."

"Don't know how fair a trial it was. I heard tell that Ann Melton kilt that Foster gal. Not Tom."

"I guess we'll never know. You say you was raised by kin?"

"They took me in when I was a young 'un after my folks died from the Consumption."

"We share a similar fate. I lost my folks when I was a boy. Uncle Billy here took me in and has cared fer me ever since." He leaned forward. "Step a bit closer. My sight ability is lacking as you mighta figgered. When I was maybe two, my ma had pulled my crib to the window one mornin' so I could see the snow that had fallen overnight. Well, the sun was a bright one that day, and the glare off that powder was mighty powerful, and I must a stared at it a bit too long. Was more than my eyes could handle. Since that day, the world is a pale blur."

"Sorry you were put in such circumstances," Nick said, not sure whether to look the boy in his eyes, or to glance elsewhere so as not to give the impression he was staring at the man's unfortunate disposition.

"Can't be helped." He held his fiddle and bow in front of him, raised above his head. "I don't need good sight to play this fiddle."

"From what I just heard, you seem to have quite a mastery of it."

"Thank you, kindly. Would you care for me to play you a song?"

Nick looked at Billy, who nodded approval.

"We got time," Billy said. "Besides, it will give Earline here a chance to catch her breath." He stroked the horse's neck.

G.B. placed the fiddle to his shoulder, and when he touched the bow to the strings, a melodic sound arose that Nick never imagined could emanate across that remote land. Chords rose and fell in smooth pitch, and the musician led into humming as if it were a separate instrument he possessed. Nick closed his eyes, and it sounded as though two fiddlers were sitting on the back of that splintered wagon. Nick caught his foot tapping to the beat, and when he opened his eyes, he looked about the mountain, a perfect marriage of setting and song. The music reverberated through the trees, and the land softened, and when the fiddler sang about some short life of trouble, it was as though this man had acknowledged some acceptance of the fate bestowed upon him. Nick cast his eyes toward the valley, the music penetrating his soul as if to verify that misery came to all who resided below. As the song continued, the music man alternated between words sung and spirited humming, as though not sure which way the music was supposed to guide him.

G.B. finished the song and lowered the fiddle to his lap. "Still working on the lyrics for this one as you mighta deduced. Short Life of Trouble is what I'm a callin' it. We all have trouble in our lives, but it's unique to each and no one can know or share the trouble another has suffered." He gently placed the bow alongside the fiddle. "What would your name be, mister?"

"Nick," he said. "Nick Grindstaff." The name sounded foreign as it had been years since he had spoken it aloud.

G.B. tilted his fedora back from his head and scratched his forehead. "I reckoned all the talk about you was purely mythical. You are legendary down in the valley."

"There's nothing legendary about me. I just live free from the burdens of the world below. The hardness of the land up here don't compare to the meanness in the valley and beyond."

"I think you're castin' a wide net," G.B. said as Billy seemed enthralled in the nature and direction of the conversation. "I think you have to take the heart of a man on a case-by-case basis. Maybe it's because I don't have the years behind me as you do, and so I can't speak from experience in a manner like you. I guess I'm a bit sheltered in that most of the people I come across are at events I been asked to play. The settings are festive, and maybe that's in part because of this fiddle. Maybe I won't have the right to speak of what's in the hearts of men until I play a somber song at a gravesite, or in the field where the farmer toils to feed his family."

"Might be wise to keep playing events that are jolly in nature. Keep your distance from the harshness."

"If a man hides behind the mask of merriness, that will keep him from experiencing the spectrum of emotion. To be honest with you, I ain't yet experienced the love of a young lady, and I worry that my lack of sight has created a mask that keeps others from seeing what's behind it, from seeing into the depths of me. And I think I'd rather chance the possible heartache that might foller just to know I've felt the experience, at least for a short while. To be honest, I want to know what it feels like to learn what's in a young gal's heart. I don't mind sayin' there's a hollowness inside when I play for others to sing and dance to, without ever bein' one who gets to participate. It puts a sadness on my heart I can't explain."

"Well, I'm not one to take advice from. I know the joy a woman's love can provide. But I also know the pain when that love is taken away and given to someone else. And I can't say which emotion affects the heart more. Looking back, I wish I had never had to weigh the two. So, take that for what it's worth. As you said, no man can share in another's happiness or sadness. Each walks his own path. And my path stays on this mountain. Godspeed in the path you choose, whether it's filled with joy or heartache." Nick nodded at the uncle. "I need to be checkin' my traps. Thank you kindly for the music. Best of luck with your fiddle playing and I hope someday people from all over will get to hear what my ears just did."

G.B. extended his hand once again, and Nick took it. "Goodbye, Nick. May you find music in the mountain breeze, in the rustling of the leaves, in the voice of the songbirds." The fiddle player grinned. "I mighta just found lyrics to a new song."

Nick and Panter entered the woods and headed to the creek.

There was movement in the rippled water. Nick was crouched behind a spruce pine, Panter watching intently as the beaver scampered across the shallow creek. The two were trying to guide the animal toward the trap, mentally. The plump creature seemed drawn to the musk oil scent. It sniffed the steel trap, hesitant, its coat sheening under the noonday sun. When it stepped onto the trap, it became ensnared, and Nick scampered to the creek. The weight of the trap's claws kept the beaver under the water until Nick had determined the creature was drowned. He raised the trap and opened it, soon sliding the animal into his burlap sack. Panter danced about Nick as though he wanted to make sure the animal was still in the sack.

Nick headed toward the cabin, the wet, bulky sack flung over his shoulder. This phantom among the hardwoods, a myth to some, trekking through the backwoods. Someday, his boot prints would fade into the gray of the world as would his story. A man relegated to debate on his existence. His shadow accompanied him, fading and reemerging under the heavy timber canopy like some voiceless companion. The land was as mesmerizing as the first time he walked upon it. The hardwoods stood barren, tall, lifeless. He came upon a chestnut tree, the sheer width of it larger than his cabin. The air contained a sharpness, and it tickled his lungs when he inhaled.

Spring would soon arrive, and the view of Doe Valley would blur except through narrow gaps where limbs didn't reach. The sun had risen to its midday position. Nick came upon the switchback he'd carved out well over thirty years prior to ease scaling the rise of the land. Growing up in the valley, he assumed the top of Iron Mountain was an even plane. It was the peak of the mountain, after all. He hadn't noticed the dips and rises from below. It had always appeared as one massive divide, surely designed to protect Doe Valley and its inhabitants. He had no clue then that the divide was a charcoal-gray mirage. His time on the mountain revealed layers within it, disclosing that mere observation of something or someone revealed nothing. Iron Mountain had revealed more and more tiers, and not just of the mountain, but within himself.

He took a seat on a narrow bank, keeping in mind the limited time he had to get the beaver dressed, the meat processed. Panter sat beside him, and Nick rubbed the dog's chin. What was time, anyway? He had come to realize the finiteness of it all. Of his life, to be exact. He pondered how quickly the path he'd carved would fade after he was gone from the world. How many seasons of change, the falling of leaves, the strong winds, the bitter snow, before the path was erased? Would he be considered a legend, a myth, or perhaps something in between? Would he be considered at all? As surely as the trees around him would someday fall to the earth, slowly rotting in the soil, removing all traces they existed, surely the same would apply to him. No matter the path he chose, in the end, it would fade to nothing more than a faint memory. He glanced toward Doe Mountain, studying the skyline and noticing the slight variations in elevation, and pondered what layers might be revealed on that mountain. He'd not heard of others living on it, but he wondered if the mountain had a replication of him. Of *the Hermit*. He sometimes pondered the meaning of the title given him. The world could label him. He couldn't stop that. He didn't care what they thought. They held no dominion over him. Only the mountain could. And only God in the afterlife.

Patches of moss clung to the scattering of rocks around him. Panter lay at Nick's feet, asleep. Nick studied the vast number of stones, their manner of location, and the wide array of sizes. Had God placed them there, one by one? Had He made a clean brushing sweep and stirred the mountain so that the rocks were jarred loose from the base of the land? Questions stirred within him that he reckoned would never have entered his thoughts had he still lived in the valley. But they were questions of creation, not of the inner workings of mankind. What answers the mountain provided he gladly accepted. What it didn't, he reckoned, was something that would come in its due time, or perhaps, not at all. And that gave him peace.

He regarded his companion and snapped his fingers. "Ready to go home, boy?"

They headed down the trail to the cabin.

Nick sat on his bed, the firelight illuminating the pages of the book. His fingers ached from carrying firewood from the barn earlier. *The Call of the Wild.* He'd found the book in a store in Damascus. One morning, he had decided to gather cranberries from the marshes in Shady Valley. He had brought his fish trap to gather up the fruit. When he had filled the trap, he recalled what William Dowell had told him about the giant wall known as Backbone Rock. It had been blasted by engineers to create a tunnel for trains to pass through. And so, he had found where the train exited Shady Valley, following it to Backbone Rock. When he reached the formation, he stood on the track under it, the aroma of the basket of cranberries easing through the narrow, twenty-foot tunnel. He studied the proximity of Damascus from Shady Valley, and a wandering itch overcame him. The day was still early, and he had time to explore. Finding a cool spot to hold his cranberry-filled trap, he made the four-mile trek to Damascus. Gentry's Mercantile was the place that caught his eye when he entered the town.

He had found the collections of items in Gentry's to be an odd and interesting assortment. Tiny porcelain figurines brightly decorated from the Old Country. A souvenir spoon from the 1893 Chicago World's Fair, an engraved ship in the curvature of the spoon. Another from Boston with an engraving of The Old South Church. He wondered the tools necessary to create such tiny images. And there was the book. The title alone caught his eye. He noticed the published date on the front page. Nineteen-zero-three. Twelve years had passed since the release of the book. Nick brushed his finger along the worn pages, wondering who might be the original owner. How many hands had held it in those years? He spotted the three-cent asking price for the book and wished he had carried some sort of barter. A cold Johnnycake with cured squirrel in his coat pocket was not a likely bartering chip. When the offer was made to the store owner, the man simply nodded and told Nick to consider the book a gift.

When he was a boy, Cora told him that the mind needed to be worked like a plow. It was one of the reasons Nick excelled in school. *Call of the Wild*, *The Last of the Mohicans*, and the Bible were the only books in his cabin, and he had spent many days reading by the fire while lying on his bed. The setting of the Yukon in *Call of the Wild* seemed to Nick a great frontier, and he wondered how it compared with Iron Mountain. As he began to read the book, trees creaked above the cabin, singing a forlorn tune. He heard something peculiar outside of that melody. He placed his book on his lap, turning his head to listen more clearly. There was a stirring, and he leaned out the door. Evening was coming on, the land heavy in shadow. He spotted silhouettes in the distance. Someone holding a lantern. A barrage of apples came his way, one making direct contact under his eye, knocking him to the dirt floor. On his knees, he wiped the liquid from his face. When he was able to steady himself, he peered out the doorway again. Four shapes, four silhouettes, reaching into the bin. Nick exited the cabin, curious as to what kind of gathering his apple stump had aroused. A tall, lanky boy took aim at Nick, and the apple hit the side of the cabin. Panter slipped out the door and ran toward the interlopers, barking hysterically.

"Panter! Come back here."

Panter stopped, his head and tail erect, barking as though to alert the world that ill intent had arrived. An apple landed at the dog's paws, making the pup skitter. Nick called Panter, and it reluctantly ran to Nick's side.

"What are you boys a doin'?"

"What's it look like we're doin'?" the boy said before tossing another apple at Nick. The apple smashed against a nearby maple, and Panter again barked furiously.

"Easy, Panter." He gathered the dog behind him. "You set right here." He approached the group warily. "I am happy to share, but there's no call for tossing them into the trees. They are meant to be eaten, not tossed like stones. And there's surely no call to throw them at me or my dog."

"Shut up, you old bastard," the lanky one said. He pointed his chin at a much younger boy who held the lantern. "George, here, didn't believe some crazy hermit lived all the way up this sorry ass mountain, and I wanted to show him that I ain't a liar. The climb made us hungry, so we figured we'd help ourselves."

George was on the frail side. Timid, as though aware he was in some place he ought not be. "Okay, Wiley, you ain't lying. Let's leave that man alone and go home."

Wiley responded, "Shut your mouth, George. You're the one who wanted to see him. Well, take a good look, cause there he stands. He's one grubby looking sumbitch, that's for sure."

George glanced at his feet. "I see him. Let's go on home now."

"We spend the day climbing to the top of the world, and now you want to turn round and head home. We ain't leavin' until we have some fun." He tossed another apple at Panter.

George looked at the dog, and tears formed. "This ain't right. I want to leave."

"I ought to cut your ass right here and now, you mama's boy." He raised his hand as though he was going to strike George. The young boy cowered.

"Do not harm him," Nick said. He stepped between Wiley and George. The other two boys watched silently as though waiting for instructions. One was heavy set with a buzzed haircut, and he cut his eyes at Nick.

"Keep quiet, old man," he said. "Take that mangy critter and get your ass back to that piece of shit shanty, or Wiley and me will whoop you soon as we're done with George." The boy who had remained silent nodded as though confirming he was ready to help.

Nick studied them. A misplaced unit seeking validation into manhood perhaps. "You will not lay a hand on the boy. Take his advice and head back to the valley. And put those apples back in the stump."

"Looky here, pole cat," Wiley said. "A man outnumbered such as yourself would be wise to show some respect." He pressed his forefinger into Nick's chest. "Now, are you gonna do what Marvin told you? If not, it's about to turn mean."

"Leave him alone," George said, his eyes filled with fear. "We done seen him. Let's go home without causin' no more trouble."

Wiley struck the boy across the shoulder, causing him to fall into the ferns. "Stop bitchin' like a little girl."

George grabbed a rock that was lying beneath the ferns and, from his knees, threw it at Wiley. The rock caught Wiley below the knee. Wiley lunged forward and yanked George by the shirt. He delivered a blow to George's jaw, and the boy fell limp. Marvin stepped forward and kicked George in the midsection. Wiley landed another blow, and the young boy curled into a fetal position, whimpering. Nick pulled Marvin by the shirt so that the boy fell backward. Nick stepped forward toward George. When Wiley turned and took a swing at Nick, his fist was caught by Nick's thick hand. Wiley's eyes grew big. Panter ran into the fray, growling. Nick bent Wiley's fist downward, and the boy fell to his knees. Marvin leapt on Nick's back, and they tumbled into the ferns. The thick-waisted boy landed a blow to Nick's back, and Panter pulled the boy by his shirt. Dormant memories of the train attack resurfaced, and a rage rose within Nick. He tossed Marvin against a hardwood. Wiley took a swing that Nick was able to deflect, and Nick pushed him to the dirt. The boy fell hard to the ground, wincing. The fourth boy kicked at Panter, and Nick swiped the underside of his leg, knocking the boy on his backside. Wiley tried to stand, and Nick took him by the arm, twisting it until it was behind Wiley's back. Wiley cried out.

"Enough!" Nick shouted. He took Wiley by the shirt. "I want you off my land. Now!" Nick looked at George. "You okay, little 'un?" George rubbed the dirt off his sleeves and nodded. With a firm grip on Wiley's forearm, Nick said, "By God, this is the end of it. I better not see you on my land again. I guarantee it won't end well for you." He looked at George. "Boy, you need to find a different group to run with. These here fellas will only lead you to trouble."

Nick let go his grip on Wiley. "Go on, now." Wiley cut a mean look at Nick, tears welling. He attempted to speak, but Nick stopped him. "Go, while you're still able."

Panter pranced and circled the group, growling. Nick called the dog to his side. Reluctantly, the boys slipped away into the fading backdrop of the woods. George led the way, holding the lantern, four silhouettes walking ghostlike toward the downslope. Nick stroked Panter's head, looking toward the velvet sky beyond Holston. Nausea welled up inside Nick's gut upon the realization that the evil of man had made its way up to his land. The sanctity of it had been breached. The soil beneath him had been the one protector. The one truth. It had deemed man to be nothing more than a nuisance, something to be tolerated at a distance. In that moment, he reckoned his sanctuary was forever tainted.

Nick walked to the cabin, worried George was going to suffer repercussions from Wiley when they made it to the valley. The callousness in Wiley and Marvin's eyes rattled Nick, like a forewarning of something sinister garnering strength in the valley. Night was quickly setting in, casting the land in eerie shadow. An owl screeched somewhere in the distance, as if cursing the coming of night. As if cursing the land. Nick hurried into the cabin, seeking refuge inside the walls that might have become the final stronghold left in his world.

| 28 |

The winds of change blew, casting an unsettled aura on the mountain. The morning sun's brilliance went unappreciated, if not unnoticed. The whisper in the breeze became indecipherable. Surely evil gathered in the valley, conspiring to deliver affliction to the mountaintop. Something malign stirred below. Nick could sense it. Seasons came and went, seamless, nothing to distinguish one from the other. Nick toiled through the days, the months, a man emotionless, a being of habit who carried on for nothing more than the act of survival. The planting field became entangled in weeds. The bounty of the crops was sparse, blessings withheld from the sustenance they provided. There was little regard for the excess he needed to get him through the winters. Nick stayed close to home, foregoing the traps for beaver and trout in the creeks. His rifle accompanied him no matter how close he was to his cabin. He had ventured off the mountain only twice in the four seasons since the fracas with Wiley and Marvin, slipping down the back side of the mountain to Stoney Creek to swap ginseng and mayapple for flour and dry goods at William's store. Head down, conversing only with Panter when he traveled to and from the store. He kept his rifle tied to his sled. William would inquire about Nick's well-being, and Nick would respond that his presence was confirmation that he was still alive and breathing. Conversation was all limited to business discussions, while Nick eyed his surroundings as though he might be the target of some sinister plan. He had become a wary traveler in a world with some disdain he could not name. An interloper with no desire to interpret the world, to decipher its meaning, its purpose any longer.

He began to find conversation with himself at the fire pit, often times in the pale-rose light just before the world awakened. With rifle across his lap, readied for when evil would return. When the flames provided light to the land surrounding him in the predawn, the trees beyond were always dark and indistinguishable, and he debated the merits of the world. And with every discussion, the same conclusion arose that there were none. He sensed a darkness following him closely even when night was nowhere to be found, hanging close to his heel alongside Panter like some creature in a state of constant unrest. A creature intent on consuming the contents within Nick's soul.

He sat on his split-log bed, rubbing his index finger along the edge of his Bible. The leather book had been kept in a corner behind the bed, and years of soot and smoke from the cabin fireplace had created a gray, dusty film that Nick tried to wipe away with his thumb. So many contradictions in those words. It promised protection if he professed his faith, which he did as a young man. And yet the book acknowledged the power of the Evil One. Which view was he to believe? Had God turned his back from the evil in the hearts of those who had wronged Nick through the years? Where had the protection gone when evil bent their hearts and minds, guiding them like strings of vile marionettes in some morbid play? Why had God allowed a lesser being to undermine Him, to alter His plan? Surely the Devil contained more power than God had given credit.

He regarded the fire, the flames lapping the elm logs in some ceremonious, slow devouring, and Nick hesitantly opened the book. Perhaps a re-reading was in order. Surely he had misinterpreted the message in his early years. He had mistakenly clung to the words that professed the safety of the shepherd over the flock, the words that promised that all good things worked for those who believed. He had believed since being submerged in the cold baptismal pit behind Bethel Baptist Church when he was a boy. Why had that accounted for nothing?

As he flipped through the book, straining to read the faded words lit only by the fire and his oil lamp, the winds whistled through the creaks that countless harsh winters had chipped away from the cabin's walls. The hissing from the flames battled the hum of the wind, as though contradictions had been exposed and a battle had risen. For no particular reason, Nick chose the book of Ecclesiastes and came upon the verse that confirmed what he reckoned to be the truth all along about the futility of chasing the whys and whims of God. *As you do not know the path of the wind, or how the body is formed in a mother's womb, so you cannot understand the work of God, the Maker of all things.* He read the verse again, this time aloud. Nick lay back on his bed, placed the Bible across his chest, and stared at the shadows dancing on the ceiling. He felt comfort in the clarity.

Nick laid a blanket across the ox. The winds raced as though gaining momentum since the day the world began. Snow stung his face, his wide-brimmed hat pulled low on his forehead. Panter watched with unsure patience, his black fur almost completely white from the snow. The overhang of the barn hardly shielded the onslaught of the winter storm, and once he had secured the blanket, Nick hurried to the cabin. Panter ran alongside in a high gallop to scale the mounting snow, his legs disappearing into the powder with each leap.

Smoke twirled from the chimney before fading into the gray mist that smothered the cabin. Nick slipped under the poplar-limbed lattice and shook the snow from his coat and hat at the doorway. Panter shook himself of the wet powder, and when they entered the cabin, Nick sat in front of the fire. The wood supply was dwindling, and he barely gave thought to whether he had enough to get him to springtime. In years past, spring brought an end to the bitter days of winter. It brought a rebirth of the land. But it held no favor for him now. What rebirth was there? It was all pretense. Let winter be eternal, let it be the reason for permanent isolation.

The cabin shook, the winds slipping through the crevices of the cabin. Panter lay at Nick's feet, his eyes dancing red from the light of the fire. Though the fire blazed, their breaths rose in smoky haze. Man and beast. A fire that barely warmed them, they had no need or desire for anyone other than themselves. The trees outside the cabin creaked and moaned, rattling like bones of some ancient beast unsettled in its resting place. It was a melody surely no one in the valley of the disillusioned could hear or comprehend. He pulled the wool blanket over him, lay back, and studied the sturdiness of the cabin. He tried to recall the exact distance of time since he'd built it. The past a vague distortion, a sketchy collection that might carry the same weight as hearsay. The details of the cabin's creation were about the only surety contained within him, but the details of the countless days from that day forward had become a vision, some dream that could not be recalled. He tried counting back from the present by the number of winters, but all he could do was feel the reckoning the winter storm outside was inflicting. Miss Veta's pies. Jerico's passing. Marvin and Wiley. Annabeth. Someone had told him Annabeth had passed four years ago. A retelling. But who had told him of her death? Was it a dream? He wondered if she ever regretted casting him aside for Cody. The creek beside the plot of land he'd chosen. The plan to marry her on that spot. What if he had not left her for St. Louis? The money gained in big city life was powerful. Was that the only draw? Was money an excuse to experience something Johnson County could have never provided? He closed his eyes. Visions rose and faded, as though battling for control. He finally faded into a restless sleep.

He walked along a bottomed-out road. He was in a valley, and on all sides, hills rose slowly into higher ridges until they faded into the blue sky altogether. The road he walked soon turned into a field of tall grass where white blossoms sat flattened atop the reeds like butterflies stuck in some sort of animated flight where their only motion was determined by the breeze. He waded through the grass, and in the distance he spotted a tall, white house set on a hill carved out of the thick hardwoods. Smoke rose from its chimney, and there was familiarity in the setting.

He walked through the tall grass, and the sun warmed his shoulders, though the sun was nowhere to be found above. There was a familiar gen-

tleness to the air he could not name, and with each step he took toward the house on the hill, tranquility surrounded him. As he neared the home, he spotted people standing alongside the earthen road. The valley was behind him now, the woods becoming thick and prominent. The land began to climb, and the mountain range beyond the house now rose in such steep fashion that the sky became hidden. The land about him darkened, and the people alongside the road were now shrouded by some gray mist rising from the ground. He came upon the first one, a petite shape whose face was hidden by a shawl. He held some desire to speak as the need arose to ask where he was. To find out where he was going. He placed his hand on the shoulder of the small woman. "Can you tell me what place this is? I don't know where I am."

The woman lifted her head and removed the shawl. Her green eyes were calming and she smiled before placing the shawl about her face. She turned to walk away, and after a few steps, he called out to her. "Can you not tell me where I am?"

She slowly turned toward him, raising the shawl. There were deep crevices where her eyes once were, blackened holes with no depth. When she smiled, it revealed a mouth without teeth. Her chin and nose almost touched. She pointed toward the house before covering her face with the shawl. She faded into the darkness.

His heart raced as he hurried toward the house, illuminated brightly inside from oil lanterns, night suddenly down upon the land. Those along the roadside had fallen back into the darkness as well, though some held a presence of light within their bodies. When he had made it to the house, someone sat on the porch steps. He wore a narrow, low rim hat and was dressed in some pedestrian manner, sunk low on the porch, legs crossed, resting on his elbows, as though there was something important that he had reluctantly passed on to stand guard over the steps.

When Nick had reached the bottom of the steps, he looked through a window of the home. A young woman stood, holding a small boy. She appeared to be singing to him, and she would twirl gently as she sang, and the boy cackled and held close grip on her sleeves. He soon was able to hear the voice, and he knew it without reservation. As she sang, Nick softly sang along. "One for the master, one for the dame, one for the little boy who lives down the lane." He began to climb the tall steps to see his mother, and the man on the steps leaned forward.

"Hidy."

"Hidy," he returned.

"This here's an invite only soiree."

He stopped at the man's feet. "That's my mama in there." And he pointed to the child. "And that's me."

"Don't see how that can be. Ain't likely you can be two people at the same time. No matter, you have no clearance to walk on past."

"Who are you to decide who passes?"

The man pushed the bill of his hat upward, exposing himself for closer inspection. His face was that of one who had appeared to have seen much strife in his life, even though he was not an aged man. His brown eyes stood bold, even under the darkness that had fallen around them. Those eyes took fierce aim at his. "You might say I'm the one who decides anything. Everything. Done so since that serpent made that gal eat the apple."

He looked up at the window again, and a man now had his arms around the woman and the boy. His father now smiled at Nick. Tom appeared at the door. "Nick!"

Tom appeared the age of about seventeen. "Tom!" Nick climbed two steps higher, and the man on the steps leaned back on his elbows again.

"You goin' to have to leave the premises."

"I'll be damned."

"That you just might be."

Nick looked at the door and they all stood there now, motioning for Nick to come. A rage rose. "Move aside," Nick said, "or I'm going to rip your ass off these steps." He looked at the door and saw himself in the little boy. Ma and Pa calling him to come in the house. Nick climbed two more steps, and the man rose from his prone position. He stood to where he was face to face with Nick. His breath smelled of something long dead, as though a crypt freshly opened. The ground shook beneath them, and the earth began to separate. As if on a wave raised from the ocean's bottom, the steps began to separate from the house. Nick took hold of the railing and looked below the steps as they drifted from the house. There were visions of people beneath the steps, too many to count. They had their arms raised toward him, trying to latch hold of the steps that passed above. There was wailing and calls of desperation, and the man in front of him on the steps stared blankly at Nick as though the event unfolding was just a task assigned from one of a more supervisory role for which he had no choice but complete.

In the distance, the house faded into the backdrop of the mountain, swallowed by the darkness. A faint whistle blew, and the wave that carried the steps dissipated. Nick noticed the steps rested on a weed-laced train track. The steam engine roared as a train approached. Nick looked about as how to disembark before the train made impact, but all about and below were the souls of those who pleaded for him to pull them from the abyss. He grabbed hold of the protector of the steps. "Do something, you chickenshit bastard."

"Cain't undo what's already been done."

"It ain't done. It's unfolding right in front of us."

The man pointed toward the train. The conductor wore a wry smile. Rose. Her face was illuminated red from the coals shoveled by her cousins. The steam building, the speed of the train increasing, the imminent impact about to take place. Nick looked for options, but there were none. The orchestrator of the macabre play stared at Nick as though to gauge the level of fear. With Rose's face growing closer and clearer, her beauty unable to hide the evil in her eyes, Nick jumped into the abyss.

Panter's tongue licked Nick's face furiously. When he opened his eyes, he found himself kneeling behind the split-log bed, trembling. He rolled onto his backside and took Panter into his arms.

| **29** |

The black-and-yellow butterfly danced about Nick as he sat in his chair. The sun was high above the treetops, slipping through the trees so that the land was a kaleidoscope of light and shadow. The ferns and ivy on the mountain floor, the trunks of the hardwoods as they stood arrow straight, awash in the contrast of colors as though caught in the battle between winter and the impending arrival of spring. Winter had bored down on the mountain in relentless fashion, harder than Nick could remember. Perhaps age had something to do with it. The thinning of blood and the hardening of joints. He studied the back of his hands. The wrinkles, the brown spots. Fingers bony and deformed. He used them to pet Panter, who lay beside the chair, the dog now content in simply lying beside his companion. How long might those snow-laced days and nights have been without his companion at his side? A friend to listen to rambling thoughts, always turning his head slightly as if to make sure the words spoken could be interpreted correctly. With the winter snows, the soil had moistened and recharged. Perhaps the crops could be plentiful enough to feed him through the year, but he had no concern about it one way or the other. He lost all desire to travel to Stoney Creek for supplies. Cross Mountain Road had become active as horse-drawn buggies came and went. Some in the manner of business, perhaps others for the purpose of leisure. On occasion, he had spotted automobiles. Nick never thought the day would come where a machine would power someone up the side of Iron Mountain. It was surely considered progress to many, but to him, all it did was shorten the chasm between the world and the mountain. All it did was ease the effort for those to come who had no true appreciation for what the mountain stood for. If the time came to where he could only scale the mountain by automobile, it was time to be laid underneath the hickory above his cabin.

Through the tree line a stranger approached, slipping in and out of shadow, a rifle leaning against his shoulder. Nick rose from the chair and took hold of his own weapon that lay across the stump.

"Hold it right there," Nick said as he spoke from a tree's edge. "Put down your weapon."

"If it ain't the king of Iron Mountain hisself," the man said as Panter trotted to greet him. "Still looking after your kingdom, I see."

Nick studied the interloper. "What business have you here?"

With one hand on the gun, he raised the cap from his forehead with the other. "It's Sam. Sam Lowe."

Nick lowered his gun but eyed the man closely. "Set the rifle down before you step closer." Searching for familiarity. Seeking something concrete in a room of ambiguity of this man who had wandered upon his land. Sam carefully leaned his gun against an elm. He became hesitant in his steps and appeared to regard Nick in curious manner.

"State your business," Nick said.

Sam wore a curious frown. "It's me, Nick. Bear-Huntin' Sam Lowe."

"There's to be no bear huntin' on this mountain."

"I recall that proclamation you put down, what, pert near forty years ago. And I'm proud to say I've not hunted bear one on this mountain since. I just come to check on you. Winter was a hard one and I wanted to make sure you was a doin' all right."

"I can't distinguish one season from another. I'd say this land has fallen into a state of constant winter."

"I don't know. Seems like we had some days where the sun beat down in the worst kind of way." He stooped to pet the dog. "Hello, there, Panter, you old son of a gun."

"How do you know the dog's name?"

"You told it to me a decade ago. Are you all right?"

"I got no cause to complain."

Sam eased onto the stump and took a seat. "I been a huntin' coons of a night. Had no success and was ready to say the hell with it all and head home. I wonder if it's about time for this old, tired body to give up huntin' for good. But I got to put supper on the table, so to speak. So, no rest for the weary, as they say. Might I bother you for some spring water?"

Nick handed him a ladle. "Drink your fill."

Sam took a sip. "This is sweeter than any sassafras ever made. This is the kind of drink that should be bottled."

"That's a peculiar statement. I don't think you should bottle something so pure."

He took another sip and regarded Nick. "You seem a might frail. More so than my wrinkled, old ass. Your food supply get cut during the winter?"

"I don't require much in the way of food these days."

"Well, you look like you need a pot of grits and spring taters to add some meat to your bones."

Nick waved the comment off. "I got food."

Sam looked about. "I ain't heard talk of any sightings of you in years down Stoney Creek way. You doin' your barterin' somewheres else?"

"Been stayin' close to the homestead. World seems to be a closing in on me these days. All them horse-drawn buggies, and especially them automobiles coming up and across the mountain. Beats anything I ever saw. I used to could hide from troubles up here. Now, I'm exposed to the world and all its troubles."

"I roam all across this land and I don't come across trouble, other than when them boys wander up from Gentry Creek, full of liquor, ready to shoot anything that moves."

Nick ran his hand along Panter's back. "My time on this earth is winding down. I don't dwell on it. When it's time for God to call me home, I won't question it. I just hope someone will look after the pup. Would you take him?"

"That implies I'll outlive you. Roamin' around the backwoods wears on a fella. But if I am still alive, I'll fulfill your request." He scratched his chin. "You ever thought of spending your last days down in the valley, amongst kin who can help tend to you should you need it?"

"I don't need or want anyone to tend to me. When the day comes where I can't take care of myself, I hope the Lord takes me swiftly. When that time comes, I won't exactly be able to put myself under the hickory up yonder peak, so I'll need some assistance there." He looked about the land. The tall trees, the cabin, the barn in the distance and the dormant planting field. "My wish is that a hundred years after I'm dead and gone, this place is as unknown and pure as it is now. I hope my living quarters, my barn, will fall back to dust and this land will look like it's never had a body step foot on it."

"Sounds like you don't want any trace that you ever existed."

"Some men want to be immortalized. Put their mark on the world forever. That's vanity. The less a man remains known, the less his imprint, the less his name could be slandered."

"My guess is you will be talked about reverently. You might inspire others to live in such a manner."

Nick studied the land about him. A curious surveyor. "Can't see this as being a desired manner of living. It takes a certain hardness. Some surely consider me a madman." A man measuring his worth, pondering the outcome from the path he had chosen. Nick closed his eyes. He searched his memory, and the sound arose of the ax felling the trees that made the foundation for the cabin. He recalled the silence of that first night as he lay on his puncheon bed, the only sounds the pop of embers in his fireplace. Opening his eyes, he said, "Rather just fade away unremembered."

"Unremembered, maybe, once the generations who knew you also pass away. Unnoticed. That depends. I believe a tombstone with some sort of story etched into it should be erected. No idy how many people might stumble upon it way up here as time goes on, but those that do would surely be interested in your story, curious to why you inhabited this land. Maybe you will become legend one day. The tale of Nick, The Hermit, Grindstaff. Maybe books will be penned about you. All the world might know who you were. And you wouldn't have any say so in the matter."

"At that point, anything written would be pure conjecture."

Sam waved his hand in the air as though shooing away some invisible nuisance. "Enough of this talk. Would you happen to have any johnnycakes or catheads and preserves? I am overwhelmed with hunger."

"I can lather up a couple biscuits with apple butter."

Sam entered the cabin, and Nick ambled to the apple stump for a jar of apple butter. His last jar. There was a deep aching in his bones when he walked. His body was wearing thin, and he reckoned he might carry on just a while longer. When he shut the lid to the stump, a shot rang out from inside the cabin. Panter barked from outside the house, and Nick hurried along the path. He spotted Sam exiting the doorway, a bloodied rattlesnake hanging limply over his rifle barrel.

"What have you done?" Nick asked.

"A damn snake slid out from the bed, ready to strike. Would surely have sent me to the grave."

"You had no right."

"I saw it and reacted, Nick. It's a deadly creature."

"It appears the deadliest is the one holding the rifle. I'd appreciate it if you leave. And I don't care for you to return."

"Nick, it appeared ready to lunge. Self-preservation made me shoot."

"Leave this mountain."

"Nick..."

"Go."

| 30 |

Veta's fingers ached as though her bones might crumble underneath her skin. The grip she had on the jar slipped, and she placed it between her legs, tapping against the top with the dull side of a knife. After a few taps, the top loosened, and she was able to pour the pole beans into a pot. She rubbed her fingers and turned her head toward the window. The deep hum of metal rubbed against the road. An ox moved slowly toward her house. A dog ran ahead of it, head high, as though a scout for possible ambush. Nick walked beside the ox, a sled dragged behind them.

She stirred the pot to spread the beans before heading out the door. Nick brought the beast to a stop, the dog barking at Veta until Nick told him to hush. "Well, you'll never pull a surprise attack a draggin' that thing," she said. He quietly tied the ox's rein to a fence post and untied a sack from the sled.

"You be willing to trade rhubarbs and taters for a hot meal?" he asked.

"You ain't never got to trade anything for a meal. You should know that. But I'll say this--I ain't gonna turn down what you got in the poke. My tater bin ain't nothin' but bugs and dust."

She regarded him as he approached. His gait was slow, and there was a frailness to his frame. His face was sunken, and his thinned hair matted and pure silver. His walk told of a body worn by more than just time.

"Would you have a need for my ox? Getting harder to feed him and he don't pull the plow no more. Not much of a garden left to plow anyways. Maybe you could sell him if you have no need for him."

"Well, I reckon I can come up with a use for him. To tell you the truth, that ox appears older than me."

"He's still got some usage left in him. I want him to be useful and needed instead of just wasting away on the mountaintop. He'd surely enjoy a full belly."

"Lead him to the barn. Gilly Shoun just dropped off several bales, day before last. We can fatten him up a bit. While you do that, I'll slice up a couple of these taters."

He tended to the steer, Panter walking beside him. She couldn't help but study him as he led the animal to the barn. Reality of life. The wearing of the body. She wondered how much wearing had been placed on his spirit.

She was busy at the stove when he walked in. The aroma of sour sweat and old smoke overpowered the smell of food cooking on the cast-iron stove. She raised her hand to her nose to lessen the scent. Nick sat.

"Do you have anything that needs tending to?"

"Nick, you and me is gettin' to the age where we gotta let the young 'uns do the heavy lifting, the chores. Larry came to visit a couple weeks back and pretty much got things caught up. Besides, you need to save your strength for the journey back."

"I may be long in the tooth, but I can still work a farm tool."

"I'm sure you can. But you're a guest, so work is not an option."

"Well."

She kept to the stove in hopes the flavors of the food would mask the stench, but the odor was overpowering. After checking the cornbread in the stove, she took a deep breath. "Nick, I don't know any other way to say this, but you's in bad need of bathin'. I'm going to fill the tin pail on the porch with hot water. I got some lye soap and a towel. They's some of Larry's clothes he left behind you can wear while I wash the ones you got on."

"There's no need to go to that trouble."

"Listen to me when I say this is as much for my benefit as yours. When's the last time you bathed in the spring water on the mountain-top?"

He shrugged. "Don't seem that important."

"Well, it's important to those you might come around. Now, you fetch the pail from the barn, and I'll boil some water and get the necessaries."

While he bathed, she took the clothes to a wash pail behind the house. She hurried to scrub them in the wash soap, stopping to catch her breath and take in the fresh air so she could finish the task. She tied them to the line to dry.

They ate with little conversation. Nick seemed embarrassed at the stir he had caused. He appeared out of place in another man's clothes, like one forced to wear a mask at a festive ball. In the silence, she wondered if he was just content being in her presence at the table. Perhaps, they were just a pair of old bodies with yet older souls that didn't have much need left for conversation.

Veta took a sip of buttermilk. "I wish I had more to offer than cornbread and soup beans. Thank goodness you brought the taters so I could fry some up in the skillet."

"This was worth the struggle to lead the ox it off the mountain."

"Speakin' of the mountain--you ain't no spring chicken. Have you give thought to movin' on back to the valley? You know, to make it easier on you. To be where others can tend to you if need be."

"If you rely on another, you lose your worth."

"At some point, we all need help. I couldn't make it without folks like Bud Johnson, Gilly. Ole Baxter McEwen. There's no shame in accepting the assistance of another. We were put on this earth to help each other."

"I prefer to go it alone is all."

"It seems you been goin' it alone since Eve baked that apple pie for Adam. Don't you think a change of scenery might be in order?"

"The only time the scenery will change is when I'm buried beneath the mountain soil."

"And I thought my mule was stubborn."

"That mule would high tail it up the mountain if it had the option."

"That mule knows it's got it made right here."

Their tongues tired, both saying what was on their mind, they returned to the comfort each other's presence brought and continued their meal. At least for a brief while, the hardness that life had laid upon them vanished.

The house sat on top of a bald, a faded-wood sentinel. In a slice of holler barely wide enough for the structure, slopes rose angular from either side of the khaki-colored knob, as though designed not to hinder the view of Doe Mountain beyond it. The charcoal backdrop beyond the house was tinged white in the upper region where ice clung to the hardwoods. Nick approached on the grassy road, walking in the burrow of dirt tracks left by horse-drawn buggy and carts. In front of the two-story house was a porch partially hidden by a wide-branched maple. There was no movement, no sound, and Nick gave thought that maybe the home stood empty. There was a dreariness brought on by the low ceiling of clouds, as though the world had fled the holler, and other than the pale wooden home, it appeared as though the world had passed it entirely, a castaway land that served no useful purpose. When Nick entered the yard, he struggled to climb the sharp upslope. Painful were his steps. He pondered the reasoning behind such an angled yard. He made it to the porch, and when he approached the door, a long rifle barrel appeared from the darkened entrance. Nick took a step back and raised his hands.

"What are you doin' in this holler?" the gruff voice asked.

Nick squinted as he studied the large silhouette in the doorway. "John?"

The figure stepped forward, the rifle still aimed at the interloper. "Who's askin'?"

"It's Nick. Your brother."

The man lowered his aim and cautiously stepped outside the door and onto the porch. The pale light could not hide the age in his brother's face. Could not hide the boldness of the brown eyes. "What brings you up the holler?"

"You been on my mind of late."

"Why now? Our lives have passed us by, and no word from you. I just hear rumors and reports from those in Doe Valley. Some say you are some sort of hermit, some misfit."

"I pay no attention to what others say."

"You just swore off the world it appears. Swore off family. Forty years and nothing from you."

"The trail to Iron Mountain runs both ways, you know. Never saw you set foot on the mountain to visit, to see if you wanted to dispute the rumors should you see me face to face."

"Never saw a need to climb to the doorstep of Heaven just to verify you was alive."

"Can I come in?"

John pointed to two rusty metal chairs at the corner of the porch. "Set there. The indoors ain't exactly up for visitors."

They sat, regarding each other in silence, as if to verify that they were indeed brothers. "So, why after all these years?"

"I been searching for recollections of Ma and Pa of late. Can't come up with many."

"That's because you were a small young 'un. Couldn't been no more than four."

"Three, to be exact. The recollections I have are more of a feel, not a concrete memory, of their faces, their voices. You got to be around them for nine years. Surely you have memories."

"I do. But I don't dwell on them."

"What was Ma like? Was she happy? Was she gentle in the way she raised us? I seem to recall Pa as being one whose purpose was to provide what was needed to survive. Not of the emotional kind."

"Pa was always working the farm. He was concerned with our physical bein', not our emotional well-bein'." John looked toward the valley below the house. "I do remember one time when Pa let me ride on the steer while he ran the plow. He bound me upright on the back of it so I couldn't fall off. I couldn't have been but maybe six. I remember his hands seemed the size of a bear claws. He was a tall 'un, and yet he was soft spoken. Kept his talk to a minimum." He glanced at the ceiling. "Ma was always at work. The kitchen. Preparing the meals. Keeping our clothes clean. At least that's the way I remember it." He regarded Nick. "Why do you want to know this now? They been laid in the ground going on seventy years."

"It's a finality of things, I guess." Nick leaned forward in his chair, resting his elbows on his knees. His face resting now in his hands. "Our days are limited. Coming to an end. An end to what, I ain't sure. Once I'm gone, the only sign I ever existed will be an old cabin and a rickety barn. When they fade back to the mountain floor, there will be no trace at all." He searched the holler beyond the house, not in the manner of seeking an answer. Rather, for the question. "My time on the mountain ain't just been hidin' in a cabin. Though I ran from the world, I observed its intricacy from a distance. When you're part of the world, it swallows you up, so that what you see as truth is actually imagined. With Ma and Pa, I don't want it to be imagined. I want concrete evidence. When I think of them, it's become a blank canvas. I thought you'd be the one who could take that canvas and add depth. Add color."

"I don't know how much depth I can provide. Hell, could be the passage of time has rendered me unable to distinguish between memory and imagination."

They studied each other, as though artists preparing to paint what sat before them. But there were no brushes, no paint. Nothing they could bring to life. Nothing to create. If they could, what tones would the palette contain? What story could the subject's eyes tell? Would it display anything other than the weariness of life?

The brothers sat, mostly in silence. The search for memories a struggle, the search for words even more elusive. But as the day progressed, the sun content to remain hidden behind the impassive clouds, a presence arose in that lonely holler. Voices from long ago stirred. Still photos of the mind were set to motion. The abstract flew away as if on the wings of the monarch, carried about on a summer breeze, content in seeking new worlds if the wind could lead it so.

The brothers conjured up the past in a manner where verification was not sought, not needed, as though the mere mention of something made it so. For a few moments, there were shards of innocence, of a time without sadness. A feeling of family, of connection. Of the might-have-beens.

| **31** |

Veta guided the horse down Campbell Creek Road. The fields, rich in green fescue, bent lazily with the breeze under the morning sun, the summer flowers scattered about in strips of purple and gold. She reckoned a more beautiful sight never existed. She brought the horse to a halt and regarded the rolling hills melting into the base of Doe Mountain. So much time had passed, so many hard events. Snippets of joy between, keeping her world from being a constant yoke of burden. Perhaps in other worlds, life was easier. In Johnson County, life wasn't designed for easy. At least not for her kind.

Sitting on the buggy in the quiet, the only sounds bees buzzing along the nettle-leaf Sage that grew along the roadside, she thought of Ray, and how she still missed him so. She stirred up a vision of him walking toward her from a grassy knob on the back side of the creek running alongside her, a wide grin as though a prank had just been pulled at the gates of Heaven that he had come to share with her. She wondered if he saw her from those gates. Did he miss her? Did he wait impatiently for her? Perhaps he'd been deprived of cathead biscuits and sausage gravy; she the only angel who could cook such a meal. Possibly stoves were made of gold instead of iron.

She pondered the first people who witnessed the beauty of Doe Valley. Was it the splendor of these fields set between purple-laced Iron Mountain to the north and Doe to the south? The sun warmed her shoulders. In the distance, an automobile sputtered toward her. The horse began to stammer, and Veta pulled on the reins gently. "It's okay, boy. It's okay." She guided the horse and buggy to the edge of the dirt road so the vehicle could pass. The black, flat-topped car rolled to a stop.

"Hidy, Miss Veta," Tom said.

"Well, well. Look-a here at Mr. Big Shot hisself driving that fancy automobile."

Tom patted the steering wheel. "Sure beats trudging along on a bouncy, buggy seat. You should look into getting one. It'll sure get you to where you want to go, and a lot faster, I guarantee." The sun exposed the age in his weathered face.

"I ain't rid in one and don't think I will. Seems too easy to lose control and end up agin' a tree. I rightly prefer transportation that works off of oats instead of petrol."

"It takes a while to get the hang of, but after you do, it's the only way to go." He removed a charcoal-colored fedora and ran his hand through his gray hair.

"You heard from Nick? I ain't seen hide nor hair of him in a coon's age."

Tom shook his head. "It appears he's climbed inside that cabin and shut the door off to everything. I never did understand why he just quit on life."

"I don't think he quit on life. He quit on the meanness of the world."

"I surely do miss him. I was putting out hay for the cattle the other day with Nicholas, thinking back to when Nick and I were boys, working the farm together. And now so much time has passed, Ma and Pa both gone. My daughter moved to Neva since her ma passed. Now the old farmhouse seems so empty."

"Time is a movin' on for sure," Veta said. "I'm glad you have your young 'un to help you. When would you say you last saw Nick?"

"I'd say a good five years. Spotted him passing through Timothy Branch. Had some mutt with him. Guess that's his family now."

"Everyone travels their own road. If you think you ain't undertakin' it alone, you'd be wrong. In the grand scheme of things, that is. So, it don't do no good to sit back and chew on the life someone else chooses. Nick did what was right for him. And I'll tell you this—I don't know of any man who coulda gone the route Nick took. That place ain't for the faint of heart. I wouldn't have lasted through the first winter. And if a body could feel more cut off from the world, I don't know where that place exists."

"But we grew up together. Would have liked for him to have been more a part of my life. I know he used to stop by your place from time to time. So, if you see him, tell him I said, hidy."

"You know, you could make the effort to go see him. Specially with Cross Mountain Road making the trip easy."

"Last time I visited, he didn't appear too happy about it. He was disheveled and aloof. No, if he wants to see me, he knows where to find me."

"Well, I'm on my way up Cross Mountain now. Going to Shady to visit my sister, Corrine. Maybe I'll spot the old boy when I head up the road."

"Completing that road across Iron Mountain has been mighty helpful to folks on both sides of the mountain. What used to be a two-day trip to Shady don't take but the course of a morning and part of an afternoon."

"I aim to test that statement right now."

"You take care, Miss Veta."

"You too, Tom."

The steady clomp of the horse's hooves kept Veta company as she headed down the quiet road. The hardened lane was laced with dust, confirmation that summer rains were needed. Veta hoped if rain fell, it would be after she'd climbed and crossed the mountain. A muddy slope on such a steep incline would make for precarious travel. The climb began, the chert road turning up in a constant series of S's making her appreciate the work Nick put in to forge it. The climb to the top was slow but steady, and it was surely easier than when she climbed it when it was barely a path. When they had eclipsed the top, she halted the horse and scoured the land to the west in hope that she might see Nick wandering about. She pondered the idea of tying the horse to a tree and walking the trail to Nick's house, but she didn't want to appear unannounced. And the ache in her tired bones dissuaded from making the trip. She certainly needed to make it to Shady before sunset as she'd not carried a lantern and knew the dangers of being a woman all alone in the dark around Stoney Creek.

Cross Mountain Road flattened and took her between fields tinted flaxen. Such a peacefulness to their appearance, and she never had imagined such wide-open beauty on top of the mountain. She wondered if Nick had ever given thought to living in this region. The land was easy to traverse, and surely planting fields could have been cultivated more easily. When the road turned gently downward, Veta observed Shady Valley below, the mountains beyond tinted purple, the valley green and gold. She had never witnessed it from that viewpoint, and the beauty of it gave her pause.

She eased the buggy along the flattening road, and she approached a small gathering of clapboard houses where it appeared no forethought was given to symmetry or proximity, as if one house begat another and so on. The only commonality was the simplicity of the structures. On the narrow porches sat inhabitants, wary-eyed toward the woman who was passing through. Veta nodded and softly spoke, "hidy," but there was no reciprocation or acknowledgement except from a smattering of chickens that milled about the grassless yards. She came upon three silos where cattle grazed in what seemed an endless supply of alfalfa. The land there flat, fields interwoven like some enormous quilt, varying shades of green. The gold in the fields had faded to a yellow hue.

By late afternoon she came upon a small farmhouse. Corrine waved from the porch. "I been looking for you most of the day," she said, approaching the buggy.

"I can say this is the shortest trip to Shady I ever made," Veta said. "Cross Mountain Road is a blessing."

"It sure beats riding to Mountain City and taking them switchbacks across Iron Mountain."

Veta rolled on her side and opened her eyes. The bedroom was filled with light and warmth, and the aroma of flour and butter filled the air. She searched her mind to remember the last time she woke up after the sun had risen but couldn't come up with such a memory. Guilt washed over her as she imagined Corrine busy in the kitchen while she lay in bed. But she had not awakened to a cooked meal since she was a little girl. By the time she was old enough to gather up her schoolbooks each morning, she was expected to assist in the cooking process.

She entered the kitchen, wearing the green robe Corrine had laid out across the bed. She gave thought to brushing her hair by running her hand through it, but decided that it was a little late in life to worry about making a good impression.

"Lord-a-mercy, I feel like I slept the day away. You shoulda woke me so I could have helped you with breakfast."

"You just take a seat and let me worry about breakfast," Corrine said. "You are a guest and it comes with benefits. Let me start you off with some coffee."

"Well, don't I feel like the Queen of Sheba." Veta sat at the table and took hold of the ceramic mug Corrine had set in front of her. She glanced out the window to a cornfield drenched in sunlight and took a slow sip. "I don't know how to act. Can't I help you at least set the table?"

"No, you can't," she said with a smile. "You aren't allowed to do anything physical on this visit." She brought her sister a plate filled with fried eggs and biscuits covered in sausage gravy. "Eat it while it's hot."

"I'll wait on you."

When Corrine brought her plate and took a seat across from Veta, she lowered her head and Veta followed suit. "For this food and all the blessings in life, we are always thankful."

"Amen," Veta said.

The sisters ate, wrapped in fellowship and a comforting silence.

"My, this is some mighty good vittles," Veta said.

"I'm just glad to have a reason to fix it. I usually just have cereal or oatmeal. Seems kind of foolish to fix a big breakfast for just one."

"Sure would be nice to have Ray and Leonard here at the table with us, even if it was just for a little while."

Corrine studied a picture of her and Leonard hanging on the kitchen wall. "It sure would be." She sighed. "Time sure is a movin' on, Sis. You ever think of the finality of things?"

"Seems like the day is filled with enough worries than what lies ahead. As the Bible says, 'tomorrow will worry about itself. Each day has enough troubles of its own.' So, instead of ponderin' what waits down the road, I guess we best just worry about makin' it through today."

"Do you ever think about dying?"

"It's only natural to think of our own mortality."

"Are you afraid of it?"

"I don't look forward to the actual dyin' part. Once that's done, then bein' dead don't bother me, cause when that happens, what's left to worry about?"

"I just hope I go in my sleep. Never even know the process is taking place."

"Now, that would be the perfect way. There are so many ways to go. Why, lawd, it's like the world is one big bear trap. I remember when John Gambill got crushed by his own tractor when he was pulling stumps from his alfalfa field." She sighed. "I guess we'll never know what the method will be till it gets here."

"Say, what's the latest on old Nick? Is he still living up on Iron Mountain?"

"I've not seen him in a while. Unless he snuck off to parts unknown, I'd say he does."

"Now, that is one of life's mysteries. Moving up on that cold, deserted mountain. Makes no sense to me at all."

"I don't give it thought. It takes all my effort just takin' care of my own self." She took a sip of coffee. "And I've decided that I'll not worry about mine anymore. No sir, at my age, it's time to let the good Lord take over. In fact, I should have done that years ago."

The day held a gloom, fog clinging low as though steam had been released beneath the land, unable to rise. The horse appeared to part the mist as he trudged down the road. Iron Mountain appeared as something from a dream, vague and consumed by opaque skies. The road was free of commerce and travel, Veta guiding the horse quietly on. The trip home would be a sad one. She wondered if she would make her way back that way again. Time and age convinced her it was the last time she would see her sister.

She came upon the Shady Valley General store at the crossroads to Mountain City and decided to give the horse rest and water before heading back up to Cross Mountain Road. She tied the reins to a post that bordered a water trough. "Okay, buddy, you fill your belly and I'm gonna go get a root beer to eat with the buttered biscuit Sis packed in my sack."

She entered the store. It was damp and cool with a low ceiling that seemed to suppress light from entering through the windows. There was a long glass counter with meats and various tubes of cheese. An aroma of something cured caught her attention, and she spotted hams hanging from small twine from the ceiling. Several men sat on stools behind the counter, and it appeared as though a story of some kind was being shared that the others found amusing. She nodded toward them as she made her way to a metal case with a sliding glass top where glass bottles huddled as though trying to prevent anyone from removing them. A cooling air rose from the box when she removed a bottle of *Hires*. She found an opener on a wooden post. It didn't take long to find what little change she carried in her money pouch. Five cents was a lot but she decided it was worth it.

"Hidy," she said when she laid the coin on the counter.

The man behind the register took Veta's coin. His fat, wrinkled fingers looked arthritic and worn. He wore blue overalls over a colorful flannel shirt of red and gold. "How do?" he asked.

"Can't complain." She looked on the wall to a strange beast mounted in some form of evilness. "They lawd, what in the world is that?"

The man looked at the mount to verify what she was asking about. "That there's a wild boar from down South Georgia way."

"I'll be a suck egg mule if that ain't the ugliest creature I ever saw."

"I certainly wouldn't want to come across one out in the wild."

"You and me both." She took a sip and nodded. "Well, time to head across the mountain."

"Safe travels."

She stood outside the door, taking a long sip as she sized up the distance she still had to ride before she got to Cross Mountain Road. The drink was satisfying, though her eyes watered from taking a bigger sip than planned. She heard a scraping sound and walked in front of the store to get a look at the source. A man in heavy beard, a beaver cap pulled tightly on his head, dragged a small sled. A dog tagged along beside him, both slow in their gait. There was an air of suspicion in the way the man walked. Veta approached the road, well pleased in her sighting. "Well, hidy, stranger," she said.

The man tightened the grip on the rope to the sled, his eyes on the road ahead.

"Nick, it's me, Veta," She waved and stepped closer. The smell of stale sweat and what seemed to be human excrement rose heavy in the air. The man kept to the same gait and continued past the store. Veta took to walking and caught up to him. "Nick, how you been?" She knelt to pet the dog. "Hello there, pup."

He stopped and regarded her, and there was a manner of distance in his eyes, as though he was observing something far away with no clue how to determine what he studied. His face wore the look of worn leather, and lines ran deep along his cheek and forehead. Silver strands of hair hung from underneath his hat. His thick beard grew long down his neck. His pants hung loosely, and he appeared as a refugee with no homeland. Veta wondered if she had aged so poorly as him. It seemed she was addressing someone ten years old than her when it was the other way around.

"Nick," she said, moving to where she stood in front of him, making him stop. She studied him intently. "Lordy, you seem off kilter to say the least. I was just talkin' about you with Tom, day before last. We was both wonderin' how you been as we ain't seen you in forever. Are you doin' all right?"

He studied her curiously. "Veta."

"That's right. Looks like you got your mind set on gettin' somewheres in a hurry. Where you a headin'?"

"Tradin' Post down past Shady. Got ginseng freshly dug. Taters and apples. Trading for ammunition. Dangerous times we're in."

"The bears givin' you trouble?"

Nick took to dragging the cart. Veta placed her hand on his arm. "You ain't got time to talk a spell with an old friend? How you a doin'? Lordy, you look a bit ragged." She patted her chest lightly. "Course, I'm no beauty myself. I just hit the ripe old age of seventy-eight. Some days it feels like I'm a hundred and seventy-eight."

Nick gave a slight nod and again took to pulling the sled. Veta stepped in front of Nick and studied his eyes, a faraway look in them as though they were detached from the mind that made them operate. As though a whitewashing to some degree had rendered all that had occurred prior to that moment as something incalculable. She kept a firm hold of the sleeves of his arms. "Nick? You rightly look like one who's been defeated. Where's that fire that used to burn in those eyes?"

His eyes softened, as though some faded memory had been recalled, a look of some wayfaring sailor regarding a land long sought. In that look, Veta saw an innocence that she wished she could grab hold of. As quickly as it appeared, it vanished, like a candle extinguished by a cold wind. And in that moment, the steely look returned, a cold realization of the truth taking hold like a plague. He looked downward briefly as though to hide his shame. "I need to be a movin' on."

She reluctantly loosened her grip. As he headed away, she placed her hand across her chest, fighting tears as she watched the shell of that once strong, proud man walking, head now hung in defeat. She walked to where the horse stood and unraveled the harness. When she climbed on the buggy, she turned and glanced toward Nick, the familiar hum of the sled dragging the ground. As she regarded him, the sled came to an abrupt halt. Nick turned and regarded Veta. He formed a sad smile, nodded, as though the words she had spoken minutes prior had found hold in the old hermit's heart. He raised his hand, a wave suspended in air. She responded in kind, her hand held in front of her, palm facing Nick.

He lowered his hand, his head, and returned to pulling the sled. His narrow shoulders slumped, his gait as one who walked through winds of suspicion. Vague, ghostlike he faded into the morning haze, the only verification he was not something conjured in the mind the hum of the sled dragging against the hardened soil.

| 32 |

Veta pumped the steel handle. Water sprayed into the bucket. She peered in the pail and hardly recognized the reflection that looked back at her. The movement of the water could not hide the deep wrinkles. The tired eyes. Silver hair, wild, and disheveled. She carried the bucket to the house. At the back door, she stopped, turned, and studied Iron Mountain. A soft shade of purple, the mountain was a contrast of beauty and power. The cloudless sky beyond held such clarity that made it appear as though a deep chasm existed between the mountain and the sky. Falsehoods revealed. Uneasiness penetrated her soul. She couldn't shake the vision of Nick walking away from her at the crossroads of Shady Valley. He was a shell of the man she had known for forty years. The one she'd seen that morning was not one she recognized, and she wondered if some traumatic event had changed him, or if the simple passage of time in such remote and lonely conditions had changed his head and heart completely. Had he become tetched from the isolation? She'd seen others lose their faculties through time, but with Nick, it appeared as though some unnatural force had consumed him.

She sat at the kitchen table, eating a cold biscuit filled with blackberry preserves. Time had frozen still all around her, the pots and pans hung on nails on the wall, the two small paintings of redbirds resting on a limb above a mountain creek, the blue and white plate that covered the stove pipe vent. But time outside that room had rolled on as some wave pushing across a vast sea in search of rumored shores. The observance of wrinkled skin that covered her arthritic fingers reminded her how time had been stolen away as though stockpiled away by some otherworldly accountant who planned to sell the days back when the world came to an end. She recalled the first time Nick had entered her store two years after Ray's death. There was something fiercely independent about the young man, a distrust in his eyes. She reckoned it took a hardened state to take on the cold isolation of Iron Mountain as though choice was not an option. She walked to the window and searched for entrails of smoke from the mountain top, but it was eerily still.

Veta guided the horse up Timothy Branch to the base of Iron Mountain. Again, she looked skyward as though signs might present themselves. She headed to Baxter McEwen's farmhouse. She found him at the hog trough, a small litter of piglets following mama to dinner.

"Howdy, Miss Veta," he said as she pulled the buggy to a stop by an elm limb fencepost.

"Looks like you're gonna have your fill of sausage till Jesus himself reappears."

"If he appears on my farm, I'll be happy to offer him some. In the meantime, I've got plenty to spare, and more curing in the barn." Baxter placed the bucket beside the fence. "How you been getting along?"

"Some days better than others. Each day I wake up is a blessing." She looked toward Iron Mountain. "You seen Nick passing through Timothy Branch lately?"

"Can't say that I have."

"I came across him down Shady Valley way a few months back. He looked plumb terrible. His mind was cloudy. It took a while for him to even realize who I was. He had no desire to carry conversation. Just dragged his sled with the pup by his side. It was the saddest sight. I can't stop worryin' about him."

"I've wondered why he hasn't come down the mountain this way. I'd say it's been four or five years since I saw him come down Timothy Branch."

"What do you say we head on up and check on him? I've got some biscuits and pole beans for him. Even got a few jars of pickled beets."

"Well, we can certainly scale the mountain a lot faster than we used to thanks to Cross Mountain. You want me to hitch up a pair of horses to the wagon?"

"No need. My horse can get us up there quick-like."

"Let me tell Elsa. Don't want her thinking I skipped off to fish Doe Creek."

They traveled the switchbacks up Cross Mountain. The horse led them on, steadily climbing, with each switchback, Veta noticed mountains to the west, layer upon layer, fade into the gray horizon as though swallowed up by the edge of the world, and she wondered if Tennessee went on forever.

When they made it to the top, a breeze cut into the humid July air, and Veta was glad the horse was able to rest in windy shade. She tied the rein around a sapling. "Be back soon."

Baxter offered to walk to the cabin alone to save Veta from making the trek. She took that as something of an insult and hoped she wouldn't have to slow down to wait on him. They began the three-mile hike, along the steady rise and fall of the mountaintop. The thick canopy of hardwoods kept them deep in shade except where sunlight found slender creases. An odd silence accompanied them. Nick's well-being weighed heavily on Veta, and there was not much in the way of conversation between the lifelong friends. She had known Baxter even before she married Ray, making them cousins by marriage. Perhaps Baxter could awaken Nick's memory, as he had been friends with Nick since they were boys.

She glanced over the ridge. The depth of trees appeared endless, the valley below completely hidden. "Sure glad Nick forged a good trail. Imagine climbin' up from down below us. You tumble down off this side, you'll bounce off ever tree until you splash into Timothy Branch."

"Nick did the whole county a favor by forging that road."

"I don't know about the county, but he sure did you and me a big favor."

"I hope the ole boy is home. I would hate to arrive unannounced with no one there to validate our efforts."

"When did you say was the last time you saw him?"

"Five years, maybe six. He brought me rhubarb and the sweetest apples. I give him some cured meat."

"I've had some of them apples. Made great pies."

"Nick's story is a curious one."

"Some would reason that *he* is a curious one. I can see why that might be. He got kicked in the head by the proverbial mule one time too many. Course, we all have had our share of troubles."

"But we didn't let it send us runnin' to the hills."

"Maybe we didn't have the courage to try."

The cabin was draped in deep shade, with ferns and undergrowth bordering the walls like some flora army preparing to invade. The chimney was quiet, and there were no remnants of recent smoke or fire. No smell of embers in the air. No barking dog. Veta took a deep breath and regarded Baxter.

"Maybe Nick and his dog are off on some expedition," he said. He followed the slope upward about fifteen feet and looked to the barn.

"Do you see him in the field?"

Baxter stepped a little higher up the slope. "Field looks like it's in a state of abandon."

"His crops are what's carried him."

Baxter walked back down the slope toward Veta. "Let's take a look inside."

They stood outside the cabin door. Veta leaned forward as though some stirring would let her know he was okay. She tried to will noise of some sort, verification of some form of activity from inside. "Well, I hear something. Sounds like the pup stirring about."

"Nick?" Baxter called out.

Panter barked, and Veta nodded. "I was right."

"Nick?" he said again before slowly opening the door. The room was dark except for the gray sliver cast on the dirt floor by the light of day. Panter growled. "Wait outside, Veta."

There was something in Baxter's tone that gave Veta pause. She stepped back from the doorway, putting her hands together at the palms, her fingertips touching her chin, a brief prayer offered up.

Baxter eased inside and Veta crept up to the doorway, pleading silently for Nick to respond. Panter's growls grew in intensity, still the only sounds coming from inside. An odd rustling sound of some manner. Baxter spoke softly, "It's all right, pup. It's all right." The dog whimpered. "Nick, ole boy. You okay?" A moment of silence. "Nick."

A few minutes passed, and Baxter came to the door. His expression told her what she needed to know. What she didn't want to know. Baxter removed his hat and ran his hand through his white, flowing hair. "I'd say he's been gone a few days."

"Were his eyes open or closed?"

"What?"

"Were they open or closed? If they were closed, surely he died peacefully."

"They were closed. He looked like he was asleep. A bridle and rope were a layin' across his arm. Not sure why since he no longer has the steer."

"The pup lyin' at his feet?"

"No. He's a layin' on Nick's chest. There to protect him."

"I had a bad feeling deep down in my insides. When I saw him down Shady, it was like seeing a body without spirit. When one loses their spirit, the body is soon to follow suit."

"He was a true hermit. Living away from the rest of the world, hid for what, thirty-five years?"

"Got to be at least forty. Ray died forty-two years ago last November, and Nick first walked into my store a couple of years after that to buy an ax."

"We best fetch Doc Raley to pronounce his passing as official. Years back, Nick picked a spot under that hickory yonder where he wanted to be laid to permanent rest. I'll fetch help to dig the grave and transport him from the cabin. Even in this elevation, the heat has placed him in a state where, if you'll pardon me a sayin', he needs to be placed in the ground soon."

"I'll go see Reverend DeVault about setting up a service for folks who want to come pay their respect. What about the pup?"

"Let's take him on back. I got three dogs already. Don't see where one more will make much of a difference. That is, if he'll go. He's been by Nick's side for a good ten years or so. No telling how long he's been lyin' on Nick's chest. Poor pup has to be starving."

"I guess eating is the last thing on his mind."

"Let's get back down the mountain and round up who we can. We'll bury him as soon as possible and then worry about a service later."

"Ready when you are."

She regarded the cabin, and the silence contained a strange reverence. In that moment, she felt more distant from Doe Valley than she had ever ventured. As though all paths from the cabin had been wiped clean, with no map on paper or in the mind to lead her home. And yet she wanted to hurry from that place. They took to walking, and the trees moaned melancholy as a breeze rose from the backside of the mountain. The trail was still lattice-shadowed, and Veta and Baxter walked back as though conversation might disturb the newly dead.

| **33** |

The horse led Veta up Cross Mountain Road, following closely behind a dozen other buggies. She glanced behind and counted at least a dozen more following. The day had warmed in the valley, and the cool breeze of the mountain was welcome relief. She thought it peculiar that two years had passed since Nick's death. The oddity of such a long gap between the man's being laid in the grave and the official service over that grave puzzled her. But Baxter explained how it took time to raise money to buy the materials, and the time it took Asa Shoun and Vaught Grindstaff to construct the monument.

When she had made it to the top, the three Shirey boys waited to assist the attendees from their buggies and to secure the reins of the horses to trees. Veta was caught off guard, not because of the numbers who had come for the service, but for the ladyfolk who were making the trek down the trail to the gravesite. Conversation was light as they walked, some carrying flowers. She noticed how the trail had thinned, and she reckoned it was because Nick's bootsteps were long dormant. The trail had more the look of a deer path. It was as though it had regained its wildness, making the trail harder to scale. Steps were cautiously taken as though they were trespassing on grounds for which they were not wanted. A breeze blew, and nebulous clouds approached as though summoned to mirror the mood. As they walked, fog rose from the valley. Laurel hell lined the downslopes, conspiratorial, brooding clusters of limbs and oblong leaves. A formidable barrier to the deeper backwoods.

Nearly an hour had passed by the time the attendees made it to the cabin. Veta paused when she saw the decrepit structure, caught off guard by the swiftness the mountain showed in reclaiming the shack. Branches clung to the roof. Weeds and vines and sumac crawled up the side walls. She inhaled deeply in hopes embers from the fire pit might spark a memory of dinners cooked long ago. But the cabin was absent of all reverence, and it saddened her. She looked to the crest above the cabin, spotting Reverend DeVault standing next to what appeared a stone chimney. The gravesite. She climbed the angled land, working her way carefully to the monument. She smiled at the craftsmanship the volunteers had put into assembling rocks into a stone shrine. The structure stood eight feet tall, with the top narrowing as though it looked like Nick might start a fire from the grave on snowy nights if he had the means. On the backside of the monument, Nick's pots and pans, skillet, and utensils had been laid in a slab of concrete. It gave the site a festive look.

Those who had made the journey migrated around the gravesite. The preacher motioned them closer. Baxter stood nearby and took Veta by the elbow to escort her closer. The floor was rich green from ferns and mayapple, a bold contrast to the mist that hung in the air. The land sloped downward all about the tomb, the fog presenting the gravesite as something bold and illustrious. The preacher thanked those in attendance, commenting that the effort would have touched Nick, but adding that he probably would have rather them gather somewhere off the mountain. He led the attendees in singing the song, *America,* which echoed hauntingly across the mountaintop. When the words *Sweet Land of Liberty* were sung, Veta thought the words most appropriate. It was indeed Nick's liberty that the mountain provided. After the song was finished, words were spoken of Nick's life, and how he had found peace not in the world, but outside of it. Veta studied the setting about her. The spot Nick had chosen as his eternal resting place was a cathedral of the most primal kind. Strong tall hickory bordered by chestnut and elm, their trunks tall and arrow straight.

She had been told Panter was buried at the feet of where Nick had been laid. Baxter had told her the dog had to be put down as he wouldn't let anyone near Nick's body when they tried to prepare him for burial. He became uncontrollable. The thought of the dog's loyalty leading it to be the cause of its death bothered her. Yet, she reckoned it was the proper thing to do as the dog would not have wanted to leave the cabin, would not have been able to settle for living with someone else in the valley.

Those who had gathered were but temporary interlopers in a place they surely could not fathom. Their presence was not in dispute, but theirs would soon evaporate into only blurred memories they would surely try to recall when telling others about the day they attended Uncle Nick Grindstaff's graveside service. Nothing save Nick's presence would remain there on that mountaintop. And Veta prayed that nothing would remove that presence.

After the preacher prayed for God to bless Nick's soul, to give him comfort man had not, a red-tail hawk cried out as it circled above the trees. A farewell calling perhaps. A slight murmur rose among those gathered as they walked to the far side of the monument to take a closer look.

"Not sure if Nick would be happy with so many people on his land," Veta said to Baxter.

"He was a man separate from the world," Baxter said. "Makes you wonder if that roughing up he got on that train years ago just warped his mind."

"I think in some ways he had the clearest mind of us all. The world had wronged him, and he figured the best way to keep it from happening again was to make his own. In a way, he got to lord over his own world. I'm just glad I got a little peek into the window."

She waited patiently as the mourners began the walk back to the horses and buggies that awaited them at Cross Mountain Road. Baxter had stayed beside her watching as Reverend DeVault placed the Bible under his arm to follow the others. He nodded at Veta and Baxter as though any dominion he held was now complete, and the land was free for rule by anyone who chose to lord over it. But Veta imagined that no one else would assume that role, to follow in Nick's footsteps. Only one man was able to complete that role, and he was in a permanent state of rest below the rugged soil.

"You ready, Miss Veta?" Baxter asked.

"You go on ahead, Bax. I want to stay a while. Offer up my own condolences in the peace and quiet of it all."

"You okay to walk by yourself? I don't want to leave you in the lurch."

"Lordy, these bones ain't so brittle that they can't handle a leisurely stroll."

Baxter let out a snigger. "Your version of leisurely is a lot different than mine, Miss Veta. If you're sure you're okay, I'll leave you be."

She patted him on the shoulder. "I'm sure Nick will watch over me."

Baxter bid her goodbye and slowly disappeared into the fog. She walked above the burial site and turned back to the monument for a closer look. She rubbed the smooth head stone buried within the wall of the stone shrine. A tear slid down her cheek. She sighed. When she read the inscription, a smile caught the tear. She touched the stone with her finger before she read the words aloud –

Uncle Nick Grindstaff
Born Dec. 26, 1851
Died July 22, 1923
Lived alone, suffered alone, and died alone

She walked to the cabin and stood in quiet observance. She pressed her hand against the door. Searching for a pulse. Seeking something that might revive Nick's presence. She would not open the door as it might unlock the crypt she felt was truly Nick's final resting place. She bowed her head and sighed, disappointed she could perform no ceremony, no rite, worthy of honoring the life of her friend. When she turned to leave, she spotted a shapely rock leaning against the wall on a narrow shelf. She removed it, examining the smoothness, the shape covering the length of her hand. She turned it over and noticed a carving lengthwise across it. Faded, hard to trace. She had been told years ago that rocks on Iron Mountain would light up like blood veins when wet. She touched her tongue to the rock, moving it about until the underside was moist. Deep red veins rose immediately, illuminating the carving. She made out the word and then held the rock to her chest. With tears welling, she looked again at the rock and traced the writing.

isolate

She placed the rock on the shelf. The walk down the footpath would be a lonely one.

ACKNOWLEDGMENTS

To my wife, Sandy – thank you for supporting me throughout the writing journey and reminding me that with God, all things are possible. Your unwavering faith fueled my desire to write this story in a way that would adequately honor the life of Nick Grindstaff.

To my daughter, Jessica – for your belief in me as a father, for your view that life is a constant competition, and that "Dad" will always come out with the win. I hope to always make you proud.

To Mary Ellen Morris and Lynnè Bell Reeves - your invaluable insight to the storyline of the book was a tremendous help. Your dedication was evident with the suggestions and observations you made in helping shape the original draft into a completed work. I might need to put you on permanent retainer.

To Daniel McEwen – thank you for accompanying me to Nick's gravesite, and for leading us down that slanted Iron Mountain to the valley afterwards. It gave me a deeper appreciation for the physical demands living on that remote mountain presented to Nick, though I think he surely had a better route to descend than the one we chose.

To my agent, Diane Nine - thank you for your tireless efforts to bring this book to life. I can't adequately express how fortunate I am to have you to lead me down the difficult path of the publishing world. May this book be the first of many book adventures together.

Note to the Reader

~Lived alone, suffered alone, and died alone~
- Epitaph on Nick Grindstaff's tombstone

Nick Grindstaff's life was one shrouded in mystery. Perhaps not to the few who knew him or crossed paths with him at some point in their life. But for those who lived outside the secluded area of Johnson County in the northeast corner of Tennessee, or those born after Nick died in 1923, the only known facts are his date of birth, date of death, and the location where he is buried on Iron Mountain. The tombstone erected at his grave site confirms those three facts.

There were articles written about Nick stretching back to 1940, from local newspapers to the New York Times. In each article, the story of Nick's life varied significantly. When I was six, my mother gave me a copy *of "Nick the Hermit - A True Story," written in poetic form of Nick Grindstaff of Johnson County, Tennessee.* It was a 26-page poetic tale written by A.M. Daugherty in 1926. Daugherty conferred with Asa Shoun (a friend of Nick's) and R.B. Wilson (a relative of Nick's) before writing it. I still have that copy. Daugherty's poetic rendering, the various newspaper articles, and word of mouth passed down from family members who grew up in Johnson County (Nick did business at my grandfather's store in Doe Valley) helped shape the storyline of this book. And yet, much of this book is conjecture.

Throughout the writing process, I wanted Nick's life to be presented as something to be respected and admired, and not one to be pitied. By all accounts, Nick was a good and honest man who had tragic misfortune, from the death of his parents from tuberculosis (The Consumption) when he was a young boy, to the robbery and beating he endured when he was a man. For readers related to Nick, or who grew up in Johnson County or nearby Carter County, where stories of Nick were passed down by older generations, surely the versions are different to varying degrees than mine. Again, it is a work of fiction inspired by various accounts of Nick's life, and it is intended to honor the life of a man who did not let the cruel fate of the world beat him down. Nick didn't so much run from the world; rather, he created his own.

Chuck Walsh is a novelist from Columbia, South Carolina. He is the author of ***A Month of Tomorrows, Shadows on Iron Mountain, Backwoods Justice*** (the sequel), ***A Splintered Dream, A Passage Back***, and ***Black Mingo Creek.***

A Month of Tomorrows chronicles the life of Samuel Gable, a WWII war hero on his deathbed revealing the brutality he endured in the war. This book rose to #6 on *Amazon's Best Seller* list for Historical Fiction in 2014. ***Shadows on Iron Mountain,*** a tale about a killer that roams the backwoods of East Tennessee, was a top 10 Finalist in the *2015 Independent Authors* book competition in the Murder/Suspense category. ***Backwoods Justice*** is the sequel to *Shadows on Iron Mountain,* where a killer motivated by revenge terrorizes hikers on the Appalachian Trail.

A Passage Back is about a man who suffers an accident following the death of his mother, causing him to awaken back in 1972. He gets a small window of opportunity to be a child again, reunited with his mother in a time when sickness and death were non-existent. ***A Splintered Dream*** is a heartwarming "comeback story" of a baseball player and his journey to be the best to ever play the game. ***Black Mingo Creek***, a murder/suspense that takes place in the Lowcountry of South Carolina, reveals what a man will do when everything has been taken from him.

Walsh graduated from the University of South Carolina and lives in Columbia, SC with his wife, Sandy. He has taught creative writing and currently works at Columbia College.